Luca was   ...   't want. He was dangerous.

He was a man who was used to people doing what he wanted them to, and he was willing to take whatever measures were necessary to make it happen.

They would come to a coparenting arrangement that suited them both, but that was it. That's all there could be.

Claire looked up to notice Luca was watching her as he held their child. His gaze flicked over her casually, and yet she could feel the knot in her belly tighten. She wasn't misinterpreting this. Luca made it plainly clear that he was attracted to her, as well. It might just be a negotiation strategy to soften her up, but when he looked at her that way, it almost made her feel like resistance was futile.

Luca was a man who got what he wanted. What would she do if he decided he wanted her?

* * *

The CEO's Unexpected Child
is part of Mills & Boon Desire's no. 1 bestselling series, Billionaires and Babies: Powerful men… wrapped around their babies' little fingers.

THE CEO'S UNEXPECTED CHILD

BY
ANDREA LAURENCE

First Published in Great Britain 2016
By Mills & Boon, an imprint of HarperCollins*Publishers*
1 London Bridge Street, London, SE1 9GF

© 2015 Andrea Laurence

ISBN: 978-0-263-91851-9

51-0316

Our policy is to use papers that are natural, renewable and recyclable products and made from wood grown in sustainable forests.The logging and manufacturing processes conform to the legal environmental regulations of the country of origin.

Printed and bound in Spain
by CPI, Barcelona

Andrea Laurence is an award-winning author of contemporary romances filled with seduction and sass. She has been a lover of reading and writing stories since she was young and is thrilled to share her special blend of sensuality and dry, sarcastic humor with readers. A dedicated West Coast girl transplanted into the Deep South, she's working on her own happily-ever-after with her boyfriend and their collection of animals.

To Those Battling Cancer —

You never expect the C word and when it shows up, your whole life turns upside down. Things that seemed so important are suddenly trivial compared to getting through this disease. I can't even imagine the full scope of emotions that go through a person as they face that uncertain future. My wish is that this book provides you a welcome distraction and gives you hope for a happy ending of your own.

One

"I don't care, Stuart. I'm not letting a total stranger just take my daughter from me."

Claire Douglas's lawyer, Stuart Ewing, patted her on the hand. He had a grandfatherly way about him, an easygoing attitude that belied the fact that he was a courtroom barracuda. She had a lot of faith and money invested in the man, but that didn't mean she wasn't terrified deep down.

"We'll work something out, Claire. I just need you to keep your cool when we go in there. Don't let your emotions get the best of you."

Claire frowned. Keeping her emotions in check was not exactly her specialty. She'd been bombarded with emotions over the past two years. Her life had become a roller coaster from the moment she found out she was pregnant. After years of failed fertility treatments, it had been their last chance. That moment had been the highest of highs.

Her husband dying in a car accident when she was five months pregnant was the lowest of lows. Especially the painful revelations that followed it. The birth of her daughter had been the only thing that pulled her out of that dark place, giving her a reason to be joyful and live her life again.

But she'd never expected this. The disclosure of the mistake they'd made at the fertility clinic had changed her whole life. It had made her a millionaire, and at the same time had threatened the stability of her small family.

"Mrs. Douglas? Mr. Ewing? They're ready for you." The receptionist at the front desk gestured to a set of double doors that led to a conference room.

There, Claire presumed, waited the man who was trying to take her child and the lawyer he'd hired to help him. She felt her stomach roll, threatening to return the coffee and bagel she'd forced down her throat that morning.

"Come on, Claire," Stuart said, pushing up from the waiting-room chair. "Everything is going to be fine. You're not going to lose your daughter."

Claire nodded, trying to act calm and assured, though she was anything but. There were no guarantees. They were marching into a room where Edmund Harding was waiting for them. He was the kind of lawyer every billionaire in Manhattan had on speed dial. Harding had such a level of prestige and influence that he could probably get the courts to do anything he wanted.

Scooping up her purse, she forced her trembling

hands into tight fists at her sides and followed Stuart into the conference room.

The room was elegant and intimidating, with a large rectangular glass table that cut it in two like a blade. There was no question that it divided everything into their side and their opponents' side. There were plush leather rolling chairs lining the table, but at the moment all of them were empty.

Claire's gaze drifted to the large, floor-to-ceiling windows on the left side of the room. A man stood in front of it, looking out over Central Park. She couldn't make out any of his features, just the hulking shape of his broad shoulders and narrow waist. The man was tall, his arms crossed over his chest. He emitted an intense energy that Claire picked up on immediately.

"Ah, Mrs. Douglas," a voice called. "Mr. Ewing, please have a seat."

Claire turned toward the voice and found a man on the other side of the room. He was gathering paperwork in his hands and carrying it to the table. The man had a certain studious look about him that convinced her that he was the infamous Edmund Harding. That meant the man by the window had to be...

"Luca, we're ready to begin," Edmund said.

As Claire settled into her seat, the man at the window finally turned. When he did, Claire was very glad she was already sitting. The face that regarded her was like a Florentine masterpiece of the Renaissance. He had a square, clean-shaven jaw and high cheekbones that looked as if they were carved out of marble. Dark brows hovered over narrowed eyes that crinkled at the edges.

Those eyes ran over Claire for a moment, then

turned away, disinterested. He strode to the conference table and sat beside his lawyer.

This was the father of her child?

She almost couldn't believe it, and yet her daughter's dark curls and olive complexion certainly hadn't come from her.

"Before we begin, can my assistant bring anyone anything? Water? Coffee?" Edmund asked.

"No, thank you," Claire said quietly.

"Coffee, black," the man across the table demanded. No niceties, no please or thank you. He seemed very much to be the kind of man who was used to getting what he wanted.

He wouldn't get his way this time. Claire was determined not to let this man get his hooks into her daughter. He didn't even know Eva. How could he possibly get custody of her?

The assistant brought Luca a mug of black coffee and silently disappeared as quickly as she arrived.

"Thank you for coming today," Edmund began as the door clicked shut. "We asked to meet with you in person because we feel as though our prior communications aren't having the impact they should. Mr. Moretti is very serious about pursuing his joint custody filing."

Being served with papers that said a stranger was demanding custody of her daughter had nearly floored her. When she had learned the truth about the mix-up at the fertility clinic, a part of her had hoped that the biological father would be disinterested in Eva. She found out quickly that was not going to be the case.

"Don't you think that filing was premature?" Stuart

asked. "He hasn't even met the child, but he thinks he should have joint custody?"

"He would've met his daughter weeks ago if your client had cooperated with our requests. We had no choice but to do something Mrs. Douglas couldn't continue to ignore."

The two lawyers continued to argue, but Claire found her attention was drawn to the silent force sitting across from her. While his lawyer did all the talking, Luca Moretti leaned back in his chair and studied Claire. His dark hazel eyes ran over every inch of her. She did her best to hold still, not wanting to squirm or show any sign of weakness in front of him.

Instead, she focused on studying him just as closely. It was so easy to see pieces of him in Eva. When her daughter was born, Claire had been confused by the baby they handed her, with the head of dark, curly hair. Claire had dark honey-blond hair. Her husband, Jeff, had light brown hair. Neither was olive skinned nor had a cleft in their chin, but Eva did.

But all her confusion and worry disappeared the moment she looked into her daughter's gray eyes. She fell in love that instant, and no longer cared what Eva looked like because she was perfect. For all Claire knew, Jeff had Spanish or Italian blood he'd never told her about.

The doubts hadn't arisen in her mind again until the clinic called three months later. They'd informed her that their last vial of sperm was due for destruction in three months if they didn't use it. They hadn't opted to pay the lifetime storage fees because they'd intended to use it all fairly quickly.

The call confused her because they'd used their

last dose when they conceived Eva. That information had raised red flags, and it wasn't long until they discovered the truth—her husband's sperm had a number transposed on the paperwork and another client's sperm was used instead.

Luca Moretti's, to be exact.

The thought sent a chill through her. The man had never touched her and yet a part of him had been inside her. What was a man like Luca doing at a fertility clinic, anyway? Putting himself through college by selling sperm for cash? Every inch of his body, from his broad shoulders to his hard jaw, screamed the kind of masculinity she hadn't been exposed to in a very long time, if ever. With the right look, Claire was certain he could make a woman's ovaries explode. If a man like Luca needed the services of a fertility clinic, a lesser man didn't stand a chance with his own progeny.

And yet, he was there. When the news broke, Luca had focused his attention on the fertility clinic. He'd sent Edmund after them and before Claire knew it, the clinic was begging to settle out of court and keep the scandal quiet. She had instantly gone from a comfortable middle-class woman, to someone who didn't need to work another day in her life.

But then Luca turned his legal bulldogs on her. Claire wouldn't back down, though. She didn't care if it cost her every penny of her settlement battling in court. Eva was her baby. It was hard enough trying to deal with the revelation of her daughter's paternity. She was still trying to work through her anger and confusion about Jeff's death. How could she tell Jeff's parents that Eva wasn't their biological granddaughter? She had a lot on her plate already. She didn't need

Luca coming out of nowhere and making demands about *her* child.

"There's got to be a happy medium," Stuart said, pulling her attention back into the conversation.

"My client isn't open to negotiating any terms that don't involve providing him with visits with his daughter."

"*My* daughter." Claire spoke up with all the force she could muster. She felt Stuart's hand covering hers, trying to calm her, but it wasn't going to help. "Eva is my daughter. I'm not just going to hand her over to some stranger. I don't know anything about this man. He could be a serial killer or some kind of pervert. Would you just hand over your child to a stranger, Mr. Harding?"

Edmund was startled by her outburst, but the sound that caught her attention was the snort of laughter from the man beside him. It was the first noise Luca had made since he demanded his coffee. When she turned to look at him, she noticed a sparkle of interest in his eyes and a hint of amusement curling a corner of his full lips. He was no longer just studying her, he actually seemed…intrigued by her.

"I can assure you that my client is no criminal, Mrs. Douglas. He is the CEO of the nation's largest family-owned Italian restaurant chain, Moretti's Italian Kitchen."

Claire turned away from Luca's intense stare. It was unnerving her, and this was no time for her to be compromised. So, he was a hotshot restaurateur. Good for him. But what difference did that make when it came to his character? Success didn't make him a saint. "So you're presuming that rich businessmen can't be murderers or child molesters? I counter that they just have better lawyers."

"My client is willing to cooperate to soothe your concerns, Mrs. Douglas. We're not the bad guys here. We're just trying to ensure that Eva is in Mr. Moretti's life. We welcome you to have a background check conducted. You won't find anything questionable. But when you don't find the skeletons you're looking for, you're going to have to let him see Eva."

"And if Mrs. Douglas doesn't cooperate?"

Claire held her breath, waiting to see what they would say. Would they push her or back down until their court date?

"Then," Edmund explained, "we stop playing nice. I'll file an emergency visitation motion to compel access to Eva and let the courts decide. You can be certain the judge will give my client even more time with his daughter than we're requesting. It's your choice, Mrs. Douglas."

So this was Claire Douglas.

Luca had to admit he was surprised. Her name had been on his mind and crossed his desk a hundred times since the mix-up came to light. He didn't know what he was expecting the widowed Mrs. Douglas to look like, but young, slender and blonde had not been on the list. It had taken everything he had to hold his composure when he turned from the window and saw her standing there.

Her practical gray suit clung to every delicious curve and almost exactly matched the shade of her eyes. Her honey-colored hair was twisted back into a professional bun at her nape. He wanted to pull out the hair pins and let the blond waves tumble over her shoulders.

The longer he sat watching Claire, the more curious he became about her. How had a woman so young become a widow? Was she always this uptight, or was it just because she didn't like him? He wanted to run his thumb between her eyebrows to smooth the crease her serious frown had worn there.

It made him wonder if their daughter looked more like him or her. Did she have Claire's porcelain skin and pert nose? Did her ears turn red when she got angry the way her mother's did? The furious shift in Claire had immediately caught his attention. There was more fire in her than the bland gray suit would indicate.

"Can they do that?" Claire asked, turning to her lawyer. She looked completely panicked by the thought of Luca having access to their child.

Their child.

It seemed so wrong for him to have a child with a woman he'd never met. Luca hadn't even given any serious thought to having a family. He'd only stored his sperm to make the doctors and his mother feel better. He hadn't actually expected to use it.

But now that he had a living, breathing child, he wasn't about to sit back and pretend it didn't happen. Eva was probably the only child he would ever have, and he'd already missed months of her life. That would not continue.

"We can and we will." Luca spoke up at last. "This whole thing is a mess that neither of us anticipated, but it doesn't change the facts. Eva is my daughter, and I've got the paternity test results to prove it. There's not a judge in the county of New York who won't grant me emergency visitation while we await our court date. They will say when and where and how often you have to give her to me."

Claire sat, her mouth agape at his words. "She's just a baby. She's only six months old. Why fight me for her just so you can hand her over to a nanny?"

Luca laughed at her presumptuous tone. "What makes you so certain I'll have a nanny for her?"

"Because…" she began. "You're a rich, powerful, unmarried businessman. You're better suited to run a corporation than to change a diaper. I'm willing to bet you don't have the first clue of how to care for an infant, much less the time."

Luca just shook his head and sat forward in his seat. "You know very little about me, *tesorina*, you've said so yourself, so don't presume anything about me. Besides, even if I have a nanny, it doesn't matter because Eva is my daughter, too. I'm going to fight for the right to see her even if all I do is pass her off to someone else. Like it or not, you don't get any say into what I do when I have her."

Claire narrowed her gaze at him. She definitely didn't like him pushing her. And he was pushing her. Partially because he liked to see the fire in her eyes and the flush of her skin, and partially because it was necessary to get through to her.

Neither of them had asked for this to happen to them, but she needed to learn she wasn't in charge. They had to cooperate if this awkward situation was going to improve. He'd started off nice, politely requesting to see Eva, and he'd been flatly ignored. As each request was met with silence, he'd escalated the pressure. That's how they'd ended up here today. If she pushed him any more, he would start playing hardball. He didn't want to, but he would crush her like his restaurants' competitors.

"We can work together and play nice, or Edmund here can make things very difficult for you. As he said, it's your choice."

"My choice? Hardly." She sniffed and crossed her arms over her chest.

The movement pressed her abundant bosom up against the neckline of her jacket, giving him a glimpse of rosy cleavage. Her blush traveled lower than he expected. It made him want to know exactly how much lower.

"Mr. Moretti?"

Luca jerked his gaze from Claire's chest and met her heated stare. "I'm sorry, what?"

"I *said*, you have my hands tied. You aren't even listening to me. How can we negotiate when you aren't listening?"

Luca swallowed his embarrassment, covering it with the confident, unaffected mask he usually wore. It had been a long time since he'd lost his focus during business discussions, much less because of a beautiful woman. Apparently, he had been working too much and needed some companionship so he didn't lose his edge. "And how are we to negotiate when you refuse to move from your position? You won't listen to anything that isn't just the way you want it."

"That is not—"

"Claire," her lawyer interrupted in a harsh whisper. "We need to consider what they're offering."

"I don't want to consider it. This whole thing is ridiculous. We're done here," she said, pushing up from her seat to stand.

"That's fine," Luca said, sitting back in his chair. Time to turn the screws. "I think you'll look lovely in orange."

"Orange?" Claire asked, some of her previous fire starting to cool.

"Yes. Prison jumper orange to be exact. If the judge orders visitation and you don't comply, you could end up in jail. That's fine with me, really. That means I'll get full custody of Eva."

"Sit down, Claire," Stuart said.

Her brave facade crumbled as she slipped back down into her chair. Finally, he'd gotten through to her. The last thing he wanted to do was to send a young mother to jail, but he would. He was not the kind of man who bluffed, so it was a wise time for her to listen.

Claire sighed and leaned forward, folding her delicate, manicured fingers together on the glass table. "I just don't think you understand what you're asking of me. Do you have nieces or nephews, Mr. Moretti?"

Did he? He was from a big Italian family. With five brothers and sisters he had more nieces and nephews than he could count on two hands. The newest, little Nico, was only a few weeks old. "I do."

"And how would you feel if one of your sisters was in my position? If her husband died and she was blindsided by the news that he wasn't the father of her child? Then to be forced to hand over your niece to a stranger because of circumstances outside her control?"

That made Luca frown. He ran the family enterprise with his brothers by his side. His whole life revolved around Moretti Enterprises. Family—blood—was everything to him. That's why Eva was so important. Regardless of circumstances, she was family. The idea of letting Nico go off with someone they didn't know was unnerving, even if that man had the right. Perhaps he needed to change his tactics with Claire. Bullying would not change her mind any more than it would change his sister's mind.

"I understand how hard this must be for you. Despite what you might think, Mrs. Douglas, I'm not keen to snatch your baby from your arms. But I do want to get to know my daughter and be a part of her life. I'm not backing down on that. I think you will be more comfortable with the entire situation if you get to know me better. A lot of your concerns about me and how well I'll care for Eva will be gone if we spend some time together. By that I mean time with all of us together, so you can be there for every moment and be more at ease with my ability to be a good father."

Claire's frown started to fade the more he spoke. "Do you mean like playdates? I appreciate what you're trying to do, but it's going to take a long time for me to be comfortable if we're just spending an hour or two together every Saturday afternoon. How much can I learn about you during the occasional walk through the park?"

Luca shook his head. "Actually, no, that's not what I mean. You're right. It's going to take more time than that."

"What are you suggesting, Mr. Moretti?" her lawyer asked.

"I'm suggesting we both take a little time away from our jobs and spend it together."

"Tiptoeing around your penthouse apartment?" Claire asked.

He shrugged. He hadn't given much thought to where or how. "Why not?"

"I would prefer more neutral territory, Mr. Moretti. I won't be comfortable in your home, and I doubt you'll enjoy the mess a baby and all her things can make in your fancy apartment. You're not going to be happy coming to Brooklyn, either."

"Okay. What do you think about us taking a vacation together? Renting a beach house or something?"

"Luca, I'm not sure that's such a good—"

"I'm listening," she said, interrupting Edmund's complaint. Claire's delicate brows then drew together in confusion. "It sounds nice, but how long of a vacation are we talking about, here?"

If they were going to do this, and make it work, they couldn't skimp. She was right; a few hours here and there wouldn't get them anywhere. He needed to get to know the mother of his child, to bond with his daughter and to make Claire at ease with him and his ability to care for Eva. That would take time.

"I think a month ought to do it."

Two

"A month?" Claire was stunned. "Mr. Moretti—"

"Please, call me Luca," he said with a smile that made her pulse quicken in her throat.

That was a dangerous smile. It was charming. Disarming. Combined with his movie star good looks, it was enough to make her forget that he was the enemy, not a potential paramour. She almost preferred that he return to his cold, businessman expression.

"*Luca*, I have a job. I'm a curator at the Museum of European Arts. I can't just leave for a month, especially on short notice."

"Do you think it will be easy for me to simply turn over the reins of my family company for a month? It will be a hardship for both of us, but it has become very clear that it is a necessity to make this work. We need time away, just the three of us, to get comfortable with one another. Don't you think Eva's welfare is worth the sacrifice?"

Nice. Now Luca was the good guy and Claire was the one being unreasonable because she wouldn't do whatever it took for her daughter. "Of course she's worth the sacrifice. My daughter is my whole life."

"Then what's the problem? The way I see it, our court date with the judge is in six weeks. After spending four of those weeks together, perhaps we can come up with an arrangement that makes both of us happy and can present that to the judge."

Claire felt Stuart squeeze her knee beneath the table. She didn't have to look at her lawyer to know that he liked this idea. No one wanted to go up against Edmund Harding in court if they could avoid it. Going to see the judge with both parties on the same page would make things easier on everyone. Including Eva.

That was the thought that won her over. Her boss wouldn't be happy, but he would understand. He knew what she had been going through the past two years. He'd be the first to tell her she deserved a vacation. Maternity leave was hardly a break. That was just a six-week introduction to the hard life of a single mother.

"Okay. If you agree to take the emergency visitation filing off the table, I'll agree to your proposal."

Luca nodded slowly and gestured to his lawyer. "Okay. I'll make the arrangements for a location."

"I'd prefer it not be too far away," Claire said. "Long trips with a baby are difficult, and I'm not sure I'm ready to take her on a plane."

"I have an old friend from college who has a place on Martha's Vineyard. Would that suit you?"

Claire tried not to react. Martha's Vineyard was the

summer playground of the rich. Until recently, she'd been solidly middle class, and a vacation locale like that had always seemed out of her reach. The sudden increase in her checking account balance hadn't changed her mind-set along with her tax bracket. "That would be suitable," she said, coolly.

"Very well. I'll speak to Gavin and make sure it's available. How long will you need to prepare for the trip and arrange the time off?"

It was Monday. At the best, she could leave this weekend. "I'm not sure, but it will take a few days."

"I'll give you my contact information. Let me know when you find out, and I'll have a car sent to pick you up."

"That's not necessary. I can arrange my own transportation." Claire was never the kind of woman who sat back and let people take care of her. Not Jeff, and certainly not Luca. She had the capacity and the money to handle this herself.

"Ridiculous. We'll ride together and start getting to know each other as soon as possible."

Claire clenched her jaw. He spoke as if everything was law. It made her crazy. She had to pick her battles, though. If he wanted to send someone all the way out to her brownstone in Brooklyn to pick them up, then fine. "Very well. Are we done here?"

Luca's lips twisted into an amused smile. "We are."

Good. Claire was in desperate need of getting out of this room. The spacious conference room closed in on her the longer Luca stared at her. Those dark hazel eyes had the slightest hint of gold twinkling mischievously in them. He seemed to look right through her, seeing all the secrets and shame she was desperate to hide.

Picking up her bag, she pushed up from her seat and turned her back on Luca Moretti. She needed some distance between them. She wanted to breathe air that wasn't scented with leather and the spice of his cologne. Claire moved with purpose out of the conference room, exiting Edmund's law offices with Stuart on her heels. She didn't stop until she was standing on the sidewalk, looking at the traffic buzzing down Lexington Avenue.

Claire took a deep breath and felt the muscles in her neck and shoulders finally start to loosen. It wasn't just what he saw in her. It was how he made her feel. Luca lit a fire inside her that licked at her cheeks and made her think about the needs she'd ignored for longer than she could remember.

When she and her husband decided to have a child and it didn't happen easily, sex with Jeff became a chore. Mechanical. When that didn't work and they went to the clinic, it was even worse. Desire and arousal went out the window with sterile rooms and medical procedures. Their relationship changed as their failures became all they could focus on.

It was no wonder Jeff strayed.

Claire had been so wrapped up in getting pregnant, and then obsessed with preparing for the baby's arrival, she didn't notice anything was wrong. Jeff was working later, going on more business trips, but a lot of people worked long hours. Even she did from time to time, especially when a new exhibit was getting ready to open at the museum. But she also ignored the fact that he took a shower the minute he got home, the distant look in his eyes and the complete disinterest in physical contact. She was so adept at justifying every red flag that if his mistress hadn't died in the car with Jeff when he wrecked, she might never have accepted he was having an affair.

It had taken time to come to terms with the truth, but knowing that her relationship with Jeff would've ended no matter what had helped her cope with his death. She had lost her husband long before that night. If Jeff had lived long enough for the truth about his infidelity to come to light, they probably would've divorced. And if by some miracle they had fought through the rough patch, finding out that he wasn't Eva's father would've been the end. His ego never could've taken a hit like that.

Realizing all this had been a major blow to her confidence in her ability to make good choices. She had thought Jeff was the perfect man for her and she'd been wrong. She'd thought a baby would help give her what she was missing from her life and her marriage, and it wasn't. She loved Eva more than anything and didn't regret having her, but a baby hadn't been the answer to their problems. In the end it made them worse.

Being attracted to Luca Moretti was another bad decision. Even as she could feel his gaze raking across her skin, she knew it was a terrible idea. And yet, she hadn't felt that alive in years. He hadn't even touched her and she'd reacted to him like no other man before him.

"Claire, are you okay?" Stuart came up behind her, placing a soothing hand on her shoulder.

"Yeah, I was just ready to get out of there."

He nodded, looking out at the passing cars. "Let me take you to lunch." They turned and started walking down the sidewalk. "All things considered, I think it went okay today. Edmund's not filing an emergency visitation petition, so that buys us some time. He's willing to work with us to come up with an agreement before we go to the judge. It isn't going to get any better than that."

"Yes, but it cost me four weeks of my life." She would pay more than that for Eva and her well-being, but she was still a little shell-shocked from everything that just happened.

"Claire…it could be worse. You're going to spend a month at a beach house on Martha's Vineyard."

"With Luca Moretti," she pointed out. Somehow that made it seem like less of a vacation and more of an obstacle course she needed to survive.

"So what? Between you and me, I think you need the break. Get out of New York, sit on the beach and breathe in the sea air. It's beautiful up there this time of year. It's early in the season, but that means it won't be too crowded or hot. Let Luca take care of Eva under your watchful eye and be grateful for the time off. How does Japanese food sound for lunch?"

This trip sounded good on paper, but she was certain that the reality would be very different. She'd barely made it through a half hour with Luca with both their lawyers present. What would she do when she was alone with him for a whole month?

Luca strolled down Park Avenue, heading toward his apartment. He could've called a car to pick him up, but he needed the walk. It helped him focus, or in this case think about something else. It took about ten blocks before he could get the sound of Claire's sigh from his mind. Her steel-gray eyes haunted him.

He hadn't expected to have a reaction to her like this. He didn't want to, either. That woman had been nothing but difficult, despite how politely he'd tried to handle this mess of a situation. And yet, he couldn't help pushing her buttons just to see the fire in her. Under that prim suit and tightly wrapped bun was a passionate woman, he was certain of it.

Of course, what did it matter? He was pretty sure that Edmund would advise him strongly not to get romantically involved with Claire. He knew it was the smart thing, but Luca didn't always follow the advice of others.

Turning the corner, Luca finally reached his building. Standing beneath the dark green awning was Wayne, the second-shift doorman.

"Good afternoon, Mr. Moretti. You're home early today. I hope everything is okay."

Luca smiled at the doorman who had worked here longer than he had owned the apartment. "No worries, Wayne. All is well. I'm actually home a little early to start planning a vacation."

"You, sir? I don't think you've had one of those since you moved in."

Was it that obvious that he was a workaholic? "Probably not. I've been working pretty hard lately. I'm going to be gone for a month, though, up to Martha's Vineyard if all goes to plan. Will you let the building manager know I'll be away? I'll need my mail and packages held until I return."

"I will, sir. May I ask if you're doing something fun on your trip?"

The thought of the rosy blush running over every inch of Claire's porcelain skin instantly came to mind.

That could be fun. Or it could be four weeks of bickering by the beach. "Maybe. It depends on how it goes. I certainly hope so."

Wayne pulled open the shiny brass door and took a step back. "Well, I hope you enjoy your time away. You've certainly earned it, sir."

"Thanks, Wayne."

Luca crossed the marble lobby floor to his private elevator. He smiled as he pressed the button that would take him up to his apartment. Claire thought she knew so much about him, but she was wrong on several counts. For one thing, he didn't live in the penthouse. He lived on the tenth floor of his building. The penthouse apartment was just too large for his needs. His apartment had three bedrooms and an unused maid's quarters. That was more than enough.

When he'd purchased the place a few years ago, he was pretty certain he would live there alone for the rest of his life. Despite the fact that he had bent to the will of his doctors and his mother as a teenager by storing the potential for future children at the clinic, he had no intention of ever using it.

A wife and a family were the furthest thing from Luca's mind. He'd found that people who lived through what he had reacted one of two ways—they were either desperate for family or terrified by the idea of it. Luca fell into the latter category, although he hadn't always felt that way.

The doors of the elevator opened to the marble foyer of his apartment. He unlocked the door, stepping into his living room. Luca slipped out of his coat and headed for his study. There, he poured himself a finger of Scotch and settled down in his favorite leather chair.

As the oldest of six kids, he'd presumed he'd have a family of his own someday. He enjoyed the camaraderie and the chaos of his childhood home. Then, at age sixteen, those presumptions went out the window when his whole life was derailed by an unexpected illness. The illness turned out to be testicular cancer. The treatment for his cancer was aggressive—surgery and several rounds of chemotherapy and radiation. The majority of patients who went through the treatment were sterile when it was over. Although the idea of it was mortifying, he'd made several donations to be frozen at the fertility clinic for the future. His mother paid the clinic big money for them to hold on to it for as long as Luca might be in need of it.

Luca knew when he was doing it, however, that he would be storing, but not using it, forever. Despite assurances to the contrary, he knew he was a damaged commodity. At any time, the cancer could come back or spread. Physically, he wasn't the complete man he'd once been. Plastic surgery had corrected the aesthetics, but he knew the truth. He couldn't knowingly go into a relationship with a woman knowing that he was limited in what he could offer her.

And he was limited. He knew that in his heart. The one time a woman had claimed to have given birth to his child, he'd let himself get his hopes up. His whole family got their hopes up. When the miracle baby turned out to belong to someone else, everyone was disappointed, including the baby's gold-digging mother, Jessica. He had always been adamant about using protection, just for safety reasons, but after that he was almost militant. He didn't want another woman to even get the idea that she could have his child.

Sipping his drink, he looked around his study. It was a part of his perfect bachelor pad, decorated with masculine touches of leather and dark wood. The shelves were lined with books he'd never read. On one wall was a framed portrait of the world, reminding him of all the places he'd never been. He'd gone from being a child, to a cancer patient, to a college student, to a CEO. That didn't leave room for much else.

It was just as well that Jessica's baby hadn't been his. Even if he wanted a family, he didn't have time. From the day he was born, he'd been groomed to take over Moretti's Restaurants. His great-grandfather had started the company eighty years ago with a small restaurant in Little Italy. By the time his grandfather took over, they had another restaurant in Brooklyn and one in Queens. It snowballed from there. His father's goal of having a Moretti's in every state had been achieved not long after Luca was born.

After he got sick, his mother had homeschooled him from the hospital to help him keep up with his studies while he received his treatment. When he graduated from high school in remission, Luca went to Harvard to get his business degree and started working at the corporate offices with his father. His MBA earned him the title of vice president, and his father's retirement two years ago had turned the reins over to him entirely.

Luca had put his own stamp on the empire by diversifying their restaurants. Not everyone had the time for a long, sit-down Italian feast. He started a fast-food Italian chain called Antonia's, after his mother. That had exploded, becoming one of the fastest growing chains in that market.

Overseeing this monster took all the time he had.

And he liked it that way. When his life was so full, he didn't miss the family he was lacking.

And now, suddenly, he found he had a family he never expected—one that had been confirmed as actually being his. Thankfully the apartment could accommodate Eva, in terms of size and space. There would need to be some childproofing and redecorating, but that was the least of his worries. The harder part would be seeing to it that the rest of his life could accommodate his newfound daughter, as well.

That started with this trip. The first thing he needed to do was to call his old friend Gavin Brooks. He and Gavin had met at Harvard and hit it off immediately. Like Luca, Gavin was the heir to a family empire of his own—Brooks Express Shipping. They both understood what it was like to have that kind of pressure on their shoulders. The difference was that Gavin had managed to run BXS *and* have a family. He and his new wife, Sabine, had two small children, including a baby girl named Beth, who was only a few months older than Eva.

Perhaps Gavin could offer Luca more than just a vacation house. He could use some advice, as well.

Reaching for his phone, he dialed Gavin's number.

"This can't really be Luca Moretti calling me," Gavin answered abruptly. "I mean, that's what my phone says, but my friend Luca never calls me."

Luca sighed. "That's because your friend Luca works too much and is never sure when he can call without waking up your kids."

Gavin laughed. "It's a crapshoot. Jared is an early bird and Beth is a night owl. We pretty much never sleep around here. How are you, Luca?"

"To tell you the truth, I'm overwhelmed." It was nice to be able to talk to someone who truly understood what his days were like. He and Gavin were members of an elite club of young, successful businessmen in Manhattan.

"The restaurant business giving you trouble?"

"No. Work is fine. I called because I need your help for a more…personal matter."

"I thought you didn't have personal matters."

"So did I, then it got dropped in my lap." Oddly enough, this was another situation that Gavin could sympathize with. He didn't learn about his son, Jared, until the boy was almost two years old. "I need your help, Gavin."

"Sure, anything. What is it?"

"Okay. If I tell you something, will you promise not to tell anyone?" At this point, Luca couldn't risk the news of Eva's existence getting out. He'd worked hard to keep the lawsuit under wraps so far.

"Sounds serious," Gavin said. "I'll keep it to myself."

"Thanks. I'm trying to ensure this whole situation stays quiet for the next few weeks, primarily because of my family. You know how they are. I need to deal with all of this without their interference."

"Your cancer has come back," Gavin said in a grave tone.

"No, thankfully. I've actually found out that I'm a father."

"A father? For real this time?"

In retrospect, Luca had wished he'd kept the situation with Jessica quiet until he knew for certain. He'd never expected her to lie about it. He should've known when he saw the look on her face after Edmund demanded a paternity test. As though he'd just take her word for it. "Yes, this time it is tested and established to be my child. I have a daughter named Eva."

"But wait," Gavin argued. "I thought you couldn't…"

"I can't," Luca confirmed. "But I had some sperm frozen before my treatment. There was a mix-up at the clinic and a woman ended up pregnant with my child instead of her husband's."

"Holy hell. What are you going to do?"

"Well, first I sued the crap out of the clinic. Now I'm trying to negotiate custody terms with the mother. I can assure you it hasn't been easy. She's not happy about all this."

"I can imagine her husband isn't that happy, either."

"I'm not sure if it makes all this easier or more complicated, but her husband is actually deceased. Apparently he was in a car accident when she was pregnant."

"I thought my situation with Sabine was complicated, but you take the cake, Luca."

"Thanks. This brings me to the favor. I've proposed that all three of us spend some time away to get to know each other. She's not very confident in my ability to take care of a baby and I've got to convince her everything is going to be all right."

"Why don't you just tell her that you helped raise your younger siblings and have spent time with a dozen nieces and nephews? The last time you came over, you handled Jared like a pro."

That was a good question. "I doubt she would believe me. She's a feisty woman, and to tell you the truth, it's more fun to aggravate her."

"It sounds like this vacation might prove a little dangerous. Where are you going?" Gavin asked.

"That's where you come in. I was hoping that we could stay at your beach house for a couple weeks. A month, actually."

Gavin only hesitated a second before he answered. "Sure thing. We're not going back up there until after Memorial Day. But why wouldn't you stay at your family's place in the Hamptons?"

That had occurred to him. They had a huge place in Sag Harbor where the family liked to gather. But it was too big. And at this point, he didn't want to run the risk of crossing paths with his family. "To do that, my mother would find out. As it is, I've got to feed my brother an excuse to run the business while I disappear for a month. I will tell them, and soon, but I need to spend time with Claire and Eva without Mama circling like a shark around her granddaughter."

Gavin laughed. "Fair enough. When are you going up? I'll have the place cleaned and the pantry stocked before you arrive."

"I'm not exactly sure. We both have to make arrangements with work, but I'm hoping in the next week."

"So, four weeks in a beach house with the woman you accidentally impregnated and the child you've never met? And the woman doesn't like you, at that."

Luca sighed. "That pretty much sums it up."

"Well, good luck to you, man," Gavin said. "I'll have a bicycle messenger bring you the key tomorrow. And just in case, I'll have the cleaning company hide anything breakable."

Three

Claire paced nervously around the living room of her Brooklyn brownstone. After her meeting with Luca Moretti and his lawyer, things had moved faster than she'd expected. Her supervisor at the museum had been understanding about her situation. The exhibit she'd been working on the past few months had opened the week before and everything was going smoothly. It was actually the perfect time for her to take a vacation, so he'd practically shoved her out the door. With no excuses, she'd called Luca and told him that she could leave as soon as Saturday.

Then her conscience got the best of her. Despite their battles over the past few weeks, Luca had yet to meet Eva. She doubted that the ideal place for their first meeting was the back of a hired car on their way to Martha's Vineyard. She could hear the voice of her lawyer in her head, telling her to play nice. Before she could stop herself, she'd invited Luca over Thursday night.

He should be there any minute.

At the moment, Claire was practically buzzing with nervous energy. Since she'd gotten home, she'd barely held still. She'd already cleaned downstairs, fed and bathed Eva and put her in her footie jammies so she'd be ready for bed when the time came. Eva was currently lying on her jungle gym mat, babbling at the brightly colored lion and monkey toys dangling overhead. She could lie there for hours, contently slobbering on a plastic ring striped like a zebra.

The sound of the doorbell nearly sent Claire leaping out of her skin. She didn't know why she was so anxious about having him over. It wasn't just the idea of a billionaire in her home, although that was intimidating enough. It was a billionaire with an influence on how she raised her child. Would he think their home wasn't good enough? Would he argue her neighborhood was unsafe? That she wasn't providing well enough for Eva? Any of those things could tip the scales in court to Luca's favor.

Truthfully, she didn't know how he could complain. She and Jeff had bought and restored this beautiful brownstone a few years earlier. It was in a safe, trendy part of Brooklyn with great schools. Even then, it wasn't the Upper East Side. She didn't have a doorman or co-op board to keep the riffraff from moving in nearby.

Claire forced her feet across the parquet floors to the front door. She glanced through the peephole, seeing Luca waiting impatiently on her front stoop. Just a glance at him, knowing he was about to step into her home, sent a shiver through her whole body. She wasn't quite sure if she was excited or terrified by the prospect. She unlocked the door and opened it as she took a deep breath to push all those feelings aside. "Good evening, Mr. Moretti," she said.

He smiled and stepped through the doorway. He had a pink chenille teddy bear in his arms and a more relaxed expression on his face than at the lawyer's office. "Please, I told you to call me Luca," he insisted.

She knew that was what he wanted, but she didn't like the idea of it. It was too casual, too intimate. She preferred to keep some formality between them, at least for now. It felt as if it would make things easier over the next four weeks if she had that emotional buffer, even as the scent of his cologne was making her pulse spike in her throat. Ignoring his request, she shut the door behind him and returned to where he was waiting for her in the foyer.

Luca took the opportunity to study her home, admiring the architectural details she'd worked so hard to preserve. Claire much preferred her view of him at the moment. He was looking very handsome tonight in an expensive navy suit that was tailored to highlight his broad shoulders and narrow hips. He'd paired it with a blue-and-brown geometric tie that seemed to capture the same shade of milk chocolate as the waves of his hair.

Chocolate waves of his hair? Claire squeezed her eyes shut for a moment to rid the image from her mind. Why was she cataloging his good looks, anyway? That was not what tonight was about. Or any night from now on. Luca might be Eva's father, but it didn't happen the old-fashioned way. Thinking of him like that was dangerous while their custody arrangement was still up in the air. She couldn't afford to make a mistake when it came to Eva and her welfare.

"I wanted to thank you for inviting me over tonight," he said as she took his coat and hung it in the entryway closet. "I realize this is difficult for you."

Claire forced a smile. "It was the least I could do," she said. "After all, you're treating us to a month at the beach." *Or trapping us with you for a month at the beach.* Same difference, she supposed.

"You can thank the CEO of Brooks Express Shipping for that, actually. We went to college together. It's his beach house we're going to be staying at as a favor to me."

"Of course it is." She chuckled dryly. Apparently rich guys just hung out together. Claire hadn't been around many superwealthy people, but she wasn't surprised to think they all knew one another. They certainly weren't spending their time with people like her. At least until now, when he had to.

With a shake of her head, she turned away from him and led Luca out of the entryway and into the open expanse of her living room. "Well, this is Eva," she said, holding her arm out in front of them to where she was playing.

Luca turned in that direction and froze in place the moment his eyes fell on their daughter. For a powerful CEO who was always in control of everything, he seemed to be at a total loss in the moment. He didn't take a step toward Eva; he just kept watching her from a distance.

Claire decided to help by easing him into his new

role as father. She walked across the room and scooped Eva up off the floor. Cuddling the baby in her arms, she turned back to Luca. "Look who's come to visit, Eva. You have a new friend here to see you."

Eva turned her head to look at Luca, her big gray eyes taking in the new person and processing it however her little baby brain operated.

Luca finally loosened up, leaning in to the baby with a wide, friendly smile. "Hello, *bella*."

Eva rewarded him with a slobbery grin, showcasing her two new bottom teeth. She was usually a little shy with strangers, but she seemed to warm up to Luca immediately. When he reached out to stroke her chubby little arm, she grabbed his finger and held on tight.

"You've got a good hold of me, don't you? How about I trade you my finger for a fuzzy bear?" Luca held up the pink bear and Eva's eyes immediately shifted to the new pretty.

She let go of his finger and reached out for the soft toy with a cry of delight. Luca handed it over to her, laughing as she immediately put the bear's ear in her mouth.

"Everything is a teething toy these days," Claire said. "Thank you for the gift."

"It's long overdue," he said with a touch of sadness in his voice.

Claire noted it, feeling guilty for her role in that delay. Her lawyer had been right; none of this was Luca's fault. He just wanted to be a part of his child's life, and he deserved to be. As much as she didn't want to admit it, the time together at the beach would make this situation workable for both of them. They needed it. "Would you like to hold her?" she asked.

"Yes," he said with a touch of excitement in his gold and brown eyes.

"Here we go," Claire said in the soft baby voice she used for Eva. Lifting her off her chest, she moved Eva over into Luca's waiting arms. He scooped her up like a professional. Perhaps it was beginner's luck.

"You are a sweet little thing," he said, cooing at his daughter. "I'm going to be wrapped around your little finger before too long, I can tell."

Claire took a step back to let Luca have his moment with Eva. After a few minutes, he moved over to her couch and settled Eva on his knee. It didn't take long for her to see that he was right. Luca was completely enamored with his daughter and they'd only just met. She understood. The minute she'd laid eyes on Eva, she was totally and completely in love. Luca looked just as she imagined she did then.

The reality of the moment was like a fist to her gut. She stumbled back a little, bracing herself against the doorway to the kitchen. Luca didn't notice. He only had eyes for Eva. As a new father should. It was the inescapable realization that she should've had this moment months ago, in the hospital with Jeff at her side, that threw her off balance. She should've gotten to watch her husband hold their daughter for the first time with that same look of wonder and adoration on his face.

Instead, her moments in the hospital had been bittersweet. She'd cradled her baby, alone in her room, and cried. They were tears of joy, tears of sadness, tears of loss. She wouldn't have that moment with Jeff because he'd gotten himself killed while he was out with his mistress. She wouldn't have that moment with Jeff because in the end, Eva wasn't even his daughter.

How had her life gone so far off the rails? Claire had done everything right her whole life. She'd graduated at the top of her class, going to college on an academic scholarship that left no time for boys. After school, she'd married the safe guy who would love her and care for her and their family. Jeff hadn't been the exciting choice, or the man who made her heart race and her insides melt, but she thought he was a stable, responsible man who would make a good father. She'd made all the right choices and did everything her family had expected her to do. And yet, everything had gone wrong.

Watching Luca on the couch with Eva, she saw nothing but sharp contrast between him and Jeff. It wasn't just the difference between Luca's darkness and Jeff's All-American good looks. It was a difference on the inside at a biological, maybe even cellular, level.

She'd spent almost no time with Luca at all, but she reacted to him like no other man before. There was an intensity in the way he watched her that got under her skin and made her cheeks turn flame hot. Everything from his commanding presence to his sharp sense of style caught her attention. Even the smell of him was enough to send an unwanted spike of need through her.

Luca was everything she shouldn't want. He was dangerous. Not in the traditional sense, but she knew she had to watch herself around him. He was a man who was used to people doing whatever he wanted and was willing to take whatever measures were necessary to make it happen. He also seemed like the kind of man who left a trail of broken hearts in his wake. Claire was determined that she wouldn't be one of those women no matter how he made her feel.

They would come to a co-parenting arrangement that suited them both, but that was it. That's all there could be. Claire would shelve any attraction she had for Luca, and maybe in time she would find a more suitable man to be in her life. Suitable hadn't done her much good the last time, but she wasn't about to throw caution to the wind because Jeff decided to stray. He was just one man with his own issues to cope with.

Claire took a deep breath to center herself and looked up to notice Luca was watching her as he held Eva. His gaze flicked over her casually, and yet she could feel the knot inside her belly tighten. She wasn't misinterpreting this. Luca made it plainly clear that he was attracted to her, as well. It might just be a negotiation strategy to soften her up, but when he looked at her that way, it almost made her feel like resistance was futile.

Luca was a man who got what he wanted. What would she do if he decided he wanted her?

Two days later, Luca rang the doorbell of Claire's brownstone and waited for her to answer.

"One second!" he heard her shout from the depths of the house. A pounding of footsteps got louder as it came across the hardwood floors to the door.

"You can take these bags and the playpen," she started as she whipped open the door, then stopped cold. "Luca?" She flushed that becoming rose color and covered her mouth with her hand. "I'm sorry. I thought you were sending a driver."

Luca shook his head. He occasionally used one around town to simplify the issues of parking and traffic in Manhattan, but he wanted some privacy and control over how today went. They'd need a car at the beach, and he certainly didn't want a chauffeur loitering around and interfering on their time together. He was fully capable of driving them and actually looked forward to it. He didn't get out of the city as much as he'd like these days.

"I changed my mind." Luca reached down and picked up the bags she had closest to the door. "I'll go put these in the car."

She nodded at him, still not quite recovered from his unexpected appearance. "I've got Eva's car seat here. It will take a few minutes to install it."

"That's not necessary. I have one in the car, ready to go."

Claire frowned at him, but Luca simply turned away and headed down the steps with her bags. He knew he shouldn't enjoy surprising Claire, but he did. She made far too many presumptions about him, and he liked shattering them one by one. As he loaded the bags into the back of his Range Rover, he noticed Claire approaching the car with Eva in her arms. Without saying a word, she opened the back door to investigate the car seat.

She wouldn't find any flaws with it. It was a top of the line model for Eva's age and weight. She was facing the proper direction with all the correct support. It was installed per the manufacturer's specifications. He even added a little mobile that hung overhead from the handle to occupy her while they drove.

Luca didn't say any of that, though. He simply loaded the bags, returning to the house to pick up a few more before waiting on the sidewalk for her judgment. "Will it suit?" he asked at last.

Claire turned to look at him with a sort of befuddled expression on her face. "Yes, it's perfect."

"Don't look so surprised, Claire. I manage a billion-dollar corporation. I can buy and install a car seat."

Her mouth dropped open in protest. "I didn't— I mean, I don't think that—"

"Are there any more bags that need to go?" he asked, saving her from herself.

"No, that's all of them. I'll put Eva in the car seat, and then I'll lock up."

From there, it wasn't long for them to get on the road. Once they got out of the city congestion and onto I-95, it was a smooth, albeit longer, drive. He'd been tempted to book a charter flight out of the heliport, but he knew better than to spring something like that on Claire. She said she didn't want to fly with Eva, and that meant she certainly wouldn't want to take a helicopter.

Claire spent the first part of the trip in the back with Eva. When they stopped for a break and some food, Eva had just fallen asleep, so Claire moved to the front. They passed the time chatting about his restaurants and her exhibits at the museum. By the time they drove off the ferry onto Martha's Vineyard, Luca was anxious to be there already.

"Finally," he said as he turned into the driveway and stopped to let both of them get a good view of the house. It was a two-story gambrel-style home with strong Dutch influences on the design. It had gray shake siding with white columns and a deck that extended off the second floor. It was charming for a beach cottage. He pulled up beside the front walkway and they got out of the car to investigate further. "Well, what do you think?"

Claire's mouth was agape as she took in the house, then turned to admire its views of Katama Bay and the Atlantic Ocean beyond. "It's beautiful. And huge. I can't believe this is just for us. Your friend doesn't need it for a whole month?"

Luca shook his head and opened the back of the Range Rover to start unloading. "Gavin works as much as I do. He bought the place so they could spend some time here in the summer. This is early season for the Vineyard, so he wouldn't be up here for at least a month anyway."

Claire returned to the car to unlatch Eva's carrier and take her toward the front of the house. Luca followed with a piece of luggage and the keys to the front door. He unlocked it, swinging the door open for her to go inside ahead of him. They stepped into a small den area with a fireplace and an office. To their left was a staircase. "Gavin says the main living area and master bedroom are upstairs to take full advantage of the views."

They climbed the stairs ahead of them until they revealed an open concept living area. It really was a stunning place. It had arched white ceilings with wooden beams and windows that gave floor-to-ceiling views of the bay. The furniture was soft and comfortable with the rustic sort of country charm that city people gravitated to while on vacation. While someone in Manhattan wouldn't think of having a pillow with a rooster on it in their trendy Greenwich Village loft, it was somehow more acceptable out here.

Claire wandered through the large, bright living

room to the kitchen that was big enough for a large family to pile in and cook a feast. Six barstools lined the kitchen island, with copper pots hanging overhead. Beyond it was a dining area with French doors that opened out onto the deck and showcased the view of the water.

"I'll be right back." Luca headed downstairs and made several trips to bring all the bags inside before parking the car in the garage. By the time he came back upstairs, Claire had Eva out of her carrier and perched on her hip. They were standing on the deck, enjoying the sunshine and letting the cool spring breeze blow over them.

Luca wanted to join them, but he was hesitant to interrupt this moment between a mother and her child. There was an expression of absolute joy on Claire's face as she looked down at her baby. Her dark gold hair whipped around in the wind, the sunlight making her porcelain skin almost glow. She looked like an angel standing there in her sundress. He felt a tightness in his chest as he watched her cradle his daughter and point out birds flying overhead.

Learning of Eva's existence had been a shock, but until a few days ago, she'd been more of an idea than a reality. Seeing Eva for the first time had changed everything. When he held her in his arms, he felt something flip inside of him. A protectiveness was roused in him, almost instinctual in its ferocity. After only a few moments together, he would've done anything for his little girl.

It surprised him after suppressing the idea of a family for so long. There was a part deep inside Luca that had still wanted children, but he had avoided finding out if it was a possibility for him. Somehow it was easier to avoid the doctor and not know whether it was off the table than to get tested and know for certain that he had only two frozen chances at biological fatherhood.

Make that one chance, now that one of the samples had been used to create Eva. It was a mistake, malpractice at best, but at the same time it was hard to be angry about it. He'd been sleepwalking through his days, working hard to fill the void in his life, then boom—he had a daughter. Nothing else seemed quite as important as doing whatever he could to keep Eva happy, safe and in his life.

"How many bedrooms are there?"

Claire's voice roused him from his thoughts. He hoped she hadn't noticed him staring at her so intently. "Four. The master suite is to the left off the living room. There are three other bedrooms downstairs."

Claire looked around, awkwardly shuffling her feet as she studied the house. She probably wasn't sure how they were going to work out the arrangements here. Obviously they wouldn't be sharing a room, as much as he'd like to. They were here together as a family, but also to become friends and soothe her concerns about him caring for their daughter. She might be the most alluring woman he'd laid eyes on in a long time, but sex would most certainly complicate their already complicated situation.

"You and Eva should take the master," he said. "Gavin said there's a crib in there because they got the place not long before their daughter, Beth, was born. There's also plenty of room for the playpen and all of Eva's things there." Luca opened the door to the master suite and gestured her to go inside ahead of him.

"Are you sure?" she asked as she stepped inside and surveyed the room with its cheery yellow walls and iron king-size bed. There was a crib and changing table along one wall and a large dresser along the other. "We'll be just as comfortable downstairs."

"Nonsense. This is perfect for you." And it was. The room suited Claire as though it was made for her. Elegant and cheerful, comfortable and effortless. Claire was all that and more. Her beauty was natural, not forced like that of so many other women. She wore just enough makeup to highlight her features, not disguise them. Her clothes looked comfortable, but stylish. Even the scent of her was perfection—like vanilla and cinnamon. It all came together into a distracting and enticing package.

It didn't stop at looks, either. Driving out here, he was impressed by how intelligent and articulate she was. Working at a museum with a degree in art history, she could just as easily discuss impressionist pieces as ancient Egyptian tomb paintings. He hoped their daughter would be as beautiful and smart as her mother. He doubted he could've picked a better woman to have his child if he'd done it himself. The Fates worked in mysterious ways.

The Fates? His mother's superstitious ways were creeping into his thoughts today. With a dismissive shake of his head, Luca went back out to the living room and started bringing Claire's bags inside. "I'll let you get settled in. I'm sure you could use a nap or something after that long drive."

Claire chuckled and settled on the edge of the bed with Eva. "I doubt I'll get a nap, but maybe there will be some quiet tummy time in our future."

He nodded and slipped from the room. Luca stomped down the staircase to the first floor. Once there, he took a deep breath and exhaled Claire's scent from his lungs. If only his thoughts of her could be expelled so easily.

Grabbing one of his bags, he went into each bedroom, selecting the one the farthest from Claire. He dropped the bag on the floor at the foot of the bed and flopped down onto the queen-size mattress. The room was tidy, with blue walls and distressed furniture. In the end it didn't really matter. All he needed was a bed and space away from Claire to keep a clear head.

Four weeks was a long time to be alone with her here. With the longing she stirred inside him with only a glance, it would feel even longer.

Four

The morning light shone through the window and roused Claire from her sleep. She yawned and stretched, feeling luxuriously lazy for not setting an alarm. She could get used to this vacation thing. For the first time in a long time she felt well rested. She'd slept like a rock last night. She hadn't done that since before Eva was born.

Wait a minute… Eva!

Shooting up in bed, Claire looked over to the crib. If the alarm didn't wake Claire up, the baby usually did, so if she was still sleeping, something was wrong with Eva. Her eyes scanned the unfamiliar crib, but there was no baby to be found.

"Eva?" she called out with an edge of panic in her voice.

Claire whipped the blankets back and leaped from

the bed. A quick search of the crib and the surrounding area confirmed what she already knew. Eva was missing. "Eva!" she shouted again, throwing open the door of the master bedroom and skidding into the living room. She came to a sudden stop, not quite sure she could believe what her eyes were seeing.

"Good morning. Are you hungry?"

Luca was standing in the kitchen with Eva perched on his hip. Together, they were cooking breakfast. The billionaire CEO was mixing pancake batter while playfully gumming at her infant's fingers and making yummy sounds. Luca looking so casual holding her daughter was a surreal sight after their tense conference room showdown. Was this the same man who had threatened her with prison time? "We've been enjoying our morning, haven't we, *bella*? We had a bottle and coffee out on the deck and watched the seabirds, and then we decided to make pancakes for breakfast."

She was happy to find Eva safe, but she didn't appreciate the fright he'd given her. Luca's brows drew together. "Claire, are you okay?"

She didn't answer him. Marching across the living room, she took Eva from his arms and cradled her to her chest. Then, and only then, could she respond to Luca. "Please don't do that," she said.

"Do what?"

"Take her without telling me."

"You mean take her like she's my child and care for her as a father would do?"

Claire frowned at him. He might technically be her father, but he hadn't earned the right to just wander off with Eva without her permission. Her daughter barely knew him. "The point of this trip was so that I could get comfortable with you handling Eva. It's been less than twenty-four hours and I can assure you that I'm not comfortable yet."

"I'm sorry," Luca said, coming around the kitchen island with a mug of coffee in his hand. "I get up early, so I came and got her so you could sleep. It defeated the purpose to wake you up and ask if you minded. Would you like some coffee? I made this cup for you, but again, I didn't ask permission first, so you may not want it."

Claire ignored his sharp tone. He was annoyed, but she didn't care. It was far too early for him to start ignoring boundaries. Being temporarily under the same roof didn't turn their situation into some family sitcom. Of course, neither did her snapping at him.

"Sure," she replied quietly, still a little off-kilter from her scare and not entirely pleased with how she'd handled all this in that state. "Thank you."

Luca set the mug on the counter within her reach and turned to the kitchen. With his back turned, Claire did a quick assessment of Eva and found her to be fed, changed and clean. She seemed happy and not at all concerned to be away from her mother with a strange man. Claire had obviously underestimated Luca when it came to caring for children. He knew more about it than he let on in their previous discussions.

"Do you want bacon?"

Claire turned back to Luca. He seemed to have cast aside their little skirmish and refocused on breakfast. "That sounds great." She slipped onto one of the stools at the kitchen counter to watch him work at the range. The in-control businessman appeared to have stayed back in Manhattan and in his place was a man enjoying his vacation. He was wearing a blue T-shirt and flannel plaid pajama pants with bare feet. His hair was slightly messy, and morning stubble lined his sharp jaw.

She imagined that this was a sight few people outside his immediate family got to see. She liked it. More than she wanted to admit. She wondered what his rough stubble would feel like against her cheek. Against her thighs…

Claire squeezed her eyes shut for a moment to send that sensation out of her mind. She wasn't allowed to snap at him, then fantasize about him a moment later. That was craziness.

When she reopened them, she focused on Luca's cooking. Even in his pajamas, he moved around the kitchen with purpose and fluidity. Luca certainly knew what he was doing. For some reason that surprised Claire. There was a lot about this man that wasn't what it appeared. "I knew you ran restaurants, but I never thought about whether you could actually cook," she admitted.

Luca flipped a pancake, then looked at her with a disarming smile. "In my family, food is life. All our family gatherings revolve around the meals we make together in the kitchen. Once a kid is old enough to peel a potato, they're put to work helping with Sunday suppers."

"Do you have a large family?"

Luca chuckled and flipped over another pancake. "Yes. I'm actually the oldest of six kids. My father is the oldest of five. When we all gather together with the cousins and spouses, there's easily forty or fifty of us."

"Did you help with caring for your siblings?"

He nodded. "Have I surprised you with my ability to handle an infant without completely melting down?"

Claire twisted her lips into a guilty smile. "Yes. I'm ashamed to admit it."

"In addition to my siblings, I have a dozen nieces and nephews that I see from time to time. I have cared for my fair share of children of all ages. Eva is in good hands, I assure you."

"Why didn't you say that at your lawyer's office?" That would've significantly reduced her stress level over this decision. She still didn't want him taking Eva without her permission, but knowing she wasn't the first baby he'd held made a difference.

Luca shrugged. "You made incorrect assumptions about me and I let you. Now that we're here—as you mentioned a moment ago—we can get to know each other as we are, not as others perceive us to be. You'll find most of your concerns are unfounded." He slid four perfectly golden pancakes onto a plate and added a few crispy pieces of bacon on the side. He placed the plate in front of Claire.

"That's a ton of food!" she exclaimed as she eyed the plate-sized pancakes.

"Well, that's the only problem I have in the kitchen. I don't know how to cook for two people. I cook for an army or not at all."

Claire couldn't even imagine having that much family. She had almost none. Jeff's family had been her own for many years and now… Eva was really all she had. She scooped the baby off her knee and put her into her high chair so she could eat. After she snapped on the tray, Luca put a handful of Cheerios out for her to pick up and nibble on while they had breakfast.

"What about you?" Luca asked as he made his own plate. "What is your family like?"

Claire frowned into her coffee mug. "Nothing like yours," she said. "I'm an only child. My parents were only children, as well. I didn't really grow up around our extended family. My father traveled with his job, so it was really just the three of us my whole life."

"And now?"

It seemed like a simple question, and yet it wasn't. Claire had family, and yet she didn't. It was a strange limbo to be in. "And now, it's really just Eva and me. My father had a heart attack and died when I was in college. My mother remarried, and since I was grown and gone, her life became more about her new husband. I don't see or talk to her very often because she lives in San Francisco now. I married Jeff not long after she moved, so I didn't notice the absence. His family was really good about including me for gatherings and holidays even before we got married. They were my family for many years, but now I've lost all that."

Luca settled beside her at the counter with his plate and coffee. "You mean they haven't included you since your husband died?"

Claire shrugged. "It's not that simple. His death was hard on us all. And the circumstances made it that much more awkward for everyone. I don't think they know what to say to me."

Luca looked at her with concern in his dark eyes. "May I ask what those circumstances were?"

She took a moment to butter her pancakes and pour maple syrup over the top. Claire had told this story enough times now that it shouldn't bother her anymore, but it did. The truth never got easier to take. "My husband died in a car accident with his mistress. He told me he had to go out of town on a business trip, but he was really with her. I would never have even known the truth, but they went off the road and hit a tree, killing them both. The police seemed to think she was… distracting him, somehow. I didn't have the heart to ask them why they thought that.

"I was five months pregnant at the time, after years of trying to have a baby," she continued. "It's hard to lose someone you love and yet be angry at him at the same time. There's so many emotions tied up in Jeff's death for me and for everyone else. I just don't think his family knew how to face me after that. Whenever they came to see Eva, his death hung over our heads like a dark cloud. And now they don't have to face it anymore. I haven't heard from his parents since I told them about the clinic mix-up. Apparently both Eva and I are disposable since we're no longer their blood relatives."

Spitting out the last of it, Claire shoveled a large bite of pancake into her mouth. There was something about admitting her pathetic story to Luca that made it worse than telling anyone else. She didn't want him to see her for the lonely, pitiful woman she felt like when she told her sad, sordid tale.

"That means it's just you and Eva now."

It was a statement, not a question, but Claire nodded as she chewed nonetheless. It was true. Eva was everything she had, which was why she'd fought so fiercely not to lose her daughter to a mysterious father. "Someday, I hope to have another chance at marriage and maybe another child if it's at all possible. But if that never happens, I'm thankful that I have Daisy, Eva's nanny. She's like family to me."

Luca's brow went up. "A nanny? After all the grief you gave me about handing Eva off to someone, you have a nanny?"

"It's not the same," Claire argued. "I didn't want Eva handed off and ignored. Daisy just watches Eva while I'm at the museum. When I get home, Daisy leaves and it's just the two of us. She gets one-on-one attention and care, and I thought that was better than putting her in day care while she's still so small. I plan to send her to a good preschool when she's older. I've already submitted a few applications."

"Where did you find this Daisy?" he asked. "Did you do the proper checks into her background to ensure she's trustworthy before you brought her into your home? Did you get several references from other clients?"

Claire sighed. "Yes. I did all that. She came highly recommended, and I haven't had a bit of trouble with her. She's been a godsend over the past few months."

Luca chuckled low and popped a bit of bacon into his mouth. "I know you did all that and more, I'm sure. I was just giving you a hard time, *tesorina*. It is only fair, don't you agree?"

She had given him a lot of grief, she knew that. Claire looked over at Eva as she studiously tried to capture a piece of cereal between her chubby fingers. "I'll do whatever it takes to keep her happy and safe, Luca. Do you blame me?" she asked.

Luca's gaze drifted from the baby back to Claire. There was a fierce fire of protectiveness there as he shook his head. "I do not."

In that moment, it was easy for Claire to believe that Luca would do anything for his young daughter, even after just a few short hours together. He seemed so deeply affected by his child it made her wonder why he hadn't married and started a family of his own by now. He was obviously comfortable with children and took to Eva immediately. Had running the family business really taken up that much of his time that he hadn't found someone to settle down with?

Or was there something he wasn't telling her?

"What's this?"

Luca looked up from making dinner in time to see Claire standing at the entrance to the kitchen. She was holding up the draft custody agreement his lawyer had given him. He'd left it on the coffee table so they could discuss it. "That's a love note from Edmund. It's the custody proposal we sent to Stuart a few weeks ago. I wasn't entirely sure if you'd read it, so he wanted to make sure we had something to redline while we're here."

A guilty expression wrinkled Claire's nose as she winced. "I didn't read it," she admitted.

Luca wasn't surprised. The woman who sat across from him at his lawyer's office hadn't been interested in his offer. Judging by the expression on her face, not much had changed. He poured dressing onto the bowl of salad for dinner and started gently tossing it. "Would you like to discuss it now?"

Claire eyed the folder and then set it on the kitchen island. "No, not really."

"May I ask why?"

With a sigh, she leaned against the counter. "Because I'm in a good mood. I'm enjoying this trip and I'm not ready to ruin it with our heated arguments. Besides, at this point, my position hasn't changed. You're still a stranger. A stranger who's good with kids, but not one I'm ready to hand over my daughter to."

"*Our* daughter," Luca corrected. She always said "my daughter." Claire seemed to have some kind of mental block where their daughter's paternity was concerned.

Claire ignored him. "My point is that I'm not ready yet, so there's no point in talking about it. I will read it," she added. "So when the time comes, I'll be well informed on your demands."

Demands? Luca wondered whether Claire knew just how her words sounded to him. They were both used to getting their way, but Luca was wise enough to realize they both couldn't win this battle without compromising. "We'll table the discussion, then. Dinner is about done. How about you choose a red wine for tonight?"

Claire went to the wine rack and looked over the selection. "The chianti or the merlot?" she asked.

Luca pulled the tray of lasagna from the oven and rested on the stovetop to cool. "The chianti," he said. No question. "We haven't tried that one yet."

Their first week at the beach had gone by in a blur, as vacations often did. Although they'd come here to work out a custody arrangement, they'd both carefully avoided that subject so far. Today, he'd finally gotten out the paperwork to broach the topic, but Claire obviously needed more time. That was fine. Instead of pushing, he took his cues from her, and it had worked. Day by day, Claire had loosened her reins on Eva. He had no doubt that by the end of the trip she would have no problem with him spending time with their daughter alone.

They'd spent a lot of time lounging by the beach and taking walks along the shore. Claire read a couple books and Luca checked in on his work email, although he knew he shouldn't. They cooked amazing meals together, spoiled Eva together and learned more about each other. It was exactly what Luca had hoped for when they made these arrangements.

Claire had turned out to be a delightful companion. After their first meeting with the lawyers, he had been dreading this trip, but he had been very wrong about her. She was fiercely protective of Eva, but once he got beyond her mother bear instincts, he was pleased to see the more easygoing side of Claire. Once she let her hair down and let the sea air into her lungs, she was just the kind of woman he'd want in his life…if he was ever going to have a woman in his life.

"I can't believe you got Eva to sleep so quickly," Claire said as she carried the bottle of red wine over to the dining-room table.

Luca had been surprised, too, but Eva had had a full day to wear her out. They'd gone down to the beach for a long walk along the bay as they'd done each day. They ate at a seafood shack by the shore where Luca got an amazing fried clam po'boy and Claire got a crab roll. Eva, sadly, got a squeeze pouch of blended chicken, peas and carrots. She took a short nap, then played on the floor for a good while with Claire while Luca assembled their dinner. By the time she had her bath and got put in her pajamas, Eva had heavy eyelids.

"Thanks for letting me put her down tonight," Luca said. It had been the first time he'd gotten to do that since they arrived. He'd stood by her crib, transfixed by his tiny child. He'd even tried out a verse of the lullaby his mother used to sing. Eva was asleep in minutes.

"You're welcome," Claire replied. "I think she likes your singing better than mine, anyway."

"I doubt that. Vacations can be tiring," he said. "She could've slept through anything at that point. To be honest, I'm not sure how much longer I'll last myself. A plate of lasagna and a glass of wine might put me right out."

Claire poured the wine into two glasses at the table beside the place settings she'd already arranged. She grabbed the bowl of salad and walked with Luca to the table to start their feast. "This all smells amazing," she said.

It was Sunday. There was no way that Luca could let the day pass without making an Italian feast that would make his mother proud. "It smells like my mama's kitchen. Garlic, spices, tomato sauce, cheese... Sunday dinner is served."

He cut a large square of lasagna and placed it on Claire's plate, then cut another for himself.

"I am going to gain so much weight," she said as she eyed her meal. "You cook too well and too much, and I can't resist it. It's only been a week, and today my shorts felt a little snug."

"Enjoy yourself," he insisted. "You are so tiny you can afford to put on a few more pounds without worry."

Claire laughed and sipped her wine. "I'm still battling my last few pregnancy pounds, so I assure you that's not the case."

Luca wasn't sure where these mysterious pounds were hidden, but he didn't see them. He actually thought Claire seemed a little thin. He assumed it was the stress of the past year taking its toll on her. "I don't know what you're talking about. You look amazing to me. My mother would insist you're too skinny and force food on you if I were to bring you home to her."

He flinched inwardly as the words slipped from his mouth. Claire seemed to stiffen in her chair beside him, and he knew it felt strange for her to think of him that way, as well. He'd never considered what it would be like for Claire to meet the rest of his family. And really, bringing Claire to the house wasn't the same as bringing home a girlfriend. It was far more complicated.

Claire finally relaxed when he didn't push the subject and just shook her head. "I can't even imagine," she said. "How did your family take the news about Eva?"

"I haven't told them yet," Luca admitted.

"Why is that?"

Luca sighed, exhausted by the mere idea of telling his family, much less doing it. "Well, as I told you before, I have a big family. I also have a loud, pushy, smothering family. I think my mother has very nearly given up on me ever having children. Finding out about Eva would be earth-shattering. They would swarm on us like bees on a honeycomb. I wanted us to have a little space first. Getting away from Manhattan was a part of that. They'll find out soon enough."

As far as Luca was concerned, they were already on borrowed time. He'd been very careful, but he awaited a leak any day now. Every time his phone buzzed at his hip, he expected to see his mother's number on the screen.

"Where do they think you are now? I mean, you

had to get someone to run the company while you're gone all these weeks, right?"

"I told my brothers that I was taking a beautiful woman away on a vacation. They agreed to handle things and not tell anyone. Probably because they're as desperate as Mama to see me find a woman."

"Do you feel bad about lying to them?"

Luca's brows drew together in confusion. "No. I'm not lying."

"But you said—"

"I said I was taking a beautiful woman on a vacation." Luca looked at her across the table. "That's absolutely true."

That rose blush spread across Claire's cheeks again, distracting him from his plate. "Quit it. You don't have to butter me up."

Luca set his fork down. Claire might be a fierce competitor in their lawyers' offices, but when it came to romance, she seemed almost broken by the idea of it. "I'm not flattering you, *tesorina*. I'm serious. Are you not aware of how attractive you are?"

Her mouth fell open, a flustered conglomeration of nonsense words coming out of her as she tried to gather her thoughts. "I mean, I think I'm pretty enough. I'm no supermodel or polished Upper East Side housewife."

"Fake," he said. "All of that is fake, crafted by makeup artists, plastic surgeons and photo-altering software. I will take a real, soft, naturally beautiful woman over one of those fantasies any day."

"I think you're in the minority, Luca."

Luca couldn't stand the uncomfortable expression on Claire's face. Was this just Jeff's doing, or had every man in her life treated her poorly? "Did your husband never tell you how beautiful you were?"

Claire looked down and anxiously moved her food around on her plate for a moment. "Not really. I mean, he chose me, so he must've thought I was pretty, but he wasn't the type to lay on praise. Especially near the end."

Luca sat back in his chair for a minute and tried to absorb everything she'd just told him. He would never have a wife of his own, but he knew if he did he would cherish her. "I'm sorry," he said at last.

Claire's eyes widened with surprise. "You're sorry for what?" she asked.

"I'm sorry that your husband didn't treat you the way he should have." Just hearing her talk about Jeff had made his blood boil. Not only had he been reckless with his marriage, he'd been reckless with his life when he had a child on the way. Then to find out that he'd never given his wife the love and praise she deserved even in the early years of their relationship... It was inexcusable in his eyes.

"We were having trouble," Claire argued. "I was so wrapped up in the idea of having a baby that I forgot about having a marriage. I think he was lonely."

"That is no excuse," Luca said, leaning in to her and covering her hand with his. "It is natural for a woman to want a child. When there are difficulties, her husband should be more attentive and supportive than ever. To stray from your bed because he felt like he wasn't getting enough attention is absurd. I was always raised to believe that a woman is meant to be treasured. She is a gift, an angel sent into your life from the heavens. To treat her as anything less is an abomination."

Claire watched him speak with a mix of disbelief and wonder in her gray eyes. She leaned into him, her lips parting. They were soft, plump lips that had gone too long without kisses. That was a tragedy in Luca's eyes. A few kind words and she was melting like butter. She deserved better. Unfortunately, Luca was not the man to give it to her. He sat back and pulled his hand away.

She snapped out of her trance and moved her hand down into her lap. "Do you really believe all that?" she asked.

"I do. My parents have been married for over thirty years keeping that philosophy in mind."

"May I ask why you haven't married, then? I'm sure there are plenty of women out there who would love you to treat them like a precious gift."

Luca tried not to stiffen at her question. He had done his fair share of prying into her personal life; it shouldn't be out of bounds for her to do the same. But there were land mines in this field he didn't want to hit. Not tonight and not ever. Instead, he shrugged and relied on the story he had told again and again over the years.

"Since the day I was born, I was groomed to take over the family business. Moretti's has always had the oldest son running the company. I went from high school to college to grad school to the boardroom. Once my father retired, I had this huge weight on my shoulders to keep the company running and profitable, or I would be letting everyone down. That hasn't really left me much time for anything else. Not just relationships, either. I never travel. I have almost no hobbies or interests outside of work. I have my business. That's it."

What Luca left out was that it was all by design. His father had managed to run the company while having time for his wife and children, so he knew it could be done, but keeping busy was the only way Luca could get through the lonely times. Claire wouldn't understand that, though, because she didn't realize he was damaged. She only saw the successful, confident businessman he portrayed to the world.

"You've never been in love before?"

Luca considered his answer before speaking. "No," he lied. "I got close, but I was wrong."

"That's kind of sad," Claire said. "For all your money and success, all you have to show for it is money and success. You don't even get to enjoy it with someone. When was the last time you took a vacation?"

"I'm on a vacation right now," Luca argued.

"No. Before this one."

Luca thought back, but he knew there wasn't really an answer. "I've never taken a vacation as an adult. Not a real one, at least. Occasionally my family gathers for a long weekend in the Hamptons during the summer."

"It sounds like you're going to be an old, lonely bachelor before too long. What will your family do if you don't have an oldest son to take over after you?"

That was a question that had plagued Luca since the day of his diagnosis. In reality, there were plenty of people in the family who could take the reins. His younger brother Marcello had a son who could easily be the next CEO. But now he had a new possibility. "Well, this isn't the fifties anymore. It isn't written anywhere that it has to be a son. I may not marry or have any more children, but through a twist of fate, I do have Eva in my life. It's always a possibility that she could take over for me."

"If she wants to," Claire countered. "It's nice to have a family legacy, but I don't want her pressured into a life and a career she doesn't want."

"Of course." Luca didn't want that for his daughter, either. He hadn't been pressured into taking the company over, thankfully. It was something he'd always dreamed of doing. His family was important to him and carrying that legacy on was an honor. He'd once hoped that he could pass it along to his child, too, but that was a fantasy he'd given up years ago. "We have the next three weeks to worry about before we need be concerned with Eva's career path."

Claire nodded and turned back to her food. Luca watched her eat for a moment, sipping his wine thoughtfully. At this angle, he could see the faint gray circles under her eyes and the defeated slope of her shoulders. The stress wasn't just wearing her thin. It was eating away at her.

He recognized the look from the days his mother sat at his bedside at the hospital, worrying over him. He hadn't been in any condition to help his mother, but he could help Claire, if she'd let him. Being a single mother had to be incredibly difficult, even with resources at her disposal. She needed this vacation more than even he knew.

They had come here to get to know each other and hash out a custody arrangement, but now he had a different goal: to find a way to make Claire happy again.

Five

Claire couldn't sleep that night. Her head was spinning with everything Luca had said to her at dinner. She wasn't sure if he was telling the truth or if he had the ability to charm a woman by knowing exactly what she needed to hear. They'd spent only a week together. Was she that easy to read? Either way, it was working. A combination of gentle words and strong wine had weakened her defenses. By the time they'd finished eating and cleaned up the kitchen, she would've agreed to anything he suggested. Even the kind of things she knew were a bad idea.

Like touching him. All through dinner she wanted to run her fingers though the dark waves of his hair. She wanted to brush the pad of her thumb over his bottom lip as he spoke the words she'd longed for a man to say to her her whole life. What would he do if she reached out to him? Would he pull her into his arms or push her away? Would he call her *tesorina*? She had no idea what it meant, but whenever he said it she felt her knees soften beneath her.

Now there was a restlessness inside her, keeping sleep at bay. An ache deep in her belly. She didn't know if it was heartburn from the spicy tomato sauce or her long-dormant desire coming back to life, but neither was welcome.

She'd come here to get to know her baby's father, but not in the biblical sense. After her disastrous relationship with Jeff, she'd resigned herself to not falling in love again. It was too hard on her heart, and she didn't think she could take that risk a second time. If she did, she needed a man who was first and foremost honest, and she couldn't trust a word out of Luca's mouth right now. They were on opposite sides of this custody battle. But between the beautiful beach views, the amazing meals and the stimulating conversation, it was easy to let that slip her mind. That would be a dangerous mistake, as she was pretty certain Luca wouldn't do the same.

Frustrated, she flung back the blankets and headed out into the living room. Tonight, she'd been warm from the wine, so she'd opted for a thin, baby-doll nightgown with spaghetti straps. It was short and nearly see-through, but she couldn't bear to put on her flannel pants and top when she went to bed.

Fortunately the house was dark and quiet when she stepped into the hallway, so her attire wouldn't matter. Claire wasn't entirely sure what she was after, but she ended up in the kitchen. She didn't bother turning on the lights. Doing that would ensure she'd never sleep.

Instead, the moonlight through the windows illuminated what she needed to see. Deciding on a cup of tea, she found some in the cupboard and put a mug of water in the microwave to heat. She opened the refrigerator door, looking around for something of interest, but nothing caught her eye. When the water was warmed, she shut the refrigerator and pulled the mug out of the microwave. She let the tea bag steep, then added some honey to sweeten it.

It took a moment for her eyes to adjust to the darkness again, but when they did, she turned and noticed a large, dark figure standing at the edge of the kitchen.

A jolt of panic rushed through her as the shape came closer, until she recognized Luca's gait. Finally, the moonlight from the window lit him, and her heartbeat started to return to normal. Well, at least until she realized he was wearing nothing but a pair of boxer shorts.

The silver light highlighted the curves of his muscular arms and cut of his chest. The sprinkle of dark hair across his chest narrowed and ran down his belly. Her eyes followed the trail along his hard abs, and she felt the heartburn start to rage more intensely inside her.

Okay, it wasn't heartburn, she admitted to herself. It was desire. She'd almost forgotten what that felt like.

When her gaze drifted back up to Luca's face, there was a faint curl of a smile on his lips. Could he tell she was checking him out?

"Are you okay?" he asked.

"Yes. I just couldn't sleep."

"Me, neither." His gaze drifted over her thin nightie with appreciation in his eyes. His jaw clenched tightly, making her wonder if they were both suffering from the same cause of insomnia.

"Would you like some tea?" she asked, distracting herself. "I just made myself some chamomile with honey."

"No, thank you."

As he continued to stand there, Claire felt herself at a loss. She could sense the tension in the air between them. It was electric, yet neither of them seemed willing to do anything about it. Probably because they both knew it was a bad idea. And yet…

Claire needed to go back to her room, drink her tea and go to sleep. That was the *only* thing she needed to do. She just had to get past Luca's hulking figure blocking the path between the fridge and the kitchen island. "Well, good night then," she said. Dropping her gaze to the mug in her hands, she pressed forward, expecting Luca to move out of the way.

But he didn't.

Instead, she felt his hand catch her waist. The heat of his skin burned through the thin fabric of her gown, nearly branding her with his touch. "Claire?"

She stopped cold, her breath catching in her throat. Using just one word, he'd asked a hundred different questions at once. She turned her head to look up at him. He was looking down at her, with his own ragged breaths making his chest rise and fall as though he'd been running. He swallowed hard, the muscles in his throat contracting. She watched his tongue snake over his bottom lip. All the while, his intense eyes were devouring her.

Claire knew in that moment that whatever question he was asking, the answer was yes. Setting down the mug of tea, she turned to him. "Yes."

Luca didn't hesitate. He scooped her up into his

arms and pulled her hard against his chest. His mouth met hers with the ferocity of a man dying of thirst and she was his glass of water. He drank her in and Claire was powerless to stop it. She didn't want to. It had been too long since she'd been desired. Wanted. Jeff had never once in their years of marriage kissed her with as much passion as Luca did in this moment. She didn't want to let that go.

Claire wrapped her arms around his neck and arched her back to press her hips into him. She felt the evidence of his desire there, insistently nudging against her. He groaned her name against her mouth when they made contact, then spun her around until her back was touching the cold stainless steel of the refrigerator. The chill did little to dampen the heat building inside her. With every stroke of his tongue and graze of his hand along her body, he stoked the flames that she'd once thought had died out for good.

When she felt his hand slip beneath her nightgown and his fingers brush the lacy trim of her panties, she felt the slightest hesitation. Like a lightning bolt, it startled her out of the hormone-driven haze she'd fallen into. Things had moved fast. Too fast. Was she really ready to have sex in the kitchen with a man she barely knew? The man who was trying to take Eva from her?

Before she could answer, the sharp, angry wail of her daughter interrupted her thoughts. It wasn't Eva's usual cry for hunger or a wet diaper. Something was wrong.

Luca stilled and pulled away, his lips a fraction of an inch from hers. He was breathing hard, likely cursing his bad luck and hoping that Eva would fall back asleep. That wasn't going to happen.

Claire pushed against Luca's chest and he took a step back. "I'm sorry, I have to go check on the baby." She fled the kitchen as quickly as she could, both out of concern and awkwardness. That situation had quickly gotten out of control, and thankfully Eva woke at just the right time to keep things from going too far.

Entering the bedroom, she turned on the lamp and scooped her red faced and teary daughter from her crib. "What's the matter, baby?" she asked, but the second Claire's cheek touched Eva's, she knew what was wrong.

Eva was burning up with fever.

Claire started frantically searching through her diaper bag for the baby thermometer. Her desire-addled thoughts were scrambled by the sharp cries in her ear. "Shhh, you're okay," she soothed, but Eva could not be comforted. Poor, sick baby.

"Is she okay?"

Claire turned to find Luca in her doorway. "She has a fever." She finally located the thermometer and placed it inside the infant's ear. "One hundred and three."

That seemed high. She felt the panic start to well up inside her. She hadn't brought her baby book. She was hours away from Eva's pediatrician. She knew that the seriousness varied by age and temperature, but she didn't recall what the cutoff was for calling the doctor. The louder Eva cried, the harder it was for her to try to focus.

"Here," Luca said, gently taking Eva from her arms.

"What do you think you're doing?" Claire asked.

"I'm taking care of our sick child." Ignoring her irritable tone, Luca immediately started unsnapping

Eva's onesie. He seemed unfazed by the sharp screams of his daughter, so in control when Claire felt anything but. "I'm going to put her in a cool bath to make her more comfortable. Do you have any medication to bring down her fever?"

She nodded. "It's in the diaper bag. I'll dig it out."

Luca disappeared into the master bathroom and Claire quickly dug around in the bag until she found the medicine. By the time she joined Luca in the bathroom, Eva had started to quiet down. She was lying in her bath chair in a shallow pool of water while Luca rubbed a damp sponge over her skin. The lukewarm water and lavender scented bubbles seemed to soothe her. After a few minutes, the tears were dried, and while she still seemed a little cranky and uncomfortable, they'd made good progress.

At last, Luca lifted Eva up into her yellow bath towel with the ducky hood and bundled her up. He squeezed the dropper of medicine into Eva's mouth and handed the bottle back to Claire. "While I get her dried off, can you make her a bottle with cool water in it? She might be a little dehydrated from the fever, and it will make her more comfortable."

Claire nodded and wandered off toward the kitchen, feeling oddly useless as Luca took charge. She wasn't even entirely sure what had just happened, aside from the fact that in a crucial moment she'd choked and given Luca the window of opportunity he'd been waiting for. When she reached the kitchen, she eyed her abandoned mug of tea and the smudged refrigerator and shook her head. Apparently tonight was a night of missteps.

At the same time, she was happy to have someone

here with her. This was Eva's first real fever, and although she thought she was prepared for it, she'd been completely off her game coming fresh from Luca's kisses. She supposed that was the benefit of having two parents, to split the responsibility and pick up the slack for the other. She didn't know what that was like.

As she filled a small bottle with filtered water, she felt the unexpected prickle of tears in her eyes. This was just one more moment to remind her what she'd lost with Jeff's recklessness. Her dreams of having a family had been shattered, creating a new reality that was so much harder than she ever imagined. He'd left her to raise a child alone all so he could get a hand job on a winding road.

"Claire?"

Claire quickly batted her tears away and sniffed. She tightened the bottle's cap and turned to face him. "It's ready. How is she doing?"

Luca watched her with concern as he took the bottle. "I think she'll be okay. I'm not so sure about you, though."

"Me?" She must not have done as good a job of hiding her emotions as she thought.

"Eva's going to be fine, you know. There's nothing to be worried about."

Claire nodded in agreement. "I know."

"Okay, so what is bothering you then?"

That was a loaded question. "Something. Everything. Don't worry about me, Luca, really. Lately, I seem to have too many hot buttons for life to push."

Luca adjusted Eva in his arms and gave her the bottle. "Is it the kiss? Did I press you too quickly?"

"No," she admitted. "The kiss was…lovely. Probably not the best idea for us, but I don't regret it."

"Then did I overstep with Eva tonight? I'm sorry if that's it, but you seemed a bit overwhelmed and I wanted to help. My youngest sister had a lot of ear infections when she was little and was prone to fevers. I've spent more than a few nights up with my mother bathing fussy babies."

That explained a lot. Despite being a mother, Claire was learning as she went. As an only child, she didn't have any experience caring for children. Her every move was a mix between her research and maternal instincts. "No, that's not it, either. Thank you for all your help with her. You're right, I was feeling a little frazzled in the moment and was glad to have someone step in. I shouldn't need help, but it's nice to have it every now and then."

Luca placed a comforting hand on Claire's shoulder. The warmth of him against her bare skin reminded her of his earlier touches, sending a shiver running down her spine. It wasn't just about temperatures, though. The simple feel of his large, strong hands on her body was enough for her to want to pick up where they'd left off a few minutes ago.

Suddenly, she was aware of how close Luca was and how good he smelled. It had been a long time since she'd been touched by a man, even in comfort. For some reason, that combination along with Luca's radiating masculinity was more than she could take. Of course she'd given into it. Any woman in her position would have. He told her she was beautiful. They had a child together. He kissed her as if there was nothing more in the world he could ever desire. But once the spell of their kiss faded away, she knew that nothing more could come of it.

There was a wall up when it came to Luca. She could tell the moment their discussions went off into uncomfortable territory for him. Even the most harmless questions about his high-school prom seemed to set a glaze over his eyes. The answers that followed felt hollow and inauthentic. Not necessarily that he was lying, but that his response was practiced. Claire had her fair share of practiced speeches with Jeff as he successfully hid his infidelity. She wasn't about to make that mistake twice, even with a man who was ten times more thoughtful and charming than Jeff ever was.

"You're a mother, *tesorina*, not a superhero. It's okay to accept help."

"Thank you." Claire knew that, at least in theory. Putting it into practice was harder. Aside from Daisy, she didn't really have anyone to lean on for help. Despite the messy circumstances, perhaps having Luca in Eva's life wouldn't be so bad. There would be someone else she could call when she needed help, and when Eva stayed with her father, Claire would get the occasional break to recharge and relax. She didn't realize just how much she needed that until this moment. She wasn't quite ready to just give in on the custody agreement yet, but she was starting to see the silver lining of the situation.

"I'll stay up with her for a while if you want to go back to bed."

Claire immediately felt anxious about his offer. It was one thing to let him help and another entirely to let him take over. She hated questioning his every motivation, but she couldn't be naive. What could he tell the judge then? That when Eva was sick, he was the one who had to care for her? No, thanks. "That won't be necessary," she said, reaching to take Eva from his arms. "I was having trouble sleeping anyway. I'm going to stay up until she starts feeling better."

Luca didn't immediately release Eva. He watched Claire suspiciously, and she fought to swallow the onset of an unexpected yawn. "I think the sandman is ready for you now. My time will come later. We'll be fine, I promise. Go back to bed. I'll wake you up if something happens. Otherwise, I'll rock her until she falls back to sleep and put her in her crib."

Claire was resistant, but she could tell by the firm, yet gentle expression on Luca's face that he would insist. Perhaps he was just being nice and not looking for ammunition to use against her in court. Her eyelids were getting too heavy for her to argue any longer. "Okay, thank you. I'll leave the door open to the bedroom."

"Good night," he said with Eva snuggled into his arms.

She could tell that Eva would probably be asleep before she was. Not much to worry about, then. She reluctantly returned to her bedroom and burrowed beneath the down comforter. With the late night emotional highs, quickly came the lows. Before she knew it, she crashed.

The last thought as she drifted to sleep was how Luca's lips had felt as they pressed against hers. And she wondered—would she ever feel that again?

It seemed as though she'd just closed her eyes when she opened them to daylight streaming through the window. Claire sat up in bed, noticing the bedroom door was still open and the crib remained empty. If Eva hadn't fallen asleep, why hadn't Luca woken her up?

Climbing from bed, she pulled on her robe and returned to the living room. She expected to find them milling around the kitchen or out on the deck, but it seemed as though things hadn't gone as Luca planned. There on the couch under a chenille blanket, she found Luca and Eva. Both were asleep, with Eva curled into a little ball on his chest. Claire stood there for a moment, watching the two of them together. It was precious. They both made the same little grumpy faces while they dreamed, their brows drawn together and their lips pouty in sleepy consternation. She wanted to capture the memory of them together like this and never forget it.

"Good morning."

Claire was startled to notice Luca's eyes had opened, and he was watching her as closely as she was watching him. "Morning. You two look pretty cozy."

Luca looked down at the infant drooling on his bare chest. "I guess so. We must've conked out pretty quickly after you went to bed. I don't think I've moved an inch the whole night." He sat up slowly as to not disturb the baby, groaning softly as he stretched his stiff limbs. "What time is it?"

"A little after nine."

"Wow." Luca ran one hand through the messy waves of his hair and shook his head. "I haven't slept that late in years."

Claire approached him and held out her arms to relieve him of Eva for a while. "I'll take Eva. Why don't you take a shower to loosen up, and I'll make us all some breakfast."

Luca stood and handed off the sleeping infant. "Please make coffee. Strong, black coffee."

"I can do that."

He started toward the staircase, but before he could reach it, Claire said, "Luca?" He stopped and turned. "I wanted to say thank you."

"For what?" he asked.

"For last night."

He gave her a guilty smirk in response. "Which part? The part where I lost control and almost took you against the refrigerator? Or the part where I pushed you aside to take care of Eva when I could tell you didn't want me to?"

That was a good question. The words had leaped from her lips before she'd really thought them through. "Both, maybe. The combination of those two things gave me a little taste of what it's like to have someone in my life again. To help me, to hold me. It was nice."

"I know what you mean," he said. "I think you and I have both gotten too used to being alone. My mother is always reminding me that's not how people are supposed to live. I'm starting to think she's right."

"I may not know you that well, but from what I've seen you're a good man, Luca. The woman you let into your life would be very lucky."

A sadness Claire didn't understand washed over Luca's face. Why would a compliment like that steal the light from his eyes so quickly when her angry insults of the past didn't seem to make the slightest dent in his armor?

"Thank you," he said, but she got the feeling he

didn't believe it, just as she didn't believe it when he told her she was beautiful. They both seemed to have a lot of doubts when it came to their self-worth and value to the opposite sex. Claire knew why she felt that way, but Luca? He was an attractive, thoughtful and wealthy businessman with a way of complimenting a woman so her knees turned to butter. She wasn't sure why he wasn't fighting women off with a stick. He wasn't the kind of man she needed in her life, but he would be a great choice for any other woman.

Claire wanted him to know that she really meant what she'd said, that it wasn't just some flattery. "I wish I'd found a man more like you when I was younger and looking for someone to start my life with. If I had, perhaps I wouldn't be a widow wondering how her life went off track."

The sadness faded away and Luca's jaw tightened along with his grip on the banister. He looked up at her with eyes that reflected a confusing combination of regret and irritation. "If I were you, I wouldn't waste my wishes on a man like me," he said, and headed downstairs.

Six

Luca sat in a beach chair quietly scowling. Claire was with Eva as they carefully splashed in the waves. The baby was wearing a rainbow-striped swimsuit with ruffles on her bottom, although most of her was held out of the water by her mother. Eva would squeal every time the cold water rushed over her feet, then giggle as if it was the greatest thing she'd ever experienced. If Claire let go of her hands, Eva would grab fistfuls of wet sand and mush them between her fingers.

It should've been a happy and amusing sight for Luca. He should be out there in the freezing water with his daughter. Instead, he was sitting at a distance, practically pouting beneath his ball cap and sunglasses. He had no reason to pout, really. He'd succeeded in pushing Claire away. That was what he'd wanted to do, or at least what he felt he had to do when she got that moony look in her eyes. He might have slipped up the other night and let himself get carried away physically, but that didn't change the fact that he was not the man for Claire. He wasn't a romantic savior there to sweep in and rescue her from her loneliness. It was better that she learn that now rather than later.

And yet the past few days had been miserable. At first, Claire had been focused on Eva and caring for her as she got over her illness. When the baby was well, she continued to keep her distance. She wasn't rude, but she wasn't as open and chatty as she had been before.

He should've been content that she got the message. Instead, Luca was surprised to find himself missing their talks. He'd also found himself lying in bed at night thinking about the kiss they'd shared in the kitchen. Lord help him, he couldn't stop himself. Once he got a taste of her, it was as if something had been unleashed deep inside him. Every touch, every soft sound she made, urged him on. If Eva hadn't woken up with that fever, he wasn't sure what would've happened.

He could tell that Claire was relieved by the interruption. They'd been caught up in the moment. Time and perspective would prove it wasn't the best idea in their situation. It didn't change how much he wanted her, though. The next morning, when she seemed more open to the idea than he expected, he wasn't sure what to do. Claire was not a casual romance type of woman, that was obvious. He'd done a better job of charming her than he'd intended to, and suddenly he found himself in a position he hadn't expected.

So he pushed back. It was the best thing to do, really. Claire deserved a relationship with a man who could give her everything she wanted, including love and another child. That wasn't going to be Luca, no matter how badly he ached for her. It was better to put a stop to all this before it went too far.

Looking back out at the sea, Luca couldn't help but admire Claire's figure on display. Despite her claims of excess baby weight, she looked great in her shorts and bikini top. Her skin was golden from their time at the beach, and the blond in her hair seemed to be picking up some lighter streaks from the sun. Her curves were highlighted by the halter cut of the bikini, giving him a tantalizing glimpse of her full breasts.

There was nothing not to like about Claire. That was the problem. It was too easy to like her. Too easy to find a reason to touch her. His blood would sing in his veins whenever he caught a whiff of her scent. There was a restlessness in every muscle when he lay alone thinking about her upstairs in the dark. It was as if his body knew they had a child together and was ready to start on another one as soon as possible.

And if Luca could provide that for her, he might be in the water instead of sulking in his chair. But he couldn't. Luca would rather live his life a bachelor than a disappointment to the woman he loved. His only alternative would be to find a woman who couldn't have children of her own. They didn't exactly walk around advertising that fact, however.

Looking back at the water, he noticed Claire and Eva had moved to drier sand to play with the plastic bucket and shovel they'd carried to the beach with them. Looking at the dark curls of his daughter, all he could do was shake his head. What a bizarre twist of fate that would give him a child. It was like a perfectly imperfect storm that brought two people together to have a child neither of them expected to have.

Wait a minute… Luca sat up taller in his chair. Claire may very well be that woman. She hadn't spoken extensively about her fertility issues, but she had to have some or she wouldn't have been at the clinic. He'd avoided the subject, as well. He didn't like people knowing he had cancer, much less the kind he'd had.

Luca wasn't the type to really believe in fate, but life certainly seemed to be convincing him otherwise. What if Claire was the chance he'd never let himself believe in? If he let their attraction evolve into a relationship, this could be his second chance. It would work out perfectly. They already had a child together. If they were to marry, it would tidy up the whole custody situation. He'd get the full-time family he wanted, and Claire wouldn't have to be away from Eva when it was his weekend.

Claire approached his chair with a sand-covered baby in her arms. "I'm going to hose this little monkey off and put her down for a nap."

"Okay. I'll pack up and be back at the house in a few minutes."

He watched Claire disappear, their dating scenario playing out in his mind. Wooing her was the perfect solution. It had been dropped in his lap, really. They'd both benefit from the scenario. Claire would get a full-time father for Eva and a man to treat her the way she deserved to be treated. Luca would get the family he never thought he'd have, and he'd get his mother off his back once and for all. It would be nice to have someone to come home to, to talk to. His apartment was becoming unbearably empty.

Never mind the fact that he'd finally get to touch her. Seducing Claire would be the best part of this plan. No holding back, no excuses, no interruptions. He'd get to run his hands along those long legs and cup her breasts in his needy palms. Luca was hardly celibate, but thinking about Claire made him as eager as a virgin. And as nervous.

He'd only attempted to be in a relationship once before, and it hadn't ended well. Even if he'd wanted to try again, he'd hardly had the time. The best he could manage was a few dates with a woman before things got in the way and she'd break it off. Aside from Jessica, he'd never even dated a woman long enough to consider her his girlfriend, much less look ahead to her being his wife. Could he do it now for his daughter's sake?

Reluctantly, Luca got up from his chair and started gathering their things in a bag. With every toy he stuffed inside, the more certain he became that the answer was yes. He'd do anything for that little girl. She was the child he never expected, and he wanted her to have a real family. Despite what Claire thought, he didn't want Eva shuttled back and forth between households, caught up in visitation agreements and who gets which holidays. That meant taking a chance on having that real family with Claire.

But would Claire want anything to do with him? He'd pretty much told her he wasn't a candidate for any of her romantic notions. She'd had an unhappy marriage and wouldn't settle for the same this time. She'd want love and passion and everything that went with

it. Luca would happily give her the passion and attention she needed. Love was another matter. He'd already
made the mistake of giving that too freely once, and
it had blown up in his face. That could happen with
Claire, too, if he wasn't careful.

He slung the bag over his shoulder and started back
up the sandy path through the dunes. He knew that if
Claire found out what was wrong with him, she would
feel betrayed, bringing up all the emotions of her first
husband's infidelity. To protect himself from the possibility of being hit with emotional shrapnel, he'd have
to keep his emotions soundly out of the equation.

That meant she couldn't know the truth. Not about
his cancer and not about how he really felt. He'd have
to make sure he did everything right so she'd never
question his love for her. It wouldn't be hard to treat
her better than Jeff had. Just a kind word was enough
to make her melt. She deserved better than he'd treated
her. Luca might not let himself love Claire, but he'd
certainly do everything in his power to make her feel
loved.

By the time he reached the house, Luca knew exactly how he would start his bid for Claire's affections.
To do it right, he knew he'd have to take the ultimate
risk—to call his sister in Newport.

There was something different about Luca. Claire
had tried to give him his space the past few days
after their unexpected encounter. He'd given her confusing signals, so she decided that perhaps that kiss
was the result of exhaustion and bad judgment. That
was probably for the best, anyway, if this was how he

was going to react to something like that. He'd been quiet and withdrawn, almost moody.

But since they'd come back from the beach, his mood had greatly improved. When she was done bathing Eva and put her down for her nap, she'd come out of the master bedroom to find him humming to himself and cooking up something tasty in the kitchen. The dark cloud that had hovered over him the past few days had disappeared, and she wasn't sure whether she should be happy about it. It was easier to ignore Luca's charms when he was distant and scowling. The smiling, happy Luca wore away her resistance too easily.

"I have a surprise," he announced when he noticed her in the living room.

Claire wasn't that good with surprises. More times than not it wasn't a good thing. "What?"

"My baby sister, Mia, is coming to the house tonight."

Claire couldn't help the frown that instantly furrowed her brow. That was not at all what she'd expected him to say. Luca had made a point of telling her that he'd kept Eva and the whole situation from his family, and yet he seemed awfully chipper for a man who hadn't had things go his way. "Why? Did she find out about Eva?"

"Yes," he admitted, "but only because I told her. I actually invited her to stay with us for a few days. Mia lives not far from here in Newport."

She was listening, but she couldn't quite figure out what was going on. Eva was a huge secret, then suddenly he was rolling out the red carpet for his family? "I'm confused," she said. "Why did you tell her? Does your whole family know the truth now?"

"If my whole family knows the truth, I'm going to skin Mia, so no, they don't all know. I just told her and swore her to secrecy."

"Again," Claire pressed. "Why?" Was he so uncomfortable being alone with her now that he took the risk of inviting his sister here?

"So we could have a babysitter," Luca said with a smile. "I'm taking you out tomorrow. I've got a whole day planned. Mia is going to stay here with Eva so you can relax and enjoy yourself."

Taking her out? "I appreciate the gesture, Luca, but I'm not sure about this. I don't even know your sister. I don't know how comfortable I'm going to be in leaving Eva with her."

"Mia is great with kids, I promise. Not only is she an elementary school teacher, she's watched all of my nieces and nephews a hundred times. She will be fine with Eva while we're gone."

It all seemed sensible, and yet Claire felt her hackles go up with his presumptuous tone. He seemed to think Eva was an asset of his corporation, not a child she had any say in. "That's all well and good, Luca, but you didn't even ask me before making that decision. This is the kind of stuff that worries me about our arrangements. I don't mind letting you in on some of the parenting decisions, but I'm not about to get pushed out of them entirely."

Luca seemed dumbfounded by her irritation. Could he really not see what he was doing while he was doing it?

"Fair enough," he said after a moment's consideration. "I'll leave the final decision up to you. When you meet Mia, you can decide if you trust her to watch

Eva. If so, I'll take you out. If not, my sister will just be visiting for a few days."

Claire sighed with relief. All she wanted was a voice in the process, even if she already knew that in the end she'd let his sister watch Eva so they could go out. Whatever was going on with Luca had inspired all of this, and despite what he'd just agreed to, he wasn't likely to change his mind easily. He wanted to take her out, so she would let him. It might actually be nice. It had been a long time since she'd had an evening out for a little grown-up time. She worked so much that she felt guilty leaving Eva with a sitter after spending all day with Daisy.

"When will she be here?" she asked instead.

Luca glanced down at his watch. "Less than an hour. She texted me when she got on the ferry. She'll definitely be here in time to eat, so I thought I'd make her favorite chicken tetrazzini. Does that sound okay to you?"

Claire chuckled and walked past him to the refrigerator to get a drink. "Any meal I don't have to cook is great by me. It certainly doesn't hurt that you're an excellent cook."

"I'm a passable cook," Luca clarified. "My sister is an amazing cook. You'll see."

"Does your sister know you just invited her up here to watch children and cook?"

Luca laughed. "When my family gets together, that's what we do. Lots of food, laughter, playful bickering and kids. You keep an eye on whichever one is closest. It won't faze her in the slightest, but yes, I did tell her why I wanted her to come up. She's excited to meet you and Eva."

Claire wished she was as excited to meet his sister. She suddenly felt anxious about the whole thing for an entirely different reason. What would his family think of her? Would they hate her for fighting Luca for custody? Would they read something into the two of them being here together, alone? Her stomach started to ache with worry. She was a fairly quiet and reserved woman who often came off to strangers as aloof or stuck-up. What if they didn't like her?

"Are you okay?" Luca asked. "You don't look very excited about Mia coming."

"I'm fine. I'm just a little nervous about meeting some of your family, is all. I'm not really the loud, laughter type."

Luca turned away from his sautéing chicken to take Claire's hands. He pulled them to his chest and held them there. Claire's breath caught in her throat. She could feel his heart pounding in his rib cage almost in time with her own. His dark gaze focused on her. This close, she could see the gold and caramel colored flecks in his hazel eyes. Looking into them, she started to relax. He could have such a soothing effect on her one moment, then with a simple wicked smile, he could heat her cheeks and make her think thoughts she hadn't entertained in a very long time.

"You're going to be fine," he insisted. "Mia will love you, and when you meet the rest of my family, they'll love you, too. They're used to intimidating new people, so if you're quiet, they'll think it's them, not you. Besides, just meeting Mia without everyone else will be a nice icebreaker."

"Are you not worried about the rest of your family finding out what's going on?" Claire didn't care if his family found out the truth, but she knew it concerned him. She didn't know what it was like to have a large, overbearing family, so she didn't understand his issues with them. This did seem out of character for him, though. What had changed his mind? That was a big change just for the opportunity to go out to dinner.

Or was it more than that?

"There's always that risk," Luca said. "But things will be fine. I wouldn't have called Mia if I didn't think I could trust her. Carla, on the other hand, would blab to everyone. And even if they did find out, it will be okay. I think you and I are getting along pretty well and can probably work out a custody arrangement we're both comfortable with. Eva seems to have taken to me. Besides, it's not like we're engaged or something."

Claire was following along until he brought up that last point. It was true, but for some reason it bothered her to hear him say it so dismissively. It must be because it felt like something. It felt like more than it was because of their daughter and the strange circumstances. In truth, all they'd shared was a kiss. They hadn't even gone out on a date. Whatever this beach house arrangement was, it wasn't a date.

Pulling away so he wouldn't see the touch of disappointment in her eyes, she started to walk from the kitchen. "I'm going to spiffy up for company."

"Okay," she heard Luca say, but she didn't turn around.

In her suite, she changed from her yoga pants into a sundress, then sat at her vanity staring at herself in the mirror. She fussed with her hair for a while, not happy, but finally settling on putting it up in a bun. She applied a little lip gloss and mascara. They might be on a lazy beach vacation, but she didn't want to look like it when she met his sister. If Mia did report back to the family, Claire didn't want them to think she was a slacker.

As she was finishing up, she heard voices in the other room and knew that Mia must have arrived. The noise finally woke Eva from her nap, so Claire changed her and put her in a cute pink-and-yellow dress to meet her aunt.

By the time they went into the living room, Luca and a pretty young woman were seated on the couch drinking wine. Luca immediately stood up and gestured toward his sister. "Claire, this is my sister Mia. Mia, this is Claire and my daughter, Eva."

Mia looked like a petite version of Luca, with long, curly brown hair, rich, olive skin and wide, dark eyes. It made Claire wonder if that was what Eva might look like when she grew up. She didn't have long to ponder, though. Mia launched up from the couch and embraced Claire before she could prepare herself.

"Oh my goodness," she declared as she pulled away and examined Claire. "She's beautiful, Luca! Why didn't you tell me how pretty she was?"

"Because I didn't want you scheming," Luca said with a smile.

"I would never," Mia argued with an equally wicked grin. She winked at Claire, then turned her attention to the baby. "And aren't you the most precious little girl I've ever laid my eyes on!"

The next thing Claire knew, Eva was in Mia's arms, bouncing happily. "You look just like your cousin Valentina, yes you do," Mia cooed, wandering away.

Claire felt a little helpless, but she tried not to

show it. It was Eva's family after all, and her daughter seemed pleased with the adoration. It was Claire who needed to adjust to her new reality. For the first time, it really hit her that she wasn't just bringing a father into Eva's life, she was bringing in his whole family. Eva would have an identity, a sense of belonging, other than Claire. The thought made her happy for her daughter and anxious for herself all at once. She always seemed to be the outsider, so this was no different.

"Would you like some wine, Claire?" Luca asked.

"Yes." Definitely. He poured her a glass and they all gathered on the couch. They chatted for a while, then Luca returned to the kitchen to finish off dinner, leaving the ladies alone for a few minutes.

"So, Luca didn't tell me much about you, just the basics of how you two ended up having a child together. That's a pretty wild story."

"That's one way to put it."

"So if you don't mind me asking, what made you decide to go to a fertility clinic? My sister, Carla, was having some issues, too, but they were able to conceive with some medication. Now she's got three little hellions."

It seemed like a really personal question so early in the conversation, but she supposed that once everyone found out about Eva, it was a natural thing to ask. "My husband and I were having trouble and nothing was working, so we had to take the next step."

Mia's eyes widened, and she glanced at Claire's bare ring finger. "You're married?"

"Widowed."

Her hand clamped over her mouth. "I am so sorry." She turned to the kitchen. "Luca! Why didn't you tell me Claire was a widow and save me from asking a rude question?"

"I wouldn't have to if you weren't asking such nosy questions in the first place."

Mia muttered something in Italian under her breath. "I'm sorry. I was just curious about how all this came about. I know why Luca opted to go to the clinic, but not everyone has the same circumstances as he did, thankfully."

Claire perked up in her seat. She'd never directly asked Luca about his involvement with the clinic. Anytime the topic came up, he circumvented it somehow. She had no idea why a young, vibrant man would have stored his future chance at children at the clinic. Perhaps his sister could shed some light on the subject.

"I was so young at the time, but Mama told me how much he went through. She just hated to have him miss his chance at a family, too."

"Dinner!" Luca shouted with a large pasta platter in his hands.

Of course. Claire wasn't sure if Luca heard his sister talking or the timing was unfortunate, but the discussion came to a quick end with her once again not finding out the whole story about Luca. It was more than she knew before, though. He'd apparently had some kind of ordeal that might cost him a future with a family. Had he been ill? There wasn't anything lacking in the physical specimen she'd touched in the kitchen a few days ago. If he had been sick, it was a long time ago.

They gathered at the dining-room table with Eva in her high chair. She enjoyed a pouch of turkey and potato mush while the rest of them happily devoured the chicken tetrazzini. It was creamy and savory with the bite of parmesan and the fresh snap of the peas.

An hour passed as quickly as the first few minutes. Claire wasn't sure if it was the wine or Mia's easy nature, but before long they were chatting and laughing like old girlfriends. It was a relief for her, since she didn't have many friends and thought it might be a struggle. Mia was quite charming. They stayed mum on the topic of Luca, but since Mia had minored in art in college, she and Claire had a lot of other things they could discuss instead.

"He looks pouty," Mia said at last as she looked at her brother. "We should probably talk about something he likes."

Claire turned to Luca, who was politely, yet blankly, sipping his wine and listening to them chat.

He shook his head in protest. "No, please. I'm fascinated by the female bonding ritual. As long as you stay off the subject of female biological processes and grooming, I'm fine."

"Now that you mention it, I am cramping pretty badly today," Mia said.

Luca immediately stood up and started clearing plates. "And I'm out," he said.

Mia laughed and picked up a few of her own. "I'm just messing with you, *fratello*. Carla and I used to do that to the boys when they were pestering us," she explained to Claire. "I once chased Marcello and Giovanni through the house with a box of tampons. You'd have thought it was a snake."

"They would've preferred a snake. See, Claire, what you avoided by being an only child? We tortured one another until we moved out of the house."

"That didn't stop us, really. Angelo texted me a picture of a giant spider the other day. I swear that thing was bigger than my hand. My skin was crawling for hours."

Claire followed them into the kitchen and couldn't help the amused smile on her face. She didn't know what Luca was talking about. She hadn't avoided this by being an only child, she'd missed out on it. It was different, for sure, but she enjoyed the camaraderie Luca and Mia had. She'd never had that with anyone.

As she handed off her plate and the salad bowl to Luca, she realized, sadly, that Eva would likely have the same fate. She would have the benefit of all of her cousins on Luca's side, but there would be no siblings to play with or talk to around the dinner table.

Eva had been a miracle, but in that moment, she felt greedy enough to hope that she would be granted one more.

Seven

"When you said you got a babysitter and were taking me out today, I kind of imagined things going differently."

Luca laughed at Claire and pulled the Land Rover into the dim parking lot of the marina. It was just before sunrise, and the sky was a dusky gray with a hint of pink on the horizon. "What were you expecting?"

"I don't know. A spa day? Maybe a nice dinner or walking around town shopping. At the very least, leaving the house after the sun had risen."

"We may still do all that. We've got all day."

Claire glanced at her watch and nodded. "We certainly do." She looked out at the boats in the marina with a curious expression. "Are we getting on a boat?"

"Maybe." Luca parked the car and got out. When he opened the door to let Claire out, her frown was pinching her brows together. "Okay, yes. We're going out on a boat. You really don't like surprises, do you?"

"It's not that I don't like them, per se, I'm just not used to them. At least not good ones."

"I'm going to change that." Luca took her hand and led her to the dock. There, waiting for them, was a small crew on a catamaran.

"Good morning, Mr. Moretti. Are you ready to go see some whales today?"

Claire's eyes were wide as she took the sailor's hand and climbed onto the deck of the ship. "We're going whale watching?"

"That's where I'm going," the captain said. "Since you're on my ship, that means you are, too. We're about to head out into some of the best and most diverse waters for marine life. If all goes well, we should see humpbacks, fin whales, a couple species of dolphins and, maybe if we're lucky, a right whale. It feels like a lucky morning."

Luca watched as the captain joined his crew in readying the ship for departure. "Have you ever done something like this before?" he asked Claire.

"No," she said as she looked out at the gray waters. "I'm really excited, though. Are we waiting for some other passengers?"

Luca shook his head and turned back to watch the crew untie the mooring and start the engines. "No, it's only going to be us this morning. I reserved it just for you and me."

Her eyes widened with surprise. "Just for us?" She looked around the ship. "That's crazy."

"I told you," Luca explained, "that I wanted to take you out today so you could relax and enjoy yourself.

Yes, I could take you to dinner or to a day spa, but I wanted to do something different."

As the boat started to pull out of the marina, one of the crew brought them a flannel blanket. "Have a seat on the bench up front for the best views. Wrap up and I'll bring out some coffee and fresh baked cinnamon rolls."

They took their seats, and Luca wrapped the blanket around them. He put his arm around Claire's shoulders and pulled her to his side. She snuggled happily against him, resting her head on his shoulder. It was amazingly easy to be here with her like this. She seemed to fit perfectly in the crook beneath his arm, as if she was meant to be there.

Taking a deep breath, he drew in the salty scent of the air as it mingled with Claire's fragrance. Luca leaned in closer, pressing his lips into the crown of her head with a sigh. Combined with the gentle rocking of the ship, it was incredibly soothing.

After about ten minutes of quietly cutting through the calm seas, the crewman brought them coffee and warm, gooey cinnamon rolls. They ate quietly as they watched the sea around them. They were just finishing up when one of the crew shouted, "Two o'clock!"

Luca and Claire both stood and turned in the direction he was pointing. The sky was lighter now, burning away the early-morning fog. They could just make out the spray of a whale surfacing in the distance, followed by a dark hump rising out of the water. A few minutes later, they were rewarded with a stunning sight as the humpback whale leaped from the water and crashed back down in a spectacular splash.

Luca tried to focus on the amazing sight, but his

gaze kept drifting back to Claire. She was totally immersed in the moment, her lips parted softly in unexpressed awe. This moment was memorable, but more so because she was here with him.

Lifting the blanket, he wrapped it around himself, then Claire, snuggling her back against his chest. She leaned into him, her eyes never leaving the water. They stood like that for nearly an hour, watching a pod of dolphins go by and one whale after the other surface. They didn't spot an elusive right whale, but they saw a pair of fin whales and a couple more humpbacks. The whales didn't breach again, but he and Claire were entertained with displays of tail lobbing and slapping of their pectoral fins on the water.

As the ship headed back to the marina, Claire turned in his arms to face him. "That was incredible," she said. "It's the most beautiful thing I've ever seen."

"They were amazing, but they weren't the most beautiful thing I've seen."

Claire snorted at him. "I'm sure being a billionaire has opened doors to plenty of things more beautiful than this, but this is probably as good as it gets for me. Second only to seeing Eva for the first time."

"My money has nothing to do with it," Luca argued. "In fact, most of the things I see in my day-to-day life are quite tedious. At least until I met you. You are by far the most beautiful thing I've ever seen."

Claire squirmed uncomfortably. "Luca…" she complained, but he wouldn't let her.

Luca pressed a finger to her lips and shook his head. "No. No arguing with me. I know better what I've seen and what I think than you do, thanks."

Her cheeks flushed pink and her eyes focused on

his chest. "I'm sorry," she said. "I'm just not used to hearing things like that. It never feels sincere to me."

"I know, you've told me that before, but you need to get used to it because I'm not about to stop. I never say anything I don't mean, *tesorina*, so accept a compliment for what it is. If I say you're beautiful and I desire you above all else, I mean it."

Her mouth fell open again. Her gray eyes, so much like the water around them, met his. "You desire me?"

"I said it, didn't I?"

"I know." Claire bit at her lip, a line of concern forming between her brows. "I just can't help but wonder if a physical relationship between us is a bad idea."

"It probably is," Luca said with a laugh. "I told you I was honest, Claire, not smart."

"I don't know how I'm ever going to adjust to real life again."

Luca laughed at Claire as he unlocked the door of the house. "How's that?"

As though he didn't know what he'd done. "You've utterly spoiled me for reality. You take me to this beautiful island and let me spend my days listening to the waves and eating your amazing cooking. There's no alarm clocks, no bills to pay, no calls to take…"

They stepped into the house, shut the door behind them and slipped out of their coats. The cottage was dark and quiet, so Mia and Eva were already asleep. Luca wrapped an arm around her waist and pulled her close to whisper in her ear. "And what's wrong with that? You deserve to be spoiled."

Claire hesitated to respond as the heat of his touch burned through her dress. Her body was pressed provocatively against his. She wasn't sure if it was the physical contact or his seductive words, but suddenly the chill of the night was gone. A heat built deep inside her, spreading through her veins. She looked up at him, getting lost in his dark eyes.

"And then today…" she continued, pulling away and moving to the staircase.

"I thought you had a good time today," he said, following her upstairs.

"I had an excellent time today. The cruise and the whales were amazing. Walking around Edgartown and Oak Bluff was so relaxing. And then our meal at the Red Cat was some of the best food I've ever eaten."

Luca reached the top of the stairs and hesitated. An annoyed frown pulled down the corners of his mouth. "Better than my cooking?"

She wasn't getting caught in that trap. There was no right answer to that question. "They were completely different culinary styles. There's no comparison and I refuse to try."

Luca approached her again. This time, when he wrapped his arms around her waist, he held on tight enough for her to not escape so easily. Claire didn't shy away from his touch. Instead, she let herself melt into his body, each of her soft curves pressing into his hard muscles. She wouldn't lie to herself and say that it didn't feel good to be held.

She was beginning to wonder if Jeff had *ever* held her like this. The simple glide of Luca's hands over her back had more tenderness, yet more intensity, than any man who had touched her before. She felt sexy and alive with him, valued by him, and she hadn't felt that way in so long.

His dark eyes focused on her, making her wonder if he knew what she was thinking. His fingertips pressed into the flesh at her hips, leaving no doubt that he wanted her. They'd danced around this whole moment since they'd arrived at the island. Luca had gone out of his way to charm her, to reduce the stressors and barriers in her life that would keep her from enjoying herself. Claire had fought it the whole trip, but she was tired of fighting what she wanted. Now was her moment to indulge.

"Tell me, what is so bad about all of these things I've done for you today? Am I not allowed to treat you to a nice time?"

"You can do whatever you like. It's just hard to have a day like that because I know this isn't what real life is like. Before too long, I'm going to go back to Brooklyn and cook my own dinner again. There won't be a beautiful beach out my window, and I won't wake up to the sound of waves crashing on the rocks."

"You can have anything you want. You just have to ask, *tesorina*."

She wondered what he meant by that. Her mind instantly leaped ahead to a life together, where he'd give her a beach house if that was what she wanted. That, of course, was a ridiculous fantasy brought on by their discussion on the boat and a little too much wine. He wasn't offering anything but an optimistic point of view. She decided to focus on something else instead, before she embarrassed herself. "Luca, what does *tesorina* mean?"

He smiled as he looked down at her. "It literally means *treasure* in Italian, but it's a term of endearment that is used like we would use sweetheart or honey in English."

Her breath caught in her throat when she heard the definition of the name he'd called her from their very first day together. "Why do you call me that?"

His brow furrowed. "Because that's what you are, Claire—both a treasure and the sweetest, most passionate creature I've ever met."

She couldn't hold back any longer. Those words were a stronger aphrodisiac than any food she could imagine. Lunging forward, she met his lips with her own. She wrapped her arms around his neck to tug him closer to her. Claire felt his hands glide over her rib cage and along her waist. She wanted more. She wanted him to touch her all over.

She pressed her body against his. She could feel the firm ridge of his desire pressing into her belly. Rubbing against it, she drew a low growl from Luca's throat. Feeling bold, she let her palm graze over his chest, dipping lower to stroke him through his pants.

Luca ripped his mouth from hers, reaching out quickly to grip her wrist and pull her away. "Claire," he nearly groaned. His whole body tensed as he struggled to keep control. "Don't. I can't take it. I want you too badly."

"Then take me. Please, Luca. I want you to make love to me. I want you to show me what it feels like to be with a man who truly desires me."

She watched him close his eyes for a moment and draw a deep breath in through his nose. When his eyelids rose, there was a heat in his gaze.

Her hand was trembling as she reached for his. Before she lost her nerve, she turned and walked toward her bedroom. Mia had moved Eva's playpen into her room tonight, so they had the space all to themselves.

Without turning back to face him, she reached for her dress and started fumbling with the buttons down the front. Claire could feel the heat of Luca's body at her back, but he didn't touch her. At least, not yet.

She let the top of the dress slip from her arms to pool at her waist. Luca's breath was hot on her nape as he moved in closer and pressed a searing kiss on her bare shoulder. The contrast sent a shiver down her spine that met with his fingertips as he gathered the fabric in his hands and pushed it over her hips.

The sundress pooled around her feet, leaving her in nothing but her underthings. Claire held her breath as Luca unlatched her bra and slipped the straps from her shoulders. He let it drop to the floor, immediately covering both breasts with his hands.

Claire gasped and arched her back to press her body closer to his touch. She could feel her nipples tighten and harden as his fingertips stroked over them. He continued to sprinkle kisses across her bare shoulders and neck, the combination of touches building a raging fire in her belly.

"Luca," she gasped as he rolled the peaks between his fingers. She wasn't entirely sure what she was begging him for, but she knew he could give it to her.

He responded by gliding his palm across her bare belly to the edge of her panties. She tensed as he moved over the skin that hadn't quite bounced back from having Eva, but he didn't seem to notice. Luca was focused on his destination. Without hesitating, his hand slipped beneath the satin and stroked across her sensitive center.

Claire gasped, but his firm grip on her body wouldn't allow her to squirm away from the intensity of his touch. *"Sì, bella,"* he cooed in her ear from behind as he moved relentlessly over her slick skin.

She felt her thighs start to tremble beneath her. Claire wasn't certain how much of this she could take. She might collapse into a puddle right there at his feet. "Not yet," she whispered between ever more urgent cries.

To her relief and disappointment, he pulled his hand away before it went too far. Instead, he hooked his thumbs around her panties and pulled them down her legs. Now she was completely naked. Thankfully, she wasn't alone in that. She heard the rustle of fabric behind her and turned in time to see Luca slip out of his shirt.

She reached for his belt and unfastened his pants. Luca stepped out of his remaining clothes and took a step toward Claire until their naked bodies were just barely brushing each other. He cupped her face in his hands and dipped his head to kiss her.

His desire for her was barely restrained as his mouth met hers. This was a kiss that had built up during their time together here. His tongue sought hers, tasting and teasing her with his lips. Claire met his intensity, nipping playfully at his bottom lip. The bite elicited a growl in the back of his throat. He moved his hands to her hips and slowly guided her backward through the room until she fell onto the bed.

Claire crawled across the mattress until she could lie comfortably. Luca followed her, kissing and touching every inch of her as he moved up the length of her body. He paused to hover over her, his erection pressing insistently against her inner thigh. He lowered his head to kiss her again, then stopped.

Looking down at Claire, there was a flash of panic in his eyes. "Please tell me you have a condom with you."

A condom? Claire froze at the thought. She didn't have any. She hadn't used them since before she got married. "I don't. Don't you?"

"No, I didn't exactly plan for this to happen. Hold on," he said, climbing from the bed and dashing into her bathroom. "Bless you, Gavin," he shouted before returning to the bed with a foil packet in his hand.

Claire finally let out the breath she'd been holding. Thank goodness. She didn't want to stop now. Even the slightest hesitation might let reality rush in and ruin the moment. The odds of them conceiving were virtually nil, considering they'd met via a fertility clinic, but that wasn't the only worry. It had been a long time since she'd dated, but there had been plenty of things to catch then and now.

She dropped her head to the pillow as Luca sheathed himself and returned to his place between her thighs.

"Now, where were we?" he asked with a grin.

Claire reached between them and wrapped her fingers around his length. She pulled him just to the point of penetration and stopped. "Right about there, I think."

Luca nodded and pressed forward slowly. Claire closed her eyes, absorbing the feeling of having a man inside her after so long. Her muscles tightened around the invasion, making Luca hiss and clench his teeth as he buried himself fully inside her.

He continued moving at a slow and deliberate pace,

drawing out the pleasure. Claire had been nervous about doing this after all this time, but that faded away once he touched her. She drew her legs up to cradle his hips between her thighs and let her body rock back and forth with his movements. The feelings he created radiated through her like shock waves of pleasure.

It wasn't until she opened her eyes again that she realized Luca was watching her. Not just looking at her, but taking in everything. Seeing the pleasure dance across her face seemed to turn him on and make him bolder. He slipped a hand between their bodies and stroked between her thighs. Claire gasped, writhing beneath him as his fingers pushed her closer and closer to the edge. The more near her release came, the more forcefully Luca moved into her, making the climax build inside her even faster.

Luca had some kind of power over her. He seemed to know just how to touch her, just how to coax every sensation from her body in a way that should take a man time to master. All she could do was bite her lip and brace herself for it.

Then it hit her. The dam holding back the pleasurable rush inside her burst and she was swept up in it. "Luca!" she cried out, gripping at the sheets, but they failed to keep her from practically rising up off the bed.

Luca slowed down as Claire collapsed onto the pillows with heavy breaths. She felt as if all her energy had been zapped away, and she didn't care.

He lowered himself onto his elbows, burying his face in her neck. The stubble of his beard scratched against her skin as he rocked against her and whispered into her ear. "Watching you come undone like that… *Sei così bella*, Claire," he said. *"Ti voglio così male."*

She had no idea what he said, but the curly, seductive words sounded so wonderful. "Yes," she replied. "It's your turn, now."

Luca nipped gently at her shoulder, then dragged his lips across her throat before kissing her again. His gaze narrowed its focus on her again and one hand planted firmly on the curve of her hip. His fingertips dug into her flesh as he moved harder and faster than ever before. Claire felt every muscle in his body tense and at the last moment, his eyes finally squeezed shut. He roared as he poured into her with one final, powerful thrust.

And then he became unnaturally still in the thrill of the moment. She expected him to collapse or roll away, but he seemed to just freeze in place.

"What's the matter?"

He swallowed hard, his throat the only set of muscles he allowed to move. "I think the condom has broken." Luca reached over to the nightstand and picked up the wrapper. "You've got to be kidding me," he shouted, tossing it to the floor in anger. "This expired over a year ago."

In a rush, Luca pulled away and before she could stop him, he disappeared into the bathroom and shut the door. Claire sat awkwardly on the bed, not quite sure what to do. Her first foray into a renewed sex life had suddenly gone off track without warning. She clutched the sheets protectively to her chest, ignoring the pleasurable pangs that still echoed through her body.

Luca came out a few minutes later with a tortured expression pinching his face. "It did break. I'm sorry, Claire. I should've looked at the expiration date. I was just so desperate to have you that I didn't even think to look."

Claire was pretty sure there'd never been a man so desperate for her that he would forget something like that. She wasn't about to beat him up over it. There wasn't much they could do now, anyway. "Don't worry about it. I mean, I doubt I'll end up pregnant, if that's what you're concerned about. It took me years and a medical intervention the last time. And I'm clean. They did all sorts of testing at the clinic and I haven't been with anyone since then."

"I'm not insinuating that you weren't clean or even worried you'd get pregnant. That would take a miracle." Luca slipped into the bed beside her and pulled her into his arms. "I've just never had one break before, so I'm a little rattled. It's always been a hard and fast rule of mine to wear one. I've never been with a woman without it. I'm sorry."

Claire nestled into his chest, feeling a little better now that he hadn't fled the room like the scene of a crime. "You didn't know it would break. Everything will be fine, I'm sure of it."

Luca brushed her damp hair from her face and held her close. "You're probably right. Let's just put it out of our minds and get some rest. Tomorrow, I'll go to the store."

"The store?" Claire questioned.

"To buy a box of new ones. I've only just begun to worship this body, *tesorina*."

Eight

This was nice.

With his nose buried in Claire's neck, the scent of cinnamon and vanilla filled Luca's lungs. His arm curled around her, holding her warm, soft body against his. He didn't want to move. He could just lie like this for hours.

It had been a long time since Luca had woken up with a beautiful woman in his arms. His plan to woo Claire had worked even better than he'd expected. If every time was as good as last night, he'd happily propose to her right now. Not even the condom debacle could ruin his good mood.

Then a sound stopped him cold. At first, he thought he was imagining things. The echo of his mother's voice was so completely out of context that it couldn't possibly be what he heard. Just when he'd convinced himself it was his imagination, Luca caught the unmistakable sound of his mother's laughter.

No. It *couldn't* be.

Luca heard Eva squeal with amusement and the chorus of cooing voices that could only be members of his family. He groaned and pulled away from Claire, sitting up in bed. She stirred beside him, looking over her shoulder with squinted eyes.

"What's the matter?" she asked in a low, sleepy voice.

Luca wasn't quite sure how to break the news, so he just spit it out. "I think…my family is here."

Claire rolled onto her back and sat up, clutching the sheets to her bare chest. She looked so messy and vulnerable, so unlike the put together woman who stomped into his lawyer's office. He loved knowing both sides of this complex woman. Had he woken under any other circumstances, he would cover her body with his own and make love to her again. Instead he had to explain to her how his family had just crashed their beach vacation.

"You mean your sister?" she asked.

Luca swallowed hard and shook his head. "No, more than that."

The sound of his mother's laughter reached his ears again. When he turned to look at Claire, her sleepy expression was replaced with one of sheer panic. "Are you kidding me?"

"I wish I were. I think our secret is out. And that means Mia is in a lot of trouble."

Flinging back the blankets, Luca reached for his pants and tugged them on. He needed to go out there and figure out exactly what the hell was going on. He opened the door, completely dumbfounded by what he saw. In the center of the living room, his mother was holding up Eva as if she'd gotten her hands on the Holy Grail. His father was standing behind her, making faces at the baby until she squealed with delight. That was bad enough. Then, just beyond them, he saw Mia talking to his other sister, Carla. No fewer than five children were running around the living room, seeking excitement and hell-bent on destruction. He could already tell that he would have to write Gavin a fat check for everything they broke.

Luca turned just in time to see his youngest brothers, Giovanni and Angelo, come up the stairs with their wives. They were all carrying suitcases. That was a bad sign. This wasn't an afternoon visit. They were staying. What the hell was going on?

"Luca! You're awake!" his mother exclaimed.

"Do you really think I could sleep through all this?" He didn't even bother to mask his irritation. "What are you all doing here?" he asked with a pointed glance at Mia. His sister slunk behind Carla with a sheepish expression on her face. "And why, in God's name, do you have luggage?"

"You with all the questions," his mother snapped. She curled Eva to her chest and narrowed her gaze at him. "I've got a question for you, young man! How long were you going to keep our new grandchild from us?"

"A little longer than this," his muttered under his breath. "How did you find out?"

"It's my fault," Mia admitted, as though there were another choice. "Well, actually, it was Eva's fault."

"You're blaming the baby?" Luca asked with incredulity in his voice.

"Yes and no. Carla called me last night while you and Claire were at dinner. I shouldn't have answered the phone, but I did. While we were on the phone, Eva started to cry. What was I supposed to tell her?" Mia asked. "I couldn't think of a good lie fast enough, so I told her the truth and then swore her to secrecy."

"So naturally, when I got off the phone I immediately called Mama," Carla said, confirming his logic on not telling her in the first place. "This wasn't the kind of secret you keep, sorry."

"She was right," his mother, Antonia, chimed in. "How could you keep this beautiful little girl from us? Especially after everything you went through with Jessica."

"Because I've just found out about her myself," Luca said, scooping up the child from his mother and clutching Eva protectively to his chest. "And after what *did* happen with Jessica, I wanted to be sure before I told anyone. Once I got the test results, I selfishly chose to get to know Eva and her mother before all *this* happened."

His mother's hand came up to her mouth. "You don't even know the mother? At least with Jessica you two seemed to really be building toward a future together. I thought I taught you better than that, Luca. You're supposed to be a gentleman."

Luca sighed and rolled his eyes. "It wasn't like that. Mama, you know I can't…" He couldn't even say it aloud. He didn't need to. His whole family knew the truth, anyway.

"It was an accident at the fertility clinic," a woman's voice said from behind him.

Luca turned to see Claire standing in the doorway of the bedroom. In a matter of minutes, she'd dressed and transformed back into the prim and put together Claire he knew. Her dark blond hair was twisted into a bun, and her lips and cheeks were pink with a touch of makeup. She was wearing another sundress that looked amazing on her figure.

"Mama, Dad, everyone…this is Claire Douglas, Eva's mother."

"Oh, Luca." Antonia made a beeline for Claire, pulling her into a huge embrace. *"Lei è bella."*

Claire flinched slightly at the unexpected physical contact, but Luca could tell she was trying to play it off. She'd better get used to it. His whole family was very physically affectionate.

"Hello," she managed with a soft smile as his mother finally pulled away.

"It's so good to meet you, Claire. I'm sure we would've met sooner if I'd known you and Eva existed." There was a biting tone at the end of his mother's words directed at Luca. He didn't care.

"Claire, this is my family. That's my mother, Antonia. This is my father, Mario." He went around the room as fast as he could. She likely wouldn't remember all the names anyway. "You know Mia, then my sister Carla. My brother Giovanni and his wife, Nicole. My other brother Angelo and his wife, Tonia. My nephews Tony, Giovanni Jr., Matteo, Paolo and my niece Valentina."

Luca watched Claire's eyes get wider with every name he listed. "Is that everyone?" she asked.

"No," he had to admit. "My brother Marcello and his family apparently couldn't come, but they have a new baby. And it looks like Carla's husband stayed home with the kids." Luca turned his back to his family and silently mouthed the words to Claire, "I'm so sorry."

She just shook her head and pasted on a smile. "So glad all of you could come. Please, set down your things and relax. Can I get anyone something to drink? I was just about to make some breakfast. Have you eaten?"

The resounding roar of voices startled Claire for a moment, but Luca felt a touch of pride as she recovered. At the mention of food or drink, half the family headed toward the kitchen. No one bothered to tell her what they'd like; they simply took over like they would at home. She watched them for a moment in confusion.

Luca handed Eva to her and leaned over to whisper in her ear. "Just go with it. This is how they are." He leaned in to plant a kiss under her earlobe, but she shied away, heading toward the kitchen to help the others. He tried not to frown at her rejection.

Instead, he approached Giovanni as he sat in one of the overstuffed chairs. "Really?" he asked.

Giovanni just shrugged him off. "You know how they are. I got a phone call at ten last night telling me that you had a daughter and I was to be packed, ready and at the airport by six a.m. to go see her."

Luca slipped into the chair beside him. "You all took the corporate jet?"

His brother nodded. "Did you really think you could keep this a secret?"

"It worked for a few months."

"Months?" Giovanni looked stunned.

"Yes. I found out about this mistake at the clinic, and then I wanted to wait to get the results of the paternity test. You remember what happened with Jessica. I wanted to keep it under wraps until I knew for certain Eva was truly mine. After that were a few weeks of battling back and forth with her lawyer before I could see Eva. We came here to break the ice and figure out how to work together. It didn't seem like the right time to bring all of you into the picture."

"It seems understandable, but I doubt Mama will accept your excuse. Expect a tongue-lashing later."

Luca chuckled. "You mean that wasn't it just now?"

"Oh, no. You were saved by your pretty girlfriend and talk of cooking. That distracted her. You'll hear more about it when she's done pumping Claire for details and we've all been fed."

"She's not really my girlfriend," Luca argued. The way she pulled away from him a moment ago made that very clear. Last night was what it was, but she obviously didn't want his family to read into anything. "I mean, we're just…"

"You two came out of the same bedroom, Luca. And you're not wearing a shirt."

Luca looked down and realized he needed to fetch his shirt from the bedroom floor. "Yeah, but that was the first time. I'm not sure it will happen again, especially with you all showing up and breaking the romantic spell I'd so carefully crafted."

"Are you trying to woo her?" Giovanni asked.

"Not at first, but then I realized Claire and Eva might be my one shot at a real family. I'd be stupid to let this chance slip through my fingers."

"You don't know that for sure, Luca. Have the doctors—"

"No," Luca interrupted. "But *I* know. This is my chance. It could be worse. Claire is…" He found it hard to find the words in the moment. "A very special woman. And a great mother."

The two brothers turned to look into the kitchen. Their parents, Mia, Carla, Nicole and Angelo were talking all at once, bumping elbows and carrying around ingredients for the breakfast of champions. Tonia was unsuccessfully trying to corral a toddler. Claire stood on the fringe with Eva, not quite brave enough to jump in. She watched the group with fascination, like a circus performance.

Periodically, their mother would stop what she was doing to pat Claire's arm and pinch at Eva's cheeks. She'd mutter something in Italian that they couldn't make out, then she'd return to what she was doing.

"Well, dating or not, Mama seems to like Claire," Giovanni noted. "That's a huge hurdle to get over."

Their mother was notoriously picky about the women her sons dated. It was a pretty big deal to get the Antonia Stamp of Approval. Luca had never brought a woman home before Jessica, and that was only because of the baby. Even without Eva, Luca got the feeling that his mama would take to Claire. It was hard not to like her, even as different as she was.

"Does she know about your illness?" Giovanni asked.

Luca stiffened in his seat and shook his head. "No. And I don't want anyone telling her, either."

"It's not a big deal, Luca. You had cancer. That's nothing to be ashamed of. You survived. You should be shouting it from the rooftops."

Luca knew his brother was right, but he'd never felt like shouting. He only ever felt as if he'd lost something. A woman like Claire deserved a whole man who could give her everything she wanted.

Maybe, just maybe, he could fake it and be enough for her.

Overwhelmed wasn't quite the word Claire would use to describe the past three days, but it was close. She knew now what Luca was talking about when he said his family was loud, boisterous and fun-loving. They were all of those things and more. The sisters and sisters-in-law had taken Claire into their fold. She was worried they would be cold to her when they found out about the custody battle she and Luca had been fighting, but that wasn't the case. They'd taken the children to the beach and the ice-cream stand. They'd sat out on the deck together drinking wine and talking about children and men. It was surprising how quickly the sense of camaraderie had set in with these women who were virtual strangers.

Claire had barely even seen Eva since they arrived. Someone was always holding her. The only time they'd had together was when she would insist on giving Eva a bath and putting her to bed. Her room was her only sanctuary. There were Morettis everywhere else. The three couples took over the downstairs bedrooms with the kids sleeping on the floor in blanket forts. Mia and Carla shared the sofa bed.

Truthfully, there was a Moretti in her room, too, but it wasn't quite the same. She had let Luca return to her room while they were there, but only because there wasn't anywhere else to sleep. She felt guilty taking up a king-size bed while he tried to get rest on the recliner. She'd set a few rules, however. No hanky-panky. There were too many people around to hear every creak in the wood floors.

Besides that, she wasn't sure it was something that should be repeated, as much as she might like to. Luca was a complex man, and she got the feeling it would take a long time to peel back all his layers. Sex was just a distraction. If she was going to fully give herself to anyone, there had to be a level of trust and honesty between them. She didn't feel as if she and Luca had that yet. And maybe they never would. This trip wasn't supposed to be about romance anyway. It was supposed to be about family, and now, it certainly was.

On the third afternoon of his family's visit, the men had all gone out in search of fresh lobster to bring home for dinner. Mia and Carla had gone to the grocery store to replenish the pantry they'd depleted. Nicole and Tonia went to the beach with the kids, but Claire passed. She was exhausted from all the activity.

Suddenly, the house felt very quiet. Too quiet. After a while, she started to wonder where Eva was. Although she rarely had her, she did like to keep tabs on where she was. Claire meandered through the house, finally spying her out on the deck with Antonia. She slipped through the French doors and approached the deck chairs.

"May I join you?" she asked.

"Of course. My new grandbaby and I were just enjoying this beautiful day. I'm going to hate to leave tomorrow. I have so much more sugar to give these little cheeks."

Claire sat down and watched as Eva's face lit up at

her grandmother's sweet baby voice and kisses. She was really blossoming with all this attention. Perhaps not putting her in day care where she could be around a lot of different people was a bad idea. She was alone with Daisy all day, but Eva really seemed to like people. Perhaps she was more Moretti than Douglas.

"Claire, since everyone is gone at the moment, I wanted to talk to you about something. Being alone is a luxury in my family, so I've learned to take full advantage of it when it comes."

Claire bit her bottom lip to hide her frown. That sounded ominous. Was this the part where she threatened Claire not to hurt her son or keep his daughter from him? Told her to call off her lawyer? "Sure."

"I'm not sure what it is you and Luca have going. I know that whatever it is, it's early, so it's hard to say whether or not what you two have will turn into something serious, but I hope it does. I have never seen Luca as happy as he is here with you and Eva. Not even with Jessica was he like this. With her, he always seemed to be waiting for the other shoe to fall, and of course in the end he was right."

Claire wanted to push Antonia for more information, but she held her tongue, deciding not to interrupt.

"It broke my heart to see him like that. Finding out he had a child was such a startling revelation, but then he really warmed up to the idea. He was excited and nervous, but as he always does, Luca held back. We never expected to find out that the baby wasn't his."

Claire tried to hide her surprise at this revelation about Luca. He'd never once mentioned this other child or its mother. Even if it wasn't his in the end, that was an important event in his life he'd kept from her. She closed her eyes as all the pieces started to fall into place. That explained why he was so adamant about claiming Eva as his own. This time, he was certain the baby was his and he wasn't going to miss his chance to be a father, no matter what the circumstances.

"But this child," Antonia continued with a smile, "is the miracle that will bring him back to life. Whether or not he thought it would happen, he finally has a family."

"He has a daughter, yes," Claire clarified. She wasn't quite ready to commit to more than that. "And I'm going to make sure he has Eva in his life as much as he wants her to be."

Antonia's golden hazel eyes, so much like Luca's that it made her a little uneasy, fixed on Claire. "Dear, you and I both know that he's got a little more than just a daughter out of this situation."

Claire bit at her bottom lip as she considered her answer. "I don't really know. Sometimes things are going well, and I think maybe something is happening between us. Then he pulls away. Knowing about the other child explains a lot, but not everything. I still feel like he's keeping things from me, and that's a deal breaker for me. I'm not going to let myself get invested in a man I can't trust."

"Luca is as good a man as they come. He's just afraid to let himself fall for a good woman. Personally, I think you two are meant to be together. I don't believe in accidents or coincidences. Fate stepped in and scrambled those numbers on the labels so two strangers could share a child, and eventually, a life together."

That was a nice thought, but Claire wasn't quite so superstitious. Accidents happened. That didn't mean it was fate. It was just rotten luck. Or even good luck. It might not be what she planned, but at least Eva had a father and a family now. But as for him and her? She doubted this little vacation romance would last all the way back to Manhattan if he continued keeping secrets.

Luca's mother thought he was a peach, of course, but mothers loved their children blindly. He had given Claire his body, but he was holding back everything else. Unless that changed, she couldn't trust him with her heart. She'd already made the mistake of giving that away too freely in the past.

Something would go wrong. The dull ache in her gut was evidence of that. The only question was how badly it would hurt her when it happened.

Nine

"It's too quiet around here," Claire said as she washed up the last of the dinner dishes.

Luca looked up from his spot on the living-room floor. He and Eva were having fun with some fabric blocks with little tags on the edges. Frankly, he couldn't understand the appeal. He cut the tags off every piece of clothing he owned, but babies seemed completely enamored with them.

"I know what you mean," he said. His family had left a few days earlier. After three solid days of big Italian family chaos, the house almost seemed to echo with emptiness. "It always takes me a while to adjust to being alone again after we have get-togethers. Does that mean you like my family?"

Luca wasn't quite sure how his quiet, reserved Claire would handle Mia, much less the whole crew at once, but she'd done amazingly well. She fit in better than he'd ever expected. Whether or not she enjoyed her time with them was still a mystery to him, however.

Claire pulled the drain plug in the sink and strolled back into the living room while she dried her hands with a dish towel. "I love your family, Luca. They're amazing. I didn't even know a family could be like that. It's mind-boggling, really. I mean, they'd just met me and they treated me like family. Jeff's family was always kind to me, but I never felt like I was one of their daughters, even when legally I was."

Luca smiled at her. "They really liked you. I'm pretty certain they aren't like that with everyone. Even Carla liked you, and she's pretty hard to win over. And Mama. Well, you could do no wrong in her eyes. If you spoke Italian, you'd be perfect. Maybe we can work on that," he added with a grin.

"Very funny," Claire said as she sat down on the couch.

He turned back to Eva in time to see her let out a big yawn. "Uh-oh. I think she is ready for bed."

"Like me, I think she's still recovering from all the overstimulation."

Claire moved to get up, but Luca raised his hand. "You relax. I'll put her to bed. Why don't you pour us some wine, if my sisters didn't drink it all."

Luca stood and lifted Eva into his arms. Her little eyes kept slowly closing, then startling open as she tried to keep herself awake. "Don't fight it, *bella*."

It only took a few minutes to change the baby, put her into her pajamas and settle her into her crib. He turned on the mobile overhead and ran his hand over her soft baby curls. *"Buona notte, cara mia."*

Eva cooed at him for a moment, then her eyes fluttered closed. That was quick. Slipping out quietly, he closed the bedroom door behind him. "You know," he said, "it's almost time to go back to New York and we haven't done the one thing we said we came here to do."

Claire glanced up at him from her spot on the sofa with a curious look. "What's that?"

"Discuss the custody arrangement we want to submit to the judge."

An odd expression flickered in her eyes. Luca couldn't tell if it was disappointment, fear, anxiety or a combination of all three. "Okay. Let's discuss it, then."

Luca crossed the living-room floor and settled on the couch beside her. "Have you had a chance to review the proposal that Edmund sent up here with me?"

"Yes, I looked it over. There wasn't a lot that concerned me. I was surprised, honestly. It seemed pretty standard to me, and after the time we've spent here, I think most of my worries about your abilities as a father have been addressed. I only had one question. The child support seemed a little high to me."

Luca's brow went up. "High? I'm sure that's the first time anyone's ever heard that." He wondered, sometimes, if Claire underestimated just how much he was worth. Any other woman would've done her research and milked him for every penny.

Claire shrugged off his comment. "Even if I put her in one of the best schools in Manhattan and dressed her in designer clothes, I wouldn't need that much each month. We have a nice home, a caregiver. It makes me worry a little."

"About what?"

"That you're wanting more from me than the plan outlines. Is there an expectation that I should sell my brownstone and move to Manhattan? The expense of an Upper East Side apartment near you is the only thing I could imagine would justify the money."

The thought had crossed his mind a time or two, but he had learned early on that trying to push Claire would get him nowhere. He had to use his best negotiating skills to get what he wanted. "That wasn't my intention, no. But would it be so bad if I wanted that? You'd be closer to the museum. Closer to the schools we discussed. It would be easier on Eva to move back and forth between us, or for one of us to step in if the other needed them."

Luca watched the wheels silently turn in her head as he spoke. He knew it made sense, but he knew she also loved her place. "It's up to you, but as you said, that amount of money I'm offering you could easily make that a possibility."

She brushed a stray strand of honey blond hair from her face and nodded. "I'll have to think on that. I like being able to get away from the chaos of the city sometimes."

He laughed. "You act as though Brooklyn is in the middle of a hayfield. If you want, I'll buy a country house in Connecticut you can visit whenever you need to get away."

Claire's eyes widened. "Don't be silly."

Luca didn't think it was silly. It seemed completely practical to him. Despite all his planning to seduce Claire and lure her into a relationship while keeping himself emotionally removed, he'd failed miserably.

He wasn't sure he'd call what he felt for her love, but he certainly felt more than he'd ever intended to.

At this point, he was willing to do almost anything it took to get Claire to play a bigger role in his life. Having her live nearby was just one part of that. If buying a country house helped his cause, so be it. He was dreading the end of this trip. He knew that returning home would mean long hours in the office, and, if he was lucky, seeing Eva every other weekend. That wasn't good enough for him, especially when nothing in the paperwork dictated how often he'd get to see Claire.

"Well, how about this? I've been thinking a lot about all of this the past few days since my family left. If I'm being honest, I don't want to let what you and I have started slip away. I want us to build on it. It's all new to me, this relationship stuff, but I want to know how much more we can have together. And maybe if that happens and goes well, all that paperwork and custody agreements won't matter anymore. I don't just want Eva in my life, Claire. I want you in my life, too."

Claire's mouth dropped open the way it always did when he stole her prepared words from her lips. After a moment, her jaw closed and she smiled. "I want you in my life, too, Luca."

Luca leaned into her, wiping away the smile with his kiss. The minute his lips met hers, he felt that familiar surge of need run though his body and urge him on. That touch, combined with being alone again in the house, reminded him just how long he'd gone without touching Claire the way he'd wanted to. While his family was there, she had kept her distance. Now that she'd agreed to be in his life for a while longer, he wanted her back in his bed, as well.

"Luca," Claire said as she pressed against his chest with the palms of her hands. "Wait. I'm glad you're happy, but I wasn't finished. There was a 'but' coming."

But? Luca sat back against the arm of the couch with a frown. "What's wrong?"

Claire sighed. "There's nothing wrong, per se, but I wanted you to know that your mother told me something while she was here."

Luca felt the dull ache of dread in his stomach. She hadn't… Who was he kidding? Of course she had. His mother never respected his desire to keep his private past private. "What did she happen to share?" he asked, knowing full well what the answer was—she knew he was a one-balled wonder and had reservations about the two of them together.

Claire's eyebrows drew together in concern. "She told me about Jessica and the baby. Primarily, the point was how happy you seemed and how she'd wanted it so badly after everything you went through with Jessica. It worries me, Luca."

Luca was surprised. He thought for sure his mother would've spilled the cancer story. Perhaps she'd finally agreed to let him put that behind him. He breathed a sigh of relief. "What worries you, exactly?"

"That you didn't tell me about it yourself," she said, surprising him. "Since we've been here, I've told you every secret I have. I told you about Jeff, about my feelings of inadequacy and my failing marriage. You had a million opportunities to open up to me about this, but you didn't."

"It didn't seem relevant," Luca said. "It turned out to be nothing. I don't have another child you don't know about, so I didn't think it would matter to you."

"It's not about the child, but that you kept it to yourself. Secrets worry me, Luca. Jeff kept secrets. And as much as I want you in my life and I want to see how far this can go, I need to know you're going to be honest with me, even when it's uncomfortable. Even when it might expose the ugly parts of ourselves that we don't want anyone to see. It concerns me that you don't trust what we have enough to share that with me. It makes me wonder what else you're keeping from me."

Luca started to open his mouth to insist he wasn't keeping things from her, but she held her finger to his lips. "Don't. Don't tell me you're not, because I know that you are. Tell me, Luca. Tell me why you were at the fertility clinic. What happened to you? Tell me right now or I can't move forward with this."

Luca sighed. He'd been dreading this moment since he'd decided to make a future with Claire. Things could go horribly wrong from here, but he got the feeling it would be worse to avoid her questions. As much as he didn't want to, he needed to tell this story at least one more time.

"When I was in high school, I was diagnosed with testicular cancer. I missed most of my junior and senior years going through treatment. I had to have surgery to remove the tumor along with one of my testicles, then I went through extensive radiation and chemotherapy. I donated at the fertility clinic before the radiation because I would likely be sterile afterward. That's why Jessica having my baby was such a huge deal to my family. I wasn't supposed to be able to have children.

I don't like talking about it, so I avoided your questions about school earlier because it would lead into that topic. I didn't get to go to prom. I got my diploma in a wheelchair. That whole period of my life was defined by my illness."

Claire's expression crumbled into near tears as he told her the truth. He reached his arm out for her. "Come here," he said. Claire snuggled against him, and he wrapped his arm around her shoulders. With her beside him and her curious eyes turned away, it was easier for him to talk.

"Don't cry. I'm sorry. I should've told you about that, but it was so hard on me and I don't like reliving it. I was just a kid. Someone that age shouldn't have to worry about whether or not they can have children someday when they'd never even kissed a girl, much less face their own mortality. I wasn't sure if I was going to make it to my next birthday. The price of beating the cancer was high. It took more from me than a teenager my age could understand at the time. Even now, knowing what I do, I would pay it gladly, but it's not something that ever goes away. I've continued to pay to this day."

Claire could hear the pain in Luca's words and it made her heart break a little more the longer he spoke. He was right; that wasn't something a child should have to deal with.

"The physical toll was a lot to get over. I recovered from the surgery, my hair grew back after the chemo, but that really isn't the worst part of it all. The worst part is the waiting."

"Waiting for what?"

"Waiting for it to show up again."

She placed a reassuring hand on his knee. "You don't know that it will. It has been over ten years since you were sick. That's a long time to go. Don't you think if the cancer was going to come back it would have already?"

"Don't use logic in the same context as cancer. It doesn't work. Besides, I know that's not true. The treatment I received to destroy the cancer alone puts me at risk of developing a secondary cancer at some point. It also can cause a slew of other health issues later in life. I suppose I should be happy to have a 'later in life' to get sick from the long-term effects of the chemo and radiation."

"So is that why you've focused so much on work at the expense of your relationships? In case you got sick again?"

"In part," he admitted. "The children part doesn't help, either. I don't ever want a woman to give up her dream of a family because she had the misfortune of falling in love with me."

"Luca!" Claire said, sitting up to look him in the eye. "The woman who falls in love with you is anything but unfortunate. You have so much to offer. You're doing yourself a disservice by only focusing on what you can't do. Besides, there are plenty of women out there who already have children or don't want any. Or can't have any," she said with a pointed tone. "Like me."

Luca looked at her with dark eyes that reflected a pain he'd always hidden from her before. There was a vulnerability there that she never expected to see in the eyes of her confident CEO. She hated that he had been through such horrible things, but she was happy to finally feel the last walls coming down between them. He deserved to be happy.

And more than anything, she wanted him to be happy with her. Her defenses were coming down as quickly as his own. Before she could stop herself, she leaned into him, capturing his face in her hands before she pressed her lips to his.

The emotional current running through each of them connected with a spark of a desire. Luca's hands pulled her closer, his hungry mouth eager to pick up where they'd left off a few minutes ago. This time, Claire wasn't about to stop him. She eased into his touch, craving the feel of him against her.

It didn't take long for the throbbing ache of need to build inside her. Claire had been content enough to go without a man for months and months, but Luca had opened Pandora's box. She wanted him. Now.

Pulling on his shirt, Claire slipped down to the rug and brought Luca with her. Their lips never parted as they slid to the floor. Luca's heavy body covered hers, the weight of it making her feel secure, somehow. She had been drifting through life since Jeff died, but here and now, she finally had an anchor to keep her steady.

"Make love to me, Luca," she whispered against his lips. "Let me show you that you're everything a woman needs."

Her words lit a fire in him, and she was happy to receive the results of it. His hands slid over her body, pulling at her cotton dress and exposing the length of her leg beneath it. He continued pushing the fabric up until it bunched around her waist.

He sat up then, abandoning her lips at last so she could pull his shirt over his head and toss it away. Her hands immediately moved to his chest, rubbing over the hard muscles. She let the smooth crescents of her fingernails drag over the ridges of his six-pack, leaving tiny half moon imprints just above the waistline of his jeans. Before she could unbutton his fly, Luca moved out of her reach.

He traveled slowly down her body, leaving a trail of kisses across her bare skin. He pushed the straps of her dress off her shoulders and tugged at the neckline until her breasts spilled over the top. His mouth teased and tasted her, sucking hard at her puckered nipples until Claire cried out and buried her fingers in the thick waves of his hair.

The tiny fire he'd ignited in her had grown to a steady burn. She ached for him, tugging him close even as his touch was so intense that she was tempted to pull away. As the kisses moved across her stomach and he nipped at the quivering muscles of her inner thigh, she felt the need gnawing inside her with no release in sight.

With nimble fingers, Luca removed her panties. Claire sighed in relief, thinking she would finally have him, but she was wrong. His jeans were still firmly in place as he pressed her thighs apart. Her breath caught in her throat as she realized what he was doing.

"Luca?" she gasped.

He paused, looking up at her from between her thighs. "Yes, *tesorina*?"

"What are you...you're not...?" She couldn't even ask the question. Claire was embarrassed to admit that this was something she'd never experienced before. Jeff had felt it was unhygienic, although he never seemed concerned when he wanted *her* to satisfy *him*.

Luca narrowed his gaze at her just as her cheeks starting flaming with embarrassment. "What's the matter? Haven't you been pleasured like this before?"

She squeezed her eyes shut and shook her head. Claire heard only a low rumble of anger in Luca's throat.

"I see your bastard of a husband failed in yet another aspect of your marriage. I intend to rectify that right now."

Claire was torn. It seemed like an incredibly intimate thing. She wasn't certain if she was ready for something like that. "I don't know, Luca. I'm not sure I—"

Without warning, Luca's tongue flicked across her aching flesh and stole her protest. A bolt of pleasure like she'd never experienced before shot through her body. "Luca!" She gasped and arched her back off the plush living-room rug.

He waited until the muscles in her body relaxed again, then he stroked ever so slowly across her with his tongue. Claire bit at her lip to keep from shouting too loudly and waking up Eva. It was difficult, especially when Luca encircled the outside of her thighs with his arms, pressed his palms against her inner thighs and opened her even wider to him.

The sensations of the intimate caress made it easier to forget how awkward all this seemed. The touch of his silky tongue on her most sensitive parts brought her close to an intense climax far faster than she ever anticipated. She wiggled and writhed beneath him, feeling it building inside of her, yet being virtually helpless to do anything about it.

Luca eased up on her for a moment, then he pressed her knees back until they were pushed against her chest. She caught her legs behind each knee to hold them there. At least that gave her something to grasp at when he returned to her, this time with his hands free.

With renewed fervor, he devoured her. Claire could only chant "yes, yes" as he drove her closer and closer to the edge. At the perfect moment, he slipped a finger inside her and she was done. The most intense orgasm she'd ever experienced exploded. Tiny sparks of pleasure danced through her whole body as her muscles quivered and tightened.

Luca retreated, but Claire barely had the energy to open her eyes. She managed to do it just in time to see his jeans pile onto the floor and an empty condom wrapper follow it. He'd kept his promise and went to the store, even with his family's unexpected arrival.

"Keep your legs right there," he whispered as he returned to her.

Her overstimulated nerves lit up as he slowly pressed his length into her. With her legs back, he reached farther, deeper than she ever could've imagined possible. When he was finished, her knees were resting on his shoulders. She could barely catch her breath, but she didn't care. This is what she'd wanted, more than anything. She wanted to be one with him in a way she'd never been with anyone else.

Luca murmured soft words in Italian against the

sensitive skin of her inner knee as he thrust into her again. Each movement was so slow, so deliberate, so tortuous, as though he didn't want it to end. She didn't want it to end, either.

Claire opened her eyes and watched his face as he moved so she would always remember this moment. His brows were drawn together in concentration, as though he were preparing an amazing dish in the kitchen, as if this were the most important task he'd ever completed. He made her feel that way, too—as though she was a priority in his life. She'd never had that before. She didn't want to let that go. Not at the end of this trip. Not after the judge's ruling. Not ever.

Because she was in love with him.

After what happened with Jeff, she told herself she wouldn't make the mistake of falling in love again. You couldn't trust someone enough not to take your heart and soul and crush it. Claire refused to give someone that much power over her again, and yet here she was. It might not be the smart thing to do, and it might bring her nothing but heartache before it was through, but there was no fighting it any longer.

Claire could feel it down in her bones, down in her core. Even as another release built up inside of her, she knew the sensation couldn't begin to touch the feeling of love that was warming her heart.

"Yes!" she gasped over and over as she felt both of them tense with anticipation.

Yes, she was close to oblivion. *Yes*, he was doing everything right. *Yes*, she wanted him to lose himself in her. *Yes*, this was better than she could've ever dreamed. *Yes*, she wanted to be with him back in New

York. *Yes*, she loved Luca with everything she was and everything she had.

Yes to it all. He needed only ask the question and she was his forever.

Ten

It felt strange to be back in New York. Despite Luca's assurances that he wanted their relationship to continue beyond their time at the beach, Claire was anxious stepping back onto the concrete of her home turf. Her stomach was constantly fluttering like butterflies had invaded. If she thought about it too long, she hovered on the verge of nausea. She wasn't quite sure what she was afraid of.

That was a lie. She knew exactly what she was afraid of—losing Luca. It was the risk she'd taken when she gave in to her feelings for him. Manhattan didn't have the cozy charm of the island. Would they really be able to hold this relationship together among the honking cabs, demanding jobs and hectic schedules of real life?

Tonight, she would find out. They'd been home a

few days. Today had been her first day back at the museum. Luca had asked her to dinner tonight so they could put together their final custody agreement for Edmund and Stuart to submit to the judge. She was supposed to meet him at his apartment, then they'd go somewhere for dinner when they were through. Daisy was staying late to watch Eva.

Luca's apartment was just a few blocks from the museum. She walked down the massive steps to head in that direction. It was a nice evening and she wanted to make the most of the pleasant weather. She was actually feeling pretty good tonight.

At least until she caught a whiff of the nearby hot-dog cart. Normally the smell didn't bother her—sometimes it was even enticing—but tonight it was anything but. She frantically sought out a nearby trash can and emptied the contents of her stomach into it.

When she was through, she straightened and clamped her hand over her nose and mouth. Had she really just done that? She looked around to see if anyone noticed. They had. She was getting more than a few disgusted looks from tourists and locals alike.

A nearby woman reached into her purse and handed Claire a tissue. "I don't know why they call it morning sickness," she said. "More like all the damn time sickness. Those hot-dog carts always got me, too. Don't let those people bother you. When you're bringing a child into the world, you have the right to puke wherever you need to."

Claire tried not to frown at the well-meaning woman. There was no sense in dumping her life story on her by arguing that she couldn't get pregnant. She just accepted the tissue and was thankful that at least one person wasn't judging her. "Thank you."

She dashed across the street when the light changed and tried to put as much distance between her and the mess as she could. It wasn't until she reached the light at the next block that she hesitated and let the woman's words sink into her head.

Pregnant? She couldn't possibly be pregnant.

Admittedly, this did feel like morning sickness. When she was pregnant the first time, there had been days when she couldn't even get out of bed. She lost weight instead of gaining it. She went through a sleeve of saltine crackers a day. The misery of her first trimester was something she'd quickly put out of her mind as the price she paid for Eva, but in the moment it came rushing back with crystal clarity.

She pulled out her phone and looked at her calendar. Doing a little math, she realized that she'd been at the beach over a month and her period was well overdue. But that just had to be a fluke. Yes, as if her public vomiting was a fluke.

Claire crossed the street with the crowd again, feeling more and more anxious with every step. She didn't know why. It was likely the questionable chicken-salad sandwich she'd had at the museum cafeteria today. There was no way she was pregnant. Even if she *could* conceive normally and Luca *hadn't* had cancer, the condom had only broken once.

Once was all it took. The ominous words of her high-school sex-ed teacher haunted her.

There was no way she could march into Luca's apartment and act like nothing was wrong while this weighed on her mind. She also didn't want to bring up the possibility and raise both their hopes only to find out she was just perimenopausal with food poisoning. This was easily dealt with. She needed to buy a pregnancy test, take it and move on with her day without this uncertainty. It was a waste of ten dollars, but it was a small price to pay for peace of mind.

In the drugstore, she sought out the aisle she'd haunted while undergoing all those fertility treatments. She picked up her favorite brand and carried it to the counter. How many of these had she taken over the years? Dozens. Only one had ever come back positive. Tonight was probably not the night for a repeat.

After paying for it, she continued down the block to a Starbucks. It may not be her first choice for where to take a pregnancy test, but she had to know now, before she got to Luca's. She took it into the women's restroom, then nervously awaited the results. When the alarm on her phone went off, she finally let herself check the tiny window.

Pregnant.

Claire's jaw dropped open in surprise and shock. That was impossible. How could she…? It had only… She could barely complete a thought, much less a sentence. Putting the cap on, she slipped the test back into her purse and headed back to the drugstore to buy another one from a different brand, then repeated the test. The screen varied, but the results were the same—two lines instead of one.

Confused, she packed up her things and left. It took another block before the news really started to sink in. She was pregnant. After the years of trying, the tests, the shots, the invasive procedures to conceive Eva… she'd managed to get pregnant *accidentally*. She had prayed for another baby. Dreamed of it, knowing that the odds of it happening were almost astronomical. And now, if all went well, she was going to have one. Eva would have a brother or sister, and she and Luca would have a second child together. It was a miracle.

The excitement was nearly bubbling out of her as she entered his building and signed in at the desk. When she got off the elevator, she had a huge grin on her face. She couldn't suppress it as much as she wanted to surprise him with the news.

Luca opened the door. A curious expression came across his face as he looked at her. "Hi. What are you so happy about?" He stepped back to let Claire inside and took her jacket.

"I have some news," she said. "Let's sit down first."

Luca followed her over to the couch where they sat together. She scooped up his hands in hers. "I know that you and I have only been together a short while, and for anyone else, this might be an unwelcome development, but I haven't been feeling well since we got back. I hadn't thought much about it, but a lady outside the museum said something today that got me to thinking. On the way over here, I took a pregnancy test…"

Luca stiffened. Those were the last words he expected to come out of her mouth. Sitting up straight, he pulled his hands away from hers. "And?" he forced himself to ask, already knowing the answer. If it was negative she wouldn't have bothered mentioning it.

She reached into her purse and pulled out two pregnancy tests. "And it came out positive. Both of them. I'm pregnant. I could hardly believe it myself. It must've happened when the condom broke that first time."

Luca took one of the tests from her hand, studying the tiny screen and hoping for the information to change. It was happening again. The dull ache in his gut told him that much. What he didn't understand was why she would try this. She knew he couldn't have children. He'd told her that only a few short days ago. "It's not possible," he said.

"I know. That's what I thought. I mean, I would have thought it was impossible, which is why I ignored all the signs. I need to go to the doctor to confirm the results and check on everything, but—"

"No," he said, interrupting her stream of words. He couldn't stand to just sit there and listen to her prattle on when he knew in his heart it was all lies. The surprise, the excitement…it all had to be carefully crafted so he'd believe the child was his and not question it.

"What do you mean, no? You told me you wanted a family. Why are you so upset? I'm pregnant, Luca."

"I'm sure you are." He got up from his seat and walked out of the living room and into the kitchen. He needed a little space. He could feel the muscles in his neck and jaw tightening. Before too long, he'd have a raging headache.

Claire didn't take the hint. She followed him through his apartment, a confused frown wrinkling her forehead. "I thought you'd be happy."

Luca chuckled bitterly and looked down at the pregnancy test in his hand. He'd made that mistake once; he wouldn't fall for it again. It was a false hope. Instead, he tossed the test into the trash can. "If I was the father, I would be happy. But like I said, that's impossible."

Claire froze in place, not quite sure she could believe the words he'd just said. "Luca, you are the father. Who else would it be?"

To be honest, he didn't really want to consider the possibilities. He was already fighting through this storm of emotions swirling inside him. He didn't need to add furious jealousy to the list. Luca narrowed his gaze at her. "I have no idea, but I'm pretty sure it's not the sterile guy in the room."

"Look, I'm as surprised as you are. Between the two of us and our issues, it never crossed my mind that it could happen, but it did. You are the baby's father. I've spent every day and night of the last month with you. The last man I was with before you died a year ago."

Luca wanted to believe her. God, he wanted to. Claire had never given him any reason not to believe what she said before. But this story was just too farfetched. She did a good job seeming sincere, though. "That all sounds good, Claire. You must've practiced before you came over."

She flinched as though his sharp words were a slap across the face. "Practiced? Do you really think I'm making all this up?"

He wanted to say no, that he believed her and was happy, but he couldn't let himself do it. The anger he'd suppressed over the past decade bubbled inside him. There was no one he could blame for the cancer or the treatments. He couldn't direct that emotion at anyone. Jessica disappeared when the paternity results came back negative, so he never got to say what he wanted to say to her, either. But in that moment, Claire was a convenient target for the disappointments of his life.

"No," he replied coolly. "Just the part where I'm the

father. What I can't seem to figure out was where you got the time to sleep with someone else."

Luca watched Claire's face turn red and the vein in her forehead start to pulse. "I didn't need any time!" she shouted. "I didn't sleep with anyone but you. How could you accuse me of something like that after what happened with Jeff? I would never ever…" Claire's voice drifted off as though she couldn't even finish the sentence.

Luca knew that accusing her of having an affair was the lowest of low blows, but what other option was there? This wasn't a star in the east.

"You know, I'm not Jessica. I understand all that must've been awful for you, but don't take what she did out on me. This is totally different."

"Is it?" Luca asked. He wanted it to be different, but he wouldn't allow himself to entertain such a wild fantasy. He and Claire were through. It pained him, but there was no going back now. He needed to make a clean break and send her on her way before things got even uglier than they already were.

"Maybe you're right," he agreed with bitterness leeching into his voice. "Jessica was happy with just having one of my children. You're pushing for two. Wasn't having one of my kids enough? You had to get more out of me?"

Claire tried not to physically react to his insult. Now she wasn't just a slut, she was a greedy one? Where had this dark side of Luca hidden over the past few weeks? She thought he was holding back, but she never dreamed that *this* was what he'd kept from her. "More what? Money? I don't need your money, Luca."

His jaw tightened as he looked her over. "Then

what's behind it? Afraid I might leave you once we got home? Did you think having a second miracle child would convince me to marry you so we could have a happily-ever-after?" He crossed his arms over his chest, challenging her to say otherwise.

She wasn't quite sure how to respond. This whole conversation had gone off the rails and there was no way to recover it. "I will admit that I'd hoped we could have a happily-ever-after with our two children, but there's no scheming involved. It simply is what it is."

"Claire, the only thing this is, is over. I knew it was a bad idea to seduce you, but you and your sad eyes and luscious lips convinced me otherwise. I don't know why I thought that us being together was the best resolution to our situation. Well, no more. You and I are through."

A sharp pain struck Claire's chest like Thor's hammer, radiating outward. She was certain it was the feeling of her heart breaking. How could she have loved a man who could be so cruel? She didn't really know him at all. All his smooth words and charming smiles had completely disarmed her.

"I thought we really had something special between us, Luca. But if you—" Her voice cracked with emotion as she fought to hold back tears. She didn't want him to see her cry. "If you are willing to accuse me of something that terrible and then cast me aside so easily, then I was wrong. About everything."

"I'm sorry to disappoint you."

His arrogant, ambivalent tone made her angry. It was one thing for him to be so convinced that he didn't believe her without proof. It was another to be downright cruel. She wasn't going to let another man treat her like less than she deserved. Luca was the one who taught her that, ironically enough.

Claire gathered up all her nerve, straightening her spine and looking him hard in the eyes like she had that first day at his lawyer's office. "You're only disappointing yourself, Luca, because you're a coward."

"A coward?" He nearly roared the words at her, but she refused to take a single step back.

Instead, she moved closer. "Yes, a coward. You're too scared to go to the doctor and find out the truth about your sterility. You'd rather throw away everything we have, accuse me of being a whore and a liar than face the reality of your condition."

"Why would I be scared to do that? The worst they can tell me is what I already know."

"No, it's not. The worst thing they can tell you is that you've been wrong all this time. Because then you'd have to come to terms with the fact that you've been living half a life for all these years for no reason. You'd know for certain that you wasted over a decade where you could've found someone to love and started a family instead of being Mr. Busy CEO all the time. You've been hiding behind your desk instead of living your life."

Luca raised his arm, pointing toward the front door. "You take your venomous lies and get out of here before I call security and have you thrown out."

"You couldn't force me to stay one minute longer." Claire turned on her heel and marched back to the entryway where she scooped up her coat. "Since you're so certain this child isn't yours, I'm going to presume that you won't be dragging me to family court to get custody of this one."

"Nope," he snapped. "Not interested."

Claire tried not to react to his indifference. Not because of herself, but because of her child. She already felt a sense of protectiveness for it. The last thing she wanted was for the baby to feel as if the father didn't love it from the day they found out he or she existed.

"Fine. Then do me a favor and try not to be interested in Eva, either. If you don't want both your children, we don't want or need you in our lives at all," Claire said.

She flung open the front door and marched out, slamming it behind her with all the Mama Bear fury she could muster. It wasn't until she'd gotten on the elevator and the doors had safely shut that the anger subsided. With it gone, a rush of tears she couldn't stop flowed free.

How could she have gotten exactly what she wanted and lost everything she needed at the same time?

A beam of sunlight came through the window and shone across Luca's face. It roused him from his uncomfortable position on the leather couch in his living room. After a furious battle with a bottle of Scotch, he'd passed out there the night before.

He pushed himself up to a seated position and winced as the movement sent a sharp pain through his head. Bending over, he clutched his forehead and groaned. It was like a vise was clamped down on his skull, turning tighter with every movement and sound.

As pieces of the night before came back to him, he realized that even the agony of his head was miniscule in comparison to the ache of loss and disappointment that had settled in his chest.

Their angry words echoed in his head. The positive pregnancy test, the hopeful, the devastated, then the angry expressions on Claire's face, and then the slamming door flipping through his mind like a broken slide projector.

When he finally looked up, he spied the shattered remains of his cell phone. After Claire left, he'd reached for the closest thing he could lay his hands on and chucked it at the closed door of his apartment. He'd felt little satisfaction as his cell phone collided with the door and splintered across the marble entryway floor. Today, on top of everything else, he'd need to contact his assistant and have her order him a new phone.

With a curse, he leaned back against the couch and stared up at the ceiling. He'd lost it last night. That was very unlike him. He was always so in control, but Claire's betrayal had pushed him over the edge. After she left, all he could hear was his blood rushing through his veins; all he could see was tainted with the red hue of his emotions.

His child! She claimed to be pregnant with his child. Luca could hardly believe it when the words came out of her mouth. Not even the pregnancy test could convince him. How could he trust Claire's declaration that it was his baby? He couldn't. Not when he knew that it was impossible.

But did he *really* know?

As usual, morning and sobriety had brought everything into question. Not even the Scotch could drive Claire's words from his mind. She'd called him a coward because he hadn't been tested in all these years. He'd never really looked at it that way. Why did getting a slip of paper from the lab make a difference? It was just the final nail in the coffin he couldn't bear to seal. The radiation treatments destroyed his chances of fathering a child. End of story. It didn't matter how much he might want another child or how badly he wanted to believe her.

She had to know that he wanted another child. There was no other reason why she would come to him with a story like that. She'd found his weakness and did her best to exploit it.

Even as the thought rolled around in his foggy, hung-over brain, Luca knew it was wrong. Everything he'd said or done last night was contrary to what he knew to be true about Claire. It was like a monster had been unleashed inside him the moment she tested his beliefs. Once it got out, there was no stopping the flow of vile words from his mouth.

Disgusted with himself, he pushed up from the couch and stumbled into the kitchen to make a cup of coffee. That would help clear his thoughts, even if he feared it would make him realize his actions last night were that much more despicable.

He busied himself with his chore and sat down at the breakfast bar. Staring at the tile backsplash, he remembered the topic of Jessica coming up. He had tried and tried to put that whole situation out of his mind. That was why he hadn't told Claire about it at first. Of course, his mother didn't have any problem with sharing. Had the story his mother told her inspired Claire to come up with the lie about the baby? Or had the past simply poisoned his view of the present?

One thing he knew was that Claire was right when she said she wasn't Jessica. He knew that even as he accused otherwise. The two women were nothing alike.

Jessica had been smart, but ambitious. They'd been compatible in bed, but he knew she wanted more. He'd wanted it, too, at first, but reality sunk in and he realized he'd never give her the family she wanted. So he'd retreated. "More" wasn't on the table. He ignored her texts and calls for a few months and finally she faded from his life. Until she showed up at the door very pregnant with "his" baby.

In the end, it had all been a hurtful lie. She wanted Luca back, wanted him to marry her. Apparently she wanted it badly enough to poke holes in all the condoms they used together, not knowing he was sterile. When that didn't work, she deliberately got pregnant by an Italian guy she met at a bar right after they broke up in the hopes she could pass it off as Luca's. It was incomprehensible. He never would've thought Claire would stoop to Jessica's level.

That's when the sobering thought crossed his mind—she wouldn't.

Claire believed what she was saying, whether it was true or not. But Claire had also told him she hadn't been with a man since Jeff. That didn't leave a lot of options, although it certainly explained the confused and betrayed look on her face when he rejected the idea of the baby being his.

He couldn't help it, though. That baby couldn't be his. It just couldn't.

But if it was…he'd made a huge, inexcusable and maybe unforgivable mistake.

Eleven

"Moretti?"

Luca looked up from his brand-new smartphone when the nurse called his name. His stomach ached with dread. This was a moment he'd avoided for ten years. He'd almost called and canceled this appointment three times. The only reason he didn't was because he knew he'd have to face Gavin eventually.

His friend had listened sympathetically while he told him his sad tale. But instead of taking his side, he'd surprised Luca by pretty much saying the same things Claire had said. That he was a chicken. That his hurtful accusations were unfounded. Gavin had finished the conversation by telling him he needed to visit the doctor. Until he was tested and knew for certain that the baby couldn't be his, he needed to hold his tongue. He'd already said a lot he'd regret if he was wrong.

Luca knew Gavin was right, but that didn't mean he had to like it. Instead, he'd scheduled an appointment and that's where he found himself. Putting his phone away, he stood and followed the nurse down the corridor.

First, Luca was taken to a private room to produce a specimen for testing. When he was finished, he left the cup in the window and was led to an examination room to wait for the doctor.

It was an agonizing wait. He watched every minute tick by, the sense of anxiety growing with each second. At last, a soft knock came at the door and the doctor stepped inside with his file. It was the moment he'd dreaded and avoided since he'd finished his radiation treatments. Now he would know for certain if he was really the damaged man he'd always believed himself to be.

The doctor shook his hand and sat down on the tiny rolling stool. "Mr. Moretti," he began, flipping through the pages. "We have done a quick preliminary test of your sample. We're going to send it out to the lab for more detailed analysis, but I'm comfortable at this point with telling you that you are, in fact, able to have children."

Luca froze in disbelief. This was not what he'd expected at all. "Are you sure?"

"I'm not saying it will be as easy to impregnate a woman as it is for men without your medical history. Your sperm counts are lower than they would've been before your treatments, but you do still have motile, well-formed spermatozoa. With the right mix of circumstances, you can absolutely have children."

Luca wasn't sure what to say. He sat dumbfounded

on the examination table as the doctor's words ran though his brain again and again.

"If you find you're having difficulty conceiving with your partner, a fertility clinic could be of some assistance."

Luca chuckled low and shook his head. "I'm through with fertility clinics, but thanks for the suggestion."

The doctor narrowed his gaze at Luca. "I'm not sure what that's about, but do you mind if I ask why you were tested today if not to start a family?"

Luca looked down at his hands. "Apparently I've already started a family. I didn't think it was a possibility, but it seems the right mix of circumstances happened."

The doctor's white eyebrows drew together in concern. "I'd say congratulations, but you don't seem very excited about the prospect of fatherhood."

"It's not fatherhood that bothers me," Luca admitted. "I'm thrilled by the idea of it, even though I still run the risk of my cancer returning someday. I'll face that if it happens. It's just that I'm going to have a lot of apologizing to do to the baby's mother."

"Ahh," the doctor said, closing his file and setting it aside. "Well, if you want to know for certain, a blood test for paternity can be conducted even early on in the pregnancy."

Luca shook his head vehemently. Edmund would probably want that, but after everything he'd said to Claire, he couldn't ask her for that. He had no real reason to believe she was lying about the baby aside from the fact that he'd thought it to be impossible. They'd hardly left each other's side for weeks; she hadn't had the opportunity to meet and seduce another man. Now that he knew otherwise, there was no doubt.

Claire was pregnant with his child. And he was an ass.

"Okay, then I think we're done here unless you have any other questions. Good luck with your situation." The doctor stood and shook Luca's hand again. Just as quickly as he'd arrived, the doctor slipped out the door, leaving Luca alone with his thoughts.

He could have children. The old-fashioned way.

The idea had never really occurred to him. The oncologists had been so doom and gloom about his prospects that he'd presumed the worst. Then he'd presumed the worst about Claire.

Claire. The woman who had been so mistreated by her husband that she had been loath to trust him or anyone else. The woman who had accepted him as he was. The woman who hadn't pushed him to talk about his past even as she struggled with her husband's dishonesty. The mother of his child. His *children*.

He'd treated her terribly. Luca never thought he could be so cruel to someone he cared about, and yet the harsh words had rolled off his tongue. Hopefully, the apology would come just as easily.

Luca sleepwalked through the motions of checking out of the doctor's office and making his way toward his apartment. Truthfully, he should've been calling for a car to take him back to the office, but he needed a little time to process all of this. That meant time away from his family. None of them knew where he'd gone or what had happened with Claire after they left Martha's Vineyard, but they would know something was wrong if they saw him right now. He was certain that shock and heartache were etched all over his face.

Stopping at a streetlight, Luca looked up and saw the Brooks Express Shipping building just ahead. Gavin would be expecting an update, so he might as well go on in and give it to him directly. Maybe he'd have a suggestion on how to make it up to Claire after everything he'd said and done.

In the lobby, he dialed Gavin and waited for his answer.

"Do you realize you've called me three times in the past month or so? I'm starting to feel special."

Luca sighed. "I'm in your lobby. Are you in?"

"I am. I've got a meeting in a half hour, but for now, I'm all ears."

Luca took the elevator up to the floor where Gavin's office was. He waved at his receptionist, blowing past her desk and into Gavin's office before she could stop him.

Gavin turned from his computer with an expectant look on his face. "So? Can your boys swim?"

Luca had to laugh at the way his friend phrased such a delicate question. "Yes, they can. They won't be winning any medals, but they can make it across the pool."

"Congratulations! Sit down." Gavin pointed to his guest chair as he got up from his own. "This calls for a celebration." He wandered over to his wet bar and poured two glasses of dark honey colored liquor.

Luca sat, eyeing his friend's desk. It was decorated with photographs from his wedding to Sabine, him holding his daughter, Beth, for the first time, all four of them on a plane, then on a beach. It made Luca want that. He wanted to litter his desk with family photos. But something kept holding him back.

Gavin carried the glasses back to the desk and handed one to Luca. Frowning at his friend, he said, "What's the matter? You look less than enthusiastic about the news."

Luca sipped the drink and winced at how strong it was. He wasn't much for Scotch, especially after overdoing it the other night. "I'm happy. Really, I am. But knowing the truth makes my fight with Claire that much worse. I've got to get her back somehow, but I don't know if she'll forgive me after what I said."

"Do you love her?" Gavin asked.

Luca nodded without hesitation. He hadn't actually thought about it, but the minute Gavin asked, the answer popped into his head as clear as day. Claire was unlike any woman he'd ever met. Since the day of their fight, he'd walked around with an aching hole in his chest. He missed her. He missed Eva. Now he even missed their baby growing inside her. He hadn't been around to take Claire to the doctor, listen to Eva's heartbeat or supply her with her strange cravings the first time. If he didn't get this fixed, he would lose his second chance at having the full fatherhood experience.

"I am madly, desperately in love with her, Gavin." Saying the words aloud made him feel better and worse at the same time.

"Okay." Gavin's brows knit together in thought. "So tell me why you're in my office telling *me* this instead of on Claire's doorstep telling her?"

Luca supposed he could go to the museum right now and track her down, but he still had reservations. "It's not that simple. I've never let myself feel this deeply for anyone before. I always felt like I was a broken toy that no one would want, so I never even let myself have the dream of something like that."

Gavin just shook his head. "You're a fool, is what you are. You're a successful guy. You're handsome enough."

"Thanks," Luca said dryly.

"My point is that you're a great catch. Even with one testicle."

Luca ignored his friend's jesting slight. "I'm not a catch. I'm a time bomb. So what if I tell Claire I love her? What if she forgives me and we get married and have the baby together? What if I do all that and my cancer comes back? She's already been a widow once. I can't be responsible for her going through that a second time."

"You can't live your whole life waiting to die, man. You've got to get out there and start living. Anything can happen to any one of us. I could get hit by a cab or have an aneurism and drop dead at my desk with no warning at all. You've been in remission a long time. Stop letting your former illness hold you back. If you don't go to her, you've virtually left her a widow anyway—she's raising your children alone."

"And what if she'd rather be alone than be with me?"

"Then that is her choice. You can't make other people's decisions for them. I went years without Sabine because she decided we weren't a good fit. I never would've let her walk out that door if it had been my choice. But you've at least got to give her the opportunity to choose."

Gavin was right. Luca knew he was right. He just

had to take all these old anxieties and put them aside. If the cancer came back, it came back. At least this time he would have Claire and the children to give him a reason to fight even harder.

He still didn't think he could march up to her and get a warm reception, however. He needed to open with a grand gesture. Not just jewelry or another flashy gift. It had to be something that would mean more than anything to her.

There was nothing in the world more important to Claire than Eva. Luca knew what he had to do. Taking another burning sip of his drink, he reached for his phone and called his lawyer.

Claire climbed the stairs of her brownstone with a heavy heart and even heavier limbs. She wasn't very far along in this pregnancy, but it was already wearing her out. That, combined with a return to her routine after a month away, left her thoroughly exhausted.

Yes, that was it. It wasn't the crushing oppression of heartache that was slowing her down.

Opening the front door, she found Daisy and Eva playing on the floor in the living room. Her nanny immediately stood and went over to give Claire a hug. "Hey, Mama. How did the doctor's appointment go?"

Claire reached into her purse and pulled out the roll of sonogram pictures. There wasn't much to see, just a blurry little blob that looked something like a jelly bean. The first time she'd seen that image of Eva, her heart had nearly exploded with love and excitement. She and Jeff were finally going to be parents. This time the sight just made her sad. She would adore this baby, she had no doubt, but she couldn't help but think that she was once again having a child without a father around to love it the way it deserved to be loved. Was a mother's love enough? She hoped so.

Daisy snatched the photos out of her hand and gave a little squeal of excitement. "Congratulations. This is so exciting. I can't believe after how hard you worked to have Eva that you could get pregnant so easily."

Claire nodded absently, but she wasn't really listening. For the past week and a half, she'd been almost sleepwalking through her days. She certainly wasn't sleeping at night. She couldn't concentrate. All that ran through her mind again and again were the horrible things Luca had said to her.

"So I was thinking if we coated Eva in some flour, we could pan fry her and she'd come out with a nice crispy crust."

"Sounds good," Claire said automatically.

"Claire!" Daisy shouted in consternation. "You're not listening at all."

"I am," she argued.

"And what did you just agree to?"

Claire sighed and shook her head. "I have no idea."

"Sit down," Daisy demanded, pointing toward the couch.

She didn't feel like arguing, so she did as she was told. Daisy sat beside her, Eva playing with soft blocks on the floor in front of them.

"Just a tip, you might not want to agree to anything while you're in this state," Daisy said. "Now tell me what's going on? This isn't plain ol' pregnancy brain, is it?"

Claire opened her mouth to answer, but before she could say a word, the tears rushed to her eyes and all that came out was a strangled sob. Daisy hugged her to her chest, letting her get all the pain and heartache out of her system. It took several minutes and a soaked-through blouse, but eventually Claire was able to sit up, wipe her eyes and tell her sad tale.

"He doesn't believe the baby is his. I don't know how he could say that. I've spent the past month alone with him. Whose baby could it be?"

"I think he'll come around," Daisy said, holding her hand reassuringly. "Like you said, it sounds to me like he's spent too many years thinking that it could never happen. To believe he's the father means that everything he knows is wrong. If he's thrown away the past ten years of his life, too afraid to fall in love and disappoint his wife, it's got to be a serious blow. It's easier to push you away with angry accusations than to face the fact that he was too chicken to find out if he was sterile all this time."

Claire listened with a slow nod, but she wasn't convinced that Luca would realize he was wrong. Luca was stubborn, and that same stubbornness might keep him from finding out the truth and admitting he was wrong. It might take a court mandated paternity test after the baby was born to convince him of the truth. At that point, he could apologize until he was blue in the face and it wouldn't make a difference. She didn't know if she could forgive him for how he'd treated her.

"The worst part is that I let myself fall in love with him, Daisy. It was so stupid of me. He just seemed to know how to get past every barrier I had. It had been so long since I felt like a man really cared for me. I must've been desperate for affection. Look where it got me…pregnant and alone."

"You are not alone, Claire." Daisy clasped Claire's chin and turned her so she was forced to look at her. "You've got me. You've got Eva. You've got this new baby. We're going to make this work, with or without this deadbeat billionaire."

"How?" It seemed like a ridiculous question to ask, but she felt so bogged down in all of this, she could hardly come up with an answer.

"I'm going to move in," Daisy declared. "I'm going to be your live-in nanny to help take care of both the children. We are two strong, smart, capable women. We will be just fine without a man. Frankly, we only need them to start the baby process, after that they're kinda useless."

Claire chuckled, wiping away the last of her tears. "You're right. We will be just fine. No matter what happened between Luca and me, I'm coming out of this with another beautiful baby. I never dreamed I could ever have another, so I need to start thinking about this as the blessing that it truly is."

"That's the spirit," Daisy said with an encouraging tone. "Now, there's a roast chicken and vegetables in the oven for your dinner. Eva has already eaten her dinner and had her bath, so you two can take it easy tonight. Eat, relax and try not to beat yourself up too much about all this. I'll see you in the morning, okay?"

Claire nodded. "Thank you for the pep talk, Daisy. You deserve a raise."

Daisy laughed as she got up off the couch. "I'll remind you of that when you write my next paycheck." She walked over to the front door, slipping on her coat and waving good-night.

When the door clicked shut, Claire took a deep

breath and tried to do what Daisy had told her to do. She scooped up Eva off the floor and carried her into the kitchen. She placed her in her swing and set it to a soothing rhythm the baby liked best. That kept her daughter occupied long enough for Claire to remove supper from the oven and make herself a plate.

Pulling up a stool at the breakfast bar, she took a few bites of chicken and started sorting idly through the stack of mail Daisy had left there for her. Bill, junk, bill… She stopped when she noticed the notepad that Daisy used to leave messages about phone calls.

Stuart, her attorney, had called. She'd had a missed call on her cell phone while she was at her doctor's appointment, but it had come at a critical time and then she'd forgotten to check it later. Searching through her purse, she found her phone and she was right. Her screen declared she'd missed a call from Stuart Ewing. She pressed the button to listen to the voicemail message.

"Claire, this is Stuart. I really need you to call me back tonight. It doesn't matter what time. There's been a development."

He left his personal number for her to call him. Claire's hand was shaking as she copied the number onto Daisy's notepad. She wished he hadn't been so vague in his message. "A development" could be anything. It could be that Luca decided to backpedal on their agreement and sue for full custody. She didn't think a judge would go along with that, but she couldn't be sure. The last time she saw Luca he'd been angry enough to do almost anything. Would he try to take Eva knowing she was the only thing Claire had? Just to spite her?

She had to stop speculating and just call Stuart back. She was going to make herself crazy if she didn't.

"Claire," Stuart said as he answered the phone. "Thanks for calling me back. We've received a request to meet with Luca and his lawyer tomorrow morning."

"Do we know if it's good or bad news?"

"I have no idea. I wasn't really expecting to hear from them when I did. Do you have any thoughts? How did the trip with Mr. Moretti go? I haven't spoken with you since you got back from Martha's Vineyard."

That was a loaded question. "It was a nice trip. I think we had everything worked out between us, so maybe it's just a finalization of our agreement to submit to the judge."

Stuart hesitated on the line. "What aren't you telling me, Claire? There's something about your tone that tells me you're leaving something out."

"Well, that's because I am. Things have gotten a little complicated since we left Martha's Vineyard, so I can't be certain that Luca will stick with the agreement we made." Claire could hear Stuart sigh heavily on the line.

"What happened when you got back?"

"I found out that I'm pregnant with Luca's child." She spit out the words as quickly as she could and waited for the fallout.

"Pregnant? I should've known you two going away together for a month would lead to trouble. Are you two an item, now? I hate to say it, but that would probably help the cause if you were."

"Not anymore," Claire admitted, dashing her lawyer's hopes. "He didn't take the news about the baby very well. He stated pretty bluntly that he didn't think it was his and got quite angry about the whole thing. So like I said, I don't have any clue what we'll face tomorrow."

"You know, I've been thinking over the past year about retiring. You may be the client that puts me over the edge."

At that, Claire had to laugh. She knew Stuart would work until he dropped dead in the courtroom, but he was a curmudgeon about it anyway. "Look at it this way, Stuart—you just have to represent me in court. This is *my life*."

"You're right," he agreed. "I'll meet you at Edmund Harding's office at 8:45 a.m. tomorrow."

Twelve

"Are you sure you want to do this, Luca? You only have a few minutes left to change your mind."

Luca turned away from the window overlooking Central Park to gaze at his lawyer. "Yes. I have to do it."

"Actually, you don't," Edmund argued. He'd been irritated with Luca since he came in and started changing the arrangements they'd worked so hard to put together. "There's nothing that says giving up custody is the punishment for being mean to the mother."

"I'm not giving up custody," Luca argued. "I'm just setting the terms that will make her happiest. It's the least I can do after everything else."

"And what about you? What will make you happy? These are your children we're talking about. The children you never thought you'd have, I might add."

"Seeing Claire happy will make me happy," he answered without hesitation. It was true. As hard as this was on him, he needed to see Claire smile more than anything. That look of hurt and devastation on her face from that night at his apartment had haunted him for days. He was willing to do whatever it took to fix that, even giving up most of his rights to his children. He didn't want to do it, but it was the punishment he deserved after rejecting the baby as his own.

A soft knock came at the door and the receptionist stuck her head inside. "Mr. Harding, Mrs. Douglas and Mr. Ewing are here for your nine o'clock."

Edmund nodded sadly and looked at Luca. "Last chance."

Luca just waved away his concerns. He knew what he had to do, and he didn't care if his lawyer liked it or not.

"Send them in."

Luca took a seat at the table beside Edmund. For the first time in a long time, he felt nervous. He wasn't quite sure where to look as the door opened. He didn't know what he would see in Claire's eyes. Taking a breath, he looked up to see her as she slipped into the office behind her lawyer. Her gaze met his, and he knew that he was making the right decision. There wasn't the slightest hint of animosity there. She was anxious, exhausted, sad, but not angry. He had been the angry one, the one to lash out. She was just here to see what kind of punishment he was about to hand down because he thought she was lying to him.

They took their seats, and Luca squirmed slightly in his chair. Edmund eyed him suspiciously, but Luca ignored him. His focus was entirely on Claire. She didn't look good. He thought pregnant women were supposed to be radiant, but perhaps that was later on. Now she just looked run-down, like she had when he'd first taken her to Martha's Vineyard. A month of good food, sun and loving had changed her, but now it was like they'd never gone.

"Are you feeling okay?" he asked.

Everyone at the table, including Claire, looked startled. Edmund reached out to grip his forearm and silence him, but he pulled away. This wasn't about negotiations. It was about Claire.

Her gaze narrowed at him for a moment before she nodded. "I'm fine. I'm just having a rough first trimester. It was the same with Eva. Thank you for asking." Her tone was cold, and he deserved that.

"Mr. Harding, my client and I are curious what today's meeting is about. We go before the judge on Thursday. It's a little late to start making changes to the agreement that Mr. Moretti and Mrs. Douglas came to on their trip."

"I understand that," Edmund said. "As I'm sure you're aware, the agreement was made regarding Eva. The addition of a second child to the equation made it necessary for us to have another discussion."

"Wait a minute," Stuart said. "My understanding is that Mr. Moretti refused to acknowledge the child as his and vowed to Mrs. Douglas that he would not seek visitation. Are you saying that Mr. Moretti is acknowledging that Mrs. Douglas's second child is his, as well?"

"Yes, he is," Edmund replied.

Luca's gaze was set on Claire's face as his lawyer delivered the news. Her gray eyes widened with surprise, then she turned to him with her mouth agape. He could only nod, hoping his contrite expression let her know just how sorry he was about all of this.

"Is Mr. Moretti requiring any kind of testing to confirm the paternity of this child?" Stuart continued.

"No, he is not." Edmund's irritation was clear in his voice.

Stuart sat back in his chair, completely deflated by the whole situation. Apparently, they had come here expecting a battle and were caught off guard. Luca watched Claire's lawyer lean into her and say a few words. They quietly conversed for a moment with Claire's eyes meeting his a time or two.

"I'm sorry," Stuart said at last. "The last time our clients spoke, it was very clear that Mr. Moretti believed the child was not his. While we appreciate that your client is no longer accusing Mrs. Douglas of lying, may we ask what caused the sudden change of heart?"

Edmund turned to look at Luca. His lawyer had been strongly opposed to sharing Luca's private medical information with the other side, but Luca insisted. He nodded and Edmund took a deep breath. "Mr. Moretti has undergone medical testing to confirm his previous diagnosis. It was determined that he is a valid candidate for fathering Mrs. Douglas's second child."

Claire's mouth dropped open. There was a momentary light of excitement in her eyes, as though she wanted to congratulate him on the amazing news. The light dimmed quickly. She already knew he could have children, considering she was pregnant. The only thing that had changed was that he acknowledged it, as well.

Stuart ignored both clients, trying to focus on the confusing negotiations. "Now that Mr. Moretti is acknowledging the child, how does this change the custody agreement?"

Edmund slid the folder of paperwork across the table with their updated agreement. "You can take your time looking it over. We presume that your client will find these new terms acceptable."

Luca watched as Claire and Stuart reviewed the paperwork, talking quietly between one another. It was agonizing to sit silently and watch as Claire shook her head and her gaze flickered curiously over him from time to time.

He wasn't entirely sure what was taking them so long to make a decision. He had given Claire everything she wanted. He'd granted her sole physical and legal custody of the children. He'd asked for minimal visitation, less than half of what they'd agreed to, as to not cause an interruption to the children's routines. He'd tripled the amount of requested child support—even though he knew she wasn't interested in his money—and offered to pay for the private schooling of her choice. He'd even set up large, generous trust funds for both of the children. What more could she possibly want? He didn't want to walk away entirely or the children would think he didn't care about them. He did. More than anything. There was a fine line between giving Claire what she wanted and abandoning his children.

Finally, Stuart shook his head. "I'm sorry, but this offer is unacceptable. My client wants more."

Claire watched Luca's expression crumble at her lawyer's declaration. She knew it was a risk, but it was one she had to take. Yes, the offer was everything she could've hoped for when they first started this process, but now everything had changed. It was missing once crucial element—Luca.

With what he was offering, she could easily raise the two children on her own. She could hire Daisy as a live-in nanny and even give her a bigger raise than she could ever afford on her own. They could attend the best schools in New York and have everything they ever wanted. Everything but a father.

"What do you want, Claire? Do you want me to open up a vein and bleed for you? Because I will."

It was the first time he'd spoken since he'd asked how she was. There was a pleading in his eyes that made her chest ache. It felt so awkward to have these legal mouthpieces between them. Everything felt so stiff and official with Edmund and Stuart doing all their talking for them. She wished she could just make the lawyers go away for ten minutes so they could talk—really talk—without all the legal protections in the way.

With them here, all she could do was lay her heart on the line and see if he bit. Luca had acknowledged this baby was his. This updated offer was as close to an apology as he probably knew how to offer. But she wanted more. He'd spent weeks telling her she was worth more than what Jeff had given her. She'd finally decided to believe him, and she was going to demand it.

"This isn't nearly enough. Your money doesn't mean a damn thing to me. I want you to apologize for all the terrible, hurtful things you said to me. I want you to say you're sorry for accusing me of sleeping with someone else and threatening to have security throw me out of the building. And then, when I'm satisfied, I want *you*, Luca."

His sharp gaze met hers for a moment. He swallowed hard, then adjusted his posture in his seat. "Gentlemen, may we have a moment alone?"

"Luca, I don't advise you to—"

"Alone," he reiterated in a firm voice that left no question of his demand.

Claire squeezed Stuart's hand reassuringly, and both men got up from the table. They made their way out, shutting the door behind them.

There were a few quiet, strained moments before Luca spoke. "I'm sorry, Claire."

She wanted to respond, but she held herself back. With the lawyers gone, she wanted to know what he had to say.

"I'm not saying any of this because you're demanding it. I'm saying it because it needs to be said. You're totally right. I'm sorry I doubted you. I'm sorry I said all those horrible things. I just never believed that I…" His voice trailed off as he shook his head and looked down at the table. "For so long, I've felt incomplete. Having cancer robbed me of so much. Not just my childhood and my youthful sense of immortality, but my self-worth. My sense of safety."

Claire watched as he pushed up from the glass conference-room table and walked over to the window. "Everything you said that day was right. I was scared. I'd put off knowing the truth for so long because it left me a glimmer of hope. Once I knew for certain, it was done. But I went to the doctor after our fight."

He turned away from the view and looked at Claire. "I can have children. I never dreamed a doctor would tell me that, but he did. In that moment, I wasn't happy, though. I felt terrible because I knew that you didn't deserve any of the things I said to you that day."

Crossing the room in four long strides, he stopped in front of Claire. "Did you really mean what you said before? That you still want me after everything I've said and done?" Luca dropped onto one knee in front of her and scooped her hands into his own.

Claire felt her chest tighten with each word he said. "I meant every word. I don't want your money, Luca. I never have. And I do appreciate your offer of giving me full custody of the children. I know that's a huge gesture for you. But it's just not enough. I want my children to have a father. I want them to have you in their lives."

Luca's posture relaxed, and his dark gaze fell to their intertwined fingers. "And what about you? Do you want me in your life, too, Claire?"

At that, Claire sighed. She'd gone over this a thousand times in her mind. Should she be happy to have a child and some good memories from her time with Luca? Did she dare ask for more? Was more even possible? "I don't know. A lot of that depends on you. A very smart man once told me that a woman is a gift to be cherished. I've spent far too long being treated as less than enough. I'll want you in our children's lives no matter what, but to be in mine, I want it all. I'm not going to settle this time, or ever again."

Luca nodded slowly. "I don't want you to settle. I've never wanted a woman to settle for me, and I don't want you to have anything less than you deserve. Selfishly, I'll tell you that I love you, Claire. The time we've spent apart has been agonizing. I absolutely want our children to play a part in my life, but I'll be honest when I say it will kill me to see you every time we pass the children from one household to the other. It's not at all what I want. I want us to be a family, together, but I'm worried."

"About what?"

"I'm worried that I'm going to get sick again. I know I shouldn't let it affect my decisions and how I live my life, but I need you to know that it's a real possibility. If you can accept that and want us to be a family, okay. If losing you is the price I pay for my sins, I accept that, too."

"Sins?" Claire's eyes were overflowing with tears as she listened to him speak. He was already punishing himself far more harshly than she ever would have. "You haven't committed any sins, Luca. You've just been hurt. We've both been hurt. We let that disappointment get between us. We can't let that happen again."

A spark of hope glimmered in Luca's eyes as he looked up at her. "Does that mean there's a chance of us being a 'we' again?"

Claire nodded through her tears. "I love you too much to just walk away."

A wide grin broke out across Luca's face, making her chest ache. She couldn't help returning the smile. "You love me?"

"I do."

Luca looked up at her with a suddenly serious expression. "We're in love, you're having my baby and I'm already down on one knee. I guess there's just one thing left to do, Claire."

She stiffened in her seat at his words. Did he mean what she thought he meant? Was he actually…?

"Claire Marianne Lawson," Luca began, "you came into my life in the most unexpected of ways and you gave me the greatest gift I could ever imagine—our beautiful little Eva. Being with you has been some of the happiest times of my life. Every day I want to get out of bed and find a way to make you smile. I want to do that for the rest of my life. Will you allow me to do that by giving me the honor of becoming my wife?"

Before she could respond, Luca reached into his pocket and pulled out a small, velvet box. He lifted the lid, and Claire found a beautiful oval diamond solitaire inside. On one side was a round, dark blue sapphire. On the other was a lighter blue stone.

"The sapphire is for Eva, since she was born in September," he explained. "The blue topaz is for the new baby. By my calculations, he or she should arrive in late December. If I'm wrong and the baby doesn't show up until January, we'll change it to a garnet."

Claire's eyes blurred with tears to the point that she couldn't make out the details anymore. It didn't matter. It was the most perfect ring he ever could've given her. She didn't care how many carats it was or how much money he'd paid. It represented not only their commitment to each other, but their children. That made it the most precious piece of jewelry she could ever wear.

"Yes," she said at last, realizing she hadn't yet answered his very important question. "Yes, I will marry you."

Luca took the ring from the box and slipped it onto her finger. She glanced at it for only a moment before reaching out and pulling Luca's face to hers. Their lips met, giving her the thrill she craved more than a ring.

He didn't disappoint. Wrapping his arms around her waist, he stood up, pulling Claire out of the chair with him. She laced her fingers at his nape and pulled him closer to her. She couldn't get enough of him. She'd come far too close to losing his touch forever.

Finally, Luca pulled away, still holding her tight in his arms. "We'd better stop. I don't think Edmund would be too pleased with me making love to my fiancée on his conference-room table."

Claire beamed at his use of her new title. "Well," she argued, "considering how much *my* fiancé has paid for his services, we should be able to do whatever we'd like."

"Soon," he promised, planting another, shorter kiss on her lips. "We've just got to call off the dogs and I'll whisk you home and make love to you all afternoon."

"Before we go, I just have one question. How did you know my maiden name?" Claire asked as she looked up at him.

Luca gave her a sly smile. "You ran a background check on me, so I ran one on you. It's only fair, right?"

She smiled wide. "Absolutely. Did you find out anything interesting while you were nosing around?"

"Just that you got a D in freshman chemistry, and your favorite food is listed on Facebook as Thai. Thai? Really?"

"I may need to update that," Claire admitted with a smile. "I'm pretty partial to Italian lately."

"You'd better be. So," he continued with a heavy sigh. "Are we ready to let the sharks know the good news?"

Claire nodded. "Let's get it over with so I can get you home and out of this suit."

"Edmund!" Luca shouted toward the conference-room door.

A moment later the door burst open with both lawyers standing anxiously in the doorway. They looked curiously at Luca and Claire, wrapped in each other's arms.

"Yes?"

"Withdraw the custody motion. We don't need to go to court." Luca kept his dark hazel eyes focused only on Claire as he spoke. Her heart fluttered in her chest when he looked at her that way.

"We don't?"

"No," Claire said with a sly smile. "We're headed to the wedding chapel instead."

Epilogue

"It's not going to zip." Claire was in full-blown panic mode. The wedding started in less than a half hour and her blossoming belly and swelling bosom were causing a major issue with her dress.

"It's going to zip," Daisy assured her. "You did the final alteration a week ago. You haven't gotten that much bigger in the last week."

Claire held her breath as she felt Daisy tug and groan slightly, then the rush of the zipper as it raced to the top. "Thank goodness," she said with a sigh of relief.

Her first wedding dress had been a princess extravaganza that made it impossible for her to use the restroom alone. This time, she'd opted for something more appropriate for the beach. It was strapless with a sweetheart neckline and a beaded bodice. The flowing organza gathered under the bust and draped to the floor. It was light and ethereal, yet sparkly enough to feel special. She loved it.

"Oh, Claire." Antonia Moretti came into the master bedroom of the cottage that was doubling as the bridal suite. "You look so beautiful. Luca will be beside himself when he sees you."

She hoped so. They had put together this wedding plan quickly, which made her nervous, but she didn't want to be eight months pregnant and huge in all their wedding pictures. Thankfully, most of it had come together easily. Gavin had offered the beach house at Martha's Vineyard as the wedding location. It was the perfect choice, since they'd fallen in love here. The wedding and reception was taking place on the beach with a roaring bonfire, a local band playing and a stellar fireworks show to wrap up the night. The seafood shack up the road was catering a traditional New England boil on the beach with loads of fresh clams, mussels, shrimp, spicy sausage, corn and potatoes.

That wasn't what Claire was looking forward to the most. She was anxious for the cake. Well, the cheesecake. They'd opted out of the traditional cake and brought in a dozen different cheesecakes from their nearest restaurant in Newport. Food hadn't been very kind to Claire's stomach for the first few months of her pregnancy, but she was finally getting her appetite back. She couldn't wait for Luca to feed her a bite of creamy cheesecake with fresh strawberries on top.

A soft tap sounded at the door. She almost didn't

hear it over the chatter of Luca's sisters as they did their hair and makeup. Daisy opened the door and to Claire's surprise her mother was standing there with Eva in her arms.

"Mom?"

Her mother smiled and stepped into the room, looking so familiar, yet so different than she remembered. "Hello, Claire. Just look at you. You're even prettier than I ever dreamed."

Claire rushed over to hug the mother she hadn't seen since right after her marriage to Jeff. "I can't believe you made it."

"Living across the country, I might be horribly neglectful in many ways, but I'm not going to miss my only child's wedding. It's bad enough that this is the first time I've seen Eva." She placed a kiss on the baby's fat cheek. Eva was wearing a little white dress with a tulle tutu as the honorary flower girl. "That's all going to change, though. Your stepfather and I are moving to Connecticut next month. Plan on seeing me a lot more often," she added with a smile.

Claire could hardly believe it. She'd been content in gaining Luca's large, loud family as her own, but to have her mother close again made tears start to pool in her eyes. She looked up and breathed through her nose. If she messed up her eye makeup, Carla would get onto her.

"I hate to break up the family reunion," Daisy said, "but it's time to get this wedding going."

The Moretti sisters scrambled to gather their things and slip out of the room. Daisy was carrying Eva down the aisle, so she took her from her grandmother's arms. "Follow me and I'll have the ushers seat you."

Then, just as quickly, Claire found herself alone. She gave herself one quick glance in the mirror and picked up her bouquet. Her stomach was fluttering, but for the first time in weeks, it was just nerves, not nausea. She took a deep breath and the anxiety faded. There was no reason to be worried about this wedding. She'd never been more sure of anything in her life as she was about marrying Luca.

Glancing out the window, she saw all the parents seated and Daisy followed. It was time to go.

Stepping carefully downstairs, she stopped at the deck to await her music. There, she could see several rows of white chairs lining the sandy path to the archway, filled with faces of friends and family, eager and happy to witness this moment. Beneath the archway of white flowers stood the officiant, Daisy, Eva and Luca.

His gaze was glued to her as she came outside. For once, it was his jaw that dropped open with amazement and his eyes that shone glassy with tears. He was wearing a white linen suit without a tie, keeping the look casual. Even then, he was still the most handsome man she'd ever seen in person. It was hard to believe this man—the father of her children—was about to be her husband. It was more than she ever could've hoped for.

The music started and everyone stood and turned to look in her direction. Claire stepped barefooted into the soft golden sand and headed down the path to her happily-ever-after.

* * * * *

"You can do this," she muttered under her breath. **"He's just your boss."**

Lies, her mind whispered. All lies. Not even very good ones. The sad truth was, Sean Ryan was so much more than the man she was currently working for. He was the first man in years who'd been able to…not just sneak past her well-honed defenses, but obliterate them. One smile from him and her knees quivered. One glance from his summer-sky blue eyes and her long-dormant hormones began a dance of joy. Oh, that was humbling to admit, even to herself.

She really didn't need this.

Kate had a good life now. She'd built it carefully, brick by brick, and damned if she'd allow attraction to ruin it all.

Of course, standing strong against what Sean Ryan made her feel would have been much easier if he'd just been able to leave tomorrow as scheduled. But with the blizzard, they could be trapped together for days.

Which brought her right back to the sinking sensation in the pit of her stomach.

* * *

Snowbound with the Boss
is part of the Pregnant by the Boss trilogy:
Three business partners find love—
and fatherhood—where they least expect it.

SNOWBOUND WITH THE BOSS

BY
MAUREEN CHILD

MILLS &
BOON

First Published in Great Britain 2016
By Mills & Boon, an imprint of HarperCollins*Publishers*
1 London Bridge Street, London, SE1 9GF

© 2015 Maureen Child

ISBN: 978-0-263-91851-9

51-0316

Printed and bound in Spain
by CPI, Barcelona

Maureen Child writes for the Mills & Boon Desire line and can't imagine a better job.

A seven-time finalist for a prestigious Romance Writers of America RITA® Award, Maureen is an author of more than one hundred romance novels. Her books regularly appear on bestseller lists and have won several awards, including a Prism Award, a National Readers' Choice Award, a Colorado Romance Writers Award of Excellence and a Golden Quill Award.

One of her books, *The Soul Collector*, was made into a CBS TV movie starring Melissa Gilbert, Bruce Greenwood and Ossie Davis. If you look closely, in the last five minutes of the movie, you'll spot Maureen, who was an extra in the last scene.

Maureen believes that laughter goes hand in hand with love, so her stories are always filled with humor. The many letters she receives assure her that her readers love to laugh as much as she does. Maureen Child is a native Californian but has recently moved to the mountains of Utah.

To my daughter Sarah—a gift for
which I will always be grateful

One

Sean Ryan's dreams were of hot beaches, ten-foot waves and ice-cold beer.

His reality was just ice-cold.

January in Wyoming was just…wrong, he told himself. A California guy had no business standing knee-deep in snow. And if he'd had a choice, Sean wouldn't have been there at all.

But it was his turn to change a run-down hotel into a role-playing fantasy based on one of his company's bestselling video games. "Why I couldn't have gotten a damn hotel in Tahiti is a good question, though."

But then, Celtic Knot video games were all based on ancient legends, and as far as Sean knew, there were no legendary Celtic tales set around a beach in Tahiti. Too damn bad.

A tall man, with thick black hair that hung past the

collar of the brown leather jacket he wore over sweaters, Sean tucked his hands into the pockets of his jeans and gave a quick look around. The great room of the old hotel was gigantic and echoed with the sound of his footsteps every time his scarred brown boots hit the wooden floor. There were enough windows in the room to make the snow-covered outside feel like the inside. Double-paned glass kept most of the cold out, but even then, so much glass was enough to chill the cavernous room.

The place wasn't huge, only a hundred and fifty rooms, yet it gave the feeling of more. Probably all the wood and glass, Sean told himself. He could see how the hotel would be once the renovations were complete. And God knew there would be plenty of those. Every room needed to be freshened, brought up-to-date and then stocked with gaming systems and flat-screen televisions. They'd get their artists in to do the murals on the walls, bringing the "Forest Run" video game to life and making this a prime destination for gamers from around the country.

And, he had to admit, the setting was perfect to mimic "Forest Run." The hotel sat on two hundred acres of land, with forests, meadows and a wide, beautiful lake. But he couldn't imagine people *wanting* to come to the middle of nowhere in the dead of winter when everything was covered in snow. Who the hell would pick *snow* over *sand*?

Not him, that was for sure. But he had to hope that there were plenty of gamers who actually enjoyed freezing temperatures. As for Sean, he couldn't wait to get back to Southern California. Shaking his head, Sean reminded himself that this trip was almost over. He'd been in Wyoming a week and now that all of the "consultations" with his contractor were finished, he'd be hopping into his company jet that afternoon and getting back to the real world. To his *life*.

Turning his back on the view, Sean glanced toward the ceiling at the sound of footsteps overhead. Instantly, a buzz of awareness shot through him. Scowling, he deliberately pushed aside the feeling, buried it deeply enough that he wouldn't have to acknowledge it.

Nope. When he left, Sean wouldn't miss the cold. Or the solitude, he assured himself. But the woman… that was a different story.

Kate Wells. Businesswoman, contractor, carpenter and current pain in his ass. He was only in Wyoming in the dead of winter because Kate, his contractor on this hotel job, had insisted they needed to meet on-site so she and her crew could get started on the interior renovations.

And from the minute he first saw her, construction work was the last thing on Sean's mind. Instead, he was focused on thick black hair, usually pulled into a ponytail, lake-blue eyes and a mouth wide enough to give a man crazy, sex-fueled dreams.

It had been too long since he'd indulged himself in a really fiery affair, he assured himself. That's the only explanation for why his body was burning for a woman who wore a damn tool belt, of all things.

He looked toward the ceiling again, the scowl on his face deepening as she moved around upstairs with quick, sure steps. He'd never met a woman as sure of herself as Kate Wells. He'd always admired strong women, but she took things to a whole new level. She argued with him on everything and as irritating as that was, Sean also sort of enjoyed it—which only went to prove that all this cold had frozen and killed off too many of his brain cells.

Shaking his head, he turned on his cell phone and gave silent thanks that at least he had reception out here. Hitting the video-chat button, he dialed and then waited.

On the third ring, his brother Mike's face appeared on the screen.

"I hate Wyoming," Sean blurted.

Mike laughed and leaned back in his desk chair. Right behind his brother, Sean could see the view of the garden behind the old Victorian in Long Beach, California, that served as Celtic Knot's offices. "Don't hold back, tell me how you really feel."

"Funny." Easy for his older brother to be amused, Sean told himself. He wasn't in the middle of a forest with a woman who both attracted and infuriated him. Thinking of Kate, Sean glanced over his shoulder, just to make sure she hadn't sneaked up on him. When he was satisfied, he shifted his gaze back to the phone. Easier to not think of Kate when he was talking about something else entirely.

"It hasn't stopped snowing since I got here," he said. "There's like three feet of snow piling up out there and it's still coming down. I don't think it'll ever stop."

"Sounds cold." Mike gave a dramatic shudder.

"Ha!" Sean snorted. "Beyond cold. Beyond freezing. I'm wearing two sweaters under my jacket—*inside.*"

Chuckling, Mike asked, "What's it like when you're not complaining about how cold you are? Have you managed, in all your misery, to check out the land and the hotel?"

Trust Mike to stay on topic. Sean sighed, then grudg-

ingly admitted, "Yeah, I looked it all over. It's pretty.
Lots of trees. Lots of open land. And who knew the sky
was so big when you get out of the city?"

"Yeah," Mike said, "I discovered that for myself
when Jenny and I were in Laughlin…"

Narrowing his gaze on his brother's image, Sean
wondered what the hell had happened exactly between
Mike and Jenny Marshall, one of the company's top artists. Mike hadn't talked about it and before Sean had
had a decent chance to really interrogate him over it,
he'd had to leave for Wyoming.

"Something tells me there's more to that story," Sean
mused, promising himself that as soon as he got home
again, he'd take Mike out for a few beers and pry the
truth out of him.

"If there is," Mike told him, "you're not hearing it."

Not long-distance, anyway. But Sean had never been
one to give up easily. And there was definitely something going on between his brother and Jenny. Still,
that was for then, and right now Sean was more interested in getting out of Wyoming before he turned into
a Popsicle.

"What's the hotel itself like, Sean?"

"Big. Cold. Empty." Sean blew out a frustrated
breath and pushed one hand through his hair. He gave
another quick look around and gave Mike a better answer. "The previous owner left some furniture downstairs, but the bedrooms are a refit from the ground up.
No beds, no chairs, tables, *nada*."

He shot a glance at the battered leather sofa and two
matching chairs that were drawn up in front of a massive fireplace in the great room. Sean didn't think much
of the furniture, but since he and Kate were going to be

stuck here for a while, he was grateful there was more than the floor to sit on.

"It's no big deal," Mike told him. "We would have redone the bedrooms the way we wanted anyway."

"True. And the bones of the place are good." Sean nodded to himself. "A lot of work to do to turn it into a 'Forest Run' fantasy, though."

"And is Kate Wells up to the task?"

"To hear her tell it," Sean muttered. He'd never met a woman so supremely confident in her own abilities. Just as he'd never come up against anyone so willing to argue with him. He was more accustomed to people who worked for him actually *working* for him. But this woman seemed to think *she* was in charge, and that was something he'd have to take care of real damn soon.

"Anyway," he said, once again forcefully pushing Kate out of his mind, "there's a hundred and fifty guest rooms, and they all need work."

Mike frowned. "If we go with your idea to hold our own 'game con' on the property, we'll need more rooms. Are there other hotels close by?"

"No. We're ten miles from the closest. It's a small town with two B and Bs and one motel right off the highway."

Mike's tight scowl deepened. "Sean, we can't go with a big conference if there's nowhere for people to stay." He took a breath and added, "And don't say people can pitch tents."

Sean laughed. "Just because I like camping doesn't mean I want strangers staying all over the property. Anyway, there's a bigger city about twenty-five miles from here, with more hotels." And that was where he was staying. A nice, comfortable, upscale hotel that he would have given anything to be in at that moment. He wanted a shower hot enough to melt the ice chips in his bloodstream. That wasn't going to happen anytime soon, though. "Kate—the contractor had another idea on that problem, too."

"What's she thinking?" Mike picked up his coffee and took a long drink.

Sean glared at his brother as annoyance sharpened his tone. "Is that a cappuccino? You bastard."

Mike grinned and took a longer drink. "I'll enjoy it for you."

"Thanks." The sarcasm was thick, but he knew Mike didn't care. Why the hell would he? Sean wondered. His older brother was at home in Long Beach with access to their favorite coffee shop, the bar down the street, ocean views and, most importantly, Mike wasn't freezing his ass off.

Damn, Sean missed civilization. Shaking his head, he said, "Kate thinks we should put in some small cabins, behind the main lodge, staggered back into the forest. Give people more privacy, a sense of being out in the wild…"

Mike nodded, thinking about it. "It's a good idea."

"Yeah, I know."

"Yet you don't look happy about it."

"Because she was so damn sure she was right," Sean told him, remembering the conversation from the day before. Kate had had him trudging through snow to inspect the property and the areas she'd already selected for possible cabin sites.

As she'd laid it out for him, he could see it as it would be. Small cabins tucked into the woods would feed in to the fantasy of the place, and he was already considering how they could make each of the cottages different, give them each an identity that would be separate from the rest.

It irritated him, too, that he'd never considered anything like she was suggesting. But damn if the idea hadn't hit home with him. The fact that Kate had come up with it was annoying, but Sean was smart enough to know a good idea when he heard it.

"Yeah," Mike mused. "It's a pain when they're right, isn't it?"

"You have no idea," Sean muttered.

"I think I do." Mike took another deliberate sip of his cappuccino. "Sounds like you're having a great time."

Sean's eyes narrowed into slits. He'd have given his car for a hot cappuccino at that very moment. Just another irritation piled on top of everything else. "Yeah, it's a laugh riot. This woman is the most hardheaded person I've ever dealt with and that includes *you*."

Mike shrugged. "As long as she does good work, that's all you should care about."

His brother was right. That *was* all he should care about. But it wasn't. Instead, Sean was thinking about her hair, how thick and dark it was, and he couldn't help wondering what it would look like freed from its constant ponytail. He thought about the summer blue of her eyes and the way her tool belt hung low around curvy hips. He hated admitting it even to himself, but whenever she talked, he was so focused on her mouth, he hardly heard what she was saying.

Damn, he had to get out of Wyoming, fast.

Sean scrubbed one hand across his face and focused on the conversation with Mike. "Yeah, yeah. She wants to get her crew in here next week and start in on the rehab, and I don't see a problem with it." He paused and ran one finger around the collar of his black sweater. "As long as I can oversee it from California."

"Okay, but since you didn't take any of the artists with you, what'll she do about the painting we'll need done?"

"Come on," Sean said sharply, "I couldn't bring an artist out here when everyone's doing the final run on 'The Wild Hunt.'"

"True," Mike agreed. "Everyone here's working around the clock."

And Sean should have been. He had to connect with marketing and their clients, check the advertising that was lined up to push the new video game once it was released. Work was piling up for him in California, but he'd had to come out here to get the reno started since he had such a fiery contractor eager for the work to begin. This trip had been bad timing all the way around, really. Every artist at Celtic Knot was focused on the finishing touches of the video game that would be released in the summer, so he hadn't been able to justify pulling them away from their work yet.

"Anyway," Sean continued, "how hard is it to leave walls blank? They can paint it white or something and then when we bring the artists in, they'll have a blank canvas to work on."

"That'll work. You still coming home tomorrow?"

"That's the plan, thank God," Sean said. "Kate's outside, bringing her truck around. We're going to head back to town now. Naturally, it's still snowing."

"If it makes you feel any better, it's seventy-five here today."

"Great. Thanks. That just caps it." A door slammed

at the front of the hotel. Kate called out something, and Sean looked to one side and shouted, "What?"

In the next second, Kate was standing in the door-way, shaking her head to send a flurry of fresh snow-flakes flying to the floor. "A blizzard's headed in," she said simply.

He covered the phone with his hand. "You're kid-ding."

"No joke," she said, shrugging. "The pass is already closed. We're not going anywhere."

"For how long?" he demanded.

There was that shrug again. "No way to know."

"Perfect."

"What is it?" Mike asked.

"Karma probably," Sean told him, expressing his dis-gust. "Kate just heard on the truck radio that the pass down the mountain is closed. I'm snowed in."

Instead of sympathy, Sean watched as Mike unsuc-cessfully fought back laughter at the situation.

"Thanks for your concern."

Mike held up one hand and tried to stop laughing. "Sorry, sorry."

"How is this funny?" Sean snapped. "I'm trapped in an empty hotel with a crabby contractor and a moun-tain of snow outside the door."

"Clearly," Mike said finally, "it's only funny from California. But have you got food, heat?"

"We're covered," Kate said, her expression telling him exactly what she thought of the description *crabby*.

"Yeah," Sean said, then he turned to Kate. "Come here for a minute. Meet my brother."

She didn't look happy with the invitation—no sur-prise there, Sean thought. The woman had a chip on her shoulder the size of a redwood. She walked briskly across the room and stopped beside him to look at the phone screen.

"Hi, I'm Kate and you're Mike," she said, words tumbling over each other. She spared a quick glance for Sean. "Nice to meet you, but we don't have a lot of time to talk. There's firewood outside, we need to bring it in before the rest of the storm hits. Don't worry, though. There's plenty of food since I make sure my crew is fed while they work and we've been out here this last week taking measurements and getting ideas about the work."

"Okay." Mike threw that word in fast, thinking he probably wouldn't have another chance to speak. He was right.

"The storm'll blow through in a day or two and the plows will have the pass cleared out pretty quickly, so you can have your brother back by the end of the week."

"Okay…"

Sean grabbed the phone and told Kate, "I'll be right there to help. Yeah. Okay." When he looked back at Mike, he was shaking his head. "She's outside bringing in firewood. I've gotta go. And I was this close—" he held up two fingers just a breath apart "—from getting outta Dodge. Now I don't know when I'll get out. Tell Mom not to worry and don't bother calling me. I'm going to shut off the cell phone, conserve power."

"Okay." In spite of the fact that he'd been amused only a few minutes ago by Sean's situation, now Mike asked, "You sure you'll be all right?"

Sean laughed now. "I'm the outdoors guy, remember? There may not be any waves to surf out here, but I'll be fine. I've been camping in worse situations than I've got here. At least we have a roof and plenty of beds

to choose from. I'll call when I can. Just keep a cappuccino hot for me."

"I will. And Sean," Mike added, "don't kill the contractor."

Killing her wasn't what he had in mind, but he wasn't
going to admit that to his brother. So instead, Sean said,
"I make no promises."

When he hung up and shut off his phone, Sean
walked across the room in the direction Kate had disappeared. Damn woman could have waited a minute,
he told himself, shaking his head as irritation spiked.
He'd already spent a week with her and was walking the
ragged edge of control. Now he was going to be snowed
in with her for who knew how long.

"This just keeps getting better," he muttered.

He walked through a kitchen that was big enough for
their needs but would need some serious renovation. His
quick glance covered the amenities he'd already noted
earlier in the week. A long, butcher-block island in the
middle of the huge room. More of the same counters
ringing the perimeter, broken only by an eight-burner
stove and a refrigerator that was both gigantic and ancient. The walls were white, yellowed with time and
smoke, and the floor was a checkerboard linoleum with
chipped-out and missing sections.

The windows were great and normally offered a view
of the nearby forest. At the moment, the wide expanse of
sky was a dull gray and snow was spitting down thickly
enough to resemble a sheet of cotton. The back door
was open and led into what Kate had earlier called the
mudroom—basically a service porch area with several
washers and dryers and a place to stow coats and boots.

Beyond was a covered back porch with a wobbly, needed-to-be-replaced wooden railing. Sean shrugged deeper into his jacket as he stepped into the icy bite of the wind. Snow. Nothing but snow. It was coming down thick and fast and for one split second, Sean could admit to himself that it was pretty. Then he remembered that the "pretty" stuff was currently blocking his only way out, and it quickly lost its appeal.

"Kate?"

"Over here," she shouted.

Zipping his jacket closed, he turned toward her voice and ignored, as well as he could, the cold sharp snap of winter. Snowflakes slapped his face with icy stings and the wind pushed at him as if trying to force him back inside.

He paid no attention to the urge to retreat and instead turned to where Kate was bent over a neatly stacked supply of firewood. She had three split logs in her arms and was reaching for another.

"Let me get it," Sean said, nudging her out of the way.

She whipped her head up to glare at him. "I can handle it."

"Yeah," he said, giving her a nod. He'd seen her stubbornness and her determination to do everything on her own all week. "I know. You're tough. We're all impressed. But if we both get the wood, we can get out of this cold that much sooner."

She looked like she wanted to argue with him, then changed her mind. "Fine. Gather as much as you can, then we'll come back for more."

She headed into the hotel without another word, leaving Sean to grab as many logs as possible. When he straightened, he took another quick look around. Pine trees stood as tall and straight as soldiers on parade, in spite of the heavy, snow-laden wind pushing at them. The lake was frozen over and snowdrifts were piling up at the shoreline. He tipped his head back and stared up at the gray sky as thick flurries raced toward him. The air was thick and cold, and realization settled in on Sean. If this kept up, he could be stuck here for weeks.

Kate laid the stack of wood in a neat pile beside the stone fireplace, then grabbed the mantel and leaned on it. "The blizzard couldn't have waited to hit until *after* he was gone?"

Of course not. That would have made her life too easy. Way better to strand her here on the mountain with a man who had shaken her nice, comfortable life right down to the ground.

Slowly straightening, she shook her head, hoping to clear out the ragged, disjointed thoughts somersaulting through it. Didn't work, but she pushed through, pushed past. Bending, she took a few of the logs she'd carried in and set them in the hearth. Then she laid down kindling from the nearby basket, took a long wooden match, struck it and held the flame to the kindling until it caught. Taking a minute to get the fire started would help her settle—she hoped.

She watched the fire catch, licking at the wood until the hiss and crackle jumped into the otherwise quiet room.

"You can do this," she muttered under her breath. "He's just your boss."

Lies, her mind whispered. All lies. Not even very good ones. The sad truth was, Sean Ryan was so much more than the man she was currently working for. He was the first man in years who'd been able to not just sneak past her well-honed defenses but obliterate them. One smile from him and her knees quivered. One glance from his lake-blue eyes and her long-dormant hormones began a dance of joy. Oh, that was humbling to admit, even to herself.

She really didn't need this.

Kate had a good life now. She'd built it carefully, brick by brick, and damn if she'd allow attraction to ruin it all.

Of course, standing strong against what Sean Ryan made her feel would have been much easier if he'd just been able to leave tomorrow as scheduled. But with the blizzard, they could be trapped together for days.

And that thought brought her right back to the sinking sensation in the pit of her stomach. Frowning, she reminded herself that she'd already survived something that would have crushed most people. She could live through a few days in close quarters with Sean.

Nodding in agreement with her silent pep talk, she pushed up from the hearth and turned to get more wood. Sean stalked into the room, arms full of more logs than she could have carried in one trip. He didn't look any happier about their current situation than she did.

Sadly, that didn't make her feel any better.

"Just stack it there on the hearth," she said, waving one hand. "I'll go out for more."

"Yeah," he said, dropping the wood with an ear-shattering clatter. "I'll get the wood. I can carry more than you, so that means fewer trips."

She wanted to argue, but he was right. Still, it was hard for her to accept help. Kate stood on her own two feet. And for the last couple of years especially, she'd deliberately dismissed anyone who thought she couldn't handle things herself.

"Fine," she said. "I've got emergency supplies out in my truck. I'll get them while you bring in more wood. Get a lot of it. It'll be a long, cold night."

"Right." He paused. "What kind of supplies?"

"Blankets, lanterns, coffeemaker—the essentials."

He gave her a wide smile. "Coffee? Now you're talking. I'd give a hundred bucks for a cup of coffee right now."

Why did he have to smile? Why did that smile have to light up his features, sparkle in his eyes and cause her already-unsteady nerves to wobble and tip dangerously? This whole adventure would be so much easier on her if she could just hate him. Damn it.

"A hundred dollars for coffee?" She nodded. "Sold."

His eyebrows shot up, and that wicked curve of his mouth broadened. "Yeah? Well, I'll have to owe you since I don't have that much cash on me."

Just too much charm, she thought. And he turned it on and off like a faucet. Her breath caught a little. "That's okay, I'll send you a bill."

"No problem." Amusement drained from his face, but his eyes glittered with promise. "We'll settle things between us before I head back to California. You can count on it."

Oh, boy. Kate watched him go, then turned up the collar of her jacket. She headed for the front door, giving herself a silent, stern lecture as she went. She couldn't believe how that smile of his had affected her. Honestly, he'd been hard enough to resist when he was miserable and complaining about the snow. But a smiling Sean Ryan was even more dangerous.

She stepped outside and welcomed the blast of cold wind and the stinging slap of blowing snow. If anything could put out a fire burning inside, it was a Wyoming winter. But even as she thought it, Kate had to admit that the slow burn of attraction, interest, was still glowing with heat.

She trooped across the wide front porch, down the steps to where she'd left the truck. Snow was already filling up the bed and stacking against the tires. If she left it sitting out here, by the end of the blizzard she and Sean would have to dig out the truck before they could leave. Jumping into the cab, she started it up, then drove around the edge of the old hotel toward the four-car garage standing behind it. She had to jump out of the truck back into the snow to open the door, but once she had her vehicle parked, it was a relief to be out of the wind.

Kate reached over the side of the truck to the metal box in the bed. Unlocking it, she dragged out her stash of emergency supplies. A heavy plastic craft box that she'd commandeered for the purpose, along with a sleeping bag and the two blankets she kept there in case she was ever stranded in the snow.

Heading out of the garage, she closed the door behind her and paused for a moment to look up at the hotel. Sean was no longer on the porch, so he was inside, by the fire. Stranded alone would be a little scary. Stranded with Sean was terrifying.

Oh, not that she was worried about her *safety*. It was more concern for her *sanity* that had her biting her bottom lip as disjointed thoughts bounced off the walls of her mind.

He was too gorgeous. Too smooth. Too rich. And not to mention the fact that he was her *boss*. This one job for Celtic Knot would give her sometimes-floundering construction company a jolt that could keep them going for the next few years.

So it was imperative she keep a grip on the hormones that insisted on stirring whenever Sean was close by. She couldn't afford to give in to what her body was screaming for. An affair with Sean was just too risky. It had been more than two years since she'd been with a man. In that time, Kate had managed to convince herself that whatever sexual needs or desires she'd had, had died with her husband, Sam.

It was lowering to have to acknowledge, even silently, that her theory had been shot to hell by Sean Ryan's appearance in her life.

She shifted her gaze to the hotel, where firelight danced and glowed behind the window glass. Only midafternoon and it was already getting dark.

The wall of snow between her and the hotel was thickening, letting Kate know that this was a big storm. She and Sean could be stuck here for *days*.

How weird was it that she could be both annoyed and excited by the prospect?

Two

Inside, the fire was already spreading heat around the wide room. Firelight flickered across Sean's features as he bent low to gently lay another log across the already burning wood. He turned his head to look at her, and Kate's breath caught. Fire and light burned in his blue eyes and seemed to settle inside her, where that heat flashed dangerously bright.

A second or two of unspoken tension hummed in the air between them, making each breath she drew a victory of sorts. When she couldn't take it another moment, Kate shattered the spell of silence by speaking. "If you bring in one more load of wood, that should see us through tomorrow."

"Right." He straightened slowly and shoved both hands into the back pockets of his jeans. Nodding at the pile of things at her feet, he said, "You carry a lot of emergency supplies."

Happy to be on safe territory, she glanced down at the things she'd brought inside. "I'd rather be prepared than freeze to death," she told him with a shrug. "You never know when your car won't start or you'll blow a tire or slide on some ice into a ditch..."

"Or get stranded in a blizzard?"

"Exactly." She gave the black nylon sleeping bag a nudge with the toe of her boot, edging it closer to the two wool blankets beside it. "Blankets to keep warm and in the box I've got a battery-operated lantern, PowerBars, chocolate and coffee..."

"There's that magic word again," Sean said with a half grin.

"Finally something we can agree on," Kate answered, a reluctant smile curving her mouth.

Sean's grin only widened, and her heart tripped into a gallop. "Yeah, we've had an interesting week, haven't we?"

"That's one way to put it." Kate sighed, bent down and opened the box to pull out her ancient coffeepot. Snatching the bag of coffee, too, she stood up again and met his steady gaze. "You've argued with every one of my suggestions for this place."

"My place," he said simply. "My decisions."

She'd never had a client fight her on nearly everything before Sean. Normally, Kate didn't mind trying to incorporate a client's wants into the required work. But she also knew what was possible and what wasn't. Sean, though, didn't consider *anything* to be impossible.

"My crew. My work," she countered.

"And here we go again," Sean said, shaking his head.

"Yeah, you'll be doing the work, but you're going to do it the way I want it done."

"Even if you're wrong."

His mouth tightened. "If I want it, I'm not wrong."

"You don't know anything about construction," she argued, even knowing it was fruitless. Her hands fisted on the coffeepot and the bag of coffee. The man had a head of solid rock. Hadn't she been hammering at it for the last week?

He pulled his hands from his pockets, crossed his arms over his chest and stood, hipshot, giving her a look of resigned patience. "And how much do you know about video games? Specifically 'Forest Run'?"

"Okay. Not much." This argument was circular. They'd had it several times already, so Kate knew nothing would be settled and still, she had to admit again that he was right.

"Or nothing."

"Fine. Nothing." Her voice sounded defensive even to her, but she couldn't seem to help it. "I'm a little too busy to be wasting my time playing video games."

Briefly, insult flashed across his features. "Thankfully, there are a few hundred *million* people worldwide who don't feel the same way."

In a heartbeat, he'd reminded her of the difference between them. He was the billionaire. She was the hired help. "You're right," she said, though the words burned her tongue and nearly choked her. "I don't know what gamers would want in a hotel designed especially for them."

He gave her a short, nearly regal nod.

"But," she added, "you don't know about construction. What can and can't be done and more importantly,

what should and *shouldn't* be done. You hired me because I'm a professional. When I tell you a wall is load-
bearing, it's not because I want to deny you the 'open
space to reproduce the sorcerer's meeting rooms.' It's
because if I take down that wall it destabilizes the entire building."

His mouth worked as if he wanted to argue, but all
he said was, "You have a point."

"Thanks, I thought so."

A brief twist of a smile curved his lips and was gone
again in a flash. "You're the most opinionated woman
I've ever met."

Kate took a breath. Strange but it was only Sean
Ryan who brought out the argumentative side of her.
Normally, she found a way to deal with clients with patience and reason. But he pushed every button she had
and a few she hadn't even been aware of. She found herself digging in, defending her position and never giving
ground, which was no way to complete a job. Especially
this job. She was going to have to learn how to deal with
Sean Ryan in a calm, rational way, and she might as
well start now. "Okay, I guess you have a point, too."

His eyebrows lifted and amusement shone in his
eyes. "Are we having a moment, here?"

Why did he have to be amiable along with irritating? Something inside her flipped over, and Kate took
a long, hopefully calming breath. She'd been so soli-
tary, so insulated, since Sam died, being this attracted
to a man was staggering. And a little nerve-racking.
But all she had to do was get through this storm. Survive being stranded with Sean Ryan long enough to
see him get on his private jet and head back to where

he belonged. Then everything would get back to normal and she could forget about how he made her feel.

"Why don't you bring more wood and I'll make that
coffee."

"And the moment's over," he muttered, shaking his
head. "I'll let it go for now, though, since I really want
some caffeine."

Kate held her coffeepot and the bag of grounds up
like trophies. "The gas is connected. All I have to do is
light a pilot light and we can use the stove."

"You're a goddess," he said with a dramatic flair.

Amused, she shook her head. "You're easily impressed."

"Really not," he told her and winked.

He winked, she thought as she walked to the kitchen
and got things started. Why did he have to be gorgeous?
she wondered. Was it some sort of trick by Fate, to send
a man like him to her when she least wanted him?

Mumbling under her breath, she filled a pan with
water and used a kitchen match to light one of the gas
burners. While she waited for the pot to boil, she headed
for the kitchen pantry to look through the food supplies
she and her men had left here over the last week.

On normal jobs, they kept a cooler on the job site,
stuffed with food, snacks and the guys' lunches. But
the hotel job was different. They would be working here
for a long time and no doubt with lots of strange hours,
so they'd more or less taken over the kitchen to store
extra supplies—including paper plates, cups, towels and
even, she saw, a plastic bag of disposable silverware.

Smiling to herself, she looked through the snacks
and realized she could identify who on her crew had
brought them in. Andy had a thing for Cheetos and

Paco always had nacho-flavored corn chips with him. Then there were Jack's Oreos and Dave's peanut butter crackers. Kate herself had brought in chocolate, tea bags and those always-had-to-have Pop-Tarts. Brown sugar and cinnamon, of course.

"Not exactly a five-star restaurant," she murmured a few minutes later, "but we won't starve."

"Yeah?" Sean's voice came from directly behind her, and Kate jumped in response. He ignored her reaction. "What've we got?"

Kate moved away, forcing him to back up, too. "Cheese and crackers. Chips, pretzels and cookies. Everything you probably shouldn't be eating." She glanced at him. "My crew likes their junk food."

"And who can blame them?"

A small smile tugged briefly at her lips. Kate closed the pantry door and opened the refrigerator. "There's more in here, too. The storm hasn't taken out the power yet. That's good. Okay, we've got lots of those little cheese sticks, plus there are three sandwiches from yesterday, too. A few hard-boiled eggs thanks to Tracy, and some macaroni salad."

He frowned. "When we brought lunch for everyone yesterday, there was one sandwich each. I didn't expect leftovers."

"Normally, you'd be right. The crew's usually like locusts, mowing through anything edible—especially if they didn't have to buy it themselves," she said with an affectionate smile for the people she worked with every day. She looked up at him and added, "But thankfully for us, Lilah and Raul are both on diets so they didn't eat theirs and Frank left early because his wife was in labor. So we've got food."

"I forgot about Frank's wife having a baby." Sean leaned against the counter. "What was it, boy or girl?"

"A girl." Kate couldn't stop the smile as she remembered Frank's call late the night before. "He's so excited. They've got four boys already, and he really wanted a girl this time."

"*Five* kids?" Sean asked, then whistled low and long. "Are they nuts?"

He looked so appalled at the very idea, Kate was insulted on behalf of her friends. "No, they're not. They love kids."

"They'd better," Sean muttered and shook all over as if trying to ward off a chill.

"Wow, really hate the thought of family that much?"

Something flickered in his eyes—a shadow—and then it was gone, so fast, Kate wasn't really sure she'd seen it at all.

"No," he said, half turning to lean one hip against the battered kitchen counter. "Just not interested in having one of my own."

"So no driving need to be a father," she said flatly, thinking this was just another insight into the man she would be dealing with for months.

"God, no." He shook his head and laughed shortly. "Can't see me being a father. My brother maybe, but not me."

Though he was brushing it off, Kate remembered that shadow and wondered what had caused it, however briefly. Curiosity piqued, Kate couldn't help asking, "Why?"

He blew out a breath, crossed his arms over his chest and said, "I like having my own space. Doing things on my own time. Having to bend all of that to fit someone else's schedule doesn't appeal to me."

"Sounds selfish," she said.

"Absolutely," he agreed affably. "What about you? If you like kids so much, why don't you have three or four of your own?"

Her features froze briefly. She felt it, couldn't prevent it and could only hope that he didn't notice. One thing she didn't want was to tell Sean about her late husband and the dreams of family they'd had and lost. "Just hasn't worked out that way."

"Hey." Sean moved closer and his voice dropped. "Are you okay?"

"Fine," she said briskly, lifting her chin and giving him what she hoped was a bright—not bitter—smile.

This was simply another reminder of the differences between them, Kate thought. Mister Billionaire Playboy probably thought having a family was like being chained in a cage. But it was all Kate had ever really wanted. She'd come close to having the whole dream—home, husband, kids—but it had been snatched from her grasp and now she was left with only the haunting thoughts of what might have been.

Something Sean clearly wouldn't understand. But that wasn't her problem, was it?

"Anyway," Kate said, "we've got enough food for a few days if we're careful."

"Right." He accepted the change of subject easily enough. "Do we have enough coffee to last?"

We. Now they were an unlikely team. As long as the storm lasted, they would be *we.* And she could admit, at least to herself, that in spite of everything, she was grateful not to be stranded up here by herself. Even if it did mean that she and Sean were going to have far too much alone time together.

But for now, dealing with their shared addiction to caffeine took precedence. "I'm on it."

The water in the pan was boiling, so she carefully poured it into the drip filter on her travel pot. She felt Sean watching her. How odd, she thought, that the man's gaze could feel as tangible as a touch. And odder still, she caught herself wishing he *was* touching her, which was just stupid.

For heaven's sake, hadn't she *just* been reminding herself how different the two of them were? How he was temporary in her life—not to mention being her *client*, so in effect, her *boss*. It was undeniable, though. This flash of something hungry between them. It was dangerous. Ridiculous. And oh, so tempting.

It was the situation, she told herself. Just the two of them, stranded in an empty hotel with several feet of snow piling up outside. Of course, her mind was going a little wonky. And the only thing wrong with that explanation was that her mind had been wonky since the moment Sean had arrived in Wyoming.

Over the sound of the howling wind outside, Kate listened to the water plopping through the filter into the coffeepot. A rich, dark scent filled the air, and behind her, Sean inhaled deeply and released the breath on a sigh.

"Man, that smells good."

"Agreed," she said and carefully poured more water into the filter. While the coffee dripped into the reservoir, Kate walked to the pantry, where she'd stored a few paper supplies for the crew. She grabbed two cups, tossed one to Sean and then turned to the now-ready coffee and poured some for each of them. The first sip seemed to ease some of the jagged edges tearing at her mind.

Leaning back against the counter, she turned to stare out the window above the sink. It was a bay window, with plenty of space for fresh herbs to grow and thrive in the sun. Right now it was empty, but Kate could imagine just how it and everything else about the hotel would look when she and her crew were finished. Still, it was what was happening beyond the glass that had most of her attention.

The snow was coming down so thick and fast, swirling in a wind that rattled the glass panes, she couldn't see past the yard to where the lake stretched out along the foot of the mountains, and the forest was no more than a smudge of darkness in the world of white.

"This happen often?" Sean asked, as he moved up beside her.

His arm brushed against hers, and Kate sucked in a gulp of air to steady herself. "Often enough," she said, determined to get a grip on the rush of something hot and delicious pulsing inside her. Another sip of coffee sent a different kind of heat sweeping through her. "Ask anyone and they'll tell you. If you don't like the weather in Wyoming, wait five minutes. It'll change."

He leaned forward and tipped his head back to see what he could of the sky. "So five minutes from now, the sun should be shining and the snow melted?"

She had to laugh because he sounded so hopeful. "Not likely. This looks like a big one. I figure we're stuck here for a couple of days. Maybe more."

He sighed, nodded and looked at her. "At least we have each other."

And *that*, Kate told herself, was the problem.

* * *

They decided to ration what food they had, so an hour later, the two of them split a sandwich and shared a few crackers. Sitting in front of the fire, with the wind and snow pelting the windows, Sean glanced at Kate beside him. They'd pulled the old leather couch closer to the hearth, and now each of them had claimed a corner of the sofa for themselves.

Kate stared into the blaze, and firelight danced across her features and shone in her hair. Her eyes were fixed on the flames, as if looking away from the fire would mean her life. Her behavior told him she was nervous around him. He liked knowing it. Made his own unease a little easier to take.

He frowned to himself as that word reverberated a few times in his mind. *Unease*. Hell, Sean hadn't been uneasy around women since freshman year of high school. Dana Foster—her red hair, green eyes and wide, smiling mouth had turned Sean into a babbling moron. Until he'd kissed her for the first time. That kiss had opened up a world of wonder, beauty and hunger that Sean had enjoyed ever since.

The women in his life—most of them—had come and gone, barely causing a ripple. Of course, there'd been one woman, years ago, who had affected him, changed him. But he didn't allow himself to think about her or what had happened between them. Ancient history that had nothing to do with who and what he was today.

Now there was Kate. And what she did to him was so much more than that long-ago woman. Admitting that really bothered him and acted as a warning bell. Kate had him tied into knots, and he didn't appreciate it. She made him feel nearly desperate to have her. And while his body clamored for him to go for it, those warning signals continued to ring out in his brain, telling him to keep his distance and to get the hell away from her as fast as he could. But that wasn't going to happen, thanks to this blizzard.

He'd avoided any kind of entanglements for years and wasn't looking for one now. But logic didn't have a lot to do with anything he was feeling at the moment.

He wanted her. Wanted her badly enough that his mind was filled with images of her all the damn time. When he was with her, his body was tight and hard, and the longer he was with Kate, the worse it got. That need clawed at his insides, demanding release. Still, sex with her would only complicate matters, and Sean was a man who didn't like complications.

His life would have been a lot easier if only he'd been able to escape Wyoming and put several hundred miles between himself and Kate. That wasn't going to happen, though, so he had to find a way to survive this enforced closeness.

"Why are you staring at me?"

He came out of his thoughts and focused on the woman now looking at him. "Just thinking."

"Now I'm worried," she said, a half smile curving her mouth. "Thinking about what?"

Well, he wasn't going to tell her the truth—that he was thinking about how soon he could get her out of her clothes—so he blurted out something that had been on his mind lately. "Wondering how you became a contractor."

Her brow furrowed, her eyes narrowed and he had

the distinct feeling she didn't believe him. But then she shrugged and answered.

"My dad is the easy answer," she said, shifting her gaze back to the fire snapping and crackling just a few feet away from them. "He's a master carpenter. Started his own business when I was a kid." She smiled in memory, and Sean noticed how her features softened. "I used to work for him every summer and he and the guys on his crew taught me everything I know about construction."

"Funny, I worked summers for my dad, too," Sean said, remembering how he had tried desperately to get out of work so he could go surfing instead.

"What's your dad do?"

"Lawyer," Sean said, bracing his hands on the floor behind him. "He wanted my brother and I to go to law school, join his firm."

"No interest in being a lawyer?" she asked.

He shuddered. "No. When you worked for your dad, you were outside, right?"

"Usually, yeah."

"Not me. Dad had us shredding old documents, sweeping, mopping and in general doing everything the building custodians needed us to do." He shook his head. "Hated being locked up inside, so I promised myself that I'd find a job where I could take off and go surfing when I wanted to."

She laughed. "Not many employers allow surfing breaks, I imagine."

"Nope." He grinned and added, "Just another reason I like being my own boss. You'd know what I mean by that."

She nodded. "Yeah. I do."

A moment or two of silence, broken only by the snap and hiss of the fire, stretched out between them. It was almost companionable, Sean thought. It was the first time since he'd met Kate Wells that they'd gone so long without an argument. It surprised him how much he was enjoying it.

"So," he asked, "who'll run things for you while you're stuck here?"

"With a blizzard this heavy, the guys will just hole up at their homes and take a few days off. They won't be expecting to work through it," she said, then looked around the room.

It was filled with shadows that moved and shifted in the flickering light. "As soon as the snow stops and the roads are clear, we'll get started on the renovations. The structure's sound, but for needing some new shingles on the roof and some of the porch railings replaced. We'll be working on the inside for now, of course, and move to the outside when spring finally gets here—"

"And we're talking about work again," Sean interrupted her. He'd noticed that whenever their conversations threatened to get personal, she "ran home to mama" so to speak and turned to talk of the job.

"Your fault this time. Besides, work is why we're here," she pointed out.

"No," he argued with a wave of his hand toward the closest window that displayed a view of swirling white, "snow is why we're here. We've talked about the job enough for today."

"Well then," she said abruptly, "what do you want to talk about?"

"Who says I want to talk at all?" he asked and gave her a slow smile.

She stiffened and her features went cool and dispassionate. What did it say about him, Sean wondered, that her reaction only fed the hunger gnawing at him? This woman's obvious reluctance to admit to what was simmering between them only intrigued him further.

So maybe, he told himself, the secret to surviving close quarters with Kate was to go ahead and give in to the sexual tug happening. If they tried to ignore it, the next few days were going to be misery.

"Yeah," she said, "that's not going to happen."

"Never say never," he told her with a careless shrug. "We're stuck together and I'm pretty damn charming."

A hesitant smile twitched at her lips briefly. "I think I can control myself."

"We'll see, won't we?" He was a man who loved a challenge. And Kate Wells was surely that.

"Right. I think I'll bring in more wood." She pushed herself to her feet and looked down at him.

"Thought we had enough." He glanced at the high stack of split logs he'd already carried in and set beside the hearth.

"Can't have too much," she said, pulling her jacket on.

He knew a displacement activity when he saw one. She was trying to get some space, some distance from him, and damn if he was going to let her. "I'll get it."

"I can do it," she said and left without another look at him.

Muttering under his breath about hardheaded women, Sean grabbed his jacket and followed. He walked through the mudroom and stepped out onto the wide, covered back porch in time to see Kate grabbing several big logs. "Let me get it."

"I said I don't need help," she countered.

Sean came up beside her just as she whirled around to face him. Her elbow caught him in the chest, and he took a step back and hit the edge of the top step. Off balance, his arms windmilled as he felt himself falling and knew he couldn't stop it. The fresh snow cushioned his fall and puffed up around him in a cloud. He was flat on his back, staring up at still more snow falling out of a steel-gray sky.

"Oh, God, are you okay?" Kate dropped the wood she held and reached out one hand to him. "I didn't know you were there, really."

Sean only stared at her. Snowflakes gathered in her hair, on her lashes, on the collar of her coat. Her hand was out toward him, and he grabbed it. But rather than take her help to get out of the snow, he gave a hard yank and pulled her down to join him.

She gave a half shriek when she landed on top of him, then immediately struggled to push herself up again. But having her body pressed along his felt so good, Sean was in no hurry to release her.

"What's the rush?" he asked, mouth just a breath away from hers.

"It's freezing."

"Cuddle up, we'll keep each other warm."

Three

"You're crazy," she said with a shake of her head. Thick, heavy snowflakes kept falling all around them, landing on his lashes, his cheeks.

"And charming. Don't forget charming."

"Right," she said, laughing. Damn it, he really was charming. Most men getting pushed into a snowdrift wouldn't have been so nice about it—though he'd made sure to yank her into the wet cold just to keep things even. "Pulling me into the snow? Charming."

He grinned. "You started it."

She had. And now that she was lying on top of him, she couldn't really regret it. "You're enjoying this, aren't you?"

He slid one hand down her spine toward her behind, and her eyes flashed in warning. "Yeah. I guess I am."

"Like I said. Crazy."

"Kiss me once and we'll get out of this snow."

Kissing Sean Ryan was absolutely not a good idea. But oh, she was tempted. Tempted enough that she knew she'd give in if she didn't move.

"I'm going in now," she told him and pushed against him again, trying to lever herself up.

Sean held on to her. "One kiss. See if we can melt all this snow."

Her gaze dropped to his mouth then lifted to meet his eyes. Temptation had never looked so good, she thought, knowing that she was in far deeper water than she'd ever been in before. No, she wasn't some shy virgin. She was a widow. And the man she had loved and married had been *nothing* like Sean.

Sam Wells had been sweet, kind, soft-spoken. An easygoing man with a ready smile and a gentle nature. Kate wasn't used to dealing with a man who wore arrogance and confidence like a second skin. And blast it, she couldn't understand why she found him so... attractive.

Then, while her thoughts were muddled and her defenses down, Sean tugged her closer and closed his mouth over hers.

So much heat. It was a wonder the snow they were lying in didn't melt into slush.

While her body lit up like a glowing neon sign, Kate's mind flashed a warning. *Melt snow?* If he kept this up, Sean would melt her *bones*.

Pull away, she told herself. Stop this now. But she wasn't going to stop and she knew it. It had been so long—*too* long—since she'd been held, kissed. That was why she was reacting so wildly to Sean's touch, she assured herself. It wasn't personal. It was simply a biological need that hadn't been so much as acknowledged for two years.

But when his tongue tangled with hers, she had to admit, at least silently, that it was this man causing her reaction. Not just a kiss, but Sean's kiss.

For a week, she'd worked with him, argued with him and, yes, dreamed about him. Now his hands were on her, his mouth was devouring hers and all she could think was *more*. This was so unlike her. So out of the realm of her ordinary world she had no idea what to do or how to handle it.

He broke the kiss, stared at her as if she'd just dropped out of the sky from Mars, then shook his head. "Well, damn. If I'd known what kissing you would be like, I'd have done it a week ago."

Gazing into his beautiful blue eyes, she blurted out before she could stop herself, "I might have let you."

One corner of his truly fabulous mouth tipped up. "Might?"

He already thought far too much of himself, so no way was she going to feed an ego that was already strong enough for three healthy men.

"I think we're way past 'might,' Kate," he said, his fingers rubbing at the base of her neck until she wanted to purr in reaction.

That realization made Kate pull back, shake her head. "No, we are not going to do this."

"Not here, anyway," Sean agreed. "We'll freeze to death."

Not the way she was feeling at the moment, Kate thought. Despite the cold, the snow, the icy chill of the wind, she felt only the heat. That was the problem. Determined to put some space between them, Kate shoved herself to her feet. Sean did the same, then caught her elbow in a firm grip.

"You're going to pretend nothing happened?"

"It was a kiss, Sean. That's all." She slipped out of his grasp, pulled off her cap, tore the band from her hair and shook it free until it lay thick around her shoulders.

"A hell of a kiss, Kate."

She felt the imprint of his fingers right through her jacket and sweater as if he was touching her bare skin. What would it be like if he *actually* touched her? Oh, don't think about that...

"Kate—"

"We need to get more wood."

"Oh, I've got plenty of wood."

He gave her a slow smile as his eyebrows arched. Kate blew out a breath. Well, she'd walked right into *that* double entendre. "Funny."

He grinned. "Told you I'm charming."

"You shouldn't waste it on me," Kate told him.

"Who says it's a waste?"

Kate sighed, tipped her head to one side and stared at him. "Why are you doing this?"

"We're *both* doing this, Kate," he said flatly. Moving in, he closed what little distance lay between them. His hands came down on her shoulders and though she knew she should shrug him off, she didn't. That stirring of bone-deep heat was too irresistible. Too compelling.

In this world of swirling white and icy cold, it was as if they were the only two people alive. As if nothing beyond this old hotel existed. Mattered. She stared up at him, into those blue eyes, and felt herself weakening further.

He was so damn sure of himself, Kate thought. And

as her willpower dissolved like sugar in hot water, she told herself he had every right to be. She'd had no intention of giving in to this attraction between them, and now she couldn't think of anything else.

"So, what's it going to be?" He looked down into her eyes as he slid his hands up from her shoulders to cup her face. The chill of his hands on her skin skittered through her and was swallowed by the building fire inside. "Are we gonna spend the next few days pretending nothing's happening between us?"

"It's the safest thing to do."

"You always take the safe route?" His mouth curved.

Yes. She'd lived most of her life trying to be safe. Her mother had died in a car accident when Kate was a girl, and that incident had marked her. She always buckled her seat belt. Drove the speed limit. Safety—caution in all things, was paramount. In everything from driving to balancing her checkbook to salting her steps during winter. She didn't take chances. Risks. She was always careful. Always vigilant. And the smart thing to do right now would be to continue being safe. To walk away from what she felt when she was with Sean.

Even while she was giving herself some excellent advice, he bent his head and kissed her. Once. Twice. His mouth was soft, his manner tender and she was lost. When he finished, leaving her breathless and just a little unsteady, he looked at her again.

Kate swallowed hard and said, "Safe is smart."

"Be stupid," he urged.

She couldn't look away from that warm, determined gaze. "I think I'm going to."

He kissed her again. This time gentle tenderness washed away in a roaring tide of clawing, greedy hunger that had been building between them for days. Even through the thick layer of sweaters and jackets they wore, Kate felt his hard, muscled chest pressed against her, and everything inside her caught fire.

It was as if embers that had lain smoldering within suddenly caught a draft of air that flashed them into flames. Her hands at his shoulders, she clung to him as he wrapped his arms around her waist and held her tight, close. Though they stood locked together in knee-deep snow, she didn't feel the cold. His mouth fused to hers, his breath filled her, his tongue twisted with hers and Kate felt the already-blazing fire inside her erupt and flash white-hot.

He tore his mouth from hers and said, "Inside. We'll freeze to death out here."

"So not cold," she told him, licking her lips to savor the taste of him.

He grinned, and her heart stumbled. "Gonna make sure you stay that way, too."

Keeping one arm locked around her, he guided her into the hotel, through the kitchen door, then slammed it closed behind them. They left the wind, the snow, the cold, and now it was just the two of them.

Nerves rose up unexpectedly and Kate started thinking. Her body was churning, every hormone she possessed was doing a cha-cha of anticipation, but her brain had clicked back on the moment he stopped kissing her and now…

"No way," he said, caging her against the counter, with his hands braced on either side of her.

"What?" She blinked up at him.

"You're thinking too much. You're starting to worry that maybe we're making a mistake."

"Are you a mind reader now?" she asked, trying to ignore the hard thump of her heartbeat.

He laughed shortly. "Reading your mind isn't that tough at the moment." His gaze moved over her face like a caress before meeting her eyes again. "You're interested. You just don't want to be."

"I could say the same about you," she pointed out in her own defense.

"Yeah, you could." He nodded thoughtfully. "The difference between us is I'm not big on denying myself and you seem to be a champ at it."

"I'll agree with the first half of that sentence. You do seem to be the type who indulges himself whenever he feels like it."

"Why not?" he asked with a shrug. "You don't get trophies from the universe for being stoic and cheating yourself out of something that could be amazing."

In spite of everything, Kate felt a rush of anticipation that fed a small smile. The man was arrogance personified. "You're so sure it would be amazing?"

His mouth curved, his eyes gleamed and he leaned in closer until their mouths were just a breath apart. "Aren't you?"

Stray snowflakes slipped from the collar of her jacket, went beneath the neckline of her sweater and snaked along her spine. Kate shivered and told herself it was the ice on her skin, not the heat in his eyes that had caused it.

"This is crazy," she murmured, shifting her gaze from his eyes to his mouth and back again.

"I'm a big fan of crazy," he whispered.

"Yeah, you would be," Kate said with a choked-off laugh.

Her insides jumped, trembled and settled into a thrum of expectancy that wouldn't be denied. Crazy is just what they were talking about here. Sex with Sean would be a mistake. A huge one. But if she let this moment pass, let him go back to California without taking the opportunity Fate had handed her, wouldn't that be a mistake, too? Wouldn't she have to live with regret for the rest of her life?

And she couldn't handle more regrets.

Kate had been so closed off for the last two years, she'd never once felt even the slightest attraction for a man. And what she felt for Sean went light-years beyond a "slight attraction." That could be a problem, too, she knew. Feeling too much was an open invitation to pain.

Kate had already had enough pain to last a lifetime.

So she'd have to keep her heart tucked neatly away. Of course, sex without love wasn't like her at all. But then again, she'd already had and lost love and didn't expect to ever have it again. So unless she wanted to live her entire life as if she was locked up in a monastery, she'd have to accept that things, for her, had changed. Affection would have to be enough. And as she met his eyes, Kate could admit to herself that as much as Sean irritated and annoyed her, she also sort of liked him. Hard not to, really. Looking up into Sean's eyes, Kate thought he really was as charming as he claimed to be. Plus he didn't cheap out on building plans, he was fair to her crew and even when he argued with her, he managed to make her laugh.

That kind of man was hard to resist. Though she'd been doing her best to do just that for the last week, she was done with it now. She took a breath and sighed heavily. She was finished trying to ignore the buzz of electricity between them.

If she was going to make a mistake, Kate preferred it be an active decision, not a mistake of omission.

"So, Kate," he murmured, pushing the edge of her jacket aside to drag the tips of his fingers along the undersides of her breasts. "Are we going to be crazy together, or are we going to be sad and lonely separately?"

She shivered again as tiny twists of heat licked at her. Her eyes closed briefly and when she opened them again, Sean was there, staring into her gaze, searching for her answer.

She lifted one hand, cupped his face and drew him to her. "Crazy," she whispered. "I vote for crazy."

"Thank God." He kissed her.

Kate's entire body lit up in an explosion of light and color and heat. She hooked her arms around his neck and hung on, drawing him even closer. Now that she'd opened the floodgates of long-banked desires and needs, she was helpless to do anything but ride the tide cresting inside her. Kate groaned as he parted her lips with his tongue. That fast, greedy dance stole her breath, blurred her mind and set fire to her body.

His hands were busy, too, pushing her jacket off her shoulders and down her arms. Free, Kate did the same for him, then threaded her arms back around his neck as he lifted her and plopped her down onto the old, worn counter. He moved to stand between her thighs, and she hooked her legs around his waist.

They were eye to eye now and when he scraped his hands up beneath the hem of her sweater to cup her breasts, even through the fragile material of her bra, Kate felt heat blossom. Tingles flickered into life deep in her belly, and the core of her ached and throbbed in time with the beat of her heart.

Want. Desperate, frantic need clawed at her, and Kate threw herself into the conflagration. Outside, snow flew in an icy wind that rattled the windowpanes and slammed a stray shutter against the side of the hotel. Neither of them noticed or cared.

"Other room," Sean muttered thickly, tearing his mouth from hers. "By the fire."

"Not cold," she assured him, leaning in for another kiss.

He indulged her, once, twice, then pulled back and shook his head. "Nope. Want you naked and," he added, "in this room, we'll both be too cold to finish what we started."

He was right. The kitchen was cold and getting colder. The light was going outside, and the snow piling up was seeping its icy touch through the walls. True, the heat inside her was only building, but the thought of being with him in front of a roaring fire had its appeal.

"Right," she said, giving him a nod, "let's go."

He scooped her off the counter and braced his hands on her behind. Kate kept her legs wrapped around his hips and held on while he carried her to the great room. At any other time, she might have objected to being toted around, but she was too busy enjoying the feel of his hard body pressed against her center. She went hot and wet, her own body trembling in wild anticipation. She wriggled against him, and he sucked in a gulp of air.

"Keep moving like that and we'll never make it to the fire."

"There's plenty of fire here already," she told him.

He glanced at her, his features tight, his eyes flashing

with purpose, then quickened his steps. Kate grinned because she felt the same way. *Hurry, hurry.*

Now that she'd made the decision to be with him, she didn't want to wait another second. She wanted him on her, inside her. She wanted him to claim what she'd only given to one other man before him.

A brief flicker of guilt sprang up in the recesses of her mind, but she smothered it. There was no room for thoughts of anyone else, of other times, other lives and loves. For this moment, there was only her…and Sean.

Sex. She hadn't been with a man in more than two years. That had to be the reason she was reacting so wildly to Sean's caresses. Always before, the best part of sex for Kate was the closeness, the snuggling that came after. She'd never before known this kind of hunger—hadn't really believed she was capable of it. Now, Kate had to fight her sense of guilt for admitting even to herself that Sean was making her feel more than her husband ever had—but that was for later. For now, all she wanted was an end to the driving demands within.

And that's when it hit her. They couldn't do this. "No. No, wait."

"Oh, no," Sean said with a dramatic moan. "Please don't tell me you're changing your mind."

"No, it's not that," she said, licking her lips, swallowing the knot of disappointment that seemed to be lodged in her throat. "I'm not on the pill, and we don't have protection—"

In the great room, he made straight for the rug in front of the hearth. He set her on her feet, grinned down at her and reached into his back pocket for his wallet, then pulled out what looked like an entire string of gold-foiled condoms.

Her eyes widened, then she smiled and shook her head. "Are you a teenager? You carry condoms in your wallet?"

"Since I met you—" he grinned "—yeah. You bet." He handed the condoms to her, then reached down for the sleeping bag she'd carried in earlier. "You have your emergency supplies... I have mine."

Kate didn't know whether to be flattered or worried. He'd planned this. Came prepared to have sex with her several times—judging by just how many condoms he'd tucked into his wallet. Her stomach jittered with nerves. She'd only ever been with one man. Her late husband, Sam. She remembered being stirred by his kisses, his caresses. She remembered the climbing tension inside her, and she remembered the soft *pop* of release that was both fulfilling and somehow disappointing.

And now, she was willingly racing down that same road with a man she barely knew. She must be crazy, Kate decided. It was the only explanation.

Sean snatched up the sleeping bag she'd carried inside earlier. Untying it, he flipped it out onto the rug, then bent to unzip it and open it to its full width.

"Not a king-size bed at the Ritz," he told her, "but it'll do."

There were those nerves again, skittering wildly in the pit of her stomach. Firelight danced and shifted across the sleeping bag and sent twisting, writhing shadows around the empty room. She watched him, caught by his steady, direct gaze, and felt the last of her doubts, her hesitation, slide away. Kate had made her decision and she wouldn't second-guess herself now.

Sean was right in that they'd come too far to stop—and more importantly, Kate didn't *want* to stop. "Works for me."

She put all thought aside and eagerly went into his arms when he reached for her. With the fire crackling and sizzling behind them and warmth slowly filling the massive room, they frantically pulled at each other's clothing. A wild, clamoring rush of need nearly choked her, and Kate couldn't even imagine why she'd been so nervous only moments before.

Sweaters were tossed to the floor, her bra was tugged free and dropped. His hands covered her breasts, his thumbs and fingers pulling and tweaking at her already-rigid nipples until Kate groaned and arched into his touch, silently demanding more. She didn't think. Couldn't have, even if she'd wanted to. There was only feeling now. Deep wells of sensation opening up inside her, spilling through her bloodstream like liquid gold.

Nothing in her memories of times with Sam could have prepared her for what Sean was doing to her. She'd never been this electrified before. Never known the sizzle of her own flesh or the burn at her center.

"You feel even better than I thought you would," he whispered, magic fingers still showering gentle torture on her breasts.

"Oh, I feel *great*," she agreed and leaned into him, sliding her hands up under the hem of the black T-shirt he'd worn beneath his sweater. His body was sharply defined muscles and warm, soft skin. She pulled at the shirt in frustration until he let her go long enough to yank it off himself. Then he drew her close, holding her against him tightly, skin to skin, body to body.

She wouldn't have thought there was more to feel, more to *want*, but there was. Sean showed her just how much. Kate had never felt like this before. Hadn't known she *could*. Her brain was muddied, her breath coming in short, hard gasps. A tingling sensation crept through her veins, making her body feel alight. Tension tightened inside her, and she yearned for that soft, delicious shimmer of release she knew was waiting for her. It would ease the unbearable pressure building within and take the edge off the desire pumping through her. She didn't want to wait another minute.

Tugging at him, she pulled Sean down to the sleeping bag with her. And the icy feel of the black nylon against her heated flesh was a counterpoint to what he was doing to her, adding yet another layer of sensation to the feelings driving her wild.

He leaned over her, stared down into her eyes and Kate's system jolted into overdrive. The man had a great face. And an amazing mouth that he fused to hers in the next instant. A muffled groan tore from her throat as she met every twist of his tongue against hers. She took his breath and gave him hers. Her hands scraped up and down his bare back, loving the smooth glide of hot flesh beneath her palms.

The fire snapped, hissed. The snow pelted the windows and the wind moaned beneath the eaves. And all of it was background music to what was happening between them. Here, in this room, there was no place for cold or ice. There was only the building heat.

He cupped her core and even through her jeans, her body responded with a jolt. Her hips lifted, rocked into his touch as she pulled free of his kiss and gasped for the air her screaming lungs demanded. This was so much more than she'd expected. That tiny shimmer of release she was hoping for couldn't come soon enough.

"You're amazing," he whispered, dipping his head to kiss the side of her throat, to drag the tip of his tongue up and down the pulse point pounding with her response to his touch.

She could hardly hear him over the hammering beat of her own heart. It was thunder in her ears, muffling the world around her. But she didn't care. All she cared about was this man's hands on her and the pleasure she knew was waiting for her. When he unzipped her jeans and swiftly tugged them down her legs and off, she was frantic.

All that stood between her and his touch were the black lace panties she wore. Helpless to do anything else, Kate lifted her hips again in invitation, in silent plea. Her body was buzzing, throbbing with a desperate need that only he could meet.

"Well, now," Sean said, smiling, "if I'd known you had something like that hidden underneath those jeans, we might have gotten to this point sooner."

She took a breath, shuddered. "I've got a weakness for lingerie."

"And I'm pleased to know it," Sean said, eyes gleaming. "Though at the moment, we really don't need these, do we?"

She shook her head as he hooked his fingers beneath the fragile elastic band and slid the swatch of black lace down her legs. Then he sat back and looked her over, up and down. His gaze was as thorough as a touch and just as sensual. Kate moved beneath his steady regard, loving the flash in his eyes as he watched her.

She reached up for him, but Sean pulled back then

stood and quickly tore off the rest of his clothes. He grabbed his emergency supply of condoms, tore one off and in seconds, sheathed himself and turned back to her. He slid his body along hers until Kate wanted to whimper with the sheer beauty of it. He was hard and strong, and she wanted him more than ever.

Reaching one hand down, she wrapped her fingers around his hard length and smiled at his hiss of an indrawn breath. She stroked him, watched his blue eyes darken and gleam in reaction and knew that he was as desperate as she to end this torment.

"That's it," he muttered thickly and moved to kneel between her thighs.

"Yes," she whispered, reaching for him again. "Please. Now."

"Oh, yeah," he vowed. "Now."

In one long thrust, he entered her and Kate's body splintered. The soft release she'd been expecting rolled through her, and she relaxed a little, knowing that the hum her body still felt was just what was expected of being so twisted up into desire. She was accustomed to this, too. The vague sense of disappointment that kept her body buzzing expectantly in spite of what she'd just experienced. In an hour or two it would fade and she wouldn't feel the frustration anymore.

Lifting one hand to his face, she smiled up at him. "Thanks."

His mouth quirked, and he held perfectly still, his body locked with hers. "You're thanking me?"

"Well…yeah."

That smile of his broadened into a grin. "Save your thanks for when we're finished."

Well, sure, she thought. He wasn't finished. He

would be soon, though, and then she could lie against him for a while, feel that warmth of the afterglow that had always been the best part of sex for her.

"Right," she said and lifted her hips as he began to move inside her. Again and again, his body claimed hers until the tension in Kate's body ratcheted up even higher than it had been before. She gasped, shook her head from side to side and clung to his arms, his shoulders. This had never happened before. Not for her. Always with Sam, there was that small release, then his body collapsing on top of hers and then the quiet while her racing heart tried to calm.

There was no calm here. Only the frantic need pulsing inside her like a neon sign. Sean slid one hand down the length of her, to where their bodies joined and he touched her. Kate's eyes flew open as he caressed that single, sensitive spot at the very center of her. Surprise, shock and a wild, raw pleasure rocked her to her bones. She shrieked his name as her body bucked beneath his. A wave of incredible, explosive sensations shattered her, and all she could do was hold on and fight to survive the ride.

"That's it," Sean whispered, leaning down to kiss her, hard. "Now go again."

"No," she gasped. Unthinkable. She couldn't take any more. "Impossible. Can't. Catch. My. Breath."

She hadn't known her body could do something like that. Feel so much. Take so much. And yet, even while she told Sean she couldn't do it again, that down-low tingle churned into life at her core. She'd never live through this, she told herself, and then a quiet, satisfied voice in her brain whispered, *Who cares?*

A heartbeat later, thought ended and her body picked

up where her mind left off. She and Sean came together frantically, each of them racing to give. To take. To feel. Seconds spun into minutes and the two of them rolled across that sleeping bag as if it was a luxurious bed.

Breathing labored, hearts pounding in tandem, they moved as one, two more shadows in the flickering light. When the next shattering orgasm slammed into her, Kate dragged his mouth down to hers and swallowed his shout, as this time their bodies erupted together... and holding each other, they tumbled over the edge of the abyss.

Later, he scraped his palms along her back and down to the curve of her behind. Kate trembled at his touch, at the still-so-fresh memory of what he could make her feel. "I'm not done with you yet," he said, his voice barely more than a low growl of promises and demands.

"Good," she said, rolling to one side and dragging him over on top of her again. "I'm not done with you, either."

He grinned. "My kind of woman."

For now, anyway, she told herself.

Four

The fire was dying, there was a warm, lush, naked woman asleep in his arms and Sean couldn't relax. Hell, he should be in a relaxation *coma* after everything the two of them had shared over the last few hours. Instead, he was wide-awake, staring into the fire, *thinking*.

So far, he didn't much care for his thoughts, either. Scrubbing one hand across his face, he tightened the hold he had on Kate when she curled into him and nestled her head on his chest. Her hair was soft and thick and smelled like strawberries. Her breath drifted across his skin and when she sighed, the small sound seemed to ripple through him.

It had been years since he'd actually slept with a woman he'd slept with—which hardly made sense and almost made him smile—until he remembered the only other woman he'd held like this in the night. Then all thoughts of smiles faded away and shadows fell across his mind. This wasn't the same thing at all, he assured himself. Kate wasn't Adrianna, and the situation was completely different.

God. Adrianna. He hadn't allowed himself to so much as think her name in years. He'd deliberately wiped her face from his memories, closing the door firmly on a past that might have haunted him otherwise.

So he wouldn't dredge up all of that now, either. This was Kate and though he didn't like admitting it, sex with her had been...*more* than he'd ever experienced before. With anyone. But that didn't necessarily mean a damn thing. Sure, Kate's responses had driven him beyond simple pleasure into a realm he'd never thought to enter—but that didn't mean he wanted to stay there.

His body stirred when Kate sighed again in her sleep and slid one arm across his chest. All right. Maybe he *did* want to stay there. At least temporarily. Sean looked down at her and admired the flicker of light and shadow that danced over her skin. Beautiful and strong and confident. She intrigued him. Worried him. Okay, he admitted, *fascinated* him. Acknowledging as much, even to himself, bothered the hell out of him.

His body had been at a slow burn since the moment he'd met Kate. But sex was supposed to have taken care of that. Eased the itch. It hadn't come close. Instead, he only wanted her again. And feeling like that wasn't in the game plan.

Frowning, Sean dragged the edge of the sleeping blanket over the two of them, as the fire died and a chill snaked through the big room. He should get up to stoke the flames, but moving would wake her up and...hell, he thought. Why bother lying to himself? He didn't want to get up because it felt too good lying there with her sprawled across him.

Outside, the wind was still shrieking, snow still pelting the window glass. Without that fire, it'd get damn uncomfortable in there. He'd have to let go of Kate soon and rebuild the fire before they froze to death. But he wasn't ready to do that just yet, and that realization bothered him, too.

This whole situation had *mess* written all over it. He'd come here to work and landed himself trapped in a snowbound hotel with the one woman who could get to him faster than anyone else had in years. He had to pull back for both of their sakes. Neither of them was interested in a damn relationship. He had to remember that as good as this was between them, it wasn't going anywhere. He wouldn't *allow* it. But that didn't mean he wouldn't enjoy this time with Kate for as long as it lasted.

"I feel…amazing," she whispered, her soft voice breaking into his thoughts. Sean was grateful.

He looked down at her and met her gaze as she lay watching him. She really did feel amazing, he told himself, and that was part of the problem. But right now, he didn't give a good damn.

He looked into her eyes, smoothed her hair back from her face. She'd slept for an hour or so. Long enough. "You know I'm still not done, right?"

A slow, incredibly sexy smile curved her mouth. "I'm really glad to hear that."

Sean took hold of her and pulled her up until their mouths met, until she sighed and he tasted her, swallowing her breath, making it a part of him. Then he rolled them over, levering himself over her, taking all she had to give. He lost himself in her, let the rest of the world outside that room slide away and closed his mind to thoughts of anything but this moment.

Tomorrow could take care of itself.

The next morning, Kate felt well used and limber. Her body ached in a good way and though she should have been exhausted, instead she felt energized—as if she could grab her tools and renovate the entire hotel by herself. She'd had no idea she could feel this good.

Smiling to herself, Kate made coffee and stared out the window at the world of white. The snow was still coming down and the straight-as-a-soldier pines were beginning to bow beneath the weight of the heavy, wet snow on their branches. This was a big storm showing no signs of ending yet—and she was glad. In fact, she'd never been so happy about being snowed in.

Logically, of course, Kate knew this wasn't the most brilliant move she'd ever made. Getting involved sexually with her boss was crazy, but at the moment, she really couldn't regret it. That, she knew, would come later. But for now, all she could do was marvel at the memories of everything Sean had done with her—and to her.

A flush of heat rushed through Kate, tingling across her nerve endings until she felt as if her skin was burning. Until she put a stop to it. Last night, she'd been so swept away by what she was feeling, there hadn't been time for guilt to grab hold of her. Now, there was too much time.

Everything she'd experienced with Sean was fresh in her mind, and Kate couldn't help feeling disloyal to the husband she had lost. As much as she had loved her husband, Kate was forced to acknowledge that Sam had never made her feel what Sean had. During her marriage, Kate had assumed that it was her own fault that somehow, something was lacking that kept her from experiencing the mind-shattering orgasms her friend Molly loved to describe in intricate detail. Of course, a part of Kate had always believed that Molly was exaggerating. Now after last night, Kate realized she owed her friend an apology. And her brain was jumping from one thought to another.

Her subconscious was probably doing it on purpose to keep her from focusing too much on what happened next. What was she supposed to say to Sean? How was she supposed to act?

"I smell coffee."

She whipped around to watch Sean walk into the kitchen. Her heart gave a hard thump, and Kate took a breath trying to calm that stir of something hot and wonderful that happened with a single look at him. His black hair tumbled across his forehead, his blue eyes were narrowed. He wore black jeans and a white long-sleeved shirt, unbuttoned. He hadn't bothered to pull on his boots, and Kate couldn't have said why she found the fact that he was barefoot so damn sexy. But she knew without a doubt that she was in serious trouble.

"Coffee's almost ready," she said, focusing on the job at hand rather than the gorgeous man headed toward her with a long, slow stride.

"Good. Need the caffeine." He leaned one hip against the counter and crossed his arms over the chest she wanted to stroke like a kitten. "You wore me out. Who knew once I got you out of that tool belt you'd be so... insatiable?"

Heat and memories rushed through her again, tangling together in her mind. "It was quite the surprise for me, too," she muttered.

"Re-al-ly?" He drawled that word into three syllables.

"It's not that big a deal," Kate said, snatching up the now-ready coffeepot and pouring each of them a cup. She needed a second or two to gather thoughts she'd only been considering for the last few minutes herself. *Insatiable*. She had been. And that had surprised the heck out of her. "I just never really cared that much about sex is all."

A half smile tugged at the edge of his mouth. "But you have such a talent for it." He paused thoughtfully, then asked, "So it must be that your former lovers weren't very good."

Kate snapped a look at him. It was one thing for her to reconsider the intimacies of her marriage, but she wouldn't stand there and let Sean insult Sam's memory. "He was just fine, thanks."

"Just fine?" Sean laughed shortly, took a sip of his coffee and said, "*Fine* is not a word you want to use about sex. Cookies maybe, but not sex." He stopped, straightened up and looked at her in disbelief. "Wait a minute. You said *he*. You've only been with one other guy?"

A new tidal wave of guilt roared over her, making Kate think she'd drown in that dark, dismal sea. Yes, before Sean she'd only been with her husband. Sam's smiling face rose up in her mind and Kate's heart ached. She couldn't talk about him with Sean. Didn't want to hear sympathetic noises or see a sheen of pity in his eyes. Kate didn't even talk about Sam with her friends or her father, so she wouldn't consider it with Sean. She was dealing with Sam's loss, but she was doing it her own way. "I don't think we need to discuss our pasts. Unless you've got something you'd like to share…"

It was gone so quickly, Kate couldn't be sure she'd seen it at all. But there was a flicker of something dark in his eyes. Apparently, he was as protective of his own memories as she was of her own. Well, good, then he would understand.

"No," he finally said, "we don't have to talk about the past."

Relieved, Kate nodded. "In that case, why don't we talk about the future instead?"

In a blink, his features went stiff and tight, his eyes glittered wildly with a typical sort of blind, male panic. "What future?"

Laughter shot from her throat, startling her and making Sean scowl in response. His expression only made her laugh harder and boy, it felt good to let go of the guilt, the awkwardness and the morning-after conversation.

"What's so damn funny?" he demanded.

Still laughing, Kate held one hand up in a silent request for time to get herself under control. Sean waited, but he wasn't happy, as evidenced by his scowl deepening.

Shaking her head, Kate realized that for the first time since awakening in Sean's arms, she felt like herself. Nerves were gone, that odd sense of guilt mingled with regret had faded away and she remembered exactly who she was. She didn't have to walk on eggshells around Sean because they weren't in a *relationship*, so to speak.

They were each strong individuals and as long as she kept that in mind, she could handle whatever came next.

Laughter, though, continued to spill from her in a long, rich torrent until she struggled to catch her breath. Looking at Sean didn't help because he looked so…irritated. Men were just amazing, she told herself, amusement continuing to bubble in her mind.

Sean was a prime example. He'd done everything he could to get her into bed…well, sleeping bag. Then the following morning, all she had to do was say the word *future* and she could practically *hear* him stepping on the metaphorical brakes. She was only surprised he hadn't tried to leave—blizzard or no blizzard. He was no doubt assuming she had visions filled with white picket fences and rosy-cheeked children. Her laughter faded away as she recalled that she'd had those very dreams once. And then they died. She had no interest in resuscitating them.

When she had the laughter under control, she said, "Relax, Sean. I'm not expecting a proposal and a vow of eternal devotion. God, you should see your face. You look like you're ready to chew off a cartoon ball and chain from around your ankle."

"That's ridiculous." If anything, his frown deepened as he took a long drink of coffee. "And I don't know what you're talking about."

"Sure," she said, shaking her head as she sipped at her coffee. "You stick with that. Anyway… I was talking about the hotel's future, not ours."

He stiffened and pushed away from the counter with a move that was too studiedly casual to be real. "I knew that."

"Please." She laughed again, waved that away and

took another hit of her coffee. "When you walked in here, you were braced for some emotional meltdown from me. You figured I'd throw myself at your feet and beg you to marry me or some weird thing."

"Weird?" His eyebrows lifted.

"Well, you have no worries on that front," she assured him, meeting those icy blue eyes squarely. "I'm not interested in a husband and if I was, it wouldn't be *you*."

He just looked at her for a long minute before blurting, "What the hell's wrong with me?"

Kate laughed again. "Wow. Now you're insulted."

"No. Yeah. I guess I am. Why wouldn't you want to marry me?"

"Let's see," she said thoughtfully, tipping her head to one side to look up at him. "For one thing, your first thought was to bolt out of the room when you thought I might be swooning over you."

"I wouldn't bolt," he told her stiffly. "It's snowing."

"Uh-huh. For another, you're irritating."

"Ha!" He flashed a quick grin. "Hello, pot? This is kettle. You're black."

"Funny," she admitted. "Fine. We irritate each other. Good enough reason to steer clear. Another is the fact that you're California and I'm Wyoming. Not exactly geographically desirable. And then there's the fact that anytime I see you in some magazine, you've got a hot blonde with boobs bigger than her IQ on your arm."

"That's sexist," he pointed out wryly.

"I'm a woman. I can say it," she said. "Face it, Sean. You're just not marriage material. You don't want a permanent woman and I have no use for a permanent man, so why on earth would I want to marry you?"

He looked at her for a long moment, then set down his coffee cup and reached for her. She went willingly enough because hey, Kate already knew how amazing he could make her feel.

"All very logical," he said, nodding. "Good points, too. But you left one thing out."

"Yeah? What's that?"

"Sex," he said with a shrug. "Between us, it's incredible."

"Not enough to build a marriage on and why are we still talking about this?" she asked.

"Because I want you to admit you want me."

"I do—just not as a husband."

"I can live with that," he said, one corner of his amazing mouth tipping up into a smile that tugged at something deep inside her. Kate felt herself melting. Sean Ryan was so bad for her. Maybe that's why she was enjoying him so much.

His gaze fixed on her mouth, and she licked her lips in anticipation. When he bent his head and kissed her, she sank into it. This thing between them was powerful, energizing, and she would be a fool not to take everything she could from this interlude before her world went back to normal.

A few hours later, the memory of Kate's laughter was sharp and bright in Sean's mind. He hated knowing that she'd been right about his reaction when she talked about a future. It was knee-jerk for most men, probably. They were, as a species, fairly suspicious, waiting for a woman to get that white-picket-fence gleam in her eye. A man had to stay wary just to make sure he had time to make a clean getaway.

Sean had had it happen to him too many times to count. Every casual relationship he'd ever been in had eventually become a tug-of-war centered around marriage. He knew what the women were thinking—a wedding. Kids. Access to Sean Ryan's fortune. Was it so surprising then that he immediately assumed that Kate was no different?

But, of course, she was, he told himself grimly. Not only was she not interested in snagging him into some kind of relationship, but she also found the very idea laughable and that just annoyed hell out of him.

"The snow's getting to you," he muttered. It was the only explanation, Sean thought. "Being trapped with a woman like Kate is bound to make a man a little nuts."

She was like no one he'd ever known. She filled his thoughts, tormented his body and, at the moment, was working him like a slave driver. Sean was used to running meetings, winning over clients and snagging huge market deals. He had meetings. Dinners. Drinks with a client at some exclusive restaurant.

What he wasn't accustomed to was swinging a hammer. He'd already helped her pull up linoleum in one bathroom, tear down some hideous paneling in what would eventually be the first-floor game room and now he'd been tasked to tear up some—God help him—*shag* carpeting in one of the upstairs suites. He tightened his grip on the worn, wooden handle, slid the claw top beneath the edge of the faded floor covering and pried it loose.

Carpet tacks gave, and Sean tossed the hammer aside to grab the rug with both hands. He pulled it up as he backed across the room and coughed at the years of dust flying into the air. It was hard, dirty work, and he was getting a new appreciation for the men and women who did this kind of thing daily.

Women like Kate. When he first met her a week ago, Sean had seen only the coldly efficient shell of the woman. She knew her job and wasn't afraid to stand up to Sean when she believed she was right. He'd admired that even while arguing with her.

Now he knew more. Knew the heat of her, the passion bubbling right beneath the surface. Knew that even while she gave herself to him, she kept parts of herself locked away. It surprised him to realize how much he wanted to know what she was hiding. And why. She would close him out expertly at the slightest threat of getting too close.

Like you? his mind whispered.

Scowling, he told himself that everyone had secrets. Everyone had pockets of regret or guilt or misery tucked away that were rarely brought out to be inspected. His were his own business—hell, even Mike didn't know about them—and so he would leave Kate with hers.

What lay between them was desire born of convenience. That was it. So he'd work, he'd sleep with her and then when they finally got the hell out of this damned hotel, he'd go home. Where he belonged and where he could put this whole situation into perspective.

"Nice job."

She moved quietly. He turned to look at Kate, standing in the open doorway. Sean didn't want to admit, even to himself, what seeing her wearing a damn tool belt did to him. She looked confident and too damned sexy for his peace of mind. Her worn jeans hugged her legs, the hem of her tunic sweater hung to her hips and her boots were as scarred as his own. The tool belt that was currently driving him insane fit her as undeniably as diamonds might another woman.

Man, he was losing it fast.

"Thanks," he said wryly. "But pulling up old carpet doesn't take a lot of finesse."

"Just time and effort," she agreed, then walked into the room and skirted around him and the roll of carpet. She went down to one knee to examine the wood floor that had been hidden beneath the ratty carpet. "Looks good," she mused, more to herself than to him. "I was hoping for this. Hardwood, even battered and scarred like this, can be sanded and brought back to life a lot cheaper than buying new floors throughout."

Nodding, he watched her stroke her fingertips over the wide planks with the same gentleness she'd used to caress his chest. His body stirred, and he gritted his teeth, ignoring the flash of heat.

She whipped her ponytail back out of her way and glanced at him. "If all the floors look this good, we'll be saving you a lot of money."

"Always a good thing," he agreed.

She stood. "I've got the rugs in two other rooms rolled up and their floors are nearly perfect, so I'm hopeful. What I'd like to do now is check out the basement, see what we've got down there."

"Didn't you already do that when you made your first inspection for your bid on the job?"

"Sure." She shrugged and rested one hand on the hammer hanging from her belt. "But it was a quick look, mainly checking for foundation issues. Now that we've got some time…"

He laughed shortly. "Plenty of that."

"Exactly. We can look at it and see what improvements can be made."

One eyebrow winged up. "We're done pulling up carpet?"

"I just wanted to get an idea of the shape of the floors. The rest my crew can do when the storm's over."

One glance at the window told Sean the snow was still swirling like a thick white veil. "If it's ever over."

"It will be. I've been through these storms all my life."

"Not me," he said with a sigh born of missing the ocean, the sand, the sea breeze. "I'm a surf-and-sand kind of guy."

"You'll be back to it soon," she told him, and their gazes locked for one tension-filled moment. "For now, though...the basement?"

"Why not?" He shrugged, following her as she headed downstairs, and his gaze dropped unerringly to the curve of her behind. Whatever else the woman was, she had a great butt and the ability to work him into an inferno without even trying. He had to admire that even while it made him a little crazy.

"The banisters will have to be tightened," she said over her shoulder. "The base is loose and you don't want it wobbly."

"Absolutely not." He gave said banister a shake and felt it wiggle under his hand. Right again, he thought, then told himself this was why he'd hired her in the first place. Kate Wells had a reputation for being a perfectionist when it came to her work, and that was something he understood and approved of.

She hit the bottom of the stairs and headed across the great room, where the fire still burned against the constant chill in the room. Through the kitchen and into the butler's pantry, she opened the door to the basement and started down the stairs.

The light spilled from two overhead lamps, illuminating a wide room that was empty but for a line of dated washing machines and dryers. There was a workbench along one wall and a pegboard above it, just waiting for someone to fill it with tools. The floor was cement, the windows were narrow and high, blocked now with piles of snow. The walls were cement blocks, which only seemed to magnify the cold outside the building.

"I always thought basements were a little creepy," Sean said to himself.

"Agreed," Kate said, throwing him a quick look as she pulled out a measuring tape and laid it down on the floor as she walked off the space. "But they don't have to be. Still, having the laundry down here doesn't seem real handy for the housekeeping staff." She paused to make note of numbers on a small memo pad she dug out of her tool belt. "Especially since they have to come and go through the kitchen."

"You're right." Nodding, he glanced back up the stairs before reluctantly admitting, "I wouldn't have thought of that. But if the kitchen staff is busy, then having housekeeping coming and going will make everyone's job harder than it has to be."

She made a few more notations, then wound the tape back into its shell. With it tucked away, she inspected the block walls and said, "A little insulation down here would make it more livable."

"Another good idea," he said. "Do it."

"That was easy." She looked at him. "And since

you're being so reasonable, what do you think about moving the laundry facilities to the old owner's suite? It's on the other side of the hotel, opposite the great room, and there's plenty of space for water and electrical hookup, plus worktables for the folding or ironing or whatever is needed."

Sean pulled the layout of the hotel into his mind and could see it just as she'd described it. "Yeah, that'd work. Be easier for everyone. But then we've got an empty basement and don't really need the insulation, do we?"

"Of course we do," she argued neatly. "Insulating down here will help keep the floors above warmer, cutting down on heating bills. And you could set this up as a tool room for the maintenance crew you'll need to hire."

He walked down the rest of the steps, stopped beside her and laughed shortly. "And they *won't* get in the way upstairs in the kitchen."

"Nope," she told him before walking across the room to slap one hand against the wall. "Because we'll cut out a double door right here, with a ramp, so maintenance can get heavy tools and machinery in and out with no problem. Gives them easy access to what they need, and you know you'll need riding mowers and at least a couple of snowblowers, as well. They can be stored down here. There's plenty of space for everything you could ever need."

He could see it once she'd painted the picture, and Sean was only a little annoyed that he hadn't seen it before. But why would he? He'd never used a snowblower in his life and since he lived in a condo at the beach, he really didn't need a lawn mower, either, did he?

Unaccustomed to having to work out solutions for anything other than how to market their next video game, he was stumbling around in the dark here. And all in all, he thought he was doing a pretty damn good job of it.

"Okay, it's a good plan."

She just looked at him for a long moment, then cocked her head and asked, "Why are you being so agreeable all of a sudden? We spent the first week you were in Wyoming arguing about everything."

She had a point there, too. But from the first, she'd gotten under his skin. Sean hadn't wanted to admit it was desire chewing at his insides, so instead he'd told himself her attitude was aggravating. Maybe she'd had some great ideas all along and he'd just been too distracted by what she did to him to hear her out. And that knowledge was lowering for a man who had always prided himself on his ability to focus.

"Things change," he finally said.

"I guess that's true enough." She came toward him, but instead of stopping alongside him, she walked past and took the stairs back up to the main floor.

"What're you doing now?"

She stopped in the threshold and was backlit by the kitchen light. Her face in shadows, he felt her smile more than he could see it. "As long as you're in such a good mood," she said, "I figured we could start tearing down one of the walls to check the wiring."

He choked out a laugh. "Seriously?"

"Okay, not the whole wall, but we should be able to at least rip away enough drywall to take a peek."

"And you want to do construction while we're trapped in a blizzard, why?"

"We can't stay in bed all day," she said.

His body burned at the thought. "Don't see why not."

"Of course you don't. And what you and I will be doing upstairs is not construction," she insisted, flipping her ponytail behind her. "It's more *de*-struction. What we in the building business lovingly call 'demo day.'"

"Great. Demo."

"Come on. You'll like it."

Well, he told himself as he climbed the stairs, if they weren't going to be having sex, at least he could take out his frustrations with a hammer.

Five

They worked together all day, with Kate keeping them too busy and occupied for either of them to consider heading back to the sleeping bag. Though the temptation of it nibbled at her continuously. How could she not think of it? Sean had opened up a world of sensations she'd never expected. And she wanted to feel them all again in spite of the fact that her mind kept warning her off. Logically, her mind was absolutely right and her body should take a time-out.

The problem was, what she was feeling had nothing to do with logic. When the day finally ended and the snow was still falling, she was out of distractions. They shared another meal from their dwindling supplies and when they were finished, Sean reached for her and she went to him. Knowing it was a mistake to continue doing what she knew she shouldn't, Kate still couldn't stop herself. There was so much to be discovered in his arms, and she wanted—needed—to know everything.

But sometime during the night, the snow finally stopped. By morning, the sky was a brilliant blue and the sunshine on all the fresh snow shone like diamonds under a spotlight. Kate should have been relieved, happy that this forced togetherness was at an end. Instead, she really wasn't.

"How long do you think it'll take for the pass to be cleared?" Sean asked.

She glanced at him standing beside her at the wall of windows in the great room. "A few hours. The county plows will get to it fast."

"Then all we'll have to do is dig out the driveway so we can get your truck out of the garage."

"We won't have to." She smiled to herself and shook her head. "Now that the storm's over, I'll call one of my crew. Raul's got a snow blade for his pickup. He makes extra cash plowing mountain roads for residents. He can get up here to clear this as soon as the county's done with the pass."

"So we're almost free," he mused quietly.

"Yep," she quipped, hoping for a light tone that would hide the yawning pit of emptiness opening up inside her. "Your nightmare ends today."

He took her arm, turned her to face him and when she did, his gaze moved over her face like a touch. "I wouldn't say nightmare."

She wished she could read his eyes, see what he was thinking, but whatever he was feeling was carefully masked. "No?"

He shook his head. "Let's think of it as a three-day seminar. Sean and Kate 101."

In spite of everything, a tiny chuckle escaped her. She had learned a lot about Sean. Maybe too much, but it was too late to go back and *un*-learn it even if she wanted to. "And now class is over."

"Almost." He moved in, set his hands at her waist and effortlessly lifted her against him until she had no choice but to hook her legs around his hips. He stared into her eyes, then gave her a slow, wicked smile. "I think we have time for one more recess."

God, he really *was* charming, she thought. She stared into those lake-blue eyes of his and knew that when he was gone, she was going to miss him. She didn't want to. She'd like to go back to her old life and leave these few days with Sean in the past, where they belonged. But that, she realized now, would be impossible.

He'd touched more than her body during their time together. He'd reached into her heart and brought it back to life again. And with that life she knew there would be pain. But for now, there was still joy to be found.

"Exercise is important," she said.

"There you go."

Two days later, Sean was back in California. He deliberately jumped back into his real life, diving into the plans and strategies for launching their next video game, "The Wild Hunt," in early summer. While he talked to distributors, marketing and the Celtic Knot website division, he was able to push thoughts of Kate out of his mind. He buried himself in work until the memory of a snowbound hotel and a tiny, gorgeous woman with a pit-bull attitude were nothing more than misty images nibbling at his brain. Which was just the way he liked it, he assured himself. His focus was on the job, where it belonged. Wyoming was a long way from Long Beach, California.

Just as well. Despite the snow and the cold and the fact that they had lived on coffee, shared sandwiches, cookies and crackers, Sean had been getting way too comfortable in that drafty old hotel. Nights spent with Kate in his arms, waking up with her sprawled across his body while a roaring fire hissed and crackled in the stillness was just too…*something*, he told himself, not really wanting to identify the feeling any more than that. Being there with her had confused the situation. Getting back to their own lives and their own work were the only real answers for either of them.

So why, then, was he in such a crappy mood? He'd already snapped at Linda, their admin, rejected their lead artist's idea for the upcoming Christmas game and managed to insult one of their biggest clients. And it wasn't even noon.

"There something you want to talk about, Sean?"

"What?" He looked up and saw his brother, Mike, standing in the open doorway of Sean's office. "No." He picked up a sheaf of papers and rattled them for emphasis. "Busy here."

"Yeah," Mike said, walking into the room and dropping into the visitor's chair opposite Sean. "Me, too. So let's wade through all of the denials and get down to whatever it is that's got your shorts in a knot."

Family could be a real pain. Especially an older brother who saw too much and knew you too well. Shooting that brother a dirty look, Sean asked, "When did you get so insightful all of a sudden?"

"When Dave tells me you eighty-sixed the sketch of the Nightmare Pooka. Linda was crying at her desk.

And oh, yeah, Dexter Stevens called to complain about your attitude."

"That's rich," Sean muttered, deliberately refusing to pick up the gauntlet of guilt Mike was tossing him. "Dave's drawing was mediocre at best—"

"Preliminary sketch," Mike added.

"Since Linda got pregnant, she cries when the phone rings—"

"And so she doesn't need *you* giving her more to be upset about," Mike interrupted.

"As for Dexter," Sean continued as if his brother hadn't spoken at all, "he's given us plenty of grief over the last two years, and we've never called him on it."

"Yeah," Mike said, "because his distribution network moved almost two million units of 'Fate Castle.'"

Sean frowned, remembering their first major best seller game. All right, Mike had a point there. Dexter had given the beta version of the game to his teenage sons, and they'd loved it. With their recommendation, Dexter's company had covered the entire northeastern portion of the country with "Fate Castle" at a substantial discount that had pushed Celtic Knot up to the next level. Was Dexter a jerk personally? Sure. But he was also hell on wheels at distribution, and they couldn't afford to offend him.

In self-defense, though, Sean scrubbed one hand across his face and blew out a breath. "Dexter Stevens is a pain in the—"

"And has been for years," Mike said, cutting him off. "Still no reason to give one of our best partners such a hard time."

He was right, but Sean didn't want to admit it. His first day back at work, and he was making everyone as miserable as he was. Upside to this situation? Dexter would be fine once Sean apologized—which he would do as soon as he could get Mike out of his office.

Normally, dealing with their suppliers, clients and distributors was something Sean enjoyed. He liked people and figuring out how to work with the different personalities he encountered. But today, he simply hadn't had the patience to deal with Dexter, and that was his own fault.

"Yeah," Sean muttered. "I'll call him later. Offer to send him an early version of 'The Wild Hunt' for his kids."

"Great. So want to tell me what's going on with you?"

"Nothing. Everything's good." Sean sat back, kicked his feet up to the corner of his desk and folded his hands on his abdomen. The casual stance didn't fool his brother.

"Sell that to someone who doesn't know you." Mike cocked his head to study Sean. "Things were fine before you got snowed in. So. Want to tell me what happened in the hotel between you and Kate?"

That'd be the day. Hell, looking back at it all from a safe distance, even *he* wasn't sure what had happened between him and Kate. And he was really trying not to think about any of it. So, instead of answering, Sean asked a question of his own. "Want to tell me what's going on between you and Jenny?"

For some reason, Mike and Jenny Marshall, one of the artists at Celtic Knot, got along as well as a lit match and a stick of dynamite. But Sean had the distinct impression something was going on between them. His first clue was the way Mike went cold and silent the minute Jenny's name was mentioned. Like now, for instance.

Instantly, Mike's features tightened and his eyes shuttered. *Ha*, Sean thought. *Not so much fun prying when it's your secrets being uncovered, is it?*

"Jenny's doing a good job at the Laughlin hotel."

"Uh-huh. Nice stall and, hey, extra points for evasion," Sean said with a knowing smile. "What's she doing to *you*?"

Mike's eyes narrowed, and he pushed himself to his feet. "Fine," he said tightly. "You made your point. You don't want to talk about Kate and I don't want to talk about Jenny, so let all of this rest and get back to work."

Satisfied, Sean nodded. "Sounds like a plan."

Mike headed for the door but stopped long enough to add, "And don't piss off any more of our clients, okay?"

When he was alone again, Sean swiveled his chair around to look out the window at the backyard. The majestic old Victorian mansion where Celtic Knot made its offices sat on Pacific Coast Highway. Just across the wide, busy street, the ocean stretched out to the horizon and from the back of the house, the view was a large, neatly tended yard. Of course now, in the middle of a Southern California winter, the grass was brown and the gardens desolate but for a few lingering chrysanthemums. Overhead, the sky was clear with white clouds scudding along like sailboats on an endless sea. He was a long way from Wyoming, Sean told himself.

So why was he daydreaming about snow?

It was snowing again.

Kate listened to the Muzak coming through her phone while she was on hold and looked through the front window, watching as a thick, white blanket fell from steel-gray skies. It wasn't a blizzard—she and her crew wouldn't be snowbound here at the hotel. It was just another Wyoming winter storm, and it made her think of Sean and how only a few days ago the two of them had been alone here.

She missed him.

Kate hadn't expected that at all. He had been such an irritation at first that all she had wanted was for him to leave, go back to California. Now? She wished he was there. She ached for him, and that was hard to accept.

"Ms. Wells?"

The music ended abruptly, and Kate dragged her mind back to work. Much, much better than thinking about Sean, which wouldn't do her any good at all. "Yes. I'm here. And I'm wondering why my Dumpsters aren't."

"Well, now," the condescending male voice on the other end of the line said, "I understand you're a little impatient, but we won't be able to haul the Dumpsters through the pass for another day or two at least."

Kate gritted her teeth, took a slow, deep breath and said, "The pass is clear, Henry, and I need those Dumpsters on-site."

He chuckled, and Kate wanted to scream.

"In case you hadn't noticed, missie, it's snowing again, and we don't want to get halfway through the pass and find we can't maneuver the rest of the way."

They both knew this storm was no issue. But Kate was also aware that pushing Henry Jackson wouldn't get her anywhere. "Fine. Then I can expect them here by Friday?"

"As long as the weather holds," he said, managing to agree and not promise a thing.

"Fine. Thank you." That cost her, but Henry was the closest supplier. If she had to arrange for someone else to deliver Dumpsters, it could take twice as long. So she'd make nice for the good of the job and hope he came through. Eventually.

When she hung up, she stayed where she was until her annoyance dropped a couple of levels. "If the snow was so bad, we wouldn't be here working, would we?" she asked herself. "The pass is clear, Henry's just lazy, which you already knew."

If the pass was still blocked, she and Sean would still be trapped here, just the two of them. A ping of something sad and sweet echoed in the center of her chest, and she absently rubbed the spot, futilely hoping to ease it. It didn't help.

"Yo, boss!"

Kate looked up, to where Raul stood at the head of the stairs. "What is it?"

"With no Dumpsters here, where do you want us to pile all the stuff we're tearing out?"

Kate scowled, glanced around the hotel, then back up to the tall man waiting for her decision. "Right now, just toss everything out a window to a clear spot in the yard. We'll load up the Dumpsters when Henry finally decides to bring them up."

"You got it."

Twice the work, twice the time, but there was nothing else to do about it. Kate figured she could do one of two things. Keep thinking about Sean and wondering what he was doing right now. Or she could get to work on this hotel and keep herself too occupied to think about the man who had so briefly lit up her world.

Grimly, she set off for the kitchen. Tearing out old cabinets ought to keep her busy enough.

Sean spent the next few weeks working on the Celtic Knot game plan. Focused, he could avoid thoughts of Wyoming and what had happened there until it was only in sleep that memories of Kate swung around to haunt him.

When he'd first returned home, he'd done his best to make images of her and those snowbound days fade from his mind by going out with other women. Lots of women. But none of them had managed to get his attention. He took them dancing, to fancy dinners and concerts, and within twenty minutes of every damn date, Sean was bored and his mind was drifting. After a few weeks, he stopped trying. Just wasn't worth the effort. He figured it was a sign from the universe, telling him to forget about *all* women for a while and concentrate on his company. Sooner or later, he'd get back to decorating his bed with beautiful women. Until then, he poured what concentration he could find into the work.

He was still talking to companies about making a set of collectible figures based on the characters from some of their biggest games. He was also in talks about developing a board game based on "Fate Castle" to capture the imaginations of those few people who preferred their games in the real world rather than the digital one.

Then there were the storyboards to go over, checking out the dialogue and scene shots for their upcoming Christmas release, and that didn't take into account setting the groundwork for the first Celtic Knot convention—along the lines of the big fantasy cons, but set solely around the Celtic Knot video games.

The Wyoming hotel was their only holding big enough to accommodate a con of any kind and now that Sean had both Mike and their partner, Brady Finn, on board with the idea, Sean had to get things rolling.

That meant, whether he wanted to or not, he had to talk to Kate about it. The fact that there was a part of him looking forward to seeing her face again was something he didn't want to think about. Over the last several weeks, they'd communicated mostly through email, except for one phone call that had been brief and unsatisfying. Hearing her voice had sparked his memories even as the distance between them had sharpened the frustration gnawing at him.

His cell phone beeped, and he glanced at it. Today would be a video chat, and he wasn't at all sure if it would be better or worse to actually see her face when he spoke to her. On the second beep, he grabbed it and answered. Kate's face popped up on the screen, and he felt a jolt of something that was part pleasure, part irritation. Why'd she have to look so damn good?

"Kate," he said tightly. "Good to see you."

"Hello, Sean." She paused as if she was considering what to say, so he spoke up to fill the void.

"I wanted to talk to you about plans for the conventions we'll want to hold at the hotel."

"Right." She nodded. "You told me a little about your plans when you were here."

"Yeah." Her eyes were direct, and so blue he felt as though he could fall into them and drown. Not easy to keep your mind on work when you were looking into those eyes, he told himself. "It's why we're going to need those extra cabins."

"Oh," she said, perking up, "I wanted to talk to you about the cabins, too."

"Okay, but first tell me how much progress you're making." Because while she talked he could enjoy watching her. The flicker of emotion on her face, the shine in her eyes, the way her mouth moved…

"Well," she said, "the interior work is going great. We've got most of the kitchen finished, and the quartz counters will be going in by the end of the week…"

She kept talking, detailing the work being done, and he knew he should be more focused on it. He, his brother and Brady Finn had each been in charge of a hotel's makeover, turning them into exact replicas of one of their bestselling games.

Fans all over the world were already lining up to stay in "Fate Castle" in Ireland, where Brady lived, and the Laughlin hotel based on the "River Haunt" game was next, probably opening around Christmas in conjunction with the latest game being released. Then there was this one.

Sean's hotel was based on "Forest Run," a game featuring soulless creatures, brave knights, sorcerers and Faery warriors. This hotel strategy was important, as it offered their gamers the chance to live out the fantasies of the games. It was one of the next big steps Celtic Knot was taking to push them into the stratosphere of success.

So yeah, Sean should be listening, making notes, but instead, all he saw were Kate's eyes, and he remembered how they looked with firelight dancing in their depths. He saw her mouth moving and nearly felt the soft glide of her kisses across his chest. She flipped her ponytail back over her shoulder, but he saw a thick mass of soft black hair spilling around her face as she rode him to completion.

"So, what do you think?"

"What?" His brain tried to catch up. To sift through what she'd said to pick out a few key words so he wouldn't have to admit he hadn't been listening. "The cottages?"

She rolled her beautiful eyes. "Yeah. What do you think about the new idea for their design?"

Stall, he told himself. *Use that charm you're always insisting you have.* "Well, it's not easy to make a decision without more than just a description."

Her eyes narrowed on him. "Yeah, I thought you'd say that. So I had my friend Molly draw these up. She's not one of your artists, but she's better at it than I am." She held up a tablet and showed him a raw, rough sketch. Intrigued, he brought the phone closer to examine what she was showing him. His first reaction was that he liked the idea very much.

Instead of a squat, square cabin as they'd first discussed, she'd come up with something that would look…almost mystical.

"It's sort of based on caravan wagons," she was saying as she flipped pages to show him more.

He could see the inspiration behind the drawings. The cabins themselves looked like half circles, resting on the flat edge. Walls and roofs curved with arched doorways brought to mind fantasy houses from fairy stories. Each one would be singular, individual, he saw, as he studied the different drawings. He could see it, the small, rounded cabins nestled in the forest, surrounded by flowers and trees, their brightly colored doors signaling welcome. Hell, he thought, people would stand in line to stay in those cabins.

When she was finished and faced him on the screen again, she asked, "So? Shall we go with these? I'm asking now because the ground's getting soft enough to start excavation. We'll have to install a new septic system, centrally located so we can connect all the cabins to it. Once that's in, we'd like to lay foundations for the cabins themselves."

"Septic system," he repeated with a short laugh.

"Well, yeah," she said. "We're too far from the county sewer lines to hook into them, and the hotel's tank isn't big enough to handle the extra load from the cabins."

He chuckled again and pushed one hand through his hair.

"What's so funny?"

"This conversation," he told her. "I don't think I've ever discussed sewers with a lover before."

"Ex-lover," she amended quickly.

A ping of something sharp and cold shot through him, but he let it pass. "Point taken. Okay, yeah. I like the drawings a lot. Make sure you leave the walls blank for our artists to come in and paint murals based on the game."

"Right," she said, all business again. "We're on that. And in the hotel, we've got acres of white walls just waiting for them. I think we should wait until most of the work's done before you send anyone out, though."

"Agreed." He turned his chair until he was facing the window with a view of the backyard and the flowers beginning to bloom there. Spring was coming, and he wondered if all the snow at the hotel had melted yet. Not the point, he reminded himself. "Fax me those sketches, will you? I want to show them to Mike and the artists. Run them past an architect and get some plans. They'll probably need refining, too."

"I'll send them this afternoon."

"Okay," Sean said and wanted to ask how she was.

"Then, I guess that's it." She looked over her shoulder and it wasn't until then that Sean keyed into the background noise of hammers and saws. "I should get back to work."

"Yeah," he said. "Me, too."

"So, good," she said, nodding. "Everything's good. I'll keep you posted with emails about the progress here."

"That'll work." His gaze locked onto her face even though he knew that seeing her like this would only feed the dreams that were already tormenting him nightly. That fact annoyed him, so his voice was brusquer than he'd intended when he said, "I'll expect those faxes today."

"You'll have them. Look," she said, "I've gotta go."

"Yeah, me, too," he said again and noticed that neither one of them was making a move to hang up. Were they twelve? That spurred him to action. "All right. Thanks for checking in and for the suggestions."

"You're welcome. Bye." And she was gone.

In the sudden silence of his empty office, Sean felt a chill far deeper than he'd experienced in a snowbound hotel.

Six

Five months later

His brother was married.

Sean was having a hard time getting his head around it, but facts were facts. Jenny Marshall was now Jenny Ryan—a new bride and pregnant with their first child. The baby had been a surprise and had really knocked Mike off his game for a while. But he'd come around, worked out his own issues and finally realized in time that Jenny was the only woman for him.

The Balboa Pavilion was the perfect spot for a summer wedding, too. He glanced around at the stately old Victorian, with its wide view of Newport Bay and the hundreds of pleasure crafts lining the docks. The dance floor was gleaming beneath thousands of tiny white lights and beyond the glass walls, a summer moon shone down on it all as if in celebration.

Sean's gaze shifted back to where his brother and Jenny were dancing, holding each other as if they were the only two people in the world. Times change, Sean told himself as he leaned negligently against a wall. Not too long ago, Mike and Jenny had been at each other's throats. Now they were pledging eternal love and about to be parents. Speaking of parents... Sean turned his head to look at his own folks. Jack and Peggy Ryan looked as happy as he'd ever seen them. He frowned thoughtfully and took a sip of the aged Scotch in his hand.

His parents' marriage had always seemed pretty damn perfect to Sean. It was only recently that he'd learned what Mike had discovered at the tender age of thirteen—that parents were people who made mistakes. It still didn't sit well with him that Mike had kept the secret of the trouble in their parents' marriage to himself for so many years. But on the other hand, Sean mused as he watched his mom lean her head on his dad's shoulder, Sean had secrets of his own.

He'd never actually lied to the family about anything, but he'd never told them everything, either. So he really wasn't in a position to complain too loud or too long.

But this wasn't the time to think about the past. This was about Mike and Jenny, who had somehow gone from antagonism to the kind of love most people never knew.

Naturally, thinking about antagonists brought him around to thoughts of Kate. But to be honest, his mind was always ready to dredge up Kate's image. Five months and he could still smell her. Taste her. Her face swam in his mind every night when he tried to sleep. It wasn't getting better. If anything, his brain seemed to be working overtime reminding him about Kate, as if to ensure he didn't forget.

As if he could. Memories of their days and nights together kept his body at a slow burn constantly. Maybe, he told himself, it was time to go back to Wyoming. Check on the hotel's progress in person rather than reading about it in faxed reports and sterile emails. And while he was at it, he could see Kate again and resolve whatever the hell was gnawing at him. He had no doubt that his memories were playing with him, convincing him that Kate was more than she really was. Making the memories of the incredible, breathtaking sex they'd shared wildly better than the reality. Seeing her again could clear up all of that. Help him put things in perspective so he could finally get her the hell out of his head.

With that thought in mind, he stepped away from the music and the crowd, pulled his cell phone out of his pocket and hit the number for a video chat. After a couple of rings, she answered and the instant her face appeared on the screen, his body tightened in response.

What was it about this one woman?

"Sean?" She didn't look happy to see him. Her eyes narrowed and she bit at her bottom lip before saying, "I wasn't expecting to hear from you." She glanced away, then back, as if she was reluctant to meet his eyes. "We're, um, kind of busy here. Is there a problem?"

He hadn't thought so, but he was changing his mind fast. Whatever else Kate was, she wasn't a game player. And judging by her expression right now, she shouldn't play poker.

"You tell me," he said, moving farther from the festivities so he could hear her better. He left the Pavilion and stepped out into the summer night, where the music from inside was muffled and the slap of water against the dock sounded like a heartbeat. "Something wrong?"

"No," she assured him quickly. "Everything's fine. Great, really. Uh, what's all the music I hear?"

"My brother, Mike, just got married. I'm at the reception."

"Oh, that's nice." She bit her lip again. "Um, I'm a little busy, Sean."

Anxious. Why?

"Yeah," he said shortly. "Me, too, so why don't you save us both some time and tell me what's going on?"

She took a breath and impatiently huffed it out again. "Fine. We're making serious progress on the hotel and—"

She kept talking, but Sean was hardly listening. Instead he watched her face and studied the secrecy shining in her eyes. There was something going on, and she clearly didn't want to talk to him about it. If it was job related, she wouldn't have a problem. He already knew that Kate took her work as seriously as he took his. She was on schedule with the remodel, so what the hell was it that could make her so clearly uneasy about talking to him? Did she have a new man in her life?

Sean really didn't like that thought. Gritting his teeth, he interrupted her rapid flow of words with one sharp question. "Why are you so nervous about talking to me?"

"Nervous?" She forced a laugh, then shook her head so hard her ponytail swung like a pendulum behind her head. "I'm not nervous, Sean. Just busy. We're at a critical stage in the job, and I should be out supervising the concrete pour for the cabin foundations. I really don't have time for this, Sean."

"Is that right?" His voice was cool, distant, but she didn't seem to notice.

She smiled, but it didn't touch the shadows in her eyes. "Absolutely. I appreciate you checking in, but everything's good. I'll contact you next week. You should really go enjoy the wedding."

"Uh-huh."

"Sorry, one of my guys is calling for me. Gotta run." Then she hung up.

Sean was left staring at his phone while behind him, music, laughter and celebration rang out. She was lying. Or if not lying then at least hiding something. The question was *what*? And *why*? Scowling, he slipped the phone back into his pocket and turned to head back into the reception. The temper he hadn't really experienced since the last time he was with Kate was back now. She had *hung up on him*. Nobody did that to Sean Ryan.

The damn woman was apparently *still* convinced that she was in charge. Giving him the brush-off? Saying she was too busy to talk to him? Yeah, that wasn't going to fly.

He turned his gaze out to the dance floor, where his brother was dancing with their mom and Jenny was dancing with her uncle Hank. And while he watched everyone, his mind was at work. After the party, Mike and Jenny were heading out for a weeklong honeymoon. The minute they got back, Sean told himself, he'd be taking another trip to Wyoming to check out the situation for himself.

"Let's see her avoid me when I'm standing right in front of her," he muttered.

* * *

"Why don't I ever get snowbound with a gorgeous bazillionaire?" Molly Feeney plopped into one of Kate's comfy chairs and picked up her wineglass from the nearby table.

"Because you're lucky?" Kate asked.

"Please." Molly took a sip of her chardonnay and said, "Women around the world would have *loved* to be snowbound with Sean Ryan. He's…" She paused and slapped one hand to her heart. "I'm feeling a little faint."

Kate laughed at the drama. "That's because you haven't met him."

"You could fix that and introduce me," Molly said.

"I like you too much," Kate told her.

Laughing, Molly said, "Come on. It's not like he's an ogre."

No, he wasn't. This would all be so much easier if he was. Instead, he was as charming as he claimed to be, along with irritating, funny, frustrating. He made her feel too many things at once, which was just one reason why she should be grateful he'd gone back home to California. Having several hundred miles between them seemed much safer to Kate.

"Molly, those three days in the hotel changed everything for me," Kate mused, grabbing her tea for a long drink.

"You don't seem to be suffering for it, though," Molly pointed out with a smile.

"No, I'm not," Kate said. Suffering, no. Worrying? You bet. Along with guilt and too many other wildly divergent emotions to even consider listing.

When Sean first left Wyoming, it had been hard. She'd gotten accustomed to seeing him every day, having him challenge her both on the job and personally. She'd thought her life would be easier once he was gone. She hadn't expected to miss him, hadn't wanted to admit even to herself how deeply he'd gotten to her. But the truth was difficult to ignore, and lying to yourself never did any good because you knew the truth no matter what you told yourself. *And now I'm officially rambling*.

"Maybe if you weren't hiding…" Molly cradled her wineglass between her palms.

"Don't start." Kate shook her head and frowned at her very best friend. Molly had been dogging her about this for months. Heck, so had Kate's father, for that matter. But no matter what anyone had to say, she knew what she was doing. She'd made a decision, and she was sticking to it. "I'm doing the right thing."

Hadn't she dreamed of this very situation for years? When Sam died, Kate had accepted that those dreams were gone. Now, she had a chance to grab hold of them, and she wouldn't let it go.

"Right for who?" Molly asked, tipping her head to one side until her long, strawberry blond hair fell in a curtain of curls.

"For me. For Sean." She paused, thought about it, then nodded for emphasis. "For everyone."

"Your life, sweetie," Molly said. "And God knows I hate to interfere—"

Kate snorted.

Molly's eyebrows arched. "*But* secrets are hard to keep. The truth will eventually jump up and bite you in the butt at the worst possible time."

Kate didn't want to believe that, so she made a joke instead. "Is that a sort of variation on Murphy's Law?"

"I'm Irish," Molly told her. "We're all about Murphy's Law and all of its subsidiaries." Sighing a little, she set down her glass on the table and braced her forearms on her knees. "At least think about it, Kate."

"Molly, I have been thinking about it. For the last five months I've pretty much done nothing else *but* think about it."

"Thinking about it with your mind closed to all possibilities but the one you want isn't really thinking, is it?"

Another quick stab of guilt. "Aren't you supposed to be on my side?"

"Oh, I am, sweetie. You know that." Molly sighed. "I'm just saying that sooner or later, all secrets are blown. And it might be better if you did it yourself. You know?"

Kate let her head fall back and her gaze fix on the heavy wood beams spanning the ceiling of her cottage-style bungalow. Her friend had a point, she knew, but it was one Kate didn't want to acknowledge. "Maybe you're right, Molly. I don't know. All I'm really sure of is I can't say anything. The gorgeous bazillionaire wouldn't be interested anyway."

"Fine. I won't say anything else about it."

Oh, she didn't believe that. Molly was like a dog with a bone, and she was very protective of her friends and family. If she thought she could help, she'd never give up. But for now, Kate sighed. "Thanks. That'd be great."

When the doorbell rang, Molly jumped up and said, "I'll get it. You stay put."

Kate sipped at her tea, heard the front door open and then heard her friend's voice go soft and flirty. "Well, hi. Where'd you come from?"

"California," a familiar, deep voice said flatly. "I'm here to see Kate Wells. Is she home?"

Stomach flipping and churning, mouth going dry as dust, Kate slowly stood up, set her teacup aside and tried to harness the wild gallop of her heartbeat. This could *not* be happening. She held her breath when Molly said, "And you are?"

"Sean Ryan."

Kate groaned and half hoped that she was having some sort of weird walking dream. If she pinched herself, maybe Sean wouldn't really be walking toward her. Molly wouldn't be behind him mouthing the word *wow*, and she herself wouldn't be wearing an old T-shirt and denim shorts.

But it wasn't a dream. Sean was right in front of her, and his gaze was locked on her belly. "You're *pregnant*?"

She dropped one hand to the swell of her baby as if to protect her from hearing her parents argue even before she was born. Instantly, she went for outrage. "Sean, what're you doing here?"

If you had no defense, she reminded herself, go for a strong offense. All those years watching football games with her dad was finally paying off.

"Seriously? That's what you have to say?" He stopped, shook his head, then shoved both hands through his hair. "Are you kidding me?"

"Um," Molly said from behind Sean, "I think I'm gonna go. Looks like you two have some talking to do—"

Kate wanted to reach out and grab hold of her friend as if she was a life preserver. But what was the point?

That would only be delaying the inevitable. Sean was here. He knew the truth. Bag open, cat out. So with absolutely no other choice, Kate told herself it was best to just put it all on the table.

"I'll call you tomorrow," Kate told her, still staring at Sean.

Sean never took his gaze from the mound of Kate's belly, so he didn't see Molly miming fanning herself because he was so hot. Okay, yes, Kate thought, Sean was truly an amazing male. But right now, it wasn't desire that was pouring through her, no matter how good it felt to see him again. Panic had the upper hand at the moment.

His blue eyes lifted to meet hers, and she saw the banked fury sizzling there. "Were you ever going to tell me?" he ground out the minute the front door shut behind Molly.

"Probably not," she admitted. "At least, not unless I absolutely had to." Kate had considered this situation from every which way for the last five months. While her child grew inside her, Kate had remembered the horrified look on Sean's face when he'd thought she was trying to trap him into something permanent. Remembered him telling her he had nothing against kids, he just had no interest in having one himself.

"Sean, don't you remember? You made a point of saying you didn't want a family. You were appalled at the thought of it. Why would I tell you about my baby?"

He took a step toward her, then stopped dead as if he was too angry to get closer. "You want to use what I said about a hypothetical situation to explain you *lying* to me for five months? Not gonna work. You should have told me, Kate. Because it's *our* baby."

Kate flushed and kept her protective hand against her belly. "Fine. Technically, you're right…"

"Technically?" he repeated, eyes wide.

She ignored that. God, she'd imagined this conversation a million times over the last few months, whenever her guilt would get the best of her, and she pictured what might happen if Sean found out. And in none of those imaginings had he looked this…ferocious.

"Maybe I should have told you."

He choked out a short laugh.

"But it wouldn't have changed the reality, Sean. The fact is, I want the baby, you don't."

He managed to look even more shocked than he had at his first glance at her, and she couldn't blame him. He was so angry, his blue eyes glinted with icy shards. Deliberately, Kate lifted her chin, met his hard gaze and prepared to do battle.

This baby meant everything to Kate. It was a gift from a universe that had already taken too much from her. She wouldn't lose this child. Wouldn't share it with a man who, if he didn't already, would one day resent its very existence.

"I've talked to you dozens of times over the last five months," he said, his voice quiet, glacial. "Emails. Faxes. Phone calls. *Video* calls. And not *once* did you find the time to say 'By the way, I'm pregnant?'"

Truth was, Kate had been in a kind of fog for the first three months of her pregnancy. At first, she hadn't believed it. Then she'd realized what a miracle had happened. She was finally going to have the family she'd believed lost to her when Sam died. She didn't need a husband, but she needed this baby.

So did Sean.

His heart was pounding, and it felt like he'd taken a hard punch to the gut. He couldn't seem to catch his breath. His gaze was locked on Kate's softly rounded belly as his brain tried to process, think, figure. He hadn't expected this. Sure, he'd known something was up, which was why he'd come to Wyoming the minute Mike and Jenny got back from their honeymoon. But Sean had thought it was a problem with the hotel. Or the crew. *Anything* but this.

They'd used condoms. What was the point of using them if people got pregnant anyway?

Hell, now he knew how Brady Finn had felt when he'd traveled to Ireland to check on the hotel there, only to find that Aine was pregnant. At the time, Sean had taken Aine's side in all of that, telling Brady to get over it and do the right thing. Apparently the universe was getting a kick out of landing him in Brady's exact position.

Scrubbing one hand across his face, Sean fought past the fury choking him and tried to steady himself. The woman who had been haunting him for months was carrying his child. That was fact. That was what he had to focus on now.

But even as he thought it, his past rose up in his mind to remind him that it wasn't the first time he'd found himself in this position. As he fought them, images from ten years before swam to the surface of his mind as if finally released from behind a thick dam.

He'd done a year of college in Italy, and there he'd

fallen in love with Adrianna. She was beautiful, smart, funny. And everything was perfect. Until the night she told him she was pregnant. He still felt shame over his reaction, though over the years he'd tried to explain it away by saying he was young. Stupid. Selfish.

But the bottom line was, she had been excited and saw a shiny, happy future for the two of them. All Sean had seen were chains. They had argued viciously and two weeks later, she miscarried the baby she had wanted so badly. Sean went to see her in the hospital, but she turned him away. He could still see her lying on that narrow bed, her beautiful face as white as the sheets beneath her. Her eyes were filled with shadows of pain and a single tear tracked along her cheek.

"Go away," Adrianna had said, turning her face to the wall so she wouldn't have to look at him.

Sean clutched the huge bouquet of roses he'd brought with him and tried again to reach her. To make her see him. To make her realize just how badly he felt. "Adrianna, I'm sorry about the baby."

She spared him a glance then, and in that brief motion he saw that her dark eyes were empty. "You are not sorry, Sean. You didn't want our child. Well, now he is gone so you can be happy. But be happy somewhere else. I don't want you here. I don't want you to come back."

The smell of the hospital, the rumble of nurses and doctors being called over the communication system, the soft moan from an old woman in a bed across the room—none of it mattered. The only thing that mattered was Adrianna, and he was losing her.

His heart breaking, Sean stood his ground, fist tightening on the flowers he held, determined to make her

understand why he'd reacted as he had. Make her forgive him. "Adrianna," he whispered, "we can get past
this."

"No." She stared at the wall, her fingers clenching
on the thin blanket covering her. "No." She took a shud-
dering breath. "I needed you and you were not there.
Now," she added, "I do not need you anymore."

Helpless, Sean had dropped the roses on the chair
by the door and left, knowing that he'd lost something
precious. That he'd thrown away what some men only
dreamed of having.

And he'd lived with the shame and guilt of that for ten
years. Never shared it with his brother—with anyone—
just carried it around like a lump of ice in a corner of
his heart. But now, he had a chance to let go of that past
by being the man he should have been when he was too
young and self-involved to know better.

Sean looked into Kate's lake-blue eyes and read her
determination to keep him out of this. To get him to
leave. To walk away from her and his child. But it wasn't
going to happen.

He wouldn't fail again.

"You should sit down," he said.

"What?"

"You're pregnant. Sit down." He steered her back to
the couch and hovered there until she sat.

"Seriously?" She flipped her long, loose hair back
over her shoulder to stare up at him. "I was on the job
site today installing new windows and ripping old paneling off walls, and you think it's too strenuous for me
to stand in my own living room?"

It sounded stupid when she put it like that. But he was
off his game. Hell, knocked off his feet. "So cut me a

break. I've known about this baby for like ten seconds. Might take a little longer to get used to it."

"That's my point, Sean. You don't have to get used to it."

"Right." He shoved both hands into his pants pockets. "You really expect that I'll just say 'take care' and walk away?"

The fact that he had done just that ten years ago had nothing to do with this.

"That's my child you're carrying," he snapped, feeling anger and frustration nipping at his insides again, "and it's my responsibility to see to it that it's safe."

"Her."

"What?"

"You said *it*," Kate said tightly. "The baby's a girl."

"A girl." Sean swayed in place as a rush of emotion filled his throat. Another hard hit in a series of them. He had a *daughter*. That knowledge alone made this all the more real. All the more vital. Sean took a breath to steady himself and looked at Kate. Stubborn fury was etched into her features. She was hostile and prepared to dig in her heels to fight him on this.

It fried him that she'd kept this secret. Kept his baby from him and clearly had had no intention of ever telling him about it...*her*. Maybe Kate had her reasons, but at the moment, he didn't give a good damn what they were. So yeah, he remembered telling her that he had no interest in children or a family. And maybe he hadn't really considered it since Italy. He might not have gone out and deliberately tried to be a father, but now that he was faced with the reality of it, he wanted his kid.

He was here and not going anywhere. Kate was going to have to find a way to deal with it. No doubt the two of them would butt heads over this situation, but in the end, Sean would have things his way. Kate had no idea what Sean could do when he was set on a certain path. Hadn't he, his brother and their friend built a billion-dollar business from *nothing*? He hadn't allowed anyone to get in his way then, and he wasn't about to start now. Sean made his living by convincing people that he was right so they would fall into line. Kate would eventually give way, just like everyone else.

First things first, though. "Is the baby all right?"

Her face softened in an instant as she stroked her palm over her belly. "She's fine."

"Good." He nodded and swallowed hard over the sudden knot of lust clogging his throat. Were *all* pregnant women this hot? "That's good."

"Sean," she said on a sigh, "I know what you're doing."

"Is that right?" He tucked his hands into his pockets. "What am I doing, Kate?"

She stood up to face him, and he felt the same surge of desire he had felt the first time he'd met her. Kate Wells affected him as no one else ever had—and pregnancy hadn't changed that a bit. But staring at her now, he wasn't thinking of the baby, or the lies, or the arguments waiting for them in the coming days.

All he saw was the woman who had been in his mind for months. Her eyes were flashing, her mouth was set in a straight, grim line and that stubborn tilt to her chin only made her look more amazing. What the hell did it say about him, he wondered, that he found a woman who looked like she wanted to rip his lips off so damned irresistible?

"You're trying to make me feel badly about not telling you about the baby."

"Don't you?"

She blew out a breath. "Yes, I do. But I did what I thought was best, just like I'm doing now. I want you to leave, Sean."

"We don't always get what we want, Kate."

"How are you even here? How did you find out where I live?" She threw her hands high, then caught herself and paused. "Never mind. Not important. What's important is that you leave. Now."

He grabbed her upper arms and held on to her, when he felt her jerk back in an attempt to free herself. "You weren't that hard to find, Kate. And now that I have found you—and my daughter—I'm not going anywhere."

She paled a little but recovered quickly and went on the defensive. "Sean, you don't have anything to prove. It's nice that you offered to be involved with the baby, but it's not necessary."

"It's not *nice*," he said, feeling that swell of irritation come thick and fast again. "That's my daughter as much as yours, so yeah, me being a part of this *is* necessary. You're not cutting me out, Kate. I'm in this."

Outside, the sun was nearly gone, and Kate reached out to flick on a table lamp. Golden light streamed through the room, and he could see her even more clearly than he had before. She didn't look happy, he thought. Well, that made two of them.

"We've got things to talk about."

"No, Sean, we don't. I'm the one who's pregnant, so I'm the one making decisions." She picked up her teacup, stepped to one side and grabbed Molly's wineglass then headed out of the room, throwing words back over her shoulder. "And since I'm only five months along, I've got plenty of time."

Sean followed right after her. It didn't take long. You could drop her entire living room, dining room and kitchen into the main room of his condo in Long Beach and still have room left over. In the tiny galley-style kitchen, he walked up behind her and, in effect, trapped her there. Backed up against the kitchen sink and hedged between the stove and the refrigerator, all she could do was stare up at him.

"We'll *both* be making any decisions necessary, Kate. I'm not walking away from my kid." He dropped his hands onto the sink's edge on either side of her. "I'm here in Wyoming for the next three days. I'd stay longer, but we've got the release of our latest game next week and I have to be there to help."

"Don't let me stop you," she quipped and ducked beneath his arm to escape him.

But he grabbed her arm and held on. "Oh, you won't. You won't stop me from doing anything." It was a warning and a declaration all at once. It was time she knew that he wasn't going to quietly disappear. She was carrying his baby, and that link bound them together.

She'd just have to get used to it.

Seven

Kate felt like she was being stalked.

Everywhere she turned, there Sean was. He watched what she ate, what she drank. He hovered over her on the job site until even her crew stopped coming to her with questions and instead spoke to Sean first. She felt the threads of control slipping through her fingers, and there didn't seem to be a thing she could do about it.

When she complained to Sean, he only smiled and shrugged, brushing off her anger as if it didn't bother him a bit. And that only made her more furious.

Molly, of course, was fascinated. While Kate stood beneath a stand of pines at the edge of the lake, she turned her face into the wind and listened to her friend's voice bubbling over the phone.

"I mean, he's even more spectacular in person than he is in all those paparazzi photos." She took a breath and heaved a dramatic sigh. "That's the kind of guy who makes women dissolve into puddles at his feet."

Kate scowled and watched two magpies swoop over the lake to disappear into the trees. "That must be why he keeps expecting me to fall in line."

"Well, why wouldn't you?" Molly asked. "He's gorgeous, rich, you're carrying his baby *and* he wants to be involved." Before Kate could say anything, Molly rushed on. "And let's not forget, you already confessed that the sex was the best you've ever had."

Now Kate winced. She had said that, in spite of feeling disloyal to Sam's memory. Her late husband hadn't been the best lover, but he'd had other, more important qualities that Sean lacked.

Sean was pushy, dictatorial, arrogant—and those were his good points. Okay, yes, he had beautiful eyes and talented hands and a wicked sense of humor that often made Kate laugh even when she didn't want to. But none of that—even including the amazing sex—was enough to build a life on. And he might not have mentioned marriage yet, but he wanted their baby so she was pretty sure he would mention it, sooner or later.

And she would never get married again. Too much opportunity for pain.

"Sex isn't everything," Kate muttered.

A deep voice behind her said, "People who say that aren't doing it right."

Kate inhaled sharply as her heart gave a hard thump. Just hearing his voice set her nerves jangling and her pulse racing—in spite of how hard she tried to rein them in. Blast it, she thought, she'd come out here to get away from Sean for a while. She'd thought she had escaped the hotel cleanly. Hadn't she waited until Sean was in the kitchen with the crew before she slipped out for a little privacy? But no, he'd managed to track her down anyway.

"I heard that," Molly said, laughing. "I'm really starting to like him."

"That makes one of us," Kate muttered. "I've gotta go."

"Fine, but I'll need a full report later. Spare no details."

Kate shook her head and hung up, then turned to face Sean. "Why are you following me?"

He shrugged and the movement stretched his black T-shirt across a chest she had reason to know was a broad expanse of muscle. "Don't think of it as following you. Think of it more like I'm walking my property. Get an idea what the land looks like when it's *not* buried under a hundred feet of snow."

She didn't believe him, even though what he said made sense. Because instead of checking out the scenery, his gaze was fixed on her. Heat blossomed in the center of her chest and sent tendrils of warmth rippling through her. His eyes were as blue as the lake behind her and the wind ruffled his black hair across his forehead. It looked like he hadn't bothered to shave that morning, so a beard shadow covered his jaw and only made him look even sexier—and she wouldn't have thought that possible.

Having him here again, on her turf, was unsettling. When Sean was several hundred miles away, she could focus on her life, her baby, and almost convince herself that Sean wasn't a part of it at all. And that, she told herself, was how she wanted it. What she felt for Sean was a tangle of emotions. The desire was still there, of course, but mixed in was annoyance and an affection she couldn't completely deny.

"Well, take a look around," she said, waving one arm to encompass the wide spill of lake behind them and the forest that ringed the lake and stretched out for miles on either side of the hotel. When his gaze shifted to the view, Kate watched him and softened at his reaction to the beauty around him.

He looked back at her and smiled. "It's a great spot. Beautiful, really. It's amazing how big the sky looks out here. Seems a lot smaller somehow in California. You know, up until now, I've always been a beach guy. Love surfing, taking a boat out." His gaze shifted back to the calm surface of the sapphire-blue lake that mirrored the white clouds overhead and the pines that stood as guardians at the edge.

She had to smile. "Boats have been known to go on lakes, too."

He grinned, and she felt the jolt of it clutch at her heart.

"Good point," he said. "Maybe we could look into getting some boats here for guests. And paddleboards would probably go over well."

She imagined they would, but said, "Not exactly in line with the theme of ancient warriors and evil creatures."

He laughed easily and tucked his hands into his pockets. "Even gamers take time out for a little reality now and then. And we could paint scenes from the game on them."

Kate sighed. It was so hard to resist when he poured on that charm. Even knowing she should be hardening her heart, keeping her distance, she was drawn to him like she'd never been drawn to anyone else. And when he smiled at her, as he did now, everything inside her softened, yielded.

He turned to scan the forest area then looked back at Kate. "Why don't you show me where you're going to position the cabins?"

"Okay." Good. This was good. Keep the conversation away from the personal. They were being calm, reasonable and talking about the job. She swallowed down the knot of emotion in her throat and pretended it hadn't been there at all. Reminding herself that he was her boss might be enough to keep her thoughts on the here and now rather than on a distant future that seemed too nebulous to negotiate at the moment.

Pointing to the closest stand of trees, she said, "You can see where we've already laid out the foundation slabs for the first two cabins." She took a few steps and stopped again. "The others complete a half circle around the hotel. While they're tucked into the forest enough to be private, they'll still be close enough to the hotel that guests can easily walk up for the restaurant or gift shops. The septics are in, so that job's done and we'll get started on putting up the cabin frames in the next week or so. Just waiting on the final plans from the architect."

He was walking right beside her, and she swore she could feel heat pumping from his body into hers.

"Sounds good. But why didn't you put a couple of them closer to the lake?"

"Risky," she said. "In a hard winter, the spring run-off could raise the water level, so you don't want to be too close to the edge or you've got flooding worries."

"Good point," he said, shifting his gaze to study the

proposed layout of the cabins. "When we get a hard storm surf in Long Beach, people are out sandbagging the sea wall to keep the shore houses from flooding."

Sometimes, it felt as if they were completely in synch. For some reason it seemed that as their personal issues got more complicated, their working relationship improved. Talking about the job, answering questions, making plans, they felt like a team. But that was an illusion. She worked for him, and it was best that she remember that. This was her biggest construction project ever and no matter what else happened between her and Sean, Kate was determined to make the most of this huge opportunity.

"Most of the cabins will have lake views," she said, walking again. The toe of her boot caught on a thick tree root, and she stumbled but caught herself. An instant later, Sean took her elbow to steady her on the uneven forest floor. Heat, raw and undiluted, roared into her body from the simple touch of his hand on her arm. Now she was more unsteady than ever but didn't want to let him know it. "I'm perfectly fine, Sean. I don't need help. I didn't fall."

He shrugged. "Shoot me. My mother raised a gentleman."

"I appreciate it, but I can walk by myself." She tried to pull free, but his grip shifted from velvet to iron in a heartbeat. And being reminded of his strength set up a flutter of nerves in the pit of her stomach.

Sean pulled her around to face him. "Look, I get that you're not used to anyone taking care of you. But you're pregnant with *my* baby now. And I'm going to take care of you—and *her*—whether you like it or not."

And there went the closeness, the sensation of teamwork. He couldn't seem to help himself from that arrogant, I-know-best attitude.

"You can't just show up out of nowhere and start throwing your weight around," Kate told him. "*You* are not in charge."

"Wrong." The word snapped from him and the heat in his eyes flashed dangerously. "From here on out, Kate, I'm giving the orders."

"Are you serious?" She matched his fury with that of her own. "I've been on my own for a long time now. I don't need you, Sean."

Something dark and pain-filled flashed briefly in his eyes but was gone again in seconds. "Need me or not, I'm here, and you're not shaking me loose so get used to it."

They glared at each other, neither of them willing to back down. All around them, the wind whispered in the trees, birds shrieked and in the lake, a fish shot from the water to dive back in with a soft splash.

Then Sean muttered, "Damn it, what is it about you anyway?"

He dragged her in tight and kissed her hard. She thought about resisting on principle, but she couldn't hold out against him. Her mouth softened against his as her blood pumped fast and thick in her veins. God, she'd missed this. The rising need, the tingles of anticipation and excitement that were bubbling through her. She held on to him, loving the feel of his strong arms wrapping around her, holding her close.

It was crazy, and all too quickly it was over.

When she opened her eyes, Kate saw Sean staring down at her and smug satisfaction shining in his eyes. "Don't need me, huh?"

Like ice water had been dumped on her head, cold-ness swamped her, putting out the fire she'd felt only seconds before.

"You kiss me then throw my reaction in my face?" Kate was practically vibrating with frustration and a simmering anger that burned so brightly she was sur-prised her skin wasn't glowing with it.

"Just reminding you of what's between us," he said tightly, and she had some satisfaction knowing that the kiss had affected him just as it had her.

"I know exactly what's between us," Kate said and slapped one hand to her belly.

He covered her hand with his. "Now I do, too. And I promise you, I'm not going anywhere."

"Am I interrupting something?"

At the sound of the deep voice, both of them turned to face the older man approaching.

"Dad?" Kate looked at her father in surprise. She'd been so caught up in Sean, she hadn't heard anything beyond the thundering beat of her own heart. "What're you doing here?"

Harry Baker was a tall man, with steel-gray hair, piercing blue eyes, a barrel chest and heavily muscled arms from years of working construction. Normally easygoing and friendly, at the moment Harry's features were tight and grim.

"Raul called," he said, answering Kate while keep-ing his gaze on Sean. "Asked me to come help him in-stall the new windows on the third floor."

Kate nearly groaned. She'd forgotten that her fa-ther would be on the job site today. Frankly, with Sean around, it was hard to concentrate on anything else. If she'd remembered, she could have prepared Sean. Heck, prepared *herself* for a confrontation that had been building for months.

She took a breath to steady herself. Her father had been after her for months to tell Sean the truth and to stop working. Ever since her mother had died, when Kate was twelve, Harry had been everything to Kate. He'd raised her, taught her, loved her and worried about her. Having her pregnant and unmarried chipped at something inside him, and Kate knew it had taken every ounce of his self-control not to call Sean himself and tell him what was going on.

"That's right. I forgot." There was too much going on, she told herself. But with most of the crew busy finishing off the main kitchen and digging out the basement to make room for the large utility ramp they'd be installing, Raul did need the help.

Her father was glaring at Sean, and she knew he'd come looking for them deliberately so he could have a talk with the man who'd impregnated his daughter. God, she felt as though she was living in a nineteenth century romance. The men in her life were suddenly becoming cavemen, and there were definite signs of testosterone poisoning.

"Well, Dad," she said, keeping her voice light and a smile on her face, "this is Sean Ryan."

"I guessed as much." He didn't smile in return.

Sean offered his hand. "Good to meet you."

Kate watched as the two men took each other's measure during the space of a handshake that looked more like a contest of wills than a polite greeting. This was so not a female moment.

As if agreeing with her, Sean said tightly, "Kate,

why don't you go on back to the hotel while your dad and I have a talk?"

Exactly what she'd been planning to do until Sean suggested it. "Stop telling me what to do."

"Kate, go away."

She looked at her father. "You, too, Dad?"

Neither of the men was looking at her, and that only infuriated her well beyond what little patience she had left. She might as well be at the hotel. These two had already dismissed her. "Fine. I'm going back to work."

"Be careful," Sean warned.

"For heaven's sake…" Her mutter carried even while she walked away.

Sean spared her a single glance, then turned his focus back to the man staring at him. Awkward, he told himself, but no getting around it.

"I didn't know she was pregnant," Sean said, once Kate was out of earshot.

"I know." Harry's eyes were narrowed on him. "I disagreed with her on that, wanted her to tell you, but she's a strong woman. Hardheaded, too."

"Yeah, I know," Sean said. "I like that about her."

Harry snorted and relaxed his stance enough that Sean was pretty sure he wasn't about to be punched. Funny how facing down the father of the woman you're sleeping with could make a man feel like a teenager caught breaking curfew.

"Kate's a grown woman and her decisions are her own, no matter how I'd like to think different."

Sean thought he could see the man's point of view and now that he knew he was also going to be the father of a daughter, he had to wonder if he'd be as reasonable as Harry Baker was in the same situation. Of course, Sean's daughter would never be in this situation because he was never going to let a man near his girl. But for now, he had to reassure Kate's father.

"She's not alone in this," Sean told the other man quietly. "Now that I know about the baby, I'm in this and she's not going to shake me loose."

Harry tipped his head to one side and studied Sean. His eyes were sharp, and Sean thought he probably didn't miss much. Made him uncomfortable having that steady gaze fixed on him, but he stood his ground and waited.

"Good to know," Harry said with a nod. "But I'm thinking it's my daughter that brought you here."

Sean frowned. He had come to see Kate. To see if he had imagined the connection between them—which he hadn't. Hell, his mouth was still burning, his body still sizzling just from that one short, furious kiss they'd shared. He didn't know what the hell was between him and Kate, but he did know they had to figure it out before he talked to her father about all of this.

Instead, he said only, "It's my hotel, Mr. Baker. I've got to keep an eye on the progress."

Shaking his head, Harry mused, "You check out every hotel with a kiss?"

Sean scowled and rubbed one hand across the back of his neck. "Yeah, you saw that."

"I did. Look, what's between you is private." Harry folded beefy arms across his wide chest and stood like a man braced for a fight. "But I'll say I want my pregnant daughter married."

Married? Amazing how that one small word could hit a man like a bucket of rocks. Nobody had said anything about getting married, Sean thought. He could understand how Harry felt, but marriage was something that seemed so...forever. *But so,* his mind whispered, *is a baby.* A child. Linking him and Kate always.

Hell, he hadn't had enough time to think things through. To make a plan. To figure out what his response should be. There was too much going on in his head right now to make sense of much of it. But he did know he wanted his kid. He wanted the chance to prove—if only to himself—that he wasn't the same man he once was. That he'd grown and changed.

Harry was still talking, though, so Sean listened.

"This is the first real sign of life I've seen in my girl since she lost her husband."

"Husband?"

Harry's eyebrows lifted. "Didn't know about Sam, eh? Well, not surprising. My girl isn't what you'd call a big sharer." He frowned to himself. "Losing Sam threw her hard. She doesn't really talk about it, but I can see it. She changed after Sam. Locked herself down." He paused and gave Sean another long look. "Until you, that is."

Sean didn't know what to say to that. She'd never mentioned being married. Being widowed. Why the news hit him so hard was beyond him. But just knowing she'd once been another man's wife was hard to deal with. What was he like, the mystery husband? As he wondered, he remembered their conversation last winter and how she'd only been with one other man.

He groaned internally. Hell, no wonder she'd been so defensive of a man who hadn't been much of a lover. He'd been her *husband.* She'd loved the guy and clearly remained loyal to him even now. There was a tightness in Sean's chest he didn't care for, so he rubbed his fist against his breastbone in a futile effort to ease the discomfort. Weird position to be in, he thought as he recognized what he was feeling. Envious of a dead man.

"She and Sam talked about having a family, but then he was gone and Kate sort of…" Harry paused then said, "Shut down. Like she pulled away from life because it was just too painful. But since you, and now the baby, she's been different. More like herself than I've seen in a while."

Was she still in love with the long-gone Sam? Sean didn't much care for that thought and didn't care to explore why the idea bothered him as much as it did. He had his own past, didn't he? He hadn't told her about Adrianna and the baby. Hadn't opened up his soul.

Passion had brought them together, and Fate had thrown them both a curve by creating a child to mark the occasion.

What the hell was he supposed to do with this information?

He was going home in a couple of days. He had to be in California for the launch of "The Wild Hunt." But how could he leave Kate and his child behind?

"Are you crazy?" Kate demanded a few hours later. "I can't go to California. We're in the middle of a job!"

Sean folded his arms across his chest and leaned one shoulder against the doorjamb. His eyes were cool, almost amused, and that just fed the outrage rushing through her. Sean and her father had walked in from their forest meeting like old friends, each of them smiling, until they caught sight of her. Then the two of them had presented a united front of keeping her in the dark.

Had they cooked this up between them?

"I told you that you couldn't march into my life and start issuing orders," she reminded him. "And if you and my dad think you can make plans for me like I'm a child who needs two strong men to take care of me, then you're both crazy."

Casually, he crossed one foot over the other and looked, she thought, not just amused, but *bored* by her arguments. "This has nothing to do with your father. I have to be back at the office to help run the launch of the new game—"

"So, go," she told him quickly, both relieved and somehow disappointed to know he was leaving. But she'd get over it. "Happy trails."

He snorted and shook his head as he watched her. She wished for an interruption. But that wasn't going to happen.

They were alone in the hotel, with the crew and her father having left more than a half hour ago. Kate had lingered behind to make sure everything was safely tucked away for the night. Tools, extension cords, coffeepots, radios. She'd checked every window on the ground floor and every door lock. They were far enough out in the country that they probably didn't have to worry about thieves or vandals dropping by, but it didn't hurt to make sure things were safe.

Naturally, Sean had stayed, too. As he'd promised earlier, she'd been unable to shake him loose. Now she knew why. He'd waited until they were alone to spring his ridiculous idea.

Outside, the light was going soft and pearly as the sky deepened toward the coming night. Inside, there were only a few lights on, keeping the shadows at bay.

"Oh, I'm going, and you're coming with me."

He looked so sure of himself, Kate wanted to kick him. "The job—"

"Is at a stage where you can leave your crew working without supervision for a few days."

"Days?"

"Maybe a week." He shrugged as if unconcerned about the time he was demanding she take.

"It's business, Kate." Before she could argue again, he said, "I want you out there to meet with our artists. They've had some ideas on the new cabins, and you can consult with them and meet with the architect in person."

"It's not necessary," she argued, already feeling as if she'd lost this battle. He looked calm and in control, and she felt the ragged threads of *her* control sliding from her fingers, but she made one more try. "As long as I have the plans, we'll get it done."

Sean sighed and shook his head. "You're going to lose this one, Kate. This is my job, and I want my contractor in California for a meeting."

He was right. She couldn't win here. He was not only the man currently driving her insane, but he was also her boss. Refusing to go with him just wasn't an option. But whatever he said, this wasn't only about business. He had an ulterior motive. She just wasn't sure what it was. To get her out of her comfort zone? To *show* her the difference in their lifestyles? To prove that if he wanted their baby, he had the money and power to take it?

Anxiety rippled in the pit of her stomach, and she had the distinct feeling it wouldn't be dissipating anytime soon.

"Pack for a week," he said casually, then glanced around the great room as if the subject was closed. "You were right about these floors," he mused. "Sanded and refinished they look brand-new and old at the same time."

Automatically, her gaze dropped to the floorboards. In the dim light, they shone golden, with a soft gleam that caught the light and held it. Yes, the hotel was looking good. Walls were painted, floors refinished, ceiling beams stripped and sanded until they looked as they had when the place was first built. But at the moment, she didn't feel like admiring her crew's work.

"Yeah, oak will do that. But back to the point—"

"The point is," he interrupted her neatly, "we leave day after tomorrow. Be ready."

Eight

It started with a private jet.

The minute she walked on board, Kate knew that she would never be happy flying coach again. There were luxurious leather seats, plush carpeting so thick her shoes sank in it and a flight attendant whose sole duty was to ensure that Kate enjoyed the trip to California. Sadly, the very efficient woman couldn't ease the knot of nerves in Kate's stomach.

That knot only tightened once they landed, and Sean drove them to his penthouse condo on the beach. Stepping into that expansive space was a revelation. Sean gave the impression of being a regular guy who liked surfing. She had known, of course, just how rich he was, but his home really defined the difference between her life and his.

The living room was wide and furnished with tasteful comfort in mind. Polished wood floors were dotted with thick rugs in neutral tones. Couches and chairs were overstuffed, inviting visitors to drop down and be comfortable. A wall of windows provided an amazing view of the Pacific, and with the French doors opened to a terrace that stretched the length of the building, a sea breeze drifted lazily into the room.

Anxious, Kate wandered through the condo and let the silence inside her, where hopefully it would settle the nerves clawing at her. She was alone now, as she had been the night before, sleeping in one of the guest rooms in this palace. Sean hadn't pushed for her to join him in his bed, and a part of her had been disappointed in that.

This morning when she woke, Sean was already gone. But he'd left her a note in the living room.

Went surfing. Make yourself at home. I'll be back in a couple hours and we'll go to the office.

So Kate made coffee in the incredible kitchen and tried not be envious of the six-burner stove, the sub-zero fridge and the miles of black granite. She was willing to bet the man never cooked anything more than a cup of coffee and maybe toast. No way he could really appreciate this kitchen for the incredible work space it was.

Sighing, she took her coffee onto the terrace and sat down on one of the cushioned chairs arranged there to enjoy the view. In June, gray skies covered the coast of California every morning, keeping the heat down and giving the Pacific a leaden look. The ocean was immense and frothed with white caps. Boats, their brightly colored sails billowing in the wind, skimmed across the surface of the water, and near the shore she could make out a handful of surfers riding the waves.

"Is one of them Sean?" Kate watched, thought about the man who'd brought her here and wondered what the hell she was going to do for the next few days.

Having him on her turf was hard enough, but being on *his,* completely pulled her out of her comfort zone… She kept losing her mental balance and wasn't sure how to get it back—or even if she would.

When her phone rang, she answered gratefully. "Molly, hi."

"Hi, yourself. How's it going?"

"Well, I'm sitting here on the private terrace of a truly awesome penthouse, staring out at the ocean."

"Wow," Molly said on a sigh. "Sounds rough."

Kate laughed shortly. Trust Molly to put things in perspective. "Okay, his home is beautiful and looks like a spread in a magazine. You should see the kitchen."

"Uh-huh, unlike you, I really don't care about kitchen goodies. What about Sean? What's happening with you two?"

"Nothing." Kate sipped at her coffee and sighed. "I don't know why I'm here. I swear, even though he insisted this trip was about business, there was a part of me that figured he was just trying to get me out here and into his bed." Well, boy, *that* sounded egotistical. "You know, keep me happy long enough that he could find a way to get our baby."

"Come on, Kate…"

"But he didn't try anything last night." Frustration jumped into life and held hands with the anxiety inside her. "Nothing. He just showed me the guest room."

And that fact, she was forced to admit, had bothered

her more than a little. She'd lain awake half the night, imagining him in the room across the hall and wishing that she was lying next to him, which made her...what? Pitiful? Crazy? Masochistic?

"Well," Molly sympathized, "that's just sad."

"It really *is*. But more than sad," Kate told her, "it's out of character. He's been flirting with me and trying to seduce me since we met. Now all of a sudden, nothing? He's been really quiet, too, and that's really not like him. Plus, I keep finding him watching me."

"That doesn't sound like a bad thing."

"Not *that* kind of watching. This is more studying, like I was a bug under a microscope and he's trying to figure out exactly what species I am."

"You're overreacting, honey," Molly said, and Kate could almost *see* her shaking her head slowly.

But Molly didn't know Sean like Kate did. Okay, they hadn't known each other for very long, but their relationship had been pretty intense right from the beginning. Being with Sean made Kate feel more alive than she did without him. She liked arguing with him, liked laughing with him and she loved being held by him. *Loved?*

That word sneaked in there unexpectedly and for the moment, Kate was going to ignore it.

"I think he's up to something."

"Paranoid much?" Molly asked, laughing.

"Molly, he told me he wants the baby." She looked over her shoulder into the living room of the condo. "Judging by this place, the private jet, if he wanted to, he could go for custody and I wouldn't stand a chance."

Instantly her friend's attitude shifted. "Don't do this

to yourself, Kate. Don't go looking for trouble. Wait for it to find you if it's coming."

"Hard to be prepared if you're waiting," Kate said, shifting her gaze back to the cool, blue ocean. On the other hand there was just no preparing for Sean Ryan. He was like a force of nature, blowing into her life and turning it all upside down.

"Kate, do yourself a favor," Molly said softly. "Just enjoy where you are while you're there. Stop worrying about what might happen before it does."

Good advice, Kate thought a few minutes later when she hung up. She just didn't know if she could follow it or not. Worry was simply a part of who she was. As a kid, after her mother's death, she'd worried that her father would die, too. She'd insisted on going with him to job sites whenever she wasn't in school, just to keep an eye on him. Later, she'd worried about classes and worried when she married Sam that something would go wrong to ruin their happiness.

That time, she'd been right.

So how could she stop worrying about the possibility of losing her child?

"Kate? You here?"

She stood up and turned to see Sean striding into the condo. For one split second, she did exactly as Molly had advised and simply enjoyed the view. His hair was still damp, his jaw shadowed with whiskers. He had a cherry-red surfboard tucked under his left arm and the wetsuit he wore had been pulled down to his waist, leaving his arms and chest bare.

Heat erupted so fast, so completely, it stole her breath. Kate dragged in a gulp of air and forced herself to lift her gaze from his chest to meet his eyes. Once she did, she saw a flash of recognition shining there, and she knew that he was aware of what she'd been feeling.

But how could he be, she wondered, when she'd just that second realized she was in love with him?

She swayed a little as the knowledge settled into her brain to stay. Kate had been fighting her own emotions for too long. She had tried to ignore them, pretend that all she felt for Sean was the closeness associated with a lover—and the father of her child. She'd even tried to ignore the feelings altogether and when that didn't work, she'd lied to herself about the truth that was even now slamming home.

She couldn't be in love with a man in the position to take everything she cared about away from her. Couldn't give him even more power over her than he already had. Panic settled into the pit of her stomach, and she swallowed hard. After Sam, she'd vowed to never love again. To never put herself in a position to experience the pain of loss again. But it seemed that life happened even when you tried to avoid it.

"Hey!" Sean dropped the surfboard with a clatter and crossed to her in a blink. Holding on to her arms and looking into her eyes, he asked, "Are you okay? Your face just went snow-white. Is it the baby?"

He smelled so good was all she could think. But she managed to tie a rope around a single active brain cell, then dragged it around until it collected enough friends that she could speak again.

"I'm fine." His eyes shone with worry. "Really. I'm fine. So's the baby." She changed the subject quickly before he could grab her and rush her off to a doctor or something. "Did you have a good time?"

"Waves weren't much, but it was good to be out

there again." He shrugged, then reached up and ran both hands through his hair. His muscled chest rippled until Kate wanted nothing more than to stroke her palms across it. Deliberately, she curled her hands into fists.

"I'm going to grab a fast shower," Sean said into the silence. "Then we'll head over to the office."

"Okay." She didn't want to think about him in the shower and wondered if he'd planted that image in her brain on purpose. But the way he walked out of the room, easily dismissing her, sort of shot down that theory.

So what was he up to? What was his plan?

Sean didn't have a plan.

He was still thinking about the fact that Kate had been someone's *wife* and hadn't told him. What the hell was that about? He'd seen the look in her eye this morning when he got home from the beach. Passion. Desire. Need. It was all there, easily enough read in spite of her attempts to hide it. But damn if he'd be a substitute for her dead husband. It had taken every ounce of self-control he had to keep from stalking across the room and grabbing her. Then she'd gone so white, anger had been swamped by a flood of panic.

He was keeping an eye on her to make sure she didn't do that again. And once Sean was sure she was okay, he would need some answers.

He watched her working with the art department and heard the deep, rich music of her laughter at something Dave said. She flipped her long, loose hair back and bent over Dave's shoulder as he made notations on a computer.

"Does she have to get *that* close?" he muttered.

"I like her."

Sean shot his brother a sour look, not pleased that he'd been so focused on Kate that Mike had been able to sneak up on him.

"Yeah, she's good. Did you see how quickly she picked up on the ideas for different rooflines on the cabins? I liked how she tweaked them, too, so each cabin will have a different look and style."

"I noticed," Mike said, giving his brother a shoulder bump, "but I wasn't talking about her work. I like *her*. She's nice. Funny. Pretty, too."

Sean rolled his eyes. Mike wasn't exactly subtle. "She is. Kate and Jenny seem to have hit it off."

Mike nodded and watched his wife join Kate and Dave at the computer. All three of them were talking over each other to the point where Sean had to wonder how they could get anything done. His gaze fixed on Kate, in her black slacks and the tight, short-sleeved yellow shirt that defined and displayed her rounded belly. Something inside him stirred, a sense of protectiveness, possession, that surprised him with its depth. And there was something else there, as well. It wasn't just the baby he wanted, it was Kate.

"You're staring," Mike murmured.

"What?" Sean shot him a quick look. "The only way you would know that is because you're watching *me*. Cut it out. Don't you have somewhere to be?"

"Nope, the beauty of being a boss. I can be wherever I want to be. And right now, I want to watch my brother drool over a pregnant woman." Mike grinned when Sean turned his head to stare at him. "Something you'd like to tell the class?"

Sean jerked his head then walked off, knowing his

brother would follow. Once in Mike's office with the door closed, Sean paced, hands in his pockets, too restless to stand still.

"So? It's your baby, isn't it?"

Sean stopped, took a breath and looked at Mike. "Yeah, it is. *She* is."

"A daughter?" Mike grinned widely. "That's excellent. Congratulations. We find out our baby's sex tomorrow."

Sean nodded, knowing just how excited Mike was about the baby Jenny was carrying. They'd made a family, they were building a future. Right now, all Sean had was the knowledge that he would be a father. He'd never really been one to look into the future. He was more of a right-now kind of guy. But a lot was changing in his life lately.

"That's great, Mike," he said, dragging one hand through his hair. "Really."

"Yeah, it is." Mike walked across the room and sat on the edge of his desk. "What's going on, Sean?"

"Oh," he said, snorting a laugh, "not much. I just found out I'm going to be a father. The woman carrying my kid wants nothing to do with me, and did I mention she used to be married but her sainted husband died two years ago?"

"Whoa. That's a lot."

"You think?" Sean dropped into a chair, stretched his legs out in front of him and folded his hands on his abdomen. "It bugs the hell out of me that she didn't tell me she was married before." He shook his head. "I mean, sure we haven't known each other long and she really didn't have a reason to tell me, but why didn't she? Hell, I don't even know *why* it bugs me so much."

"Don't you?" Mike asked.

"Is she still in love with the dead guy, Mike?"

"I don't know," his brother said thoughtfully. "Why don't you ask her?"

"Because she should have told me about Saint Sam," he snapped. This had been gnawing on his gut since Kate's dad told him about her marriage and how it had ended. He'd been biting his tongue for days to keep from saying something because damn it he wanted *her* to tell him. But it was looking like that wasn't going to happen, so he'd have to do something to end this. Did she kiss *him* and think of Sam? Because Sean wasn't going to stand for that.

"Look," Mike said, "you gave me some good advice not long ago when Jenny was making me crazy—"

"Not the same thing," Sean said, cutting off his brother. Mike had been in love with Jenny. Sean was in lust with Kate. *Big* difference.

"Right." Mike shook his head impatiently. "Anyway, the point is, you told me I should talk to her, get everything out, and you were right. Why don't you take your own advice? Talk to her, Sean. For God's sake, you're having a baby together. Maybe you should work some of this stuff out?"

"Yeah. The question is, how?" Sean jumped from the chair and prowled the office again, as if he was trapped and looking for a way out. Throwing a look at Mike, he said, "I don't have time for this right now. We've got the big launch next week, and there's a million details to refine yet."

"Uh-huh."

"We're still putting together the storyboards for

'Dragon's Tears'—and that comes out in December, we've got to get those finalized…"

"Uh-huh."

Sean stopped dead and fired a look at his brother. "Just say what you're thinking. You agreeing with me so easily is a little creepy."

"Fine." Mike came off the desk and faced him. "We've always got a launch or a new game in the pipe and hopefully, it'll be like that for the next fifty years. But you get to have a life, too, Sean, and sometimes you have to make the time for it."

He scrubbed one hand across the back of his neck. "Make time."

"Yeah. You brought Kate out here—take advantage of having her on your home court, so to speak. Figure out what the hell it is you want, then go and get it and stop giving me a headache."

Sean laughed and shook his head. Leave it to family to wrap things up so neatly. "Wow. Touching. Okay, fine. Speaking of taking some time, I won't be in tomorrow."

"Good. Improve your attitude before you do come back, okay?"

"Gonna work on that," Sean said and left.

Several hours later, Kate was sitting across the table from Sean in the most elegant restaurant she'd ever seen. Candlelight flickered on every table, white linen cloths were brightened by deep red napkins and the sparkle and shine of crystal and silver. Quiet conversations sifted through the room and soft, classical music was a whispered backdrop.

Kate smoothed her napkin across the lap of her new

black dress and looked at the gorgeous man opposite her. In jeans and a work shirt, Sean was hard to resist. In a well-tailored black suit with a sapphire-blue tie, he was amazing. He looked as if he'd been born to be in places like this. Actually, he was as comfortable in this rarified atmosphere as Kate was uneasy. Just one more reason that loving him was going to bring nothing but trouble.

"You look beautiful," he said, shattering her thoughts.

"Thank you." She'd had to go shopping, of course, since she hadn't brought anything with her that would have been good enough for a place like this.

There'd been a tension between them all day. Well, Kate admitted silently, Sean had been…different, since they'd left Wyoming. For her, realizing she was in love made her cautious, afraid she might somehow let the truth slip and set herself up for pain. So the two of them did a careful dance, where every word was weighed and measured and what *wasn't* said lay between them like a minefield.

Conversation during dinner had been stilted, and Kate felt as though she was balancing on a tightrope, trying desperately not to fall.

"How do you like California so far?"

She smiled at him. "What I've seen is beautiful. I love the view from your terrace."

He nodded, and one corner of his mouth tipped up. "That's the reason I bought it. I like seeing the ocean when I wake up."

"You can see it from your bedroom?"

One eyebrow lifted. "If you'd joined me last night, you could have found out for yourself this morning."

"You didn't invite me."

"You don't need an invitation and you know it."

Oh, if she had joined him last night, the view would have been the last thing she was interested in. Even as her body stirred, she let that go and said instead, "This is actually my second trip to California. Of course, on the first trip I was ten and my parents took me to Disneyland."

He smiled, and this time the smile reached his eyes. "Every kid should get the chance to go there."

"You probably went all the time, growing up here."

"Not really. My folks were more about going camping and exploring rather than amusement parks."

"Tonight, you don't look like a camping kind of guy."

"And you don't look much like a contractor who wears a tool belt like other women wear diamonds."

"But that is who I am." Waving one hand to encompass the restaurant, she said, "Places like this, not really a part of my life."

"They could be," he mused.

"Not a lot of five-star restaurants in a little town in Wyoming." Her heartbeat sped up, but before it could get out of hand, Kate reined it in. Her life wasn't here in California. Even if by some miracle she and Sean could find a way to make things work between them, she still couldn't stay here. She had a business, people depending on her, and besides, she wanted to raise her child where she'd grown up.

In a place with more trees than people. Summer nights of lying on a blanket in the yard watching the stars. Fourth of July town picnics, snowmen and ice skating on the lake. Small schools and big dreams. She wanted that for her child and knew she wouldn't be able to find it here in California.

His fingers tapped lightly against the table as he studied her.

"You're staring at me again," she said.

"I like the view," he said, taking a sip of his coffee.

"You're doing the charming thing again," Kate said and smiled a little. "I wondered if I'd see it again."

"What's that mean?"

"Just that I've never seen you as quiet as you have been the last two days."

His gaze dropped deliberately to her belly. "A lot to think about lately."

"You're right about that." She shifted a little under his steady stare. So much to say, she thought, and no way to say it. She changed the subject to one less personal, one less fraught with emotions neither of them was willing to discuss. "So do you come here often for business dinners?"

He smiled and in the candlelight, his eyes glittered. "Not really."

"But you brought me here." She tipped her head to one side. "Why?"

"You didn't enjoy your dinner?"

"It was wonderful, but that doesn't answer my question."

"Easy answer, then. I wanted to take you someplace nice." He stood up, came around to her side and helped her to her feet. "Now, I want to show you something else."

She slipped her hand into his and felt the sizzle of electricity that always happened when he touched her. How would she live without feeling that every day? Would she spend the rest of her life wondering what he was doing? Missing him?

Rising, she looked up into his eyes and asked, "Where are we going?"

His mouth curved briefly. "It's a secret. You like secrets, don't you, Kate?"

They drove down the coast and in his Porsche, the miles flew by. On her right, the ocean shone and sparkled in moonlight that danced on its inky surface. On her left was the man who had so thoroughly breached what she had believed to be well-honed defenses. His charm and his smile had attracted her and now his quiet distance drew her in even further. Was it the baby that had changed him so completely? Was he thinking about how to gain custody? Was he regretting saying he wanted their child?

And what had he meant when he said she liked secrets?

She glanced at him as he steered the sleek car down the crowded road that ran alongside the beach. Why was he suddenly so hard to read? When they'd first met, she'd dismissed him as an arrogant rich man—now she knew he was much more than that. But what was driving him now?

"Now who's staring?" he asked.

"Just trying to figure you out."

He laughed and it was a short, sharp sound. "I'm not that deep, Kate. You don't have to try so hard."

"I wouldn't have to try at all if you'd just tell me what's going on."

"No fun not knowing what's going on, is it?"

She bit her bottom lip to keep from responding. She knew he was making a crack about her not telling him about the baby. But she'd done what she thought was right, and that was all anyone could do. Besides, she'd apologized for that, hadn't she?

She didn't say another word as he steered the car into a right turn by a sign announcing View Point. He parked, got out of the car then came around and helped her out, as well. Tucking her hand in his, he pulled her along behind him as he walked to the short, white barrier that stood at the edge of the cliff.

Theirs was the only car in the narrow lot, and the roar from the cars on the road seemed muffled somehow beneath the sigh of the ocean below. A sharp, cold wind plucked at the hem of her dress, and the three-inch heels she wore weren't made for crossing uneven asphalt at the pace needed to keep up with Sean's long legs. But finally, he drew her to a stop beside him, with the really insufficient white fence the only thing between them and the long drop to the rocks below.

"This is one of my favorite spots," Sean said, pitching his voice to carry over the wind, the sea and the highway behind them. "Used to come here when I got my first car. I'd sit on the hood and watch the sea for hours."

"It's beautiful," she said. And only a little unnerving to be so close to the edge of a cliff.

"Yeah, it is." He pointed, and her gaze tracked in that direction. "When it's clear like this, you can see all the way up the coast. Sometimes you can see Catalina, too. On a foggy night, it looks like something from out of a dream. Most nights, though, are like tonight and from up here, the beach city lights don't look too bright, too harsh, too crowded."

Listening to him, Kate could see him as a teenager, out here in the dark, alone, watching the world. Hadn't she done the same thing when she would go to the lake as a kid and watch the moon and stars dance over the surface of the water?

"It's a lot more lights than I'm used to seeing at night."

"You have lights, too," he said, with a half smile. "They're called stars. I've never seen so many, and I've been camping in the desert."

"It's true." She looked up and saw maybe a quarter of the stars she would have seen at home. There were just too many lights here to let the sky shine as it should.

She shivered in the wind and shifted her gaze to the bottom of the cliff, where waves slapped hard against the rocks and sent frothy spray into the air.

"Cold?"

"A little." A lot actually, but when he dropped his arm around her shoulders and pulled her in tightly to him, cold was just a memory.

"When I was a kid," he said, "I'd come here, and no one would know where I was. This place was my secret."

There was that word again, Kate thought, looking up at him to find his gaze fixed on hers. "You keep talking about secrets. What is it, Sean?"

His eyes narrowed against the wind as he stared at her. After a few seconds, Kate thought he was going to ignore her question. Then he asked, "Why didn't you tell me you were married? That your husband died?"

Nine

Kate felt all the air whoosh out of her lungs, and it took her a second or two to refill them. His arm around her tightened in response to her instinctive push to back away from him. *Her father.* Kate closed her eyes briefly when she realized her dad must have told Sean about Sam.

She should have expected it. Anticipated it. Harry Baker was *not* happy that his pregnant daughter was unmarried. She probably should have been grateful that he hadn't come after Sean with a shotgun. Instead, he'd done what he could to convince the father of his grandchild to do what Harry would think was the "right thing."

Now, Sean's arm around her felt like a cage, keeping her where she didn't want to be. She needed a little space, a little breathing room. "Let me go."

"No. Talk to me."

"About what?" She shook her hair back from her face when the wind tossed it across her eyes. "Sounds like my dad already told you everything."

"Not everything," Sean argued, turning her in his arms until she was facing him, pressed up against him. "He couldn't tell me why you kept Sam a secret from me."

She looked everywhere but into his eyes. How could she have told him about her late husband? "Because my marriage had nothing to do with what happened between us."

"That's what you think?" He took her chin and tilted up her face until she had no choice but to meet his gaze. Kate didn't like the shine of anger there, but she was surprised by the layer of hurt she saw over it.

"Okay, when was I supposed to tell you, Sean? *Before* sex or directly after?"

"It wasn't just sex, Kate." His grip on her tightened. "What happened between us was more than that, and you should have told me. God knows there was plenty of time when we were snowbound."

Yeah, he was angry. But instead of convincing her to back down, his anger served to kindle her own. "Just how was I supposed to work that information in, Sean? I know, 'Help me pull out the carpet upstairs and oh, by the way, did I mention I'm a widow?'" She set both hands on his chest and gave a shove. "Let me go, damn it."

He did, and Kate stalked off a few steps before she turned around to face him again. He hadn't moved. Just stood there, a tall presence whose features now looked as if they'd been carved in stone.

"I don't talk about Sam," she blurted out. "Not to anyone. He's gone, that's all, and when he died, a piece of me died with him."

"Kate…"

"No," she snapped, holding one hand up to get him to be quiet. She'd done this. Opened herself up to this. Memories of Sam tangled with new ones of times with Sean and twisted her up into knots of pain and regret.

Damn it, why did she have to love him? Losing Sam had hurt so badly, and she knew that losing Sean was going to be worse—not only because what she felt for him went deeper than what she'd known with Sam. But because she would also be losing him and still have to live knowing that he was alive and well—just not with her.

So she struggled against the misery curled in her heart and said, "You wanted to hear it, so just be quiet and listen." She had to take a deep breath and steel herself against the flood of memories that swept through her. "We were happy," she finally said. "Sam was a sweet man with a kind smile and a big heart. We were married a couple of years, talking about starting a family. Then there was an accident on a job site and he was killed.

"He's been gone two years now. And when he died, my dream of kids, a family of my own, went with him."

Sean's eyes narrowed, and a muscle in his jaw twitched as he ground his teeth together. She felt the power of his stare slamming into her, heard the rawness of his voice when he said flatly, "Until you found out you were pregnant."

"Yes." She curled her arms protectively across her

belly. "This baby is a miracle for me, Sean. Dreams I let die are alive again because of her."

"That's why you didn't tell me," Sean said, taking two long strides that brought him right up in front of her. "As long as you didn't tell me about my kid, you could pretend that it was Sam's."

Kate's head jerked back as if she'd been slapped. Her throat filled, and her stomach churned. She fought for air and thanked God for the sharp, cold wind that batted the tears from her eyes before they could fall. Staring up into the face of the man she thought she knew and seeing none of the warm humor and charm she was so used to, Kate could only think... *he's right*.

She had done that. And now she was caught with the truth and what it had done to Sean. She had played mental games with herself. Pretended that the baby she carried was the child she and Sam had wanted so badly, because she hadn't wanted to involve Sean at all. What they'd shared had been so momentary—how could she call him later and say she was pregnant and expect anything from him?

But it hadn't been momentary at all, her mind whispered, and that's what had really scared her.

Those snowbound days with Sean had opened up her heart, her mind, her soul. He'd touched places inside her that no one else ever had, and it had scared her. Scared her enough that she'd found a way to avoid seeing him again. And now, being called on it, she could understand Sean's anger and the hurt she'd caught such a brief glimpse of.

She wanted to argue with him, tell him he was wrong, but she couldn't. The truth was hard, but lying wouldn't solve anything at this point.

"God." Shaking her head, she said, "You're right, Sean. I did try to pretend that this was Sam's baby. We wanted a family, and I felt cheated when Sam died." She threw up her hands. "We had a few days together, you and I, and what we felt and did was so far out of my normal universe that I had to find a way to protect myself, I guess.

"Plus, you made this huge point about not wanting a family and I thought, why tell him? Why bring him into this at all? And I was wrong. I should have told you."

"Yeah," he said tightly. "You should have. But some things are hard to talk about. To remember."

Was he talking about her now, or did he have secrets of his own? Was he going to tell her? Would he hold that part of himself back in some kind of retaliation for what Kate had done?

"Do you still love him?"

Her gaze snapped to his. "What?"

"Sam," Sean said, his gaze burning into hers. "Do you still love him?"

"I'll always love him, Sean," she said, knowing Sam deserved that much at least. "He was my husband, and he died. That's not something I can just tuck away and forget."

Kate had loved Sam with all the sweet promise of first love, and she would always treasure those memories. But what she felt for Sean was so much bigger, deeper, richer, there was simply no comparison. Sam had been as soft and gentle as a candle's glow. Sean was the sun—searingly bright, all-encompassing and so hot you risked being incinerated by getting too close.

Yet she couldn't stay away.

He moved in on her, and Kate shivered. It wasn't the

wind, not the sea-scented cold; it was the heat in Sean's eyes that affected her. God, she loved him, and she knew she shouldn't. Knew she should find a way to stop.

He set his hands at her waist and whispered into the wind, "Who are you thinking of when I kiss you, Kate? Sam? Or me?"

Is that what had been tearing at him for days? How could he imagine that there would be room for anyone else in her mind when he was touching her? Hadn't he felt her surrender?

Lifting one hand, she cupped his cheek and told him the truth. "Don't you know? Don't you feel it when you touch me? It's you, Sean. There's only you."

"Good answer," he murmured, then bent his head and kissed her.

Here was what she wanted, *needed*. Here, Kate thought, was everything she couldn't have. She sank into his kiss, letting the cold wind wrap itself around her as counterpoint to the heat pumping from Sean's body into hers.

His arms were like iron, his heart pounding hard against hers. The taste of him filled her, and she gave herself up to the wonder of what she had with him. Her mind raced ahead, shouting warnings that were coming too late to prevent the hurt she would feel when this time with him was over. Deliberately, she closed down her mind, shut her worries away for another time. Now was all that mattered.

All she really had.

Waking up with Kate sprawled across his chest didn't bring even the tiniest bubble of panic. Sean told himself he should probably worry about that. He never had women stay over. Hell, he didn't normally bring women to his place—he went to theirs. This condo had been a sanctuary for him. His place in the world that was inviolate. But for the last week, he'd had Kate there with him and it felt…way too good.

She stirred, woke up slowly, slid her foot along his leg and his body went from sated to hungry in a blink. Tipping her head back, she looked up at him and gave him a slow smile.

"Good morning."

He grinned at her. "Getting better every second."

Rolling her over onto her back, he looked down into her eyes and stroked his hands up and down her body, relearning every line, enjoying the new curves caused by the gentle swell of her belly. He kissed her there, above his child's heart, and then moved up, to take her mouth in a kiss that showed her just how badly he needed her. She dragged her hands through his hair and the slide of her fingers was the kind of torture, he thought, a man would be willing to die for.

Kate arched into him as he stroked her core, and she sighed his name as her hips rocked into his hand. When that first gentle release claimed her, Sean moved to cover her body with his. He felt the tremors still claiming her when he entered her on a whisper.

Dawn streaked the sky with shades of pink and violet and red as he rose over her and moved into her heat with a tenderness he'd never experienced before. She met him with the same gentle touches, the quiet sighs and the murmured words that made sense only when two people became one.

Sean stared into her eyes and watched as the climax took her. She cried out his name, and he buried his face in the curve of her neck when his body surrendered and emptied into hers. And locked together, they fell.

A couple of hours later, they were back at the office. While Sean made dozens of phone calls, checking in with distributors, shipping, retailers and wholesalers, he knew Kate was working with Jenny in the art department.

They'd settled into a routine over the last few days. Breakfast on the terrace—and how great was it that Kate not only knew how to cook, but also *enjoyed* it? His condo now always had some delicious scent wafting through it.

He liked their early-morning time together, laughing, talking, just the two of them. Sean had never enjoyed a woman as much. He loved the way her mind worked— she was smart, creative and the strongest woman he'd ever known. He admired that about her, too. She didn't want to be taken care of, or told what to do and had no problem standing up and telling him so.

Every other woman he'd ever been with had *wanted* him to be in charge. But Kate had built a life for herself on her own terms. She'd lost her husband and hadn't curled up into a ball to whine about it. She hadn't felt sorry for herself. On her own, she'd turned her construction company into a thriving business, and now she was determined to raise a child on her own. Not that he was going to stand still for that.

He frowned, kicked back at his desk and shifted his gaze to the backyard garden. Color flowed in a serpentine spill across the length of the yard. Silky vines with bright yellow flowers climbed a trellis, and the birdbath Jenny had brought home from her and Mike's honeymoon trip to Paris held center stage on the lawn.

Celtic Knot had seen a lot of changes over the last couple of years. Brady was married, living in Ireland and the father of a baby boy. Mike was married now, too, about to be the father of a baby boy and letting his wife drag him around on house-hunting missions.

"And me?" Sean mused aloud. "Having a daughter with my lover, who's already started talking about getting back to Wyoming."

He'd noticed she was getting antsy, and he knew she was ready to get home and back to work. What he didn't know was what the hell he was going to do when she left. How was he supposed to live in his condo when every corner of the place would now remind him of her? Hell, he wouldn't even be able to sit out on the terrace without thinking about homemade pancakes and syrup-flavored kisses.

No. Unacceptable. Sean made his living talking people into seeing things his way. He made deals, solved problems and always managed to come out on top. There's no way he'd lose now. Not when Kate was more important than any other challenge he'd ever faced.

He wanted Kate Wells. He wanted their child, and he wouldn't lose either of them.

In the art department, most of the artists were on computers, a few at long conference tables scattered with paper and pencils and markers in a vast rainbow of colors. Energy seemed to sizzle in the air. Kate enjoyed the atmosphere in here, with everyone working together on one project and yet separately, each doing their best to make the whole work.

It reminded her of job sites back home. Whatever project they had going at the time, each of her crew would do their best work on their own, making sure that the finished product was cohesive. She admired creativity, too, and spending the last week watching these people bring myths to life had been fascinating.

"I never realized how much work went into creating a video game," she said.

"Believe me," Jenny told her with a grin, "I know just what you mean. When I first started working here, I was overwhelmed by all of the minutiae that goes into the design and the artwork and the graphics. But now I love it." She eased back in her chair and laid one hand over her growing baby.

Kate did the same and thought how nice it was to be able to share with a friend exactly what she was feeling. Their due dates only a couple of weeks apart, the two women had done some serious bonding over the last week. "Yours is a boy, right?"

"Yep. Mike's so excited, it's adorable." Jenny smiled to herself. "Keeps bringing home footballs and baseball gloves. But you know what I'm talking about. Sean's thrilled about having a daughter. I heard him telling Mike that his girl would be the first female pitcher in the big leagues one day."

Kate rubbed her belly and smiled gently. Sean was excited. He wanted their baby as much as she did and though she was happy about that, it was also a worry. She couldn't see how they would work this out.

For the past week, it had felt as if the two of them were playing house. Sleeping wrapped in each other's arms, waking up together, sharing breakfast on the terrace, talking about their days over dinner. She'd gone to the beach to watch him surf and had felt like a teenaged girl when her boyfriend came running out of the surf to flop down onto the sand beside her.

They spent every night making love in the big bed with a view of the ocean, and every morning she woke to his kisses.

How was she supposed to go home and pretend she didn't miss it? Didn't miss him?

But she had to go home. Soon. Her crew needed her, she had a house, a life to get back to and pretending this time with Sean was real wouldn't change any of that. She knew, though, that the minute she talked about leaving, that would spawn another argument.

"How do you do it?" Kate suddenly asked Jenny. "How do you handle being with a man who's so sure of himself all the time?"

Jenny laughed, searched through the stack of artist's renderings and said, "Oh, it's not easy sometimes, but it's never boring being with a Ryan." She found the picture she was looking for and reached out to grab a deep red marker. Quickly, expertly, she added a robe, lifted in an unseen wind, to the character on the page.

"That's really good," Kate said, turning her head so she could see the whole image.

"Thanks." Jenny shot her a quick grin. "Here's one of our famous arguments. Mike insisted that the empress here should be short and twisted, your typical cartoon image of a bad witch. He wanted evil easily seen on her face." She snorted and shook her head, clearly amused. "I told him that evil is much scarier if it looks beautiful. We went around and around on it. It was a fun fight, but I eventually won."

"If it helps any," Kate told her, looking at the beautiful drawing, "I think you're right. She's gorgeous, but there's something dark in her eyes."

"Exactly!"

"Do you argue a lot? With Mike I mean," Kate asked, then added quickly, "I'm not being nosy, it's only that Sean and I seem to butt heads regularly. He's so damn stubborn."

Jenny laughed out loud this time and set the sketch aside once she was finished. "Our arguments are legendary. When we get going, everyone around here heads for cover. Mike's got a head like a rock and frankly, I'm just as hardheaded, so when we're on opposite sides, it can get loud.

"But oh, making up is so worth the battle," Jenny said on a dreamy sigh.

Funny, Kate thought now, she and Sam had never argued. They'd come from the same place, wanted the same things, it was just *easy* being with him. But if she was honest, at least with herself, Kate could admit that the fire between her and Sean was part of what made being with him so exciting.

"Kate," Jenny said, sympathy coloring her tone, "I know it's none of my business, but are you planning on staying with Sean?"

The simple question, quietly asked, suddenly clarified everything in Kate's mind. She couldn't stay. Her life was in Wyoming and Sean's was here. Staying with him, living with him, was only making the inevitable harder on both of them. She had to get back to her real life and the sooner the better, for both their sakes. Meeting Jenny's eyes, she said, "No. I'm going home. Tomorrow."

Now, she had to tell Sean.

* * *

That night, they had dinner at a local diner, went to a summer concert in the park and then took a long walk back to the condo. Sean had been making plans all day, and he knew he had everything worked out. There was really only one way to solve their situation, he assured himself. All he had to do was convince her he was right. And since he was right so often, how hard would that be?

Once inside, they took the elevator to the penthouse level and walked into his home. In the last week, he realized Kate had made some changes not only to him, but also to this place. There were fresh flowers in vases, fruit in a bowl on the counter and the scent of the chocolate chip cookies she'd made the night before still in the air. Kate's stamp was all over this once-empty space—and on him, as well.

"You want a cookie?" she asked, heading for the kitchen.

"No," he said and stopped her by snatching her hand and pulling her up tight to him. "I want to talk to you."

"Okay." She reached up and laid one hand on his heart. "I have to talk to you, too."

"Well, ordinarily I'd say ladies first, since my mother would kick me if I didn't." He grinned at her. "But I've been thinking about this all day, and I want to get it said."

She smiled at him, and her eyes sparkled. "Okay, what is it?"

"I've been giving this situation we're in a lot of thought," he said, his hands on her shoulders, his thumbs caressing her even as he held on to her. "And I think I've got the solution."

"Sean…"

"No," he said, shaking his head, "let me finish. Kate, we get along great. The sex is incredible, and we're having a baby together. I think you know there's only one real answer here. Marry me."

He'd surprised her. He could see that. But what he didn't see was excitement, pleasure. Instead, he read regret in her eyes, and a cold fist took hold of his heart and squeezed.

"No."

Sean didn't have a quick comeback. He'd expected an argument. Hell, he'd been looking forward to it. He liked fighting with her almost as much as taking her to bed. But the look on her face told him she wasn't interested in arguing. She'd already made her decision. It was just one he couldn't live with.

"No? That's it?"

"You don't really want to marry me, Sean."

"See," he said, "I think I do, since I'm the one who proposed."

"That wasn't even a question," she pointed out, shaking her head. "You said 'marry me.' Like, I don't know, 'fetch me my slippers' or something."

"I don't own slippers."

"Not the point." She held up both hands and breathed deeply before saying, "I've been married before, and I don't want to risk that kind of pain again."

"There doesn't have to be pain," he countered. "I'm not talking about love here. A marriage based on mutual need is safe. Neither of us risks more than we're prepared to lose. It's the perfect solution, Kate. You know it is."

He thought he had her for a second when she chewed

her bottom lip and seemed to be considering it, but then she started talking again. "I don't need you to take care of me, Sean. And I can take care of myself, so why should I marry you?"

He went tight and still inside. She didn't need him. Just like Adrianna.

"Besides, my life is in Wyoming and yours is here. I can't give up the mountains in exchange for crowds and traffic—not even for you. And I know you don't want to leave the ocean, so it won't work. I appreciate the offer but—"

"Spare me the appreciation," he snapped. Damn it, he was talking about marrying her, and she couldn't have been less interested. First time ever that he proposes and he gets turned down? Was it some kind of karmic kick in the butt? Was the universe at large having a good laugh at his expense?

He'd been so sure this was the solution. All the time he'd spent thinking how much he admired her strength and self-confidence, and it turned out that's exactly what was keeping her from agreeing to marry him.

"And what do we do about the baby?" he demanded.

"I promise, I will give you regular updates on how she is," Kate told him, her gaze locked with his. "And I won't try to keep her from you, either."

"That's it?" He slid his hands up from her shoulders to cup her face. "Just 'no' and we're done?"

"We'll never be done," she said and lifted her hands to cover his. "We'll always share a daughter."

He was going to take another stab at it. Sean and his partners hadn't built Celtic Knot by giving up. He had to fight for what he wanted or it wasn't worth getting.

"It's not enough, damn it. We're good together, and you know it, Kate."

"I do," she agreed and stepped back, distancing them just a little. "But you're dangerous to my heart, Sean, and I don't want to risk that again."

"Nobody said anything about *love*, Kate." He cared for her, of course he did. And she was the mother of his daughter. But he didn't *love* her. Love hadn't been a part of this at all for him. Love was something that tied a man into knots and sent him spinning off on roads he'd never planned to travel. It was having to think of someone else before yourself. And for a selfish man, that was hard to imagine.

She took a breath, blew it out and said softly, "I'm saying it, Sean. I made the mistake of falling in love with you, and now I have to leave so I can get over it."

He felt the punch of her words, saw the look in her eye and just for a second the world seemed to tilt. "What?"

"I love you, Sean. Didn't mean to, didn't want to." She shrugged and gave him a reluctant smile. "Turns out you're just as charming as you said you were. You got to me when I thought no one else ever could. But I can't be in love, Sean. I won't let myself be. So I can't marry you."

She wouldn't marry him, but she *did* love him. What the hell? Sean took a long step back, physically and mentally. He thought of his brother and how Mike's life had changed the minute he'd admitted to loving Jenny. Sure, he seemed happy, but he didn't have a pool table in his family room anymore, did he? And Brady? Hell, Brady had given up his home and moved to Ireland of all places because he was in love.

Well, Sean's world was already just as he liked it. He did what he wanted when he wanted. If that made him a selfish bastard, he'd just have to live with it.

"So when are you going home?" he finally asked, shoving both hands into his pants pockets.

"Tomorrow. I'll find the best flight I can—"

"Don't be ridiculous, take the company jet."

"I can't—"

"Damn it, Kate!" He took a breath to cool off and wondered why he was so angry. Sean didn't want love in his life any more than Kate did, so why did it make him furious that she loved him and wanted to "get over it" like a bad case of the flu?

"Don't yell at me," she said in a dangerously soft voice.

"Then don't say stupid things." Outrage glittered in her eyes, so he spoke up fast. "Sorry, sorry. Take the company jet. I don't want to have to worry about you on some crowded plane with strangers sneezing in your face and making my daughter sick."

A muffled laugh slipped from her and was gone again in a heartbeat. "Okay, thanks."

He rubbed the back of his neck then shook his head. "Yeah. No problem. You'll call me when you get home."

"Is that an order?" she asked.

"Damn straight it is," he told her, then pulled her in for a hug. And as he held her, Sean realized he really didn't want to let her go.

Ten

The next morning, Kate was gone. She left early, with a kiss and a promise to stay in touch. And Sean let her go.

What choice did he have? She was the one who'd brought love into this. He'd been after a simple arrangement between lovers. Between parents of a child they both wanted. What the hell did love have to do with this anyway?

Kate leaving was for the best, he told himself. It just didn't feel like it at the moment. But instead of thinking about her or having to spend too much time in a condo that seemed to echo with emptiness, he threw himself into the launch of the new game.

So far, "The Wild Hunt" looked to be their biggest success yet. Sean spent hours every day on the phone, tracking numbers, making new contacts and negotiating new deals with their old customers. The packagers were having a hard time keeping up with demand for the game, and that was good news.

When the first sales reports began trickling in, Sean and Mike made a video call to Ireland so all three partners could talk about the latest news.

"The European numbers are every bit as exciting," Brady told them with a wide grin. "We've got more orders than we can fill—I ordered a second run at the packagers so we can move quickly and take advantage of the buzz the game's getting."

"Good idea," Sean said.

"And," Brady added, "I'm thinking we should line up an extra packager before we launch 'Dragon's Tears' this Christmas. We don't want to be caught coming up short again."

"Makes sense," Sean agreed, looking to Mike and getting a nod in response. "I've been scouting for more packagers already, since we've had the same problem here, needing an extra run to fulfill orders. Think I've lined up a new one—in Montana of all places, so I thought I'd go and check it out this week. Get things rolling way ahead of schedule."

"Montana. Isn't that close to Wyoming?" Brady swiveled in his desk chair and behind him, they caught glimpses of the Irish countryside, complete with dark gray skies and trees twisting in the wind.

"It is," Mike told him from his chair behind the desk. "And no, he's not stopping off to see Kate."

"Why the hell not?" Brady asked. "She's having your baby, you idiot."

"Thanks for all the support, guys," Sean said tightly, aiming a narrow-eyed stare at his friend and then at his brother. "But I think I can handle my own life, thanks."

"Not from where I'm sitting," Mike muttered.

"Me, either," Brady chimed in. He scowled into the camera. "Did you learn nothing from watching Mike and I make messes of everything?"

"Yeah, I learned that being in love is mostly a pain in the ass," Sean said and took a sip of his beer.

It was after hours in the office. Everyone else had left for the day. Soon Mike would be heading home to be with Jenny, and Sean would be...alone. And that was how he liked it, he reminded himself.

"Hey, loving Jenny's the best thing I ever did," Mike argued.

"Yeah?" Sean tipped his head to one side and gaped at his brother. "How many times have you complained about losing your damn pool table? Or how many houses has Jenny had you out to look at this week?"

Mike sighed. "Eight. And I'll get another pool table when she finally decides on a house."

Sean snorted. "And you." He looked at Brady. "You moved all the way to Ireland for your wife."

"Best move I ever made."

Sean wasn't convinced. He'd watched Mike and Brady take the plunge and though he'd encouraged them both, he just couldn't see himself taking the same fall.

"Jenny told me she talked to Kate this morning," Mike said.

Sean whipped his head around to look at him. "Why? Is everything okay with her?"

"Did you see that?" Mike asked Brady, then snorted at Sean. "Yeah, you don't care about Kate. I can see that now."

"I never said I didn't *care*," he argued. "I said I didn't *love* her."

"Sell it to someone who might buy it," Brady said and even all the way from Ireland, the sarcasm in his tone rang loud and clear.

Sean took a breath and told himself not to let them get to him. "Fine. Just tell me what she wanted when she called Jenny."

"I don't know." Mike shrugged. "Something about the baby moving around a lot and Kate wondering if Jenny's baby was doing the same thing."

Moving around a lot. And he wasn't there to experience it with her. That chewed at him. Hell, it had been her choice to leave. He'd wanted her to stay, hadn't he? Asked her to *marry* him, for God's sake, when he'd never wanted to marry anyone. She'd been gone four weeks now, and missing her was just part of his life. He still couldn't walk into his own damn house without seeing her, smelling her, wanting her.

He gritted his teeth and said, "I'll call her tomorrow and check in."

"Yeah," Mike said, nodding with a smirk on his face. "Give the mother of your kid a phone call. Good idea."

"What're you riding me for?" Sean turned in his chair to glare at his brother.

"Because you're being a damn fool and it irritates me."

"Me, too," Brady said from Ireland.

"Thanks." Sean gave his friend a hard look. "Nothing like being insulted long-distance."

"What else do you want?" Mike leaned forward and slapped one hand down on his desk. "She's been gone a month, and you're more miserable to be around than ever."

Sean took a breath and huffed it out in a long sigh.

Maybe he had a point. But hell, it wasn't like Mike was a vacation to hang out with half the time.

"Look," Sean said, trying for reasoned calm, "Kate had to go back home. She has work. I have work here. It's no big deal."

Could they hear the lie? he wondered. Could they see that his tongue nearly rotted and fell off just telling that lie? She said she didn't need him. And the bottom line was what had punched at him the hardest. Adrianna had said the same damn thing, and he'd lived through it.

He'd be fine this time, too. If she didn't want him there, he'd stay the hell away. But he wouldn't walk out on his kid. That baby was *his,* and nothing would keep him from her. Not even her mother.

"So you're gonna let her make the call on this." Mike shook his head sadly, disappointment gleaming in his eyes.

Sean ignored it and gave his brother and friend each a hard stare. "My business. My life. Back off."

"Fine." Mike turned to face Brady and shrugged. "There's no cure for 'idiot.'"

"So I hear." Brady cleared his throat, checked a readout on his tablet and changed the subject. "We're already getting preorders for the Christmas game. With that video of 'Dragon's Tears' we tacked on to the end of 'The Wild Hunt,' gamers are primed. Hell, they haven't even finished this game and they're already talking about the next one."

"All good," Mike said shortly. "Sean, what's the story on this new distributor?"

He pulled out his notes and lost himself in the details he was most comfortable with. Going over plans and strategies, he focused on the work, because thinking about Kate would push him over the edge.

Kate had been back in Wyoming for two months, and she still woke up stretching her arm out across the mattress reaching for Sean. Starting every day with disappointment and misery was taking a toll. She was tired a lot of the time, and the growing baby was like a ticking personal clock. Every day brought her closer to delivery, to meeting her child for the first time. And every day reminded her that Sean wouldn't be with her.

He should have been there, experiencing it all with her. Every time the baby kicked, she thought, *Sean should feel this*. When she bought a crib and put it together herself, she thought how much more fun it would have been to have Sean helping. Even though his skill with tools was less than brilliant, they'd have been together, doing something for their daughter.

And the misery filled her.

Phone calls and video chats weren't enough. Seeing him, hearing him, only made her miss him more when the call was over. Molly did her best to distract Kate, Harry worried and hovered and her crew had all taken on more work to pick up the slack, since she wasn't at her most productive at the moment.

The familiar symphony of power tools and voices shouting to be heard welcomed Kate when she stepped into the hotel. Nearly finished now, the guys were just taking care of a few finishing touches. Today, detailed wood carvings were being added around the mantels of the fireplaces, and low cabinets were being added to the walls in the main dining room. They still had to replace some shingles on the roof and add a few hand-crafted flower boxes to the front porch railings, but then the work would be done, except for whatever the Celtic Knot artists would do to the interior walls. Most of the crew was now working on the individual cabins, and just looking at them as she walked out to the wrap-around porch made Kate smile.

They looked as if they belonged in a Faery forest, with their curved roofs, arched doors and round windows. Details were coming to life, making each cabin different. Paint colors were bright and Kate thought her favorite had to be the sapphire-blue cabin with the emerald-green door. Gingerbread trim scrolled along the rooflines of each cabin and outlined every window. Every cabin even boasted a tiny gas fireplace and whimsical chimney crafted out of either copper or brick. It was a magical spot and she wished, damn it, that Sean was there to see it all.

When her phone signaled a video chat, her heart gave a quick jump and even the baby kicked as if she knew it was her daddy calling. Had he felt Kate thinking about him?

"Sean. Hi." He looked so good, she thought sadly. And so far away.

"How's it going, Kate?"

He was in his office, she thought, recognizing the space behind him. It was harder, somehow, now that she'd been with him in California. She could picture him in the office where they'd shared a pizza one night. Where he'd held her on his lap while he answered phone calls. Kate's heart twisted in her chest, and she sighed a little at the memories.

"Everything's good," she said, forcing a smile she knew wouldn't so much as touch her eyes. "We've nearly finished the main hotel. Just some minor things left to do there. The crew's focused mainly on the cabins, and they're looking wonderful."

"Yeah?" A half smile curved his mouth briefly.

She wanted to kiss it.

"See for yourself." She turned the phone around and moved it slowly, so the camera would catch at least four of the cabins, sitting like tiny jewels among the trees.

When she was looking at him again, he said, "They look excellent, Kate. Really." He rubbed the back of his neck, and she almost smiled at the gesture. She recognized it as what he did when he was stressed. Good to know that seeing each other like this was no easier on him than it was on her.

"I wanted to let you know we'll be sending a couple of our artists out to do the work on the walls," he said.

"Great." A spurt of hope shot through her as she asked, "Are you coming, too?"

"No," he said and deflated that bubble of expectation. "I've got meetings set up for the next two weeks that can't be put off."

"Right. Okay." She nodded and smiled again, not wanting to let him know how disappointed she was. It had been two months since they were together, and it felt like two years. "When will they be here?"

"Sometime next week. They'll move into a couple of the bedrooms there so they can be on-site, get the job done as quickly as possible."

"Then I'll bring some supplies in for them."

"That'd be great, thanks," Sean said, then his voice lowered to an intimate tone. "How are you doing, Kate?"

"I'm fine," she said, lifting her chin and refusing to give in to the aching loneliness beginning to throb inside her. "Went to the doctor yesterday. He says the baby's perfectly healthy and growing just as she should."

"Good," he said, his gaze locked with hers. "That's good. Um, Jenny says her baby's moving all the time now. Is ours?"

A sting of tears burned her eyes, but she blinked them back. He should *know*, she told herself. He should be there, feeling every kick and bump their child made. Maybe she should have accepted that marriage demand disguised as a proposal. But even as she thought it, Kate knew she'd done the right thing. If for no other reason than the fact that she loved him and he didn't feel the same.

"Yes," she said, shutting down those thoughts. "She was doing jumping jacks all last night. I hardly slept."

He frowned. "That can't be good. You need rest, Kate. You—"

"I'm taking care of myself, Sean," she interrupted him quickly. "Everything's fine. We're fine." She watched him nod, then she asked, "How about there? The game still selling well?"

"Best one yet," he said, but there was no excitement in his eyes.

"Good. That's good, too." God, they sounded so stiff with each other. Both of them talking and neither of them saying anything that mattered. Anything *real*.

"Kate!"

She looked up to see one of her workers shouting to her from one of the cabins. Kate held up one finger to let her know she was coming.

"Sean, I'm sorry. Lilah's got some issue in a cabin. I've gotta go."

"Right," he said. "Me, too. Look, I'll call you in a day or two, okay? And be careful, will you?"

"Don't worry. Take care of yourself, Sean," she said and gave in to the urge to touch the screen as if she could stroke her finger along his cheek.

Then he was gone and she went back to work.

Two weeks later, Sean was at his desk when Mike stuck his head in the office and shouted, "Jenny's in the hospital!"

Panic shone in his brother's eyes, so Sean leaped up, said, "I'll drive," and raced Mike to the car. It was a wild ride through beach traffic, and Sean pulled out all the stops. He weaved in and out of the cars on Pacific Coast Highway like a driver at the Indy 500. "What happened?"

Mike looked at him, eyes stricken. "Jenny was out shopping, started feeling bad. She says she started bleeding. The doctor told her to get to the hospital." He dragged in a deep breath and blew it out again. "God, Sean, how the hell would I live without Jenny? The baby?"

"You're not going to have to find out." Sean prayed he was right.

Mike's closed fist hammered down on his own thigh helplessly, relentlessly. "I should have gone shopping with her this morning. I was busy and so damn sick and tired of looking for the perfect couch, I backed off. Let her go off alone. Idiot. What was I thinking?"

"You were thinking she'd be perfectly fine shopping on her own. This is not your fault, Mike."

"Doesn't matter whose fault it is."

Sean was panicked now, too. A cold ball of dread sat in the center of his chest, but he held it back and talked his brother off the ledge. "You couldn't have known, Mike. For God's sake, she went to the doctor just yesterday and everything was fine."

"Well, it's not *now*," Mike snapped. "Can't you go any faster?"

"If we had wings!" But Sean stomped on the gas pedal and gave it everything the car had. While he drove like a crazy man, Mike called their parents and Jenny's uncle Hank and his new wife, Betty. Family needed family when things went to hell.

Sean zipped through yellow lights, and when he turned into the hospital parking lot at last, the tires screamed for mercy. He'd barely stopped before Mike was out and running to the emergency room. A few minutes later, car parked, Sean was in there, too, looking for his brother and praying everything was all right.

It should be all right. The day before, the doctor had given Jenny a clean bill of health. What the hell could have happened so quickly?

He saw Mike at reception, then his brother was hustled into the back and Sean was left to pace through a crowded waiting room with a TV tuned to a game show with an annoying host.

Sean hated hospitals. The smell of them. The hopelessness of them. Look into any one of the faces gathered here and you'd see desperation, fear and the wish to be absolutely *anywhere* but there. Minutes ticked into hours and still Sean knew nothing. Mike came out occasionally just to tell him they were waiting for the doctor and to keep Sean from going nuts with the lack of information.

Jack and Peggy Ryan hurried into the waiting room and after hugs and whispered conversations, they sat down on the most uncomfortable chairs in the world to wait.

Sean couldn't sit. Couldn't stand still, either. He kept pacing. He walked through the room until his mother told him to go outside because he was giving her a headache. So he went and tipped his face into the ocean breeze. But there was no peace there, either, since Jenny's aunt and uncle raced up a few minutes later demanding answers.

And the whole time he waited and worried for his brother and sister-in-law, his mind kept turning to Kate. What if this had happened to her? Hell, for all he knew, it could be happening right now. He was hundreds of miles away. If she had a crisis, chances were good he wouldn't find out about it until it was over. What if she was out on a damn job site and something happened and she was alone?

Panic was alive and clawing at him as he wondered if Kate was telling him everything. What if she wasn't really okay? Or if there was a problem with the baby? How the hell would he know? He stomped back inside and saw his mother and Betty holding hands and whispering while Hank and Jack sat stone-faced.

Through the raging storm in his mind, Sean realized something that seemed profound yet it shouldn't have been. *This* was love. Families coming together in a crisis. Leaning on each other. Being there. His heart opened and heat spilled out, filling every vein in his body.

He looked at his parents, who'd come through problems of their own and emerged stronger than ever. And there was Betty, who'd been Hank's housekeeper for years until finally one day they both woke up and realized that what kept them together was *love*. Yeah, Brady had moved to Ireland, but he loved it. And Mike lost his beloved pool table, but what had he gotten instead? A woman to share his life with.

Love didn't stifle anything. It blossomed and grew and made lives richer. And Sean was certifiable for trying to avoid the knowledge that he *loved* Kate. Maybe he had from the beginning—he didn't know. What he was sure of was that night at the view point. Something major had shifted inside him and he'd loved her then and loved her now.

Someone in the waiting room sobbed, and the sound raked along his spine like nails on a chalkboard. *Kate.* Her name echoed over and over in his mind. A chant. A prayer. The last two months without her had been the longest, loneliest of his life. He'd let her go because she said she loved him but didn't need him.

"That's a damn lie," he muttered, flicking a glance toward the closed doors separating him from his family. "Of course she needs me. As much as I need her. And I'm going to tell her so the minute—"

Mike rushed through the double doors and hurried to the family. He was surrounded instantly with everyone asking questions at once. Until Hank clapped his hands and said, "One at a time."

"She's okay, so's the baby," Mike said first and on cue, Peggy and Betty wept. "Doc says she's been doing too much and lifting too much, which is what I've been telling her, but who listens to me?"

He was smiling as he complained, and Sean could see the stark relief on his face. "I'm taking her home in a couple hours, so you guys can come see her then if you want."

"We will," Betty told him and rose up to kiss his

cheek. "You give her our love and tell her I'll be there tomorrow to look after her."

"I will, thanks."

Peggy kissed her son and said, "I'll be there with Betty, and we'll make sure she stays put."

"Thanks, Mom."

When the family left, Mike turned to Sean and breathed a huge sigh.

Everything was forgotten except for Jenny and her baby. "She's really okay?"

"Yeah," Mike said, smiling. "Scared me brainless, but she's okay. Come say *hi* to her." Sean kept pace with his big brother through the double doors and down the hall until they came to a curtained-off bed in the corner. Mike pushed the drapes wide and there was Jenny, propped up on pillows and smiling. "Hi, Sean, I'm so sorry I scared you guys."

"Hey, don't worry about us." At the side of her bed, Sean lifted her hand and gave it a squeeze. "You okay?"

"I'm fine. The baby's fine, too." She rubbed her belly, then stretched out her hand for Mike, linking the three of them. "His heartbeat is strong, and he's kicking up a storm. All good."

Mike lifted her hand and kissed it, and Sean's heart ached for the fear his brother had just lived through. "So what happened?"

"Apparently, I've been on my feet too much lately and—"

"Didn't I tell you that?" Mike interrupted, kissing her hand again as if making sure she was still there and safe.

"Yeah, yeah, you were right. God, I hate admitting that," Jenny said with a laugh. "Anyway, I get to go home, I just have to put my feet up more. Take it easy and quit spending all day exploring antique stores."

"Hallelujah," Mike muttered.

"That's great, Jenny, really." Sean bent over and kissed her forehead. "You take it easy and quit scaring everybody, okay? I want to talk to Mike a second, then I'll toss him back to you."

"Take your time," she said, smiling as she waved them both off. "He'll only hit me with 'I told you so' again anyway..."

Relief was almost painful, Sean thought. When every nerve in your body was filled with tension that was suddenly released, you were left a little shaky. He walked outside, with Mike right behind him.

"Man, I've never been so scared in my life," Mike muttered, leaning back against the hospital's brick facade. "If this is what having kids is like, I'm gonna be an old man before I'm forty."

Sean slapped his brother's shoulder in solidarity. "I'm glad everything's okay, Mike."

"Yeah, me, too." He smiled, scrubbed both hands over his face. "Thanks, man. You were a rock. You came through for me."

"Always. You need me to take you guys back home?"

"No. Jenny's car's here. We're good."

"Okay." Nodding, Sean said, "Then I'm going to the condo to pack."

Mike's eyebrows lifted. "Going on a trip?"

"No," Sean told him. "I'm going home. To Wyoming."

The end of summer in Wyoming carried a hint of the fall to come in the breeze that danced in the trees and the thick, heavy clouds gathering on top of the mountains. Kate was really tired of being hot, so she was looking forward to fall and winter. Now, though, she ignored the late summer sun and picked her way carefully across the forest floor.

Seth and Billie, the Celtic Knot artists, had finished up their work on the cabins and were now busily handcrafting the murals in the main hotel. With her crew busy on a job site in town, Kate wanted to take a look at the gazebo they'd erected last week. No ordinary lakeside pavilion, this structure was as fanciful as the jewel-toned cabins nestled in the pines.

Scrollwork highlighted every pillar, and the bench seats followed the hexagonal line. There were carved dragons perched on the roofline like gargoyles and the view of the lake was just as mystical. Sean really was going to have an amazing place when it was all finished. Kate walked up the gazebo steps and sat down, because at seven months pregnant now, she was just tired.

But more than tired, she felt…sad. She lifted her face into the wind and thought of last winter and those precious snowbound days with Sean. She wished he was there with every beat of her heart.

"You know," a voice said from right behind her, "I just realized how much I missed this place."

Kate gasped and spun around to look at Sean walking toward her in long, purposeful strides. He wore a black T-shirt, black jeans and boots. His black hair blew in the wind, and his sharp blue eyes were locked on her with so much heat she could barely breathe. If this was a dream, she didn't want to wake up.

He came up the steps of the gazebo, then paused to turn and look around. "The trees, the mountains, the sky—" He shot her a look and a half smile. "God, you're beautiful. I really missed looking up and seeing all those stars every night, too."

"I can't believe you're here." Kate stood up slowly, her gaze locking with his.

"Believe it." His gaze was steady, his voice warm and strong. "I'm here because I missed *you*, Kate. Like I'd miss my right arm, I miss you."

"God, Sean—"

He shook his head and moved up to her in one long stride. Then he put one finger against her mouth to keep her quiet. "Nope. I came a long way to have my say, and I just want you to listen."

As glad as she was to see him, Kate wasn't going to stand there and be shushed. From behind his finger, she grumbled, "Excuse me?"

"There's my girl." He laughed and shook his head again. "Damn if I haven't missed that stubborn streak of yours." Before she could argue that ridiculous point, he bent and kissed her fast and hard, then lifted his head to look at her again.

Her lips were buzzing, her heart pounding. Even the baby felt like she was jumping up and down inside, as if she sensed her mother's excitement.

"We're getting married, Kate—"

She inhaled, but he cut her off.

"Before you start in on not wanting to risk more pain, think about the pain we've both been in for the last two and a half months," he stressed. "Admit it, Kate. You can't lie to yourself or to me about this. We've been too separate, lonely, miserable."

"We have, but...married?" She'd done that,

and it had ended in heartbreak. And if she lost Sean as she'd lost Sam…she didn't think she'd survive it.

Sean laughed and sighed all at once. "I can see in your eyes exactly what you're thinking, Kate. But see, the thing is, I love you."

She swayed a little and was grateful he took hold of her.

"Yeah. Surprised the hell out of me, too," he admitted. "But more than that, I *need* you. And you need me."

Kate wanted to argue that, but what would be the point? They would both know she was lying. Of course she needed him. And missed him. And loved him.

"See," he said softly, "when you said you didn't need me, that kind of gave me a hard punch." He blew out a breath and scowled. "We all have secrets, Kate. It wasn't only you in that boat. Ten years ago, I thought I was in love and she got pregnant and I…let her down." His features softened in memory then hardened in shame. "I wasn't what she needed because I was too selfish to see past my own life."

"Sean, I'm sorry…"

"She lost the baby, Kate, and then told me to leave because she didn't need me around anymore." He shrugged. "So, when you said it, I just pulled back and locked down. Stupid."

"Not stupid," she said, her heart breaking for him. They all had losses, she thought now. Everyone had pain; no one got through life with just a series of one rainbow after another. "I lied, you know. I do need you."

"Yeah," he said, with that half smile of smug satisfaction that she'd missed so much. "I know. So back to my first statement…we're getting married, Kate. And we're going to live here."

"In Wyoming?"

"Not just Wyoming, but *here*," he said. Keeping one arm around her shoulders, he turned her to point out to the strip of land that ran along the lake and backed up to the forest. "I'm hiring Wells Construction to build us a house, right there."

"A house," she whispered, looking from his face to the beautiful stretch of land.

"Our house. You're going to design it any way you want, Kate." He looked down into her eyes, and everything in her lit up like Christmas. "Make it your dream house, Kate, because all of our dreams are going to come true in it."

"But, Sean, what about the ocean?" she asked, stunned. "You love it so much. How can you give it up? And you'd be so far from your family…"

"You and the baby," he insisted, his eyes boring into hers, "are my family." His thumb stroked away a single tear that tracked from the corner of her eye, and his touch sent ripples of warmth sliding through her. Then he smiled again. "And with the company jet, we can travel as much as we want. We'll keep the condo, stay there when we visit. But meanwhile, I'll have the lake, and paddleboarding might be fun. You could even teach me to ski in the winter."

She laughed shortly. "You're crazy."

"Crazy about you."

God, Kate wanted to believe, to have everything he was offering her. To love and be loved. To make a family with him, to build a dream house on the shore of the lake and to make a lifetime of memories with this man who touched her so deeply.

"I'm just so scared of losing again." She reached up

and cupped his face in her palms. "Sean, if something happened to you, I think it would kill me."

"I can't promise that nothing will ever go wrong, Kate. Nobody can." He led her to the bench seat, sat down and pulled her onto his lap. Kate stared into his eyes and heard every word when he spoke again. "If something goes wrong, we'll handle it. Together. But Kate, what if everything goes right? What if our lives are perfect and happy and filled with a dozen kids screaming and running through the forest?"

She laughed at that even as he laid the flat of his hand on the swell of their child. "A dozen?"

He shrugged. "Negotiable. But with all this room around here, I'd say we'll need at least six."

Kate could see it all. The two of them, a houseful of kids, taking part in the conventions he would hold on the grounds every summer. Working the hotel, being with Sean every day and night and she suddenly wanted it all more than her next breath.

"What's not negotiable," he was saying, "is marriage. I want you, Kate. Forever. So say yes."

"Yes," she said and felt a huge, smothering weight slide off her shoulders. This was right. They were perfect for each other, and together they would be able to handle anything that came at them.

"Hey!" Sean's gaze shot to her belly. "What was that?"

Kate laughed, delighted in the man. Throwing her arms around his neck, she said, "That was your daughter telling you she's glad her mommy and daddy are getting married."

"That's amazing," he said, wide-eyed as he laid his hand across her belly, waiting to feel it again.

"So, where's my engagement ring?" Kate asked, feeling loved and wanted and needed.

"Ha!" He reached into his pocket and pulled out a box. "No engagement ring, you'd only get it caught on a saw or some damn thing." Opening it, he showed her a pair of stunning emerald earrings. "This is for the engagement and plain gold bands for both of us when we get married."

"Oh, Sean…" Kate smiled through her tears. How perfect was it to be loved by a man who knew her so well? So intimately? "You really are perfect, aren't you?"

"Don't forget charming," he quipped, and then he kissed her.

Epilogue

Two months later

"Kate, come on," Sean shouted, "the storm's rolling in, and I want to be off this mountain before we get snowed in again!"

He glanced around the main room in the hotel and waited impatiently for his wife. The whole place was furnished now—beds, couches, chairs and top-of-the-line entertainment systems with gaming capabilities in every room. They were ready for guests, but with the new baby coming, he'd made an executive decision to wait until spring for the grand opening. Give them a chance to settle into being a family first.

It was only early October, but winter was heading their way in a hurry. He never should have agreed to bring her up here today, but Kate was like a dog with a bone when she wanted something.

She'd been determined to get another look at the house site before the snow hit. She was working on the design so the architect could have the plans in time for the crew to get started on it as soon as winter was over. The woman was like a force of nature. She wanted everything done right and in her time.

"Kate! If you're not out here in ten seconds, I'm going back to your place without you!" An empty threat, and they both knew it.

"You know," Kate said as she came toward him, "if you were walking around with a bowling ball on your bladder, you'd move a little slowly, too."

Nine months pregnant and she still took his breath away. How could he love her more every day? She was frustrating and intriguing and everything he'd ever wanted in his whole damn life.

"Yes, you're right," Sean said, hustling her into her coat and easing her toward the door. "Men are miserable human beings and women should rule the world. Just get in the car, okay?"

"Relax, Sean," she said, stopping on the front porch to look around. "We're not going to be stuck, and I'm not having the baby here."

"Damn right you're not," he said, closing the door behind them and locking it up. Once the baby was born, he and Kate were thinking of moving up here and waiting out the winter. Kate's little bungalow was too small for the three of them, plus all of the office equipment Sean needed to get his work done for the company.

He was looking forward to the quiet. The solitude.

And even being snowed in with Kate again—*after* the baby was born.

"It's nice that Jenny and Mike had their little boy yesterday," Kate was saying dreamily as he helped her down the front steps. "Now our Kiley and their Carter will only be a day apart in age."

"Yeah," he muttered, keeping her moving toward the car, "it's great. Wait." He stopped dead when what she'd said sunk in. "How do you know Kiley's coming today?" Suspicion then panic settled over him like a radioactive cloak. "Are you in labor?"

She grinned at him, went up on her toes and kissed him. "For the last hour or two. You're going to be a daddy today, Sean! Isn't that amazing?"

Joy, wonder, then one more time, *panic*. "We've got to get you to the hospital. Walk slow. No bumps. Don't breathe too hard."

She laughed and when he got her tucked into the car and raced around to the driver's side, he heard another peal of laughter and told himself women really were the stronger sex. Why wasn't she terrified?

Sean threw the car into gear and headed down the mountain as quickly as he could. Storm clouds gathered and began to surge forward, like an army on the march. He couldn't worry about them, though, because in the passenger seat, Kate groaned.

"Are you okay?"

"Fine," she muttered and shifted uncomfortably on the seat. "That one was much stronger, though. Just hurry, Sean."

When she started the panting and breathing, Sean's heart leaped into a wild gallop so frantic he almost forgot to breathe himself. The mountain road had never seemed so long or so twisty. He had to take his time or they'd go flying off the edge, but he had to hurry because he was *not* going to deliver his first child in his car.

Twenty minutes later, he pulled into the hospital lot and parked the car, not caring if it was legal or not. Kate was wincing and moaning regularly now. When he helped her out of the car, she grabbed hold of his hand and twisted with the strength of someone twice her size.

Sean gritted his teeth and went with it, steering her inside and standing by helplessly as orderlies appeared and whisked her into a wheelchair. She looked back at him as she disappeared down a long hallway, and Sean felt that thread of panic again when he lost sight of her.

But a few minutes later, he was in the labor room with her, and she battled and raged to bring their baby girl into the world. Sean's heart twisted every time a pain claimed her, and he would have given every dollar he had to change places with her. Anything would have been better than watching the woman he loved suffer.

"Don't look so worried, honey," she said, voice broken in between gasps. "This is normal. Everything's just moving really fast."

"This is fast?" He felt like they'd been doing this for days. "I was wrong before. Not six kids. One's enough. God, I swear I'll never touch you again, Kate."

She laughed, delighted, then gasped as another pain slammed home. "I'm not going to hold you to that, sweetie. Oh, Sean, she's coming."

Doctor Eve Conlon bustled in, and to Sean the woman looked like she was fourteen years old. Lots of curly, thick hair, big brown eyes and a wide smile. "How're we doing?"

"Kate says the baby's coming," Sean blurted. "How're you?"

Eve laughed. "Take a breath, Sean. I'm just going to take a look, Kate."

When the brief examination was over, the doctor smiled and announced, "Kate's right. She's doing everything in a hurry. Your daughter's on her way."

The next half hour was nothing but a blur for Sean. He'd never been so scared and elated all at the same time. Admiration and love for his wife soared as he watched her bring their baby into the world with a fierce determination that staggered him.

All he could do was hold her hand and look on in proud amazement when the doctor laid their gorgeous, screaming daughter on Kate's chest. Kate laughed and cried and smoothed her hands over their baby's tiny body, and Kiley, as if sensing she was just where she was supposed to be, settled right down and looked directly into her father's eyes.

Reverently, he reached out to touch her tiny hand, and the baby's fingers curled around one of his fingers in an instinctive grasp that took a firm hold on his heart, as well. "Happy birthday, Kiley Ryan," he whispered.

Love rose up and spilled over inside him, and Sean was humbled by it all. She was less than a minute old and already, Sean loved her more than he would have believed possible. He'd never known he could feel so much, so quickly. He looked at his beautiful wife and realized he had never guessed what it would mean to love a woman so completely.

"Thank you," he whispered and bent to kiss Kate. "Thank you for her and for everything you've given me since the day I met you."

"I love you, Sean," Kate said.

"Don't ever stop." Sean laid his hand over Kate's and together, they cradled their daughter—their future.

* * * * *

MILLS & BOON®

Desire™

PASSIONATE AND DRAMATIC LOVE STORIES

---

sneak peek at next month's titles...

In stores from 10th March 2016:

Take Me, Cowboy – Maisey Yates *and*
His Baby Agenda – Katherine Garbera

A Surprise for the Sheikh – Sarah M. Anderson *and*
Reunited with the Rebel Billionaire – Catherine Mann

A Bargain with the Boss – Barbara Dunlop *and*
Secret Child, Royal Scandal – Cat Schield

Available at WHSmith, Tesco, Asda, Eason, Amazon and Apple

Just can't wait?
Buy our books online a month before they hit the shops!
visit www.millsandboon.co.uk

These books are also available in eBook format!

MILLS & BOON®

Helen Bianchin v Regency Collection

MILLS & BOON®

Let us take you back in time with our Medieval Brides…

The Novice Bride – Carol Townend

The Dumont Bride – Terri Brisbin

The Lord's Forced Bride – Anne Herries

The Warrior's Princess Bride – Meriel Fuller

The Overlord's Bride – Margaret Moore

Templar Knight, Forbidden Bride – Lynna Banning

_MB519

MILLS & BOON®

Why not subscribe?
Never miss a title and save money too!

Here's what's available to you if you join the exclusive **Mills & Boon® Book Club** today:

✦ *Titles up to a month ahead of the shops*
✦ *Amazing discounts*
✦ *Free P&P*
✦ *Earn Bonus Book points that can be redeemed against other titles and gifts*
✦ *Choose from monthly or pre-paid plans*

Still want more?
Well, if you join today, we'll even give you
50% OFF your first parcel!

So visit **www.millsandboon.co.uk/subs**
to be a part of this exclusive Book Club!

MILLS & BOON®

Why shop at millsandboon.co.uk?

Each year, thousands of romance readers find their perfect read at millsandboon.co.uk. That's because we're passionate about bringing you the very best romantic fiction. Here are some of the advantages of shopping at www.millsandboon.co.uk:

* **Get new books first**—you'll be able to buy your favourite books one month before they hit the shops

* **Get exclusive discounts**—you'll also be able to buy our specially created monthly collections, with up to 50% off the RRP

* **Find your favourite authors**—latest news, interviews and new releases for all your favourite authors and series on our website, plus ideas for what to try next

* **Join in**—once you've bought your favourite books, don't forget to register with us to rate, review and join in the discussions

Visit **www.millsandboon.co.uk**
for all this and more today!